sleeper

E.G ROWLEY

Jumpmaster Press
Birmingham, Alabama

Library Cataloging Data
Names: Rowley, E. G. (Eugene George Rowley) 1970-
Title: Sleeper / E. G. Rowley
5.5 in. × 8.5 in. (13.97 cm × 21.59 cm)
Description: Jumpmaster Press digital eBook edition | Jumpmaster Press Trade paperback edition | Alabama: Jumpmaster Press, 2018. P.O Box 1774 Alabaster, AL 35007 info@jumpmasterpress.com
Summary: Wizard, Oh'Raum Yulr, is drawn by his dreams to a far-off shore where he finds the key to a thousand-year-old legend which could change the course of future events.

Identifiers: ISBN-13: 978-1-949184-44-0 (ebk.) | 978-1-949184-43-3 (paperback) |

1. Fantasy 2. Mythology 3. Legend 4. Magic 5. Adventure 6. Science 7. Knowledge

Printed in the United States of America

For more information on E.G. Rowley
https://www.facebook.com/EGRowley

sleeper

E.G ROWLEY

The Ballad of Cap'Tian

Cold and black brisk East winds blew,
Through Far'Verm Pass to Western lands,
To walls of Draer dark shadows drew,
Delivered into evil's hands.

Draer King's army gave valiant defense,
Against the shadow's growing might,
As dusk Sun's light made red intense,
Draer King lay martyred that very night.

Unmatched they marched with force of arms,
Southward evil's dark armies spread,
Cross rivers and forests and trampled farms,
With misery, hopelessness, death, and dread.

When from the heart of the Western lands,
Like a brilliant star that comes to Earth,
A shining hero stalwart stands,
Raises sword and shows his worth.

Cap'Tian, pure of heart and mind of stone,
With sword and shield and spear-tipped lance,
The hero stands — one man alone,
Drives back the horde's conquering advance.

Back to the East flees evil's retreat,
With one final card yet to play,
A feast and trap did lay in defeat,
For Cap'Tian's fate ends would betray.

By victory drink was Cap'Tian betrayed,

To sleep but not to die or rise,
On windward slopes the evil stayed,
To perhaps return and claim their prize.

Foretold the hero of this song bides,
Until Draer Princess softly weeps,
When returning horde of evil rides,
Yet deep in El'Thune Cap'Tian sleeps.

Chapters

The Western Kingdoms

Part I:
The Journey to The Sea

Dreams of Young Men

Stripes of orange light shot through a small window, illuminating the plank floor of Rowan'Gaff's bedroom. Fine, ever-present dust rose from the floorboards and refracted the morning light throughout the small room. The boy sat on the edge of his bed catching his breath from the previous night's shocking dream.

In it, the stocky five-foot-three lad wore heavy black armor and drug behind him a long-sword gouging a shallow trough in the blood-stained ground. He marched with slow, hammering steps lifting each weighty boot in lurching agony. Around him, taller dark figures lumbered ever forward — great plumes of steam bursting from their helmets accompanied by grunts and growls. Fear gripped the boy and the feeling of being out of place and time spread through his consciousness like a wildfire through dry underbrush.

The company halted in lockstep and Rowan'Gaff nearly plowed into the hulking soldier to his front. Through gaps in the front lines, Rowan'Gaff shielded his eyes from a glowing figure holding back the advancing horde. Snarls emanated from figures looming over him and whispers of, "Cap'Tian," and "The hero," floated forward from within the cohort.

Cap'Tian? the boy questioned, whispering in his dreaming mind. He shuffled to get a better look at his fabled ancestor.

Since birth, Rowan'Gaff listened to stories of his heroic fore-bearer, the man that single-handedly drove off an over-powering, invading army. In his dream, the boy struggled to make out the glowing figure's features. He squinted at the dazzling light hovering in front of the company.

The ranks in front of Rowan'Gaff shouted a blood-curdling roar and broke into a sprint toward the glowing light. Rowan'Gaff lurched forward, pushed by the onslaught of immense, armor-clad fighters. He tried to slow his advance, working his heavy feet backward only to find himself at the vanguard of the assault.

Before him stood an enormous luminescent man, his face obscured by the brilliant orange and yellow light bursting from him. Rowan'Gaff stepped back, shielded his eyes, and attempted to take in the figure. It was like looking into the Sun. The figure advanced and his hammering shield plowed into the boy, dropping him to the muddy ground.

"No!" Rowan'Gaff cried. His cry burst forth, not only in his dream, but also unknowingly throughout his small bedroom. Again, Rowan peered into the stunning light. The form reared back and plunged the silvery tip of his lance deep into Rowan'Gaff's chest.

The boy shook awake, his body trembling at the memory of Cap'Tian's voracious thrust. He touched the spot on his nightshirt where, moments earlier in his dream, a spearhead punctured his heart.

The spot itched and he softly scratched at it. The irritation did not subside. From it, emerged a feeling that Rowan'Gaff no longer belonged in this place. His room looked unfamiliar — his belongings foreign. He stood and crept into the main room of his family's small farmhouse.

His father, Fere'Man Vodr, sat at their small, common room table, finishing a bowl of boiled oats. "I heard you yell," he commented through a spoonful of dripping meal. "Are you well?" The question came as more of an inquisition regarding Rowan'Gaff's fitness for the day's work, than fatherly care or concern.

"I'm fine."

Fere'Man nodded and jabbed another ladle of oats into his bearded mouth. "Then dress yourself and eat with haste. The wagon for Son'Us needs attention." He motioned to a squat brown bucket on a preparation table next to their cooking hearth.

Rowan'Gaff returned to his room, removed his nightshirt, and dressed for the day's work. The itch in his chest grew to a burning desire to immediately leave this place. The drawing force also instilled within him feelings of destiny, greatness, and fear. Behind the nightmares of black-clad warriors, Rowan'Gaff saw himself as the shining hero. He heard imaginary songs of his deeds ringing from some distant inevitability. He mustered his strength and pushed the secret desire to leave deep within himself before warming his own bowl of oats. The young man quickly finished his breakfast and joined his father at their wagon. While he hefted burlap sacks of grain onto the dray, his mind filled with the glowing form of Cap'Tian.

"Father? You used to tell me tales of Cap'Tian, the hero. Are we really descended from him?"

Fare'Man pushed a grain satchel into position and rested an elbow on the stack. He nodded, "Aye, he is your fore-bearer on your Mother's side." He waved for the boy to toss him another load.

Rowan'Gaff hoisted a bushel from his shoulder to the cart's rail. "Was he really the great hero the legends make him out to be?"

"I have no reason to doubt the songs."

"I'd like to be a hero," the boy said.

His father laughed. "If you manage to get your chores done today, you'll be a hero, bar none."

Rowan'Gaff frowned at the jibe, the longing in his chest felt as though his heart would beat its way through his ribs. He needed to go — now. *Where do I need to go?* he asked himself and heaved the final bag to the cart.

Fere'Man maneuvered the grain into position, securing the load with several runs of fraying twine. "I'll return tonight from Son'Us. I expect your tasks completed."

"Yes, father," the boy answered. Behind his composed response, Rowan'Gaff knew the instant his father crested the low hill to the South and lost view of the farm, his journey would begin.

The beating in his chest and desire to depart clouded his thoughts, removing any notion of responsibility to his father or their small Longshore farm. Rowan'Gaff moved to the house and withdrew a strapped satchel from his father's worn storage chest. On the table, he filled it with dry and salted supplies, a semi-clean shirt from his room, and a small skin of water.

Minutes later, Rowan'Gaff stood outside their cottage door watching the cart lazily draw up the southern hill's slope. Without looking back, his father crested the incline and vanished from sight. The boy looked left, then right. *Which way?* he silently questioned. He closed his eyes, bringing the vision of Cap'Tian to the forefront of his mind. When the memory of the gleaming hero focused, Rowan'Gaff winced from a sudden, sharp chest pain. For an instant, in his mind's eye, a bright lance erupted from below his chin. Rowan'Gaff opened his eyes to the brilliance of the blazing morning sun. *East*, he concluded.

ଔ   ౸

The pack's weight made Rowan'Gaff's back sore and his limited knowledge of the lands outside of those between the River Mor'Ah and the Great sea slowed his progress East. He trudged along the rolling grasslands of Longshore keeping the sun in front of him for the first half of the day and at his back as afternoon progressed. He hoped to reach Narrow Bridge, the shortest crossing point in all the great river's length, by nightfall but the unfamiliar terrain and unknown distances forced him to set camp far short of his goal.

In his haste to begin his journey, Rowan'Gaff failed to pack a flint and steel or a proper bed roll. His camp consisted of a mound of dried grass which he plucked from the side of a wind-blown rise and a small morsel of scraped salt-pork.

Mercifully, the weather remained dry and the heat of the day dissipated slowly, allowing the young man to fall asleep in relative comfort under his makeshift blanket. Rowan'Gaff drifted off when his tired muscles finally relaxed, and thoughts of his father's anger evaporated.

When his eyes closed Rowan'Gaff's mind drew him back to the corpse-strewn battlefield. Again, he stood opposite the glowing hero surrounded by grunting heathens awaiting the opening of the melee. *Why am I here? Why am I not standing beside my kin?*

Knowing the outcome of this scenario, Rowan'Gaff pushed forward to join his heroic ancestor and fight off the black horde, like the hero he should be. The ranks in front of him opened and he found himself face to face with the vibrant visage of Cap'Tian.

"Cap'Tian, I am Rowan'Gaff, your decsend..." The hero's shield slammed the boy to the ground. Cap'Tian stepped over him and raised his glimmering lance for the eventual deathblow.

Before the glimmering head of the spear penetrated Rowan'Gaff's chest, his dream abruptly wavered and he found himself laying in a meadow listening to the sounds of birdsong. He unfurled defensive arms from his face and stared into a bright blue sky.

He no longer wore the heavy black armor and his skin felt cool and clean. A soft breeze rose gooseflesh on his arms. A feeling of peace washed over him carried on the wind's soft breath. Relieved, Rowan'Gaff's dream-self sat up in the tall, green grass. In the distance a snow-capped mountain range extended as far as he could see, and an ocean of yellow and purple flowers stretched toward a towering wood line. Behind him a brook babbled, and the same gentle breeze lovingly caressed the surrounding flowers bending them from side to side like rhythmic dancers.

Rowan'Gaff stood, turned in a circle, and looked into the mid-day sky. His chest pounded as he surveyed the prairie, not unlike the grasslands of Longshore. Tall, straight trees encircled the meadow and Rowan'Gaff felt an intense desire to remain in this peaceful place. "Hello?" his dreamy voice called only to have his call vanish in the wind.

Rowan'Gaff turned again and several feet away, opposite the stream, stood an old man. The man did not startle Rowan'Gaff; the boy felt the stranger's presence before he saw him. The man leaned on a worn staff which ended in a gnarled root, several inches above his head. His gray cloak scrubbed the ground around his boots and tracks of countless travels worked up from its worn edges.

The man looked directly at Rowan'Gaff with intense eyes and a caring, yet forceful expression. Rowan'Gaff took a step forward. "Is this where I'm supposed to be? Please..."

Rowan'Gaff's foot slipped in a slight depression and he tumbled to the ground, landing on his side. He rolled to his back and stared up into the glowing image of Cap'Tian. The hero's lance slammed into his chest, smashing through his armor, and driving the air from his lungs.

The boy shot awake, clutched at his chest, and gasped for breath. He thrashed at the remaining grass-covering and stood, pacing away from his sleeping area. He convulsed and bent forward, resting his hands on his knees.

Dawn's light crested the distant mountains, igniting a burning in his chest — a longing. That is where he needed to be, he knew it now more than ever. *I must find the old man's meadow,* he told himself. Rowan straightened and allowed the eastern light to flow over him from boot to scalp. The morning heat cleansed him, and he shrugged off the night's chill before rummaging through his pack for breakfast.

The hunk of stale bread did little to fill his hollow belly and less to diminish the aching in his chest to find the old man who stood next to the bubbling stream.

Sleeper

Dreams of Old Men

The old man shook under his thin, gray sheets. The dream hit him with enough ferocity to jerk him awake and ache his joints while a thin coat of sweat chilled his exposed skin.

"Master?" a young voice called as a sliver of flickering light crept under his chamber door.

"I'm all right," the old man called back.

Slowly, the door swung open and the face of his apprentice emerged, illuminated by candlelight. "I heard you tossing. Can I get you anything?" Genuine concern in Preslovard's voice warmed the old mystic still reeling from the fading vision's impact.

"Thank you, my boy. Perhaps a cup of tea will settle me."

Preslovard moved to the wizard's small side table and lit another stubby candle, softly filling the room with its own pale light, then left the room to warm water for his master's cup of chamomile. The mystic relied on his ten years old apprentice for many of the more energetic requirements of life: tending the garden, hunting rabbits, and cleaning the cottage. After four years in Oh'Raum's service, Preslovard proved an able apprentice with a growing knowledge of astronomy, alchemy, and the sciences.

Oh'Raum slid from his cot and sat on the edge of the rickety bunk. He stretched from side to side, initially wincing from the popping and cracking in his joints, then smiling at the resulting pressure and pain release. He stood, took up the candle holder, and shuffled to a small writing desk in the corner of his room. Ancient, leather-bound books occupied the back corners of the wood-hewn desk and haphazardly shuffled papers strewed the remainder of its surface.

The magician sat, took up his writing quill, closed his eyes, and forced himself to return to the dream. He dabbed the quill in a small ink well and hovered the feather's tip over a blank page until a drop of ink splashed to the paper. When the large black spot struck the paper's top corner, the old man's mind brought the black dream forward and, as if guided by an unseen hand, the quill scribbled across the parchment.

In his mind, Oh'Raum flew high over the land of the Western Kingdoms. He saw everything from the Kingdom of Draer, far to the North, to the Southern Wastes past The Twin Pillars. To his left, the great Sea of Res'Teran slashed a blue-green gorge across his entire vision. To his right, the impassable mountain range of The Great Hooks ran like towering spikes on some enormous creature's back.

His consciousness flew north, high over King's Road which bisected the land from south to north. Rushing air screamed in his ears as he flew toward the El'Thune Hills, the southern boundary of the Kingdom of Draer. A welcoming light bathed the entire country below him and a feeling of peace and tranquility enveloped his floating consciousness.

He flew north. Ahead to his right, where Fire Worm Road disappeared into the forested foothills of The Great Hooks and Far'Verm Pass, a menacing darkness loomed. Like a slithering dark snake, the shadow spread from Far'Verm Pass, the northern passage through the mountains. Oh'Raum's feeling of peace and tranquility diminished, replaced with a swirling sickness in the pit of his stomach.

Another image flashed in his mind like a lightning bolt arcing across a cloud-filled sky — the lapping of water against a boat beached on an unknown shore. His dream-self stood facing the ocean and felt the presence of someone behind him. Oh'Raum's hand jerked and ink slashed across the page spreading like a gash in soft flesh. The old mystic dipped the quill in the inkwell again, took a deep breath, and braced himself for the dream to continue.

"Master, your tea," Preslovard softly called when he entered the sparse room. A raised hand and a, "Shush, boy," from his master stopped him in the doorway.

Oh'Raum pressed the quill to the paper and took himself back to his high vantage point above the Western Kingdoms. The darkness ahead spread like thick, oozing crude oil across the land west of Far'Verm Pass. The peaks of the El'Thune Hills slipped beneath him, and he shivered against the icy wind of their summits bathed in deep snow like a blanket tossed over one's knees.

Ahead to his left, a vast army garbed in the silver and blue of Draer marched from the walls of Holm'Stad, the Draer capitol city. The blue of their tunics appeared like a rushing flood far below and their silver shields glinted in the bright sunlight. The two spreading armies, one a rushing ocean wave and the other a darkness his eyes could not pierce, drew closer together far below him. When their lines met, an explosion of brilliance rocketed from the ground blinding him.

In that moment, another shock ran across his body and the hairs on his arms stood on end. He no longer floated high above the land. The blazing light changed to a volley of flaming arrows that flew across his vision.

Instead of seeing the green lands of Draer, his consciousness now drifted in the deep waters of a narrow fjord like a piece of discarded flotsam. Above him, arrow after arrow whistled through a black night. He watched them arc and impact a floating ship, where high amidships the supine bodies of two people lay. The boat burst into flames and bobbed in the water slowly meandering out to sea — and the afterlife.

Oh'Raum shook again and opened his eyes. A feeling of sorrow gripped his heart at the sight of the arrows striking the ship.

Seeing his mentor's eyes flicker open, Preslovard moved farther into the room and sat on the bed. "Master Oh'Raum?"

Oh'Raum's body shuddered from the replayed impression. He turned to face the young boy and offered him a thin smile. "I have had a disturbing vision, my boy." Seeing the concern on his apprentice's face, he continued, "I'm fine." He reached for the tea and inhaled its soothing vapors.

Preslovard looked at the drying parchment under his master's quill. Oh'Raum followed Preslovard's gaze to see what his free-writing exercise produced. On the paper, jagged lines of black ink scratched across the canvas at odd angles, like long incisions from razor-sharp talons. Some of the stinging quill-marks drove through the thick paper leaving black streaks on the page beneath. Written at various angles, the old magician scribbled runes and unknown letters amongst the slashes.

Oh'Raum's breathing calmed and he regarded the jumble of letters and images on the paper. "It will take some time to decipher this message the earth-spirits have given me."

"It is still before sunrise, master. I can start preparing breakfast now or wait if you'd prefer," Preslovard offered.

"We will wait for the appointed time, my boy. There is more here for me to discover. This vision is dark, and I fear a deeper meaning yet lies within the dream."

Preslovard nodded and stood ready to leave so his master could return within himself and glean answers from the visions.

Oh'Raum took the boy by the arm. "Please, stay. Your presence is comforting in the wake of these black images. Fetch yourself a drink and return to meditate with me. I would appreciate your positive energies in the endeavor."

Preslovard smiled. "Of course, master." He returned to the bunk, crossed his legs, and took several deep breaths. He locked eyes with the mystic, smiled again, and closed his eyes.

Oh'Raum returned the smile as though feeling the boy's positive thoughts and energy fill him with renewed vitality. He turned back to the desk, took another sip of tea, placed the cup on a shorter stack of books, and drew his consciousness back within his mind.

He expected to see the frightening image of the burning funeral barge. Instead he floated high over the land again. The shadow from the East pushed against the waves of blue in the highlands of Draer. Steadily the flowing darkness drove back the blue and silver, mercury-like armies of the northern kingdom, until the darkness surrounded the city of Holm'Stad. In the next instant, the oily blackness engulfed the city, wiping it from the countryside below.

Oh'Raum shuddered again and pressed the quill's nib to a fresh piece of paper. He calmed his rushing heart by synchronizing his breathing with that of his young apprentice beside him.

The darkness in his vision gushed south unhindered, surrounding the peaks of the El'Thune Hills like filthy water flowing around a jutting rock in an unctuous sewer. Oh'Raum flew high overhead again, watching the endless onslaught of the black horde. Peering deep into his mind, he forced his consciousness to fly lower and focus into the smoky blackness. Choking, thick dust rose from the boots of black-clad soldiers. Shields, as black as night, thrust forward by gauntleted arms and stomping boots trampled everything in their path on their march over the kingdoms.

A feeling of dread filled him when he looked into the advancing horde. *Are these men or beasts or worse?* he asked his floating perception. The old man's hand jerked over the paper as he sensed an unseen presence within the thundering legion. Onward the black army marched, spreading over the A'Or Plains. From his vantage point, like a bird soaring over the land, Oh'Raum looked south for anything that could stop the blackness.

From the heart of the land, near Bal'Wern, a kingdom in the middle of the country, a light flickered. It flashed and danced like sunlight reflected from one of Bal'Wern Keep's high towered windows. As the swirling dark horde moved to surround the kingdom of Bal'Wern, the light grew in intensity, becoming a large orb of dazzling orange and yellow incandescence. The old man's heart thumped in his chest, unable to keep rhythm with the steady breaths of his ward.

The oily blackness, sliding south, stopped at the edges of the light; engulfing it but unable to penetrate it. *What is this aura?*

The beacon grew in Oh'Raum's vision, pushed back against the black army, and opened a hole in the advancing infantry's lines.

The wizard forced his consciousness to stare at the splendor, peering deep into it. Squinting against its sparkling intensity, Oh'Raum saw the outline of a fighting figure. He whirled to avoid multiple enemies' attacks while thrusting his great spear forward, cleaving a path through the darkness. He drove the creatures back with crashing shield blows and devastating advancing attacks.

As though aware of Oh'Raum's presence, the great shining figure turned his face upward. Oh'Raum could not make out his features but knew throughout his being that the hero smiled up at him. How he knew this, the old magician did not know, but a feeling of awe and virtue ran through him, again raising the fine hairs on his arms.

Oh'Raum's perception shifted away from the great hero fighting back the black army. Instantly, he felt the rocky shoreline of the great sea under his feet, heard the waves gently caressing the beach, and looked around to gain his bearings.

He stood in early morning sunlight on an unknown sheltered inlet, not a deep-water fjord. Behind him a marshy coastal wetland spread into the distance. Its distinctive rank odor a reminder of long-ago travels.

Oh'Raum turned and looked out over the calm water. *Was this where I saw the barge?* His inner voice sounded isolated and tired. He squinted into the distant waters looking for any sign of a boat when the light around him suddenly dimmed. Instead of early morning, the light faded as though time ran backward and he now stood in early twilight. He turned his gaze skyward expecting to see a flock of flaming arrows arcing across the darkening sky. The light retreated further to a pallid orange glow barely illuminating the pebbles at his feet.

Oh'Raum turned in the direction of the rising sun and sheltered his eyes against an eclipsing corona. *Sköll* had found his pray. Although only a vision in his waking memory, he recoiled from the damaging direct light of the star's blinding wreath and turned back to the coastline as a noise filled his ears — water lapping against the side of a boat. He strained to make out a small boat, in the full darkness of the eclipse's shadow, drifting on the slow current.

The wizard felt himself jerked from the beach like a fish on the end of a snagging line. Oh'Raum inhaled as his body lurched high into the air, again taking flight over the land. He flew away from the sea, scanning the coastline for the inlet and the pebbled shore. To his left, the small fishing village of

Dur'Loth Harbor emerged from a craggy, fog-filled seaboard when the moon swung away from the star and the sun's full radiance returned.

Below him, the black armies from the East retreated under the intense light of the unknown hero's ceaseless advance. Light returned to the lands and the darkness pulled away from Holm'Stad, moving in reverse through Far'Verm Pass, growing fainter as it retreated. Finally, nothing remained of the black horde but the charred land. Even the light of the hero faded from Oh'Raum's view.

With a sigh, the old wizard opened his eyes. His hand ached under the constant pressure of free-writing and the intensity of his dream.

After several deeper breaths he turned to his apprentice. "You may start breakfast, Pres," he said in a calm fatherly tone.

Preslovard inhaled his own series of breaths, opened his eyes, and stretched. "Yes, Master," he replied.

Oh'Raum replaced the quill into its holder, frowning at the significant damage this experience caused to the delicately crafted nib. On the paper, several thick lines cut across the page at sharp angles similar to his first draft. Under and around these, his hand worked to draw several runes and ancient words. Along the left side of the second page a long, jagged line ran almost the length of the entire edge. At the right side of the first page, the ugly slashes formed a long series of tall chevrons. He slid the pages around the desk, examining them from every possible angle.

To the left of the first page, and one-third up the page from the bottom, a half-circle ran off the page darkening the desk's surface beneath. Oh'Raum lifted the paper in front of him and rotated it. He turned to the small window over his cot, allowing dawn's light to shine through the paper. He looked from the page in his hand to the paper on the desk and back again.

Something about the half-circle looked familiar.

"Master?" Preslovard called. "All is prepared but for drawing a flagon from the creek."

The boy left and Oh'Raum heard the cottage door open and close. He placed the paper on the desk, stood, and moved to a small stand of shelves holding numerous delicately rolled parchments. He dug through the upper most shelf, scanning the documents until he found a worn scroll tied with a thin leather thong.

The mystic moved to the desk and unrolled the parchment, revealing a roughly drawn map of the Western Kingdoms. Oh'Raum placed the first page from his free-writing experience over the map, moving it to align with the right edge. Although not to scale, the scratched, triangular teeth running the length of the paper lined up with the map maker's rendition of The Great Hooks, a vast blockade of jagged mountains. *The half-circle must represent Bal'Wern Keep*, the mystic thought.

Oh'Raum moved the second page over the map and again, his unconscious mind had drawn a similar half-circle, but on the opposite side of the page. He aligned the circles and stood back. Along the left side of the scratched map, a jagged shoreline stretched along the paper. He followed it with his finger, dipping into coves and natural harbors. North of Skorpo Fjord his finger slid past a depression in the coastline and his heart stopped. He felt a sudden, uncontrollable urge toward that spot on the map. Something pulled the air from his lungs and forced him to sit. He needed to get to that spot on the map, he knew it — he felt it. In his mind, he again stood on the pebbled beach listening to the gentle gurgle of wave against shore. Something pulled him toward the cold waters of the great sea.

The cottage door opened and Preslovard called, "Breakfast is prepared, Master."

Brought back to his chambers, Oh'Raum yelled back, "I'll be right there." He stood, pulled the map from under the ink-blotted papers and shuffled into the small cottage's main room. On the table, Preslovard set out a plate of various cheeses, a freshly sliced overly red tomato surrounded by numerous other vegetables, a bunch of red wrinkled grapes, and a half-torn loaf of grain-bread. The young man stood over the table pouring water into stumpy wooden goblets. He looked at his master and smiled at the scroll under his arm expecting a lesson over breakfast.

Oh'Raum surveyed the meager meal and washed his hands in a prepared wooden basin in the corner of the main room. Preslovard took him a thin swatch of linen as was their morning custom.

"Thank you, my boy," the old magician said and sat at the table. He allowed Preslovard to sit before nibbling on several grapes. "I need to leave for a few weeks," he said.

"Oh?"

Oh'Raum nodded. "I believe the vision has laid before me a journey and I dare not heed its invitation."

"Can you tell me your vision, Master?"

"It is yet unclear to me the true meaning of my nightmare, but I believe it musters ill-tidings for our lands. Have you paid attention to the heavens recently?"

Preslovard smiled. "I have."

"And what do the stars tell you?"

The boy's expression turned down. "I know of *Sköll's* chase, a fortnight hence, but I know not of its significance. Does the wolf devour the Sun in these days, master? I have much to learn before I can glean any meanings the stars have for me."

Oh'Raum nodded and pulled a tomato slice to his plate. "It is good at your age to simply know of *Hati* and *Sköll*. Leave the divination to wrinkled old men like me." He offered the young boy a wink.

Preslovard laughed into his mug and washed down his bite with cool water. "When must you leave and how long will you be away?"

The old wizard pursed his lips causing the top hairs of his gray mustache to push into his bumpy nose, "As soon as you get Haseth burdened. It is eleven day's walk along the road to what I believe is the spot where I am being drawn. For how long this wandering will take me away from you, I know not."

Preslovard nodded. "I will make Haseth ready when the washing is done and prepare fresh snares in the forest."

Oh'Raum sighed. "You've been a good apprentice, Pres. I see great things in your future."

"Thank you, Master." The boy munched down on a chunk of bread smothered in a jam made from berries he and his master gathered from the forest. "Where is it the visions bade you go?"

Oh'Raum moved aside the plate of vegetables, taking a small cucumber and placing it in his mouth, before unfurling the map of the Western Kingdoms. He crunched the cucumber between his teeth and pressed his finger on an inlet along the western coast. As soon as his finger hit the spot, he again felt an irresistible tug on his being.

Preslovard stood and peered over their breakfast at the cove under his master's finger. Oh'Raum withdrew his hand still reeling from the urge to stand and walk out the door.

"Rach'Ella Wash," Preslovard read. He looked at his master, sat, and licked a blot of jam that ran down his fingers. "Never heard of it," he said through the mouthful of sweet jam.

Oh'Raum slowly shook his head. "Neither had I, my boy. Neither had I."

Sleeper

The Boy in The Woods

Nine days march from his father's farm on Longshore, Rowan'Gaff staggered through a pine forest that hugged the roots of The Great Hooks. His food ran out shortly after he crossed Narrow Bridge south of Longshore Garrison — his water the day following that.

Where Peninsula Road turned north toward Long Bridge Crossing Rowan'Gaff continued East, leaving the road's relative safety. The aching in his chest to find the old man drew him forward. Each night of his exhaustive trek culminated with him collapsing at sunset, drawn into the hellish nightmare of the black army. Night after night, his drained mind drifted to either the foot of the glimmering hero, ready to be run through by his spear, or to the creek and the old man.

Many of the previous eight nights found him lying in the peaceful meadow, longing to talk to the old man. Last night, added a new dimension to his nocturnal ethereal travels — a boat beached along a rocky shore. Any escape from the black horde eased Rowan'Gaff's sleeplessness but not long enough for him to glean any meaning to the revelations.

Four days prior, he passed slightly south of Fal'Run, a thriving lake town on the southern shore of Lake Fal'Run. Rowan'Gaff passed the town only three miles south on his eastern trek at the very edges of starving and dehydrated even then.

When the ground beneath his wary legs rose gradually into the foothills, Rowan'Gaff fainted in the day's twilight under a grove of short pines. The following morning, the tugging on his heart forced him north, paralleling the mountains to his right. Two days hence, he turned north only to continue to stumble through this foreign wood.

Beyond the evil dreams that haunted Rowan'Gaff's sleep, his forlorn mind turned to dark thoughts of his own death among these strange trees. He questioned the desire to abandon his father's farm and seek his own way in the world — a decision that brought him to this far-off dark forest and the doorstep of his dwindling mortality. If only he could resist the urge to put one foot in front of the other and find the old man in the meadow.

On the ninth day since venturing from Longshore, Rowan'Gaff Vodr crumpled to the soft ground of an overgrown copse. In the light of mid-day, his eyes closed, and a dreamless darkness enveloped him.

◌   ◌

"I'd wager the hares in this part of the country know all your tricks, my boy," Oh'Raum chided his apprentice.

"Not all, Master." Preslovard wound the string around a bent sapling and gently allowed the trap to pull the string taught. He gently brushed leaves over the snare, stood, and backed away. "I caught two last week, remember?"

The old man smiled. "Remember to give back to the forest and not hunt the free creatures too much. Although nature's abundance is provided for us, we only take what we need."

"Yes, Master," Preslovard responded. He enjoyed walking in the forest with his master and felt as though around each tree, a new lesson waited for him. Knowing that his master readied to embark on a great journey and leave him alone for how long he knew not, filled the boy with trepidation. Preslovard trusted his master and knew the old mystic held his best interests at heart.

Oh'Raum stopped and poked the ground with his short walking stick. Preslovard pulled up next to him and eyed the ground at his master's feet. Small, under-ripe strawberries poked out from below a tuft of brush. Preslovard bent to examine the vine and mark the spot for when the fruits ripened.

"These will be ripe in a few..." Preslovard started. A firm hand on his shoulder cut his words short. With a single touch, the apprentice felt Oh'Raum's wordless uneasiness.

Preslovard stood and scanned the forest around his master. Neither spoke as the song of remote birds filled the air. In the distance the gurgling brook added to the forest's sounds.

Oh'Raum took a deep breath and closed his eyes. He felt the same presence that inhabited his dreams of the pebble-strewn beach. The wizard turned in a circle allowing his instincts to reach out like a *virgula divina* and tell him which path to follow through the wood.

Preslovard remained silent, knowing not to interrupt his master when such trances took hold of his consciousness. He followed the mystic through the forest toward the source of power that drew him. *Is this part of his night visions?* the boy wondered.

They walked a short distance and ducked under a fallen tree at the edge of a thicket of thin but dense conifers. Oh'Raum stopped at the clump of trees and cocked his head, resembling a forest creature, intently listening for an approaching predator. Preslovard stepped beside his master looking between the tree trunks.

Oh'Raum rested a hand on Preslovard's shoulder. The old

man whispered, "Do you see it?"

Preslovard thinned his eyes and looked deeper into the stand of trees. He shook his head, not seeing as his master did.

Oh'Raum stepped into the thick grove and all but vanished from sight. He moved through the trees with a lightness and silence that rivaled any of the other woodland creatures Preslovard had observed. The boy leaned from side to side, hoping to catch a glimpse of his master sliding through the stand of trees, but the old man moved like the wind.

"Preslovard!" Oh'Raum called, startling his apprentice. "Return to the cottage and prepare my medicines." The urgency in his voice spurred Preslovard to action. Rarely did Oh'Raum shout at the youth. When he did, Preslovard acted as ordered.

"Yes, Master," Preslovard responded.

"Quickly now!" Oh'Raum shouted.

Preslovard loped through the forest toward the meadow, his mind racing at what mystery his master discovered in the tree stand. He burst from the wood line into the meadow's light and sprinted for the cottage as ordered.

He slammed through the door, sliding to a stop in front of a large wooden box in which Oh'Raum stored his medicines. Preslovard placed the small box on the table, opened it, and removed bundles of dried herbs, several vials of colorful liquids, and spotless linen swatches. He moved a clean crock to the hook above the fire and between heavy breaths filled it with their remaining breakfast water. Preslovard rounded the house and plunged the empty water jug into the stream.

Oh'Raum lurched from the forest dragging something behind him. "Hurry," he yelled.

Preslovard ran to the house, placed the jug on the table, and met his master in the front garden. Oh'Raum's gray cloak bounced behind him with each step. One end of the cloak was wrapped around the mystics staff and the other was tied around a limp human body like a makeshift travois.

The out of breath mystic dropped his staff and marched into the cottage while Preslovard cautiously unwrapped the cloak to reveal a dirty youth, not much older than himself. The boy's gaunt, gray face lulled to one side and his tattered clothing hung to his frail skeleton by threads.

Oh'Raum emerged from the house with the water pitcher, several linen bandages, and a bundle of dried leaves. He drenched the herbs and linens in the cold water, knelt next to the boy's head, and placed a dripping linen under his chin. He crunched the herbs in his hands and set them on the wet rags. "Pres, warm some soup. Our young friend here will be very hungry should he wake."

"Yes, Master."

Oh'Raum bent his cheek over the boy's face while holding his breath against the vapors emanating from the re-hydrated rhizome. The old mystic smiled when a soft breath escaped the boy's lips and moments later, his eye's flickered awake. He moved his mouth to sound words but only managed a wheeze while clutching at his chest.

"Save your strength, young man. You've been snatched from an early boat ride to the afterlife."

The boy's blood-shot eyes surveyed the old wizard's face and tears flowed to his ears.

"Ah," Oh'Raum announced when Preslovard emerged from the house with a small bowl of warm soup, "are you hungry, young man?"

The boy's eyes fixed on Oh'Raum and he struggled a whisper, "I..."

Oh'Raum smiled.

Preslovard knelt opposite his master and handed Oh'Raum the bowl who spooned the warm liquid gently across the boy's lips. When the soup entered his mouth, the young man licked his lips and opened his mouth like a hungry, newborn sparrow. Oh'Raum dribbled more of the brown broth into the boy's mouth and with each spoonful, the young man inched closer to lucidity. After Oh'Raum spooned half the bowl into the boy, he turned to Preslovard. "Help him sit up." Preslovard wrapped his arm under the young man's head and propped his back against one knee. Oh'Raum handed him the bowl which the boy upturned into his mouth with both hands, all the while keeping his eyes fixed on the old magician.

"Slowly, young man," Oh'Raum said, "you've no need to eat like a condemned man. What is your name and how come you to these woods?"

The boy slurped the last bit of soup from the bowl, his eyes still squarely on Oh'Raum. "Rowan'Gaff," he whispered. "I," he paused, "I came here for you."

Oh'Raum glanced at Preslovard, giving him silent instructions with the slightest eye movement. Preslovard held out his hands for the empty bowl and took it into the cottage.

"For me, you say? And what master would send you to me so ill prepared for the journey?"

Rowan'Gaff looked around the meadow and eyed the cottage, expecting to be forcefully yanked from this peaceful place and impaled as he had been in his nightmares. "No master," he answered, stuttering. "I left my father's farm and..."

Oh'Raum watched the hair on the boy's arm's stand on end and his head jerk from side to side.

"I," he managed. His hands went to his chest and his breathing grew heavy as though fearing an impending attack.

"Calm yourself. You're safe here," Oh'Raum said.

The boy jerked and crashed backward. His eyes rolled into his forehead, his body convulsed, and he fell to the ground violently thrashing. Oh'Raum steadied the boy's head making sure the fit did not cause him to choke. In his mind, Rowan'Gaff again faced off against his legendary ancestor awaiting the inevitable death stroke.

With a final wheeze, the quakes stopped and Rowan'Gaff lay still, his head cradled in the old man's wrinkled hands.

Sleeper

Go West

In the many years Oh'Raum called the small cottage in the meadow home, his only companions had been, Haseth, a hinny nag, and his apprentice, Preslovard. Each morning, master and apprentice walked the quiet stream that ran through their secluded meadow in the foothills of The Great Hooks, east of Lake Fal'Run. Oh'Raum talked about the Earth, the stars, and ancient knowledge he would eventually pass to the boy.

Although considered by most to be a magical conjurer, a mysterious dark wizard, or the possessor of ancient wisdom, Oh'Raum explained to his ward the power of scientific knowledge over the ignorance of society. This insight required proficiency in astronomy, physics, chemistry, biology, botany, and a list of sciences unknown to the masses. Preslovard especially enjoyed the study of botany and excelled at tending the garden. While watching Preslovard, Oh'Raum regularly reflected on the day he decided to make the boy his apprentice.

On an infrequent trading junket to Bal'Wern, Oh'Raum came across a pregnant woman and a filthy, disheveled man giving away their son for apprenticeship on a soggy back alley. The runty, dark-haired boy looked malnourished and in need of a bath.

Apprenticeship, more akin to legal adoption in the Western Kingdoms, existed as a means for a family with too many children to make room for an expecting mother. If not for the natural urges of men and women, and the overabundance of guardian-less youth, apprenticeship would be outlawed in the kingdoms. Turning a youngster onto the street strictly went against the provisions of the Western Kingdoms Charter established between the three kingdoms and the Southern Desert Tribes.

Oh'Raum's rare trip to the walled city proved fruitful as he traded surplus vegetables and jenny milk to Mard, the blacksmith, for several pounds of scrap iron left over from shoeing Lord Bohn's newest stable horses. He also persuaded seven travelers to have their fortunes foretold for a few coins while lounging in Long Bridge Tavern, which he used at Ner'Dim's shop to replenish his stock of alkahest.

With his bartering completed and a few spare coins clinking in his purse, Oh'Raum prepared to leave the city with Haseth in tow, her sloping back laden with his new acquisitions.

"Please, sir, are you in need of an apprentice?" the pregnant woman called. "Take my boy, sir. He's a sturdy lad, despite his appearance, and will serve you well."

"Aye," announced a short man behind her who smelled of fish and ale.

Oh'Raum stopped at the sight of the boy — small, skinny, eyes downturned, wearing shabby clothing and shoeless. "How old is this creature?"

"Six, Milord," the woman answered.

"Don't call me that," Oh'Raum chastised, "I'm no nobleman, woman." He cleared his throat, withdrew a small yellow flower from inside his cloak, and held it in front of the youth. "Here boy, what does this flower say to you?" the wizard asked.

The woman looked at her husband in response to the strange question. "Sir, I know he looks small, but he'd make a good farm hand, you can count on that."

Oh'Raum leaned in closer to the lad, ignoring his mother. "What does this flower say?" he asked again in a softer tone.

The boy regarded the daisy and the weathered face of the gray-haired stranger. He took a deep breath, hoping to smell the bright flower's sweet aroma. Finally, in a meek voice, he said, "Nothing, sir."

Oh'Raum straightened, returned the flower to his pocket and released a gruff breath. "Useless," he whispered and turned, leaving them in the street.

"Please, sir," the woman begged and reached for the mage's elbow.

The boy pulled away from this mother, stepped around her, and tugged on the old mystic's cloak. Oh'Raum turned and looked sternly down at him. When their eyes met, the boy felt the full force of the wizard's hard gaze but did not allow it to diminish his determination. "It does not speak because you picked it," the lad whispered.

Saddened and embarrassed by her son's ridiculous statement, the woman put her hands on his shoulders and pulled him back to her. She glanced over her shoulder, feeling her chances of finding her son an apprenticeship dwindling with his silly, nonsensical answer. Her husband shook his head and furrowed his brow, ready to deliver the boy's punishment as soon as this cloaked old man moved on.

A broad smile crossed Oh'Raum's face. He burst into raucous laughter and nodded in praise at the child's response. The old mystic knelt in front of the boy and squinted into his tiny eyes. These were not the dark eyes he'd given the boy for grabbing his robes but the gentle, caring, questioning eyes of a mentor. "There might be hope for you yet, young man."

Oh'Raum stood. "Madam, I would like to take your boy as my apprentice," he announced.

The woman turned to her husband before tears of joyful sorrow drenched her face.

The squat, balding man stepped from around his wife, his mood for punishments abated. "He'll be a right good apprentice for you sir, won't you, son?" the boy's father asked.

"Yes, father."

Preslovard's mother knelt and turned him to her. "You work hard for this gentleman," she bid through more sobs and kissed him on the cheek. She dabbed a corner of her apron to her lips and wiped his face free of any lingering grime. With a hand on her shoulder, the husband pulled her to her feet and took a step away from the gray magician.

"Come boy," Oh'Raum ordered, turned, and continued his way to the end of the street. Preslovard did not look back, walking several paces behind his new mentor.

When the pair rounded a corner, Oh'Raum turned and looked down at the youth following him. "What is your name, son?"

"Preslovard, sir," the boy answered. "Preslovard Parn."

"And do you yet know your numbers and letters, young Preslovard?"

The boy shook his head at the question.

"Well, we shall have to remedy that straight away, won't we?"

ભ   જ

Reminiscing on his apprentice's entrance into his quiet lifestyle of self-imposed solitude did nothing to bring forth answers to the questions posed by his recent dreams. *Was I right to bring this boy into this life*? he asked himself. Oh'Raum had never asked himself that in the four years since returning with the boy from Bal'Wern. Each day since intervening in Preslovard's life filled his with joy at the teaching and the learning, experienced as a pseudo-parent. Preslovard never once shirked his duties, talked back to him, or questioned an order. He added incalculable value to life at the cottage and Oh'Raum struggled to imagine a day without his ward by his side.

Now he struggled what to do with this new boy, an even greater unknown. The power drawing him to leave his home also awakens in him the sense that Rowan'Gaff played some important role in his visions. The old wizard spent hours tending the boy's injuries while pondering what role he would play in his eventual journey west.

No matter what course his mind took to rationalize recent events, his love for Preslovard pulled his thoughts to his apprentice. The thought of leaving the boy behind hurt Oh'Raum like nothing he experienced in his long years. What power did this boy have over him? What about this journey felt different?

Oh'Raum had not returned to Bal'Wern since Preslovard came to the meadow but made the four-day supply-trading journey to D'Grath many times in the past four years. When he did, he left the boy at the cottage without question or concern knowing all would be well with him. This journey felt different to the mystic. It felt as though he would be going against his will, forced to leave his home and ward.

Between restless bouts of sleep and tending his patient, Oh'Raum scanned his route across the map of the Western Kingdoms. Each time his eyes fell on the strange, insignificant inlet on the far western coast, the drawing in his chest intensified. Unconsciously his fingers caressed the spot and in his mind he stood on that unfamiliar shore listening to low waves slosh the beach.

"Master," Preslovard softly called from the doorway, "how

many days' provisions would you like me to prepare?" The question came on an air of uncertainty and Oh'Raum felt the apprehension in the boy's voice. The old man stood, surveyed a sleeping Rowan'Gaff, and joined his apprentice in the cottage's main room. He offered Preslovard a genuine smile when he caught the boy eyeing Rowan'Gaff. "I don't know how long we'll be gone, my boy."

"We?"

Oh'Raum sat at the table across from Preslovard, feeling the uneasiness emanating from him. Oh'Raum nodded. "I've searched for signs of what path lay ahead of me and I believe this young man should accompany me."

Preslovard remained silent, trusting his master.

"I have yet to decipher the true meanings of my visions but feel this young man has a role to play. That role, I know not. But I do know one thing." Preslovard looked up at him. "You're a capable young man and we both feel the heaviness of this impending, uncertain venture. I've left you alone before and you've fared well."

"I know, but—"

"We'll need provisions enough for D'Grath. There I believe I can secure supplies for the rest of the journey to the coast."

The boy looked down. "Yes, master."

Oh'Raum sighed. "You want to travel with us, don't you?"

Preslovard nodded.

"I would also like that very much, but who would tend the house or the garden? Have you a secret friend in the forest of which I know not who can attend your daily chores?"

The boy laughed. "I will make one while you're gone, so I may join you on your next quest or even," he paused, "have my own adventure."

Oh'Raum sat back in the chair and smiled at the boy's wit. "In time, I have no doubt you will have your own adventures.

For now, I need you here looking for our speedy return."

"I will," he paused, "Master." In his heart, Preslovard wished to call this man, Father.

The cot in Oh'Raum's room creaked, drawing their attention.

"Well," Oh'Raum said and slapped the table, "we have preparations to make. You pack Haseth and I will prepare my belongings for the journey. It sounds as though our new friend is awake and my feeling to leave immediately grows with each breath. More delay adds to my impatience to at once be about the road."

Preslovard stood, looked at his mentor, smiled, and left the cottage for the small attached stable to ready Haseth for her long walk.

Oh'Raum return to his chamber where Rowan'Gaff sat on the edge of the bunk. "Feeling better, young man?"

"I'm hungry."

"I'll take that as a yes." Oh'Raum poured water from the pitcher and sprinkled in a pinch of a reddish powder. "Drink this. I'll fetch food. Drink all of it, now," Oh'Raum said before leaving the room.

Rowan'Gaff sniffed at the mug and an unfamiliar sweetness wafted around his head. He sipped at the water and looked around the room. A roughly fashioned desk, piled with ancient-looking books, took up one corner and a floor to ceiling bookshelf sat in another. Opposite this, a low table held a small water pitcher inside a carved basin. Slung over one corner lay a linen towel.

He downed the rest of the water, gingerly pushed himself off the cot, and shuffled to the desk. Stretched across the free space lay a map held open by small stones at two corners and stacks of books at the others. Rowan'Gaff traced his finger along the roads and looked at the strange markings labeling the trails and settlements.

"Does anything look familiar?" Oh'Raum's dry voice startled the boy.

Rowan'Gaff sharply turned, almost dropping the cup. Oh'Raum stood in the doorway holding a plate of colorful vegetables, a wedge of cheese, and a crumble of brown bread. At the sight of the food, Rowan's mouth watered. How long had it been since he last ate solid food?

"Since you're on your feet, come into the main room and we'll talk while you eat your fill."

Rowan'Gaff's eyes shifted between the map and the plate before straggling into the main part of the cottage. Oh'Raum placed the plate on the table and pulled back a chair, inviting him to sit. The boy sat and voraciously dug into the food before Oh'Raum could say, "Don't wait for me. Help yourself."

The old man sat across from the boy, allowing him to tear at the food like a hungry dog. He shoveled food into his mouth and washed it down with a gulp of water before returning to the frenzy.

"By your garb, you come from Longshore," Oh'Raum said.

The boy nodded in between bites, chews, gulps, and swallows.

"And you said you came here for me?"

Rowan'Gaff nodded again.

"By what road?"

"No road," Rowan'Gaff answered with a mouthful of bread.

"You journeyed overland, then?"

"Aye," the boy said. Not "yes sir," as was custom in the Western Kingdoms when addressing a person of greater station.

Oh'Raum ignored the boy's discourtesy. "Why come to me? And so ill-prepared that we find you unconscious in the wood, knocking on the doors of the afterlife?"

"I had to," Rowan'Gaff said and shook his head, searching for a more adequate answer. He spoke slowly, "I saw you. I saw you in your meadow. I woke here, in the grass, near the stream. And you were there."

Oh'Raum narrowed his eyes. "How did you see me?"

"In a vision," Rowan'Gaff replied.

"A vision?"

"Aye."

"And this vision, it beckoned you to my door?"

The boy nodded again and bit into a soft-boiled potato.

"What other sights were given to you in this vision?"

Rowan'Gaff instinctively touched his chest without noticing the watchful eyes of the old magician. "I saw," he hesitated and looked into his emptying plate.

Oh'Raum felt the boy's hesitation, he also felt the burning inside him to leave for the coast. "In time, you can tell me your story. For now, finish eating." He stood, walked to his chambers and returned with the map. In his youth Oh'Raum traveled overland at a fast clip, but for the length of his beard, this journey would proceed at a more leisurely pace. Looming thunder clouds and the aching in his joints tempered the yearning in his heart to reach Rach'Ella Wash.

He sat again, unrolled the map, and looked at Rowan'Gaff. "I, too, have had a vision. My visions bid me to journey to the coast, much as yours drew you here."

Rowan'Gaff regarded him with astonishment. "Your chest burns also?"

"I plan to make northward for the D'Grath Ferry," Oh'Raum said and pointed to a spot on the map. Rowan'Gaff leaned forward to look at the crossing of the Great River Mor'Ah which, at a mile wide in places, cut the land in two from the mountains to the tip of the southwestern peninsula. "This route means cutting through familiar forests. A four-day journey."

Rowan'Gaff followed the mountain range south to the drawing of a small hut nestled in the foothill of The Great Hooks. He looked across the map, unable to read its markings.

Oh'Raum noticed his wandering attention. "This is Longshore, where I assume you trekked from." He pointed to a stretch of green running the northern half of a long peninsula before returning to the slopes of the eastern mountains. "In D'Grath I plan to barter for supplies enough to reach to the coast, a further seven day's march along the Plains Road." Rowan'Gaff followed the old man's finger as he traced their intended route. "I believe following the road will aid in our travel."

"Our?"

Oh'Raum looked at him and nodded.

"I know nothing of these lands. I came to find you," he paused, "and I have yet to learn who you are." His breathing grew sharp and short.

The sound of Preslovard's handling of Haseth interrupted them. Her gentle nature grew restless when being readied for a long journey and saddled with canvas sacks. Through the walls of the cottage Oh'Raum heard the familiar, "There's a good girl," and "There we go," from Preslovard as he coaxed the hinny from her stabling.

"I am Oh'Raum and my apprentice is Preslovard. I am a student of this world and knower of things. I, too, have seen visions and I, too, am drawn to journey. I believe you were sent here to travel with me for a purpose I have yet to discover."

Rowan'Gaff sat quietly for a moment before leaning forward and whispering, "Did you see him?"

Oh'Raum smiled. "Indeed."

Rowan'Gaff released the breath he held and sank in his chair, flooded with emotion. "I, too, will be a great hero someday. It is my destiny."

Oh'Raum cocked his head.

"I'm not one of those black-clad horrors. I shall be like Cap'Tian, a great hero — destined for great things!" Unconsciously, Rowan'Gaff brought a hand to his chest while he grew more animated. "It's in my very blood!"

"Cap'Tian?" Oh'Raum mouthed, recalling the songs of the great hero. Memories of the glowing figure flooded him. *Cap'Tian*, he thought.

"I - I," Rowan'Gaff stuttered and shook, "not." His body stiffened in the chair and his leg kicked the table jarring Oh'Raum from his own vision. Rowan'Gaff's eyes rolled backward and Oh'Raum slowly helped him to the floor.

"There, there, my boy," Oh'Raum soothed until the boy's shaking stopped. "It'll pass soon." When Rowan's seizure subsided, Oh'Raum carried him to the bunk.

Oh'Raum returned to his map. North of where the Plains Road met King's Road, he planned to span the River Thune and turn westward, crossing north of the vast wetlands indicated on the map.

He closed his eyes and steadied his mind, thinking on the path he planned to take through the forests. Oh'Raum knew the countryside well and the cities stretching from mountains to sea, surprised to have never visited the spit of land known as Rach'Ella Wash. He had crossed the River Thune many times on infrequent visits to The Kingdom of Draer in advisory service to King Tyurn. Never once had he turned to the coast, preferring to stick to the well-marked and maintained roads that crisscrossed the Western Kingdoms.

Oh'Raum pulled a small, leather pack from a storage closet and placed it on the table. He rolled his map, tied it with a thin leather thong, and laid it beside the pack. From a wooden storage box, he removed a crock of pickled radishes and one of the small cheese wheels. To this he added several ears of corn, Preslovard picked the previous day, and the remnants of a smoked rabbit shoulder from last night's dinner. He piled the simple food-stocks into the pack along with a small book, his traveling quill, a long thin pipe, a pouch of pipe-weed, and several prepared firelighters. The latter, one of his more thrilling wizardry tricks, amazed the dull-witted and unschooled alike by allowing him to produce fire at will. In reality, through his knowledge of chemistry and experimentation, Oh'Raum learned that dipping thin sticks into a mixture of ground fish bones and tree sap sparked when struck against a sufficiently course stone. Many travelers at Long Bridge Tavern told tales of Oh'Raum's ability to ignite objects in his bare hands for the mere cost of a lesser coin.

The cottage door opened. "Haseth is prepared, Master."

"Very well," Oh'Raum answered.

"Have you deciphered the meaning of the dream?" Preslovard asked.

Oh'Raum thought about Rowan'Gaff's earlier confession but shook his head. "My dreams are pulled in so many directions, I have yet to learn how the visions are connected." He thought for a moment. "My spirit is drawn to the west, as our young friend in there," he pointed to his chambers, "was drawn here."

Preslovard sat at the table, pondering the meaning of the strange, older boy.

"Pack your satchel with supplies enough for D'Grath. The young man will be leaving with me and will need his own provisions."

"Of course, Master," Preslovard replied.

Oh'Raum entered his room to find Rowan'Gaff sitting on the edge of the cot again. "We must be on the road, young Rowan'Gaff. Your fits do not appear to wax your strength for long. Are you able to travel?"

Rowan'Gaff stood; his legs more unstable than he let on.

"Aye."

The two emerged from the back room as Preslovard finished tying the thong of his small pack. Preslovard handed the pack over to Rowan'Gaff.

"There's food for two days in here. I also added my spare water skin and flints for cooking."

Oh'Raum smiled and nodded at his apprentice.

"I have packed Haseth with five days provisions," Preslovard said to his master.

"Very well," Oh'Raum said and stepped toward the door. "I took the radishes." He patted his pack. "I know you won't eat them."

Preslovard made a face at the mention of the pickled red bulbs. He moved to the door and removed his master's gray cloak from a hook and made a show of dusting it.

"You have enough in the root cellar alone to last several months and I expect you'll have some fresh tomatoes in a few days."

Preslovard nodded. "Would you like me to fetch a portion of the smoked fish?"

Oh'Raum shook his head. "We'll be fine on what we have, my boy. You finish it tonight." He moved to the door, let his pack slide to the floor, accepted the cloak from Preslovard and shuffled it onto his shoulders.

Preslovard lifted his mentor's pack and pulled a long, well-used walking stick from the corner of the room. He handed Rowan'Gaff a waist-length, knotted tunic. "In case the night's get cold," he said in a pleasant tone.

Rowan'Gaff took the tunic and tossed it over his shoulder.

Oh'Raum smiled at his old wooden walking stick. "Thank you, my boy," he said.

"Of course, master," Preslovard replied.

Outside, Haseth nibbled on several sweet strands of grass growing at the corner of the cottage. She lifted her head when Oh'Raum approached and ran his hand along her forehead. "Ready, old friend?"

He untied Haseth's lead and turned her toward the narrow path that lead to Lake Fal'Run, a half-day's journey west. Rowan'Gaff awkwardly followed the old wizard, unfamiliar with the air of apprehension in the old man's leaving.

Oh'Raum turned to Preslovard who stood outside the door. "We should reach the coast in ten days. I don't know what to expect when we get there." He paused, looking at the boy. "I will return with all haste."

Preslovard lifted his chin to display his mustered courage. "I look forward to hearing the tale of your journey upon your speedy return, Master."

Oh'Raum smiled, seeing through the facade his ward portrayed, but feeling pride with him all the same. "Everything will be fine, my boy. I expect you to continue your studies while I am away."

"Yes, Master."

With one final survey of the cottage, Oh'Raum turned and led Haseth to the edge of the meadow where the trail broke into a thick forest. Before stepping into the dark wood, the old wizard turned and sighed at his own uneasiness of leaving his apprentice for so long. Secretly, he longed to call the boy son, as much as the boy longed to call him father.

Rowan'Gaff followed behind the animal, happy that the burning in his chest had finally subsided.

The Journey to the Sea

The sun stood overhead at mid-day when Oh'Raum and Rowan'Gaff stepped into the thick wood encircling the peaceful meadow. In his mind, he calculated where they should be when the sun dipped toward the western horizon on the far side of Lake Fal'Run.

"We should make the edge of the lake by nightfall, old girl," Oh'Raum told Haseth who clopped along behind him.

"How far is that?" Rowan'Gaff asked from behind Haseth.

Unfamiliar with having traveling companions, Oh'Raum often spoke to his hinny and had all but forgotten the young boy shuffling along behind her.

"It is but mid-day, young man. The lake lies the second half of the day away. We'll make camp along its banks while the sun is setting."

"We have to walk all day?"

"Our journey takes us across the whole country, as yours did to find my meadow. We will be on the march until we reach the western shore."

Rowan'Gaff made an unfamiliar sound and kicked at loose rocks in the path with each step.

Oh'Raum sang a walking song under his breath while they passed among the trees.

> Through seas of grass and forested green,
> This old traveler is often seen.
> He moves in song with spirits high,
> And under stars his head will lie.

He hummed the melody, only remembering a few words of the next verse. "I'm out of practice," he announced. The hinny paid him no attention and Rowan'Gaff barely lifted his head at the comment. "Haseth knows the song better than I, ay girl? Come on, sing with me!" He looked over his shoulder at the boy and improvised a new verse.

> Under gray wool cloak in hand his staff,
> He marches with young Rowan'Gaff.

Oh'Raum turned to see the boy's lackadaisical response. A raucous bout of laughter escaped him, and he returned to humming the melody of the traveling song.

At dusk, Oh'Raum, Rowan'Gaff, and Haseth emerged from the forest path on the eastern shore of Lake Fal'Run, an immense inland sea. Puffy brown cattails crowded the nearest shore and tall grasses stretched along the shoreline in both directions. Fish from Fal'Run provided a steady diet of protein when the forest rabbits eluded Preslovard's ingenious snares.

Rowan'Gaff collapsed against a tree trunk and drained his water skin.

Oh'Raum tied Haseth's lead to a small tree and eyed the young man. "Oy, there will be time enough for lounging when we've made camp. Scrounge some kindling while I prepare our bed rolls," he said. He untied two thick rolled blankets from Haseth and unrolled them opposite her tree. Rowan'Gaff crushed the water bag into his small pack, muttered something under his breath, and walked into the woods picking up small sticks.

"I have excellent hearing, my young friend."

Rowan'Gaff stopped in his tracks.

"For one who does not know his letters, you should not use such language in polite company. However, should you wish to use the proper curses in the future, I would suggest zounderkite over mumblecrust. And despite what you think, I am neither."

The boy briefly looked at his feet before continuing with his impromptu chore.

After starting a small fire, Oh'Raum crunched on several pickled radishes while a small earthen crock sat on a pair of rocks straddling his cooking fire. He offered the radishes to Rowan'Gaff who turned his nose up at the smell of the pickling brine. Haseth eyed the ears of corn boiling in the water, knowing that once the old wizard finished off the outer kernels, her snack would be the delightfully crunchy, and still warm, cob.

"I should have brought my line and hook, hey girl?" Oh'Raum remarked while carving off a thin piece of meat from the rabbit haunch which he handed to Rowan. Haseth lowered her head and sniffed the grass encircling the base of the tree.

Following dinner, Oh'Raum and Rowan'Gaff stretched out on their blankets. Oh'Raum wrapped his cloak around his legs and stared into the night's sky, quietly listening to water lap the lakeshore and distant frogs chirp for their mates.

"Tell me of your home, young man."

Rowan'Gaff sighed. "My father is a Longshoreman farmer outside of Son'Us. He smelled of manure and depression at his station," he dryly replied.

"I see," Oh'Raum whispered. "And what of your mother?"

"I have no memory of my mother, and judging the lowly state of my worthless father, nor do I desire any."

Oh'Raum remained silent and stared at the twinkling stars.

"I left that life behind for the destiny that awaits me," Rowan'Gaff said with as much hope as his tired body could muster.

Oh'Raum thought about finding the boy half-dead in a thicket. "And what destiny is that?"

"I am going to be a great hero, not some commonplace farmer."

"Then may you dream of heroes, young man. I will dream of far-off shores, for I know not my destiny," Oh'Raum said.

Rowan'Gaff shuttered. He did not want to dream at all — least of which about heroes.

☙ ❧

In Oh'Raum's dream, storm clouds crested the craggy, snow-covered tips of The Great Hooks and long lines of torch-fire poured from its northern pass. Unlike his previous night's vision, Oh'Raum felt the age of the world in his dream, an ancient version of the lands he knew so well.

The inky blackness spread across the land like an impassable fog thrust forward by driving wind. His consciousness saw the entire passage of time in an instant. In his dream-state, Oh'Raum both felt the ground beneath his feet and saw the world change from high above. Riverbeds twisted and flowed around him, yet at the same time, far below him. The Great River Mor'Ah shifted south toward the Twin Pillars then reversed, allowing the southern desert to swallow whole forests as it advanced north.

The Sun and Moon shot passed him, but also far overhead. They arced across the sky so quickly it flashed from day to night then back to day before his mind's eye adjusted to the change.

Immense northern ice sheets flowed to the sea, calving enormous chunks of itself into the waiting water. Blankets of

58

snow flowed down mountainsides only to suddenly retreat nearer the summits with the incredible passage of time.

Through it all, Oh'Raum felt the change. He watched cities and entire kingdoms sprout from the ground then crumble to ruins. Forests expanded, fell back, and burst forward again like undulating prairie grass waving in a spring breeze. From his juxtaposed vantage points, he watched the blackness retreat back across the mountains and the hero's light fade from the countryside. The world spun around him and his two viewpoints converged, dropping him again on the pebbled beach of Rach'Ella Wash.

A salty breath brushed past him from the ocean and stung his nose when he inhaled deeply.

"Hello?" Oh'Raum's consciousness called, cutting through the morning air. His bellow faded into the sound of low waves softly pushing up the beach and the crunching of pebbles underfoot as he turned in a circle.

Without warning, the vista shifted abruptly around him and caused his dream-self to stagger. He no longer stood on the shore but outside a great walled city. Fires burned along a battle-line and entire sections of the wall lay in heaps where siege engines successfully breached the city's defenses.

Oh'Raum turned and watched a cohort of men celebrating their victory. At the heart of the festivity stood the shining hero, his face obscured — as brilliant as the sun. He held a tall clay mug in his upraised hand, saluting his men. With a boisterous roar they cheered their leader, and all drank heartily from their own mugs.

Oh'Raum willed his consciousness to glide through the crowd of euphoric soldiers toward the hero. He yearned to see the man's features, to know this apparition who haunted his dreams and called him to the coast. Again, his dream swirled and melted around him, only he and the hero remained, the soldiers fading into his dream's foggy blackness. Throughout his being Oh'Raum felt something strange about the soldiers; for they were not soldiers at all. Their chosen instruments of battle were not swords and shields, but plain garden implements and wood-hewn spades.

Oh'Raum glided toward the hero. When the shining man withdrew the mug from his lips, the dazzling light surrounding him swiftly faded and the man swooned, falling on his pike for support. Oh'Raum reached for him, desperately wanting to hold him up. The man fell to the ground and his light faded to blackness, as did the world around Oh'Raum. In the darkness, he instantly found himself underwater fighting to reach the surface. With a final stroke, the old mystic broke the surface, and struggled to get his bearings. A volley of arrows lit the sky. His perspective changed from water-level to standing on a rocking boat. Fiery arrows arced toward him. Oh'Raum brought his arms up in a vain attempt to shield himself from the blazing missiles. The deck of the *langskip* erupted in flames, engulfing the wizard's awareness in yellow-orange heat.

Oh'Raum shook from his fiery dream, his chest heaving for breath. He opened his eyes, half expecting arrows to fill the sky above him. He rolled toward the remains of their fire. Across the smoldering embers, Rowan'Gaff fought an unseen demon in his own nightmare.

"No!" the boy cried and curled in a fetal position, clutching his chest. He kicked at his bed roll and rose to his knees, shaking off the dark vision. His wide eyes locked on Oh'Raum's over the makeshift fire pit. "You saw me?" he asked between ragged breaths.

Oh'Raum nodded.

"I have the same dream each time I sleep," Rowan'Gaff admitted, his pulse slowing.

"As do I."

Rowan's mouth fell agape at the old wizard's confession. "You see him too? In your dreams?"

"The shining hero," Oh'Raum said.

Rowan'Gaff fell against the tree trunk. "Cap'Tian himself. I desire nothing more to stand with him — to see his smiling face."

Oh'Raum nodded again. "He beckons my spirit to the coast. For what, I know not."

Rowan'Gaff pulled his legs to his chest and swallowed hard. "And the black army? You see them as well?"

"I do."

"What does it all mean? Why are we forced to endure these visions?"

Shards of morning light glinted from dew droplets dusting the grass on which Haseth munched.

"In time, I hope all is revealed. For now, we follow the path before us." Oh'Raum stretched under his blanket and shook off the harsh night-visions. Through a broad, lingering yawn he said, "No visions for you, I'd suspect, ay Haseth?" The nag regarded him with a tuft of grass protruding from the side of her mouth, ready for grinding between her stubby teeth.

Oh'Raum sat up, unwrapped himself from his cloak, stood, and scanned the area for an appropriate place to drain his morning water. "Slowly, the spirits are putting the pieces together in our minds. It has been my experience that when they are ready, all will be revealed." Rowan'Gaff stood and shivered. Haseth paid neither of them much attention.

Although hungry, another craving filled Oh'Raum's belly — the desire to reach the coast with all alacrity. After relieving himself, he and Rowan'Gaff rolled their linens and the old man showed the boy how to properly secure them to Haseth while choking down more pickled radishes. Oh'Raum washed down the briny vegetables with a splash from his water-skin, shook off the morning's final chill, and untied Haseth from her tree. With a few enticing clicks the hinny moved with him along the shore to a small creek-crossing leading north to the D'Grath Ferry.

Rowan'Gaff yawned. "How far today?"

"A full day's march through the wood, young warrior of destiny."

"Then what?"

"Two more days before we reach Ferry Road."

"Three days of walking? All Day?"

Oh'Raum stopped at the edge of the creek, turned, and sternly looked at the boy. "Our journey does not end until we reach the western shore of this land. Complaining about the distance does nothing to lessen it. That is why I sing." He clicked and patted Haseth's rump to cajole her through the shallow water.

Rowan'Gaff made a face and hopped from stone to stone across the gully.

On the opposite bank of the shallow creek, Oh'Raum opened into another walking song to pass the time as the traveling trio wound through the forest, hugging the mountain's foothills. The tune did nothing to erase the images burned into his mind's eye. Each bar he hummed, stumbling over the words, brought forward the vivid visions from his memory. He picked a long, thin strand of switchgrass, slid it between his lips, and tried to make sense of the jumbled images from both his and the boy's dreams. Several stood out in his mind: the shining hero suddenly fading to darkness, the unfamiliar seashore to which he felt drawn, and the burning boat. *Did this boy share the same dreams or are his different?* Oh'Raum pondered.

At mid-day, he stopped and allowed Haseth to drink from

a slow-moving stream fed by the remnants of thawing snow higher in the mountains.

"This seems like a good spot for a meal," he said.

Rowan'Gaff made up the distance he had fallen behind and crashed against a tree before slumping to one side.

Oh'Raum stretched and sat on an outcropping of rock to finish off the leg of rabbit. "Are you hungry?"

"I've never been more so," Rowan'Gaff answered, making no move to sit up.

Oh'Raum took several pulls from his skin, stood, and rummaged through one of the satchels Preslovard loaded for him. To his surprise, he found a linen-wrapped wedge of cheese the boy stowed away on Haseth's back. *Preslovard serves me well, even here*, he thought, smiling at his apprentice's caring. He cut a hunk for himself and tossed the rest at Rowan'Gaff.

"Eat. You'll need your strength for the second half of today's march — and lying down only increases the rest of the day's discomfort."

"Discomfort?" Rowan'Gaff asked. "I'll never stand again."

"You walked for nine days to reach my meadow."

"Which nearly killed me," Rowan'Gaff reminded him.

"Yet, here you lay like a wounded animal. You don't hear Haseth complaining, do you?"

Haseth drank her fill from the stream, snacked on a low tuft of sea oats growing along the creek, and looked up at her name.

Oh'Raum turned in a circle, gauging their progress for their first full day of travel. He patted Haseth's neck muscles. "We're making good time, girl. We should find ferry trail in two days, if the weather stays favorable." Haseth's reply came in loud crunches of grass.

In a moaning voice, Rowan'Gaff bellowed. "Two days?"

The next two days passed in similar fashion. Oh'Raum stopped only to eat and sleep, which drew him into a harsh world of spreading darkness, fiery funeral barges, and unfamiliar shores. Rowan'Gaff stumbled along behind him losing ground with each step only to catch the old man when he stopped to let Haseth eat or drink. The boy's grumbling grew incessant and only abated at dusk when he collapsed onto his bed roll to dream of the dark army and the inevitable spear to the chest.

Each of Oh'Raum's dream-spells pulled his spirit to the coast with renewed vigor. He felt as if he could not get there fast enough, although his destination still lay over one-hundred-fifty miles beyond D'Grath.

While he walked, Oh'Raum worked on the puzzle of the dreams. He questioned Rowan'Gaff for details of his own nightly visions, but the boy remained tight-lipped and evasive. Recognizable parts of his own visions danced on the edges of sights he had never seen. Following another dreamy trip through the reveling soldiers, Oh'Raum surmised the walled city to be Holm'Stad, capital city of the Draer Kingdom which lay at the apex of Helsem Fjord on the Northern Road. In his dream, the city lay in ruin, besieged either by the hero and his band of victorious soldiers or by the spreading blackness. Oh'Raum presumed the previous deduction to be the more accurate as the presence of the hero meant the evil had been vanquished.

He also attempted to comprehend the significance of Cap'Tian's fading brilliance. What could that mean? As one who explored both the scientific and the supernatural, Oh'Raum believed his visions carried heavy meaning — else, why would he embark on such an uncertain quest on which he now found himself?

When he first saw Cap'Tian emerge in the middle of the western lands, from his vantage point high above the countryside, it appeared as though nothing could cause such a light to subside. In his latest vision, the instant the victory mug touched the hero's lips his light extinguished, and somewhere in Oh'Raum's long memory this raised familiarity.

On the evening of the third day, Oh'Raum, Rowan'Gaff, and Haseth emerged from a shadowed wood line into a clearing, a well-known overnighting spot for travelers heading to and from D'Grath. Opposite the glade, the D'Grath Ferry Trailhead sank into the wood, signifying a single day's travel to the wood-walled outpost.

"You think we should stop here for the night, old friend?" Oh'Raum asked the hinny. As though receiving a positive, verbal response from the animal, Oh'Raum continued, "You're right. Get an early rest tonight and tomorrow night we find you a timothy-filled stable at Olva's and a soft bunk for my old bones." He patted the hinny's rump, coaxing her back to the trees where he tied her off with plenty of slack to meander among the thickets.

Moments later, Rowan'Gaff caught up to the pair, out of breath. "Is this where we camp tonight?"

Oh'Raum nodded across the clearing. "That trail indicates a single day's walk to our first destination."

Rowan'Gaff released a heavy breath at the thought of no more walking and flopped his pack to the ground.

"Before you get too comfortable," Oh'Raum started.

"I know. I know. Gather firewood," the boy sarcastically replied, interrupting the wizard.

"Perhaps among the twigs you fetch tonight, you'll find some manners."

Rowan'Gaff briefly locked eyes with the older man before trudging into the wood.

The following day's travel passed quickly along the D'Grath Ferry Trail's clear path. On the southern bank of the River Mor'Ah, a braided rope, as thick as Oh'Raum's arm, stretched into the river from the trunk of a large tree. Oh'Raum took a seat on the rocky bank and waited for the ferry to cross back to their side of the river. Rowan'Gaff saddled up next to him, sat, and rubbed his calves, mumbling about the ache in his legs.

On the far side of the wide river, the tops of D'Grath's twin towers glinted in the evening's reddening sky.

Oh'Raum looked forward to a night in a bed. He hefted his small purse and convinced himself that a hot meal might be in their future as well. "I think tonight we will find ourselves in soft beds with full bellies. How does that sound?"

"Much better than another tree root in my back."

Oh'Raum turned to the unhappy boy. "I was talking to Haseth," he said with a smile.

The boy smirked and looked across the river. "What is this place like?"

"It's a trading outpost for mountain trappers and a forgotten place where those wishing to escape the world often venture."

The thick rope danced in the water indicating the approaching ferry.

"Since you have no coin, young man, don't expect luxurious accommodations."

Three strong-armed youths tugged on the rope, pulling it through two large eyelets affixed to the front and rear of the lashed raft. A small handcart rode the raft, stacked high with brown sacks. A burly, middle-aged man stood next to the cart clicking coins in his hand, spurring the young men to pull him across the river with their remaining strength.

With a final tug, the raft beached in the loamy bank and the three lads collapsed. The merchant tossed each of them a coin for their efforts, lifted the cart, and pulled it behind him up the sloping shore. Oh'Raum clicked his tongue at Haseth who disliked stepping from solid ground to the uneven deck-planks of the raft, but dutifully followed her master onto the craft, followed by Rowan'Gaff.

The three young men stood and pulled the raft free of the bank. Several yards from shore, the oldest turned to Oh'Raum. "Two coin a piece to cross, sir."

Oh'Raum stared the boy down from under his hood. "And of course, you inform crossers of your extortion once you've brought them a ways from shore."

The boy smirked.

"You'll each get one coin, lest I inform the Ferrymaster of your swindling and word reach the Lord-Governor of this township. Now mind your rope, young man."

The other two boys looked at the third then turned themselves to the task of pulling the ferry across the calm river. The third boy cleared his throat and added his own effort to that of his companions. "One coin a piece, then sir," he said, quietly acknowledging Oh'Raum's insistence.

On the river's far side, Oh'Raum gave each boy a coin and the travelers departed the raft. A wide lane sloped from the ferry landing to the gates of the main settlement. A tree-trunk palisade encircled the entire town, making D'Grath look more like a garrison outpost than the fourth largest township in the Western Kingdoms. Traders, trappers, and traveling merchants frequented the town from north and south of the River Mor'Ah as the only western-leading road terminated in D'Grath.

As a protectorate of Bal'Wern, D'Grath's Lord-Governor, Edrus Erovad, maintained law and order in the town. Two of his uniformed enforcers manned the main entry gate, harassing vagrants and generally inquiring into everyone's business. Oh'Raum approached, tugging Haseth behind him when one of the men stepped in front of him. "Oy, what's your business here, old man?"

Rowan'Gaff eyed the guard's long spear and reflexively covered his chest with his free hand.

Oh'Raum lowered the hood of his cloak and looked up into the soldier's chiseled face. "We make for Olva's in search of a hot meal and a warm bed. Not that our business in D'Grath is any of yours, sir."

"Just doing my job, sir," the guard said. He eyed the old man's tired-looking straggler and backed away to allow Oh'Raum and his company to pass.

"Perhaps I shall speak with your Lord-Governor about your job indeed," Oh'Raum spat as he tugged on Haseth's lead.

The guard on the other side of the gate eyed his comrade. "I meant no disrespect, sir," the first guard said. "I'm charged with keeping the peace here and I do well at that job."

"Then you would do well to know when the peace is in need of your keeping and when it is not." Without a backward glance Oh'Raum led Haseth through the gate toward her waiting stall at Olva's Inn and Boarding.

After a meal of pheasant pie and halved potatoes, Oh'Raum and Rowan'Gaff checked that Haseth remained well-tended and retired to a small room containing a single bed.

Rowan'Gaff surveyed the accommodations. "Are we meant to share?"

Oh'Raum laughed. "The night maid should be delivering you a floor mattress."

"A floor mattress?" Rowan'Gaff protested and sank into the only room's chair, sulking.

Oh'Raum sat on the edge of the bed, shaking his head. "In all my years I have yet to encounter a more ungrateful youth. It's a floor mattress for you, lest you find yourself sharing a hay floor with Haseth. I doubt she is complaining about her accommodations this night." He let out a heavy breath and stared at the thankless young man. "Well? Which will it be?"

"I'll take the floor mattress," Rowan'Gaff whispered.

"Speak up, boy. I am at my limits with your insolence."

"The floor mattress!"

Oh'Raum stood and in the prepared basin washed off the dust of their pilgrimage. "I have no idea why the spirits would send me such a lad. I have half a mind to leave you here and journey to the coast alone."

Rowan'Gaff looked up at him.

Oh'Raum returned his mistrustful glare. "But for reasons I know not, you have some unfinished part to play in this story."

A knock at the door ended their argument. A short woman entered to lay out Rowan's bed.

Oh'Raum slipped under the bed's covers and rested his head on the broad bolster.

"Tomorrow we barter for supplies to carry us the rest of the way. I expect your attitude to change in the coming days. If it does, you'll see a change in mine as well. Good night, young man."

Rowan'Gaff stared at the ceiling-beams, reeling from being so callously chastised. "Good night, sir," he finally said.

Oh'Raum, blew out the candle next to the headboard and readied himself for another fitful night of unpleasant and unnerving dreams.

Sleeper

D'Grath Outpost

Oh'Raum again stood outside the walled city. *Holm'Stad*, his dreaming mind spoke to his consciousness. He turned and floated toward the group of reveling soldiers, the shining hero at their center raising his tankard in victory. He brought the cup to his shining, obscured face.

"No!" yelled Oh'Raum in his dream-world and the real.

His vision faded to blackness and the old mystic expected to wake up or end up staring out over the ocean awaiting the arrival of the charred boat. Soon, his eyes adjusted to the darkness and Oh'Raum found he stood at the intersection of two smooth stone walls. To further bring the dream into focus, Oh'Raum put a hand against the gray slab to his right. The stone's cold and musty surface chilled his fingers. *Am I in a cave?* he wondered. His circle of light grew along the walls, extending several paces before smoothly fading into the void.

"Hello?" he called in his dream, his plea echoing back at him from the darkness.

Dust and chunks of stone littered the floor. Oh'Raum stepped away from his sheltering corner, one hand outstretched although his vision extended beyond arm's reach. Each movement brought scraping replies echoed from around the room.

At the far edge of his adjusted night-vision, Oh'Raum

detected a shape in the darkness. At first it appeared to move as he moved. He stepped left and the figure moved right — he jogged right, and the apparition slid left. He took another step toward the phantom, realizing in the darkness, a second dark object hovered behind the first.

Oh'Raum put up both hands in case the figures, which stood a forearm taller than him, attacked. He inched forward. The shadowy creature remained motionless, thankfully unaware of his presence, or giving this insignificant invader no attention. A beak protruded from the beast's face and immense wings sprouted from the creature's shoulders. Oh'Raum advanced another tentative step and looked into the expressionless, stone face of a gargoyle.

Four of the protective statues stood at the corners of a large, raised sarcophagus. Oh'Raum reached for the tomb. Before his fingers touched the smooth coffin, the stone gargoyles lurched forward, driving his consciousness from the dark cavern.

The wizard woke with a shout. Lingering images of devilish creatures clawing for him stung behind his eyes.

Rowan'Gaff sat on his bedding staring at the old man. "Why must we endure these visions?"

Oh'Raum stretched and swung his legs over the side of the bed. He heaved out a breath and shook his head. "I know not. But each visit to the dream world is a piece of a larger story and we must see where it leads." Shards of sunlight beamed through the room's window and a renewed aching in his heart to leave immediately for the sea burst inside him.

"I'd prefer to skip to the end and be rid of these nightmares."

Oh'Raum sat on the edge of the bed and calmed himself by watching the sun's light inch across the floor toward Rowan'Gaff. With a groan he stood and made use of the chamber pot standing vigil in the corner.

After a small breakfast of cheese and vegetables, Oh'Raum and Rowan'Gaff checked on Haseth, who looked as though she had done nothing but eat all night, then made their way to D'Grath's main square.

Rowan'Gaff gawked at the throng of people having only imagined what a city might look like. He knew from stories his father told that Son'Us, the nearest city to his farm, also held such a marketplace but nothing this grand had entered his mind. Around a central well, no longer fit for human use, rows of stalls and makeshift tables stood ready for the opening of the market. The boy and the mystic walked among the merchants, each preparing their wares for the eyes of possible customers.

Oh'Raum found himself delayed by his companion's unfamiliarity with market etiquette and many times chastised Rowan'Gaff with a, "don't touch that," or, "put that down," and, "we don't need that where we're going." The market operated on a coin-for-goods basis, although many merchants would barter in good faith, if they smelled a deal.

"Fair morning, sir," one eager merchant called as Oh'Raum strolled past his rickety table. "Freshest fish in D'Grath, sir. Caught this very morning."

Oh'Raum turned to the man. "Fare morning, friend," he replied and eyed the array of fish.

Rowan'Gaff stepped up next to Oh'Raum, his eyes wide at the selection.

"You and your friend look like men on a journey," the fishmonger said, examining Oh'Raum from boots to hat and taking note of the boy's expression. "I'll filet your choice and salt pack it for one coin extra."

Oh'Raum nodded. "A fair offer, friend. My purse is a shy light this morning, but I have fresh vegetables if you're so inclined to trade honestly." Oh'Raum removed an ear of corn from his satchel and measured it against one of the smaller fish.

"Oh, I haven't had a fresh cob in too long, sir," the merchant said. He looked over his stock and pointed to a puny dark gray fish on the edge of the table. "Fancy a trade for this fella?"

Oh'Raum countered and touched the corn's tip to a medium-sized trout. "I'll trade for this one and pay a coin to have it prepared for travel by mid-day."

The salesman nodded and pulled the fish from the table for preparation. "By mid-day as promised," he said, readying his filleting knife.

"I'd like one filet packed for me and one for my young friend here," Oh'Raum instructed and lay two corn cobs on the table.

"As you wish, sir."

Rowan'Gaff watched Oh'Raum peruse several more stalls in D'Grath's market, wishing he had his own jingling coin purse. He stopped at a stall featuring cooking knives, an array of short swords and daggers, and other metal utensils.

"Interested in a dagger for the boy," the merchant asked Oh'Raum as he passed by. Rowan'Gaff stopped and ran his fingers along a *baselard*. He dreamed of wielding the weapon like a true soldier.

"The boy has no money of his own," Oh'Raum replied. He turned to Rowan'Gaff still fondling the short sword. "Perhaps that is a good use of your time." He stroked his beard several times.

"What is?"

"Earning some coin today. I'll request an audience with Lord Erovad and the Ferrymaster about a posting."

"A what?" Rowan'Gaff did not understand.

Oh'Raum led him away from the market, through the tight streets of D'Grath to the town's Municipal Building which also served as the Lord-Governor's residence. Two rough-looking guards stood at the entrance of the two-story, log building.

Inside, a group of townsfolk moved about the lower room

speaking with employees who sat logging and cataloging their complaints. Lines stretched from each small table — above which a sign read the duties of the functionary sitting beneath it. Through another guarded door, a group of townsfolk assembled to parlay with Lord-Governor Edrus Erovad.

The obese Lord-Governor sat on a throned dais looking bored with the townspeople's' daily petitions.

"And if I could expand my pottery shop into the storeroom next to the baker, it would not only benefit your Lordship's coffer, but—" a bent businessman pleaded.

"Oh'Raum Yulr?" Lord-Governor Erovad called, cutting off the man's request. The fat bureaucrat waved the store owner away and sat up in his chair, cloaking himself in as much obtuse dignity as he could wrangle. Many in the assembled crowd whispered at the familiar name of the mysterious mystic.

"My Lord-Governor," Oh'Raum loudly said and approached the dais. He bowed deeply, flipping his traveling cloak to one side with practiced grace. Rowan'Gaff stood behind the old man watching the ridiculous charade. When Oh'Raum stood from the bow, he looked to Rowan'Gaff several hands taller.

"To what do we in D'Grath owe such an honor, my old friend?"

"I am on pilgrimage and as is my custom, D'Grath's renowned hospitality is my first stop," Oh'Raum announced with more vigor and flourish than required.

"What can this humble servant of Bal'Wern do for you to aid in your pilgrimage?" Edrus asked and bowed slightly from his high-backed chair.

Oh'Raum smiled knowing the custom of Bal'Wern to offer lavishly in public while counting the cost in private. "Your generosity and that of Bal'Wern's Master, Lord Bohn, knows no limits, Lord-Governor. My young friend here is need of a day's work in fair exchange for coin. And although the merchants of market square are fair tradesman, I find my purse somewhat light of late."

"I see," Edrus said. "Finding work for this stout young man, is easy enough." He waved Rowan'Gaff forward. "Where can we put you to work today, my boy?"

Rowan'Gaff looked over his shoulder at Oh'Raum. "Anything that lets me carry a sword."

The crowd laughed. Oh'Raum took Rowan'Gaff by the shoulders and spoke quickly. "I was thinking about asking the Ferrymaster to enlist him as a puller."

Edrus spoke directly to Rowan. "I admire your mettle, young man, but it is not my custom to enlist such young men into the city wardens. I think your master's recommendation is the better one."

"He's not my—" Rowan'Gaff started.

"Thank you, Lord-Governor," Oh'Raum said, cutting Rowan'Gaff off and moving him backward. "And now to the other matter."

"Of course." Erovad scanned the crowd waiting to hear their petitions. A clever smile crossed his face. "If anyone here would like to aid this distinguished visitor on his journey, I would be more inclined to hear your petitions positively. I'm sure Lord Bohn would also be grateful to the people of D'Grath."

Of course, he would push his generosity on the people, Oh'Raum thought without changing his pleasant expression.

"I have food," a heavy-set man called from near the door. This set off an avalanche of support from the crowd in hopes the Lord-Governor might indeed support their petitions.

"I have supplies to trade."

"New boots would do you well, sir."

"A right cloak to replace your threadbare one."

"Please. Please," called Edrus. "I knew the generosity of our town would be at your beckon, old friend. Dev'Ris will make note of your offerings so that our friend here can visit you later to collect your beneficence."

A stern-looking, thin man to the side of the dais unrolled a scroll and dipped his quill in a nearby ink well. He spent the next few minutes scribbling on the parchment and looking at the people in the crowd as they called out goods and services.

"By your leave, Lord-Governor, I will make haste to the Ferrymaster lest he fill his tally of pullers for the day," Oh'Raum said.

"Of course. D'Grath is at your service."

Oh'Raum pushed Rowan'Gaff through the crowd and the outer room.

"A puller?" Rowan'Gaff protested. "I have to pull on that bloody rope all day? I'd rather shovel Olva's stalls than pull the ferry back and forth."

Oh'Raum glared at him. "Olva doesn't pay a coin a crossing," he paused and spread his hands, "but if you'd rather shovel sh..."

"No! I'll pull," Rowan'Gaff yelled. "I'll pull the ferry."

"It is an honest day's work, and you should end the day with a good start to your purse."

They walked through D'Grath's gate and back down the path to the river's edge. A small group of crossers stood on the bank arguing with the Ferrymaster. "We need two more lads to start the crossings today. Who hear has a strong back for a day's work?"

"Ferrymaster," Oh'Raum called. "By the Lord-Governor's leave, I bring you a puller for the day."

Rowan'Gaff stepped forward and stood straight, defiantly lifting his chin.

"I'll collect him at nightfall," Oh'Raum said.

The Ferrymaster nodded and stepped aside allowing Rowan'Gaff to board the raft. He took his place in line behind an older boy. Tight, corded forearm muscles flexed as he gripped the rope.

"I'm Rowan'Gaff."

"Tall'Bern."

"Have you done this before?" Rowan'Gaff asked and ran his hand over the thick rope.

"Aye. I'm hoping we'll get a fair bit of crossings today. Can you count?"

"Some."

Tall'Bern nodded. "Maybe the third puller will know his numbers right. I've not known old Lorn'Fin to cheat us of our coin, but..." he trailed off.

"I doubt my," Rowan'Gaff paused not knowing what to call Oh'Raum — he almost said, friend, "...companion would allow us to be cheated. He knows his numbers and I'll ask him to count for us."

Tall'Bern nodded as a third boy, about Rowan'Gaff's age boarded the ferry and took up the rope behind him.

"Alright you lot, I believe you were first to cross this morning, sir," Lorn'Fin said to an older man pulling a ladened pony.

Halfway up the path, Oh'Raum looked back at the ferry. Rowan'Gaff gripped the rope and readied himself to pull across the river. He smiled and walked back to the municipal building.

"Your list, sir," Dev'Ris said in his slimy voice. "You'll find the people of D'Grath are very generous."

"I'm sure I will." Oh'Raum took the list and scanned the coerced offers, supplies, and services.

"Is there anything else, sir?"

"I don't believe so," Oh'Raum replied and left the municipal building. He visited each name on the list, collecting most of what they offered in the presence of Lord-Governor Erovad. As he expected, most dealt with him honestly and some reneged on their promised offer of assistance, no matter Edrus' overture of preferential petitioning. At the end of the day, Oh'Raum's boarding room at Olva's held more than enough supplies and equipment to easily take the pair to the coast and back to the meadow.

Oh'Raum thought about the boy. Was it wise to continue traveling with him? What part did he play in the journey to the sea? *Perhaps I should leave him here?* the old mystic pondered.

Oh'Raum walked to the river's edge in time to see the ferry approach the shore, tugged along by three bent-backed young men. The raft landed on the D'Grath side of the river and the boys sank to the boat's deck breathing heavily.

Oh'Raum approached as Lorn'Fin, the Ferrymaster, tallied the day's crossings with the pullers. An exhausted Rowan'Gaff approached and held several coins in his hand. Oh'Raum ignored the coins and focused on the torn skin and ragged blisters on the young man's palms.

Rowan'Gaff pitifully looked at Oh'Raum. "Is this good? I don't know if this is good or not."

Oh'Raum approached Lorn'Fin. "Excuse me, Ferrymaster. Might I inquire as to how many crossings did your ferry make this day?"

Lorn'Fin looked taken aback by the question. He cleared his throat. "Well, let's see," he said making a show of opening his ledger. "I counted nine crossings today."

"I see," Oh'Raum replied. He turned to the older boy. "You there, do you know your numbers?"

"No sir."

Oh'Raum pointed a thin finger at the third puller. "And you?"

The boy shook his head.

"So, none of you know how many times you crossed this bloody river?"

The older boy stepped back on the raft. "I made a notch in the timber each time we reached a side, sir. I don't know how many there are, but surely I kept a record of our landings."

Lorn'Fin closed his ledger and scoffed.

Oh'Raum stepped to the raft and inspected the nocked timber. "By this young man's count Ferrymaster, I reckon these pullers made twenty-eight crossings. And yet, my young friend here only holds eleven coin. How do you account for this discrepancy? Have you a mind to cheat these young men of their labor?"

"I have been Ferrymaster here for eight winters and I've never—"

"I asked you a direct question, Ferrymaster," Oh'Raum said, cutting off Lorn'Fin's protests. "In my experience, anything other than a direct answer is generally the opposite answer." He stepped closer to the Ferrymaster. "We can rectify this here or we can venture to the Lord-Governor's court for recompense. However, to avoid a scandal, I suggest we examine your own purse sir, or you add the amount of seventeen coins to each man's tally. The choice is yours."

"This is robbery, sir. The boy could have notched several times a crossing. How dare you take his word over mine?"

Oh'Raum turned to Rowan'Gaff. "You stood behind him. Do you vouch for his accounting?"

Rowan'Gaff looked at Tall'Bern then back to Oh'Raum. "I did not see each mark Tall'Bern made, but I did most of them."

"You see," Lorn'Fin shouted. "Even his friend, didn't see him!"

Oh'Raum smiled at Rowan'Gaff and turned on Ferrymaster Lorn'Fin. "You don't even see honesty when it presents itself to you. The lad told us both the truth and you mock him for it.

This only solidifies their position, sir."

"What?"

"Had my young friend here said that he did see each mark, I might have been suspicious of the count. By admitting that he indeed had not been witness to each mark, speaks volumes. As does your refusal to make restitution. An honorable man would take more concern in the fair wages earned by his men. I wager you give more thought to the wellbeing of your animals than these young men."

Lorn'Fin pulled a bulging purse from his cloak and poured out a handful of coins. Each puller approached wide-eyed as seventeen more coins were counted out. Between each boy's payment, the ferry master locked eyes with Oh'Raum who stood watching.

"I've never seen so much money," Rowan'Gaff whispered as he flipped coins between his hands.

"Put your earnings away," Oh'Raum said. "You can fawn over it in the safety of the inn."

"There!" Lorn'Fin said. "Are you satisfied?"

"I am, sir," Oh'Raum replied. "If I hear of other young men not receiving their fair earnings, I will inform the Lord-Governor of your dealings. I'm sure either he or Lord Bohn won't hesitate to find another Ferrymaster."

Lorn'Fin made a dismissive noise, replaced his purse, and walked toward the city gates as a light drizzle started.

"Can we go back to the market?" Rowan'Gaff asked.

"Just can't wait to spend some coin, eh young man?"

"I want to buy a knife."

"A knife?"

"For our journey. We may meet some," Rowan'Gaff paused, searching for the right word, "unsavory people on the road."

Oh'Raum's deep laughter continued all the way to Market Square and the metal dealer's table.

Sleeper

The Plains Road North

Despite the bed's comfort and the fluffiness of the floor mattress, both Oh'Raum and Rowan'Gaff suffered through another night of visions and the burning in Oh'Raum's chest to launch for the coast hardened.

They hastily washed and ate, retrieved Haseth from Olva's stables just after sunrise, tossed the fully laden sacks on her back, and donned their own bulging packs. Oh'Raum presented Rowan'Gaff with a new pair of mid-calf leather boots to replace his work slippers and a new twill traveling robe.

"Thank you, sir," Rowan'Gaff said and marveled at his new clothing.

"You're welcome. I hope the new boots will allow you to keep up on the road ahead."

Oh'Raum paid Olva for her hospitality before setting off through D'Grath's main gate.

"How long are we on this road?" Rowan'Gaff asked not long after leaving the walled town.

"Until we turn from it for another day in the wild."

Rowan'Gaff huffed and ran a hand along the leather scabbard slapping his right hip. He liked the feel of the weapon against his leg. It made him feel larger, as though he walked a bit straighter now that he walked armed. He noticed other armed men and went out of his way to get his sword noticed. A quick eye-twitch, a short nod, or a thin smile to indicate that he, too, bore a weapon. Who cared that he lacked the knowledge of how to use the weapon, just the having of it made him feel like his entire life had taken a turn toward his unavoidable destiny. *One step closer to being the hero I'm supposed it be*, he thought.

Throughout the day, Oh'Raum turned to watch the young man straighten and puff out his chest as a passing traveler gave them greeting, only to slump again into a familiar lumbering stride.

Rowan'Gaff's new feeling wore thin as the day's march lengthened. "Did you put stones in my pack?"

Oh'Raum stopped at the remark and laughed internally at the thought of the prank — *or punishment?* "I've done no such thing, young man. Nor would I," the old magician said. *Unless you truly deserved it*, he thought. "If you put more of your energy into putting one foot in front of the other and less to your new knife, we'd be closer to stopping for the day."

"Knife?" Rowan'Gaff countered and pulled his weapon from its scabbard, inspecting it.

Oh'Raum smiled, keeping his own sword sheathed and obscured behind his cloak. "Knowledge and experience," the wizard answered.

Rowan'Gaff held the sword in front of him with both hands. He enjoyed the weight of it and how the sunlight reflected from it. He looked from the blade to the old man.

Oh'Raum's stone face betrayed none of his emotions or intentions. In a cold voice he said, "If you continue down this path, you will learn a painful lesson, young man."

"You haven't once to draw your own sword. Maybe it's a fake. I wonder if you even know how to use it. Perhaps it is you that will learn the lesson." In Rowan's mind, he saw the old man sitting in the dust after being knocked over. Rowan'Gaff would stand over the humiliated old fool and yield to his superior ability.

Oh'Raum let go of Haseth's reigns and gripped his walking staff, appearing to put his weight on it. "Without proper training, you could hurt me or yourself. If you'd like to learn to use that weapon, I'm willing to teach you."

Rowan'Gaff stepped forward, raised the short sword and swung a clumsy overhand stroke toward the wizard. He did not want to hurt the old man, only to establish that he held a sword, and the old man did not. The blade's weight carried through the stroke barely missing the boy's left foot and digging its tip in the dirt.

Oh'Raum brought the stump of his walking stick to Rowan's chest with a lightning-fast attack. The staff crashed against his chest stopping the momentum of Rowan's opening swing. Oh'Raum stepped forward, sliding the lower-third of his staff along Rowan's chest and between the boy's arms. The old mystic fluidly stepped behind the off-balance boy and rotated the walking stick over his head. Using the staff as a lever, Oh'Raum effortlessly wrenched the sword from Rowan's tight grip, sending it skidding in the dirt. With another step forward, Rowan'Gaff also sprawled to the ground.

The speed of Oh'Raum's counter stunned Rowan'Gaff and he rolled to his backside looking up at the wizard who held the walking stick in front of him ready to foil any further attack. An explosion of fear cascaded through Rowan's mind as he expected the old man to step forward and bury the end of the staff in his chest.

Oh'Raum locked eyes with the boy, smiled, placed the stubby end of the stick to the road, and returned his hunched weight to it. He stepped toward Rowan'Gaff who recoiled from the old man's outstretched hand.

"As I said, if you'd like to learn to use that weapon, I'm

willing to teach you."

Rowan'Gaff took the offered hand which helped him to his feet. "That was…" he said through an excited breath.

Oh'Raum watched him retrieve his sword and wipe it clean on his cloak.

"…unfair. The weight of the pack put me off balance and my foot slipped on this miserable road."

The old man slid Haseth's lead through his hand, turned her in their previous direction, and muttered to her, "Unfair, he says. What do you think, old girl? Too lenient on the boy? Ah, perhaps. Should he really want to learn the sword, all he has to do is ask."

Rowan'Gaff sheathed his weapon and dusted himself off before taking up the pace.

At the crossroads of Plains Road and D'Grath Trail, Oh'Raum lead Haseth off the path and secured her to a stand of bushes. He removed the bags from her back and dropped his own pack amid the thick roots of a tall oak. Haseth's skin shivered when the mystic removed her numnah allowing trapped sweat to evaporate in the cool evening air.

Rowan'Gaff approached a few minutes later, swatting long strands of grass with his short-sword like a bagging-hook.

Oh'Raum shook his head. "If you don't stop playing with that thing, you're going to hurt yourself."

The boy slid the pack off his back and slouched against a tree trunk. "I want to learn to use it."

"Then your second lesson for the day is this." Oh'Raum approached and held his hand out for the weapon. He leveled the blade on both hands in front of Rowan. "This is a tool, nothing more. If you dig a hole with it, it's a spade. If you clean a fish with it, it's a filleting knife. It's a tool. You are the weapon." He measured the weight of the short sword, took a step away from the boy, and swung the blade from side to side.

With practiced footwork, Oh'Raum slashed and thrust at invisible enemies with fluid perfection.

Rowan'Gaff watched his sword go from a shiny toy to an elegant weapon in the hands of a master. The old wizard and the sword danced together in front of him, whistling through the air in a blur of steel and glinting sunlight.

In a final move, Oh'Raum slid the blade to his side and stopped the exhibition facing the boy. "With proper training, patience, and dedication to the craft, you will learn to wield this tool as it was meant to be." Oh'Raum stepped forward and handed the blade back to its owner.

"Now clean it, sharpen it, and name it before the sun sets. I will make camp," Oh'Raum instructed.

Rowan'Gaff sat stunned and dared not accept the weapon back from the old master. After following Oh'Raum's directions, Rowan'Gaff sat with the sword across his knees contemplating into their small cooking fire. The sun's final rays peaked over the trees while two potatoes boiled in Oh'Raum's small crock.

"Thea, Beatrix, Elzbet," Rowan'Gaff whispered and stared into the fire as though meditating instead of rambling off potential weapon names.

Oh'Raum heard him mumbling. "What?"

"I can't think of a name," the boy said and patted the sword in his lap.

"Ah."

"I have some good ones, but I don't know which to choose."

"It's a tough decision, I know. What are you considering?"

"Well," Rowan'Gaff said suddenly embarrassed at his choices, "I thought about Beatrix."

"And what does that name mean to you?"

Rowan'Gaff shuffled his feet in the dirt. "It was my mother's name."

"It comes from a long ancient language and means voyager or traveler," Oh'Raum said.

"And Thea? I met a girl in Son'Us once. Her name was Thea." Again, Rowan'Gaff chagrined at his poor name choices.

"That name means goddess."

"None of my names are any good," Rowan'Gaff loudly said.

"That's not true, you just haven't found her name yet. Think about what you want to do with the sword during your life and a name will come to you."

Rowan'Gaff returned his gaze to the crackling twigs under the cooking crock while Oh'Raum stirred the potatoes. What did Rowan'Gaff want from his life? "I want to be a great warrior," he whispered, "a hero."

Oh'Raum watched him and also pondered the boy's future. Quietly he said, "Herleva? It means soldier or commander, in some tongues."

Rowan'Gaff lifted the short sword allowing flame reflections to dance from its blade. "No," he said and took a deep breath. "As you said, I am the weapon, this is but a tool. I will be the warrior, and this will be my strength." Rowan'Gaff lowered the blade to his lap and locked eyes with the old mystic. "What is the old tongue word for strength?"

"*Ealhswith*."

Rowan'Gaff stood, held the sword in front of him and in a grandiose voice announced, "I name you, Ealhsw..."

Before Rowan finished his grand pronouncement, a slinking black shadow entered his peripheral vision. He yelled and skipped away from the firelight, holding his sword at the ready.

The boy's shout and sudden movement startled Oh'Raum who nearly tipped the crock into the fire. Near his right boot, a long, gray, leathery creature crept toward the fire. It cautiously moved into the circle of light, one clawed foot inching forward at a time and its long tail swishing the dirt behind it.

Oh'Raum sat motionless, allowing the creature to move closer to the fire.

"Kill it!" Rowan'Gaff shouted.

"You're the one with the sword, great hero," Oh'Raum chided.

Seeing that the hideous creature did not devour the old man, Rowan'Gaff lowered his sword.

"Please, please, don't hurt him," a strange voice called from the wood line.

Rowan'Gaff raised his sword and Oh'Raum turned to see a short man emerge from the brush. His dark, flowing robes caught on the thick branches as he freed himself from the thicket. "Please."

Oh'Raum stood to greet the stranger.

Once able to stand upright, the man straightened his head dress and smiled at the sight of the creature nestled near the fire. He placed his right hand on his chest and bowed. "Please, forgive Munsif. He broke free from my camp, just there." The man pointed over his shoulder into the woods. "And on this cold night, sought the warmth of your fire."

Oh'Raum approached the man, placed his right hand over his chest, and bowed in return. He said something in a language Rowan'Gaff did not understand before the two straightened and shook hands.

"I am Alabash Nahamad Nurendar."

"Oh'Raum Yulr," Oh'Raum paused, "and this young man is Rowan'Gaff Vodr."

Alabash joined them around the fire and ran his hand along the iguana's spiny back. "I apologize if Munsif startled you. He rarely leaves my side."

"You are on the road from the South?" Oh'Raum asked.

Alabash nodded. "I walk the Plains Road making for the

Twins and my home beyond. I'm a trader in rare goods and have spent several months in the north part of your country."

"What news of Draer do you bring?" Oh'Raum asked. Rowan'Gaff sat across the fire cautiously eyeing the stranger. This foreigner required more scrutiny. *Anyone who travels with a dragon should be avoided*, Rowan'Gaff thought.

Alabash stroked Munsif's back again and looked deeply into the flames. "I left as soon as I heard the rumors. I'm a peaceful man and have no part in such things. Also, I haven't seen my home in many years, so the time was right for me to venture south. I'm looking forward to seeing my wife and daughter." He looked at Rowan. "She should be about your age, young man."

Oh'Raum smiled. "Forgive me, friend, I am acquainted with the nobleman of Draer so my interest in their well-being runs deep. Of what rumors do you speak?"

"Word came from Far'Verm of a vast marching army. King Tyurn sent riders to his eastern garrisons, but none returned. The energy of Holm'Stad turned sour following that initial rumor of a black army."

Both Oh'Raum and Rowan'Gaff leaned closer to the fire. "A black army?" Rowan whispered.

"Days passed and still no word came from the eastern pass. Tyurn sent more scouts into those woods, hoping for confirmation of an invasion." Alabash locked eyes with Oh'Raum. "None returned. I packed my mule and made for King's Road with all haste. I turned east, for D'Grath, as I have more to sell and would prefer to return home only carrying coin."

Oh'Raum nodded.

"I plan to spend a week in the D'Grath Market before trying my luck in Bal'Wern. From there, the long march home."

"Did you hear other news from Draer along the road?"

Alabash shook his head. "Very few walked north and the

few I walked with only heard the same as I. What news from D'Grath can you share?"

"The Ferrymaster will cheat you," Rowan'Gaff loudly said while polishing his sword. The men laughed in acknowledgement.

"The market is in need of your store. You will do well there. No word of trouble in the north has reached this part of the country. Your news to the Lord-Governor will also be welcome."

Alabash slowly nodded. "I'm sure word has reached Bal'Wern."

"I agree, but news moves slowly in the Western Kingdoms and I'm sure Lord Bohn has already dispatched riders to Draer. Sending word to D'Grath is not one of his priorities."

"I see," Alabash said.

Oh'Raum stirred the cooking crock. "You're welcome to share our fire and share a story from your homeland. It has been many years since I ventured beyond the Twins."

"You know my country?"

Oh'Raum nodded and smiled. "When I was a younger man, I held the favor of a wandering princess and that of her brother, the king."

Alabash looked impressed. "You are well travelled, sir."

"As are you."

"I appreciate your offer, but I have a fish over my own fire and have already been away from its tending too long." He scooped up the spiny dragon, stood, and slung the creature to his shoulder.

Oh'Raum stood and shook Alabash's hand, before the stranger turned back to the wood.

"Can I pet your dragon?" Rowan'Gaff hastily asked before Alabash stepped from the firelight.

Alabash looked at Oh'Raum who nodded his approval,

before kneeling in front of the boy. "He is not a dragon. In my tongue, he is called a *Har'duce*." Alabash looked at Oh'Raum.

"Here the word is *Ölda*. But I think saying we met a dragon on the road makes for a better story."

Rowan'Gaff smiled before gingerly moving his hand toward Alabash's shoulder. The animal's skin felt cold and rough to his touch. Rowan'Gaff felt Munsif's muscles twitch under his fingers. "Thank you," he said to Alabash.

Alabash stood and again placed his right hand over his chest and bowed, "I bid you both safe travels." He said something in his native language, turned, and disappeared into the dark forest.

"What did you call his animal?" Rowan'Gaff asked.

"It's an *Ölda*," Oh'Raum said as he sat and spooned out a potato from the crock. He juggled the hot potato to Rowan'Gaff who dropped it in his lap, catching it on his cloak. They both chuckled.

"I've never seen one of those before."

"There are many things in this world I'd venture you haven't seen."

Rowan'Gaff looked into the fire. "I'd like to see them all," he whispered.

Oh'Raum blew on his potato and took a small bite, steam rising from its skin. "We have several days journey to the coast. When we cross the River Thune, we leave the safety of the road. Let's finish this current quest before we see the sights of the world."

Rowan'Gaff smiled and dabbed at his own potato.

Oh'Raum nodded at the boy's sword. "So, you've chosen a name for her?"

"Ealhswith."

"Interesting."

Rowan'Gaff remained silent, waiting for the old mystic to

finish a bite.

"As I've said, it means 'temple strength' or 'strength' in old tongues. An appropriate name for your companion."

A large grin crossed Rowan's face. "Strength," he said in awe.

The pair silently finished dinner and tucked into their bed rolls. Rowan'Gaff thought about Munsif the dragon and what other amazing creatures lived in the world. Oh'Raum pondered the dark news from Draer and longed to venture to Holm'Stad as he knew he would from his dreams. In his chest, the aching for the coast burned and soon he fell asleep, pulled back into the vision-world of the shining hero.

He floated beside the gleaming hero outside the walls of Holm'Stad, surrounded by a somber army. No longer did they revel in victory but sung a low song of mourning. Oh'Raum looked around for whom they sung. A commotion among the soldiers caught his attention as they wrestled a man through the throng. The hero took up his lance in judgement of the man.

The soldiers threw the prisoner forward who pleaded with the hero for mercy. The hero's blinding light obscured the faces of those nearest the hero and Oh'Raum shielded his face from it. It grew in intensity and brilliance. With a flash, the hero advanced on the prisoner slicing his lance upon the man.

Oh'Raum's dream-self shouted and he threw himself to the ground. Beside him lay the corpse of the prisoner, impaled through the chest.

Sleeper

Into the Wild

Rowan'Gaff refused to sleep, knowing the horrific dream would come and take him away. He stared into the black sky, thinking about the strange creatures of the world and his own foggy destiny.

Beside him, Ealhswith lay against his leg, tucked securely under his blanket. After all, who knew what evil things lurked in the country's foreign parts.

What a strange twist his life took, not long ago, when he decided to leave this father's dirty, run-down farm for a grand adventure. *Had it been a grand adventure? Was it really his decision?*

Oh'Raum's dreamy grunts and murmurings helped Rowan's eyes from closing and sinking into his personal nightly hell. He rolled to his side, felt his sword press into this leg, and watched the old mystic sleep.

Since leaving the cottage, the burning in Rowan'Gaff's chest no longer itched and he felt as though he had completed his journey. *Have I?* he wondered. *What part have I yet to play with this old man?*

Oh'Raum's body shuddered and the old mystic spoke in an unfamiliar language. The words came in short, choppy bursts. "*Cho'showry Et.*" Oh'Raum's body shook again. "*Dun Lofti'nu Orbeth Alum.*" Finally, he let out a shout and his body settled into a more restful sleep.

Is your dream like mine? Rowan'Gaff wondered. Oh'Raum rolled lazily to his side and softly snored.

Rowan'Gaff rolled to his back. Small gray clouds lumbered past the twinkling lights overhead and before long Rowan's eyes fell unwillingly shut. His breathing grew deep and even, and soon the farm-boy from Longshore slipped regrettably into a deep sleep.

In Rowan'Gaff's dream, he emerged in a dense, swirling fog — a mist so thick, he barely made out his own bare feet. He stood on a pebbly beach; water lapped a shoreline, just out of view. Cold, wet air drifted past him wafting musty, peaty odors from a yet unrevealed nearby bog.

Rowan'Gaff took a step forward, crunching stones beneath his bare feet. Ahead of him, the dark figure of a man appeared from the gloom and Rowan'Gaff felt a familiar ease settle throughout his body. Another step brought the apparition into sharper focus. Stringy gray hair from the back of the man's head fell over a worn traveling cloak.

"Master Oh'Raum?" Rowan'Gaff's awareness asked.

The old magician's body rocked as though in deep contemplative prayer. Above the sound of the waves breaking against the rocks, Rowan'Gaff heard the old man whispering.

The boy took another step toward the wizard.

"Orbeth Alum. Mur Toolik Sah'yassa, Alum Et. Dur'dortha Lo Aro'um Nen'malli Fer'eth."

Rowan's consciousness reached for Oh'Raum's shoulder, but before the boy's hand fell upon the old man, the fog surrounding them whirled. The sound of the shoreline vanished, as did the pebbles crunching under his feet, and the whisperings of the old mystic.

As though the world were a painting, Rowan'Gaff felt himself pulled away by unseen hands, the oil on canvas ripped from his vision. His feet, still bare, clawed among the pebbles then slipped on a slick grassy floor. The fog burned away, and a billowing tent appeared overhead. Torchlight blinked into view from the dissipating haze and the shapes of men closed in on both sides.

Ahead, a growing brightness flared. Rowan'Gaff fought against the force propelling him toward the light, knowing the hero lived within it — the hero and his impaling lance.

"No," Rowan shouted, yet still the gripping weight threw him toward the shimmering hero.

Rowan'Gaff emerged from the fog, thrown to the floor in front of the intense circle of light. He looked away, shielding his eyes from the brightness, and stared into the horrified face of Oh'Raum Yulr.

Oh'Raum pleaded with the glimmering hero, furiously waving his hands. Rowan'Gaff put his own hands before him to ward off the unavoidable attack, bracing himself for the impending deathblow. The hero advanced on him and thrust his lance deep into his chest, throwing him to the ground. Rowan'Gaff watched the deathblow as if in slow motion and did not feel the strike's impact. From his perspective, Rowan watched the tent pivot as he fell to the ground. He did not endure any pain or feel the impact with the grassy floor. His hands went to his chest, wrapped around the protruding spear and watched his warm blood course from his body, yet he felt nothing.

Oh'Raum's dream-ghost moved to his side and Rowan'Gaff looked into the old man's face before deep-rooted remorse flooded him. "I'm sorry," Rowan'Gaff whispered as metallic-tasting blood filled his mouth and his dream-self slipped back into sleep's cold, dense fog.

The following morning, after a quick breakfast of boiled oats, the two packed Haseth and donned their own packs for another day of travel. Following a now-familiar custom, the first several miles on the Plains Road passed silently as both reflected on the previous night's dreams. Oh'Raum's analytical mind focused on the prisoner while Rowan'Gaff replayed the night's events over in his mind.

Rowan'Gaff called forward as he walked several steps behind Haseth. "What did you dream last night?"

"What?" Oh'Raum called over his shoulder, his thoughts of the prisoner broken by the boy's question.

"Did you dream?"

"I," the old mystic's pace slowed, "I don't recall."

Between heavy breaths, Rowan'Gaff said, "You talk in your sleep, you know."

Oh'Raum slowed further and looked back at the boy. "I'm sure most people do. Is it that strange?"

Still not used to the blistering pace of the old magician, Rowan'Gaff leaned against Haseth and caught his breath. "I suppose."

Oh'Raum grunted an acknowledgment, turned, and tugged on Haseth's lead to regain their pace.

"I'd wager most people don't speak in different tongues, though." Rowan'Gaff took his position beside the hinny. "Orbeth something, you said. Orbeth Alum, I think."

Oh'Raum abruptly stopped but did not turn and face the boy. His head sunk and in a low voice he repeated Rowan's words. "Orbeth Alum?" Slowly he looked back and Rowan'Gaff saw surprised sadness cross the old man's face.

"What does it mean?"

"It is from an ancient poem about betrayal. One solder betrays another for the hand of a great lady. Ultimately, neither possess her." Images of the impaled prisoner flashed through his memory.

Rowan'Gaff chuckled. "So apparently you recite poetry in

your sleep."

Oh'Raum smiled. "Apparently so." He turned and clicked his tongue for Haseth to follow.

"So, what did you dream last night?" Rowan'Gaff pressed.

"Something unpleasant I would rather soon forget."

"I dreamt of the shining hero again."

Oh'Raum did not slow his pace. "Oh?" Images of the glimmering hero filled his vision as he walked.

"Not at first, but eventually I was taken to his victory tent. A great cohort gathered around him."

Oh'Raum silently listened, recounting his own dream.

Rowan's pulse quickened. "Then I woke up."

No, you didn't, Oh'Raum thought. *There is something he is not telling me.* "It is a good sign to dream of heroes. Considering your ambitions in life, young man."

Rowan'Gaff let out a pitiful laugh, poorly hiding his lie from the mystic.

CR   SO

On the fourth night from D'Grath, Oh'Raum led Haseth off the road to a clearing near a spot on his map called the King's Crossroad. The Plains Road met the intersection of the Northern Road and King's Road just south of the river Thune. On the opposite side of the Thune River Bridge, Oh'Raum planned to leave the road and venture west to the coast.

Rowan'Gaff's ability to keep pace improved with each day and Oh'Raum's fondness for the boy slowly grew. A revision in Rowan's attitude and arrogance played no small part in Oh'Raum's change toward the boy. He continued to talk about his inevitable future heroism and almost constant pestering for sword lessons endeared the upstart to the old man. Such lessons often ended with both bruised body parts and egos.

Even so, Rowan'Gaff kept pace for the following day's march, further giving Oh'Raum hope in his young companion.

On the morning of the fifth day, following another night of traumatic, fractured dreams, both travelers ate quickly, anticipating leaving the road at mid-day. Oh'Raum rubbed down Haseth before Rowan'Gaff loaded the satchels to her sturdy back. "I am looking forward to leaving the road," he said.

Rowan'Gaff hefted the bags and slung them over Haseth. "I'm looking forward to besting you tonight."

Oh'Raum smiled at the gibe. "You've a long way to go before that happens, young hero."

Rowan'Gaff returned the mystic's smile, slung Ealhswith to his side and took up his pack. "Why do you seek the wilds? Is traveling on the road not easier?"

"Roads are a necessity, but they remove us from our element, as do most man-made things. Also, easier is not always better."

Rowan'Gaff laughed. "If you say so."

Oh'Raum led Haseth to the road, where they both stretched. The magician drew in a long breath, turned north and set off on the day's march. Rowan'Gaff took up the pace beside Haseth, replaying the previous night's swordplay with Oh'Raum.

Just south of the Thune River Bridge Rowan'Gaff smiled and said, "I am devising a riposte for the high outside lunge you used last night."

"I'm eager to see what you come up with."

"Where did you learn to sword..."

Oh'Raum held up a hand stopping Rowan's question. He cocked his head, listening. "Do you hear that?"

Rowan'Gaff's hand instinctively pressed against Ealhswith and they both stopped walking.

In the distance, the sound of fast approaching hooves came

from behind them. Oh'Raum and Rowan'Gaff turned in the direction of the charging horse.

"A single rider," Oh'Raum said. "Off the road!"

"An attack?" Rowan'Gaff asked and gripped Ealhswith's handle, ready to loose his blade from her scabbard.

"This rider moves with speed not stealth. Remain calm."

Around a distant bend a galloping horse emerged carrying an armor-clad rider. The rider pushed his steed to its limits, sending a spray of dirt from its flashing hooves. Oh'Raum steadied Haseth against the approaching horseman. Rowan'Gaff's mouth opened when the knight swept past them, his worn leather armor rippling in the late morning sunlight.

The rider eyed the pair as he hurtled by in a cloud of dust, pulling up before dashing across the bridge.

Oh'Raum and Rowan'Gaff pulled their cloaks across their faces to shield their breathing from the dust and moved back to the road.

The rider turned the heavily panting beast and dismounted as they approached.

"Forgive me, my lord." The rider removed his helmet, tucked it under one elbow and bowed low as they approached.

"We are not at court, Rider. You can dispense with the pleasantries. Where do you ride in such haste?"

"I am dispatched from Lord Bohn himself to Draer. Word reached our halls of trouble in the north. My Master set me off, not two days hence, on his fastest mount, pray I return with news of an invasion from the east."

"I, too, have heard these rumors. A traveler on the Plains Road spoke of black-clad invaders."

"Forgive me, Sire. Do you also make for Draer to assist King Tyurn, if these rumors are true?"

Oh'Raum looked at Rowan'Gaff who stood admiring the rider's armor. "We do not. We walk a different road," he said, choosing his words carefully.

The scout led his tired horse down the embankment beside the bridge to gulp river water and enjoy a bit of cool shade.

"What is your name, Scout?" Oh'Raum called from the wood line.

"Luke Fistle, Sire." He unclasped his *haubergeon*, lifted his *fauld,* and relieved himself.

"Second son of Lady Prunella Fistle. You've grown since last I set eyes on you."

Luke fastened his accoutrements and tugged his horse away from a small tuft of grass up the embankment. "I was half this young man's age when last we met, my lord."

Oh'Raum frowned. "Stop calling me that, Son." He patted the horse on the neck and held the reigns while Luke mounted the saddle. "On your way now. You have an important task at hand."

Rowan'Gaff watched Oh'Raum.

"Safe journey, Sire," Luke said from habit.

"Go carefully," Oh'Raum replied.

Luke wheeled his horse Northward and with a click of his tongue and tap to the shank, rode off at a gallop.

Oh'Raum secured Haseth's lead, gave her a similar click and coaxed her toward the bridge.

Rowan'Gaff fell into step behind them. "Why do you always do that?" Rowan'Gaff asked.

"Do what, young man?" Oh'Raum snapped.

"Dismiss people when they show you respect."

"Pray, what do you mean?"

"The rider. He paid you great respect and you did not accept it."

Oh'Raum rounded on the boy. "And where does such respect come from? What is the value of it? Does it fill your belly or your purse? Does it make the wild things grow or nurture a newborn?"

Rowan'Gaff took a step back.

"It is folly. I did not earn, nor do I want such fawning." Oh'Raum spat into the river below the bridge. "I leave it for this lord or that lady to encompass." He stared momentarily in Rowan's eyes, turned on his heels, and snatched Haseth along with him.

Rowan'Gaff watched the old man cross the bridge, turn off the road, and disappear into a grove of Emerald Greens.

"Are you coming or not?" Oh'Raum called — not the voice of an angry old man but that of apology, or at least as much apology as the angry old man could muster.

Just inside the grove, Oh'Raum waited, allowing Haseth to nibble beneath the slim conifers. "I apologize, young man. You did not deserve such wrath."

Rowan'Gaff said nothing. He knew, in these moments, allowing Oh'Raum to speak extemporaneously fared better than engaging him in further conversation.

"It's just that I," Oh'Raum paused and licked his lips. He looked at Rowan'Gaff with a forlorn expression. Finally, he smiled weakly and said, "The roots of our secrets run deep like those of the world tree."

Rowan'Gaff returned his smile, pretending to understand.

Oh'Raum put a hand on Haseth's rump. "Well, shall we be off then?" He gently tugged the hinny beside him and trudged off between the trees.

Rowan'Gaff followed at a distance. Thoughts of his father darted through his mind and an unpleasant taste entered his mouth. Growing up under such stern authority had not equipped him for this confrontation. Unlike his father, Oh'Raum had earned the boy's respect and hearing pain in the old mystic's apology solidified that respect. *There is more to this old man than is known,* Rowan'Gaff thought and closed the distance behind Haseth.

The dream-memory of Rowan'Gaff standing behind Oh'Raum on a pebbly beach replaced that of his father. The magician's long gray hair swayed in a gentle breeze while he rocked and muttered in an unknown tongue.

"According to the map we'll soon find marsh country," Oh'Raum called over his shoulder returning Rowan'Gaff to their present condition.

"Can't we navigate around the bog?"

Oh'Raum stopped, turned, and rested against Haseth. "The lowlands ahead stretch for more than twenty miles. Going around to the North would add days to our journey." He shook his head, "No, through the swamp is the faster route."

Rowan'Gaff shrugged. "Through we go then."

Oh'Raum smiled and nodded. "Time to get your feet wet, old girl," he said to Haseth and gave her pat on the neck.

Orange light bathed the sky when the pair stopped to set camp on a mound of peaty earth. Murky water, dotted with islands of knobby green shrubs, stretched as far as Rowan'Gaff could see. Toads chirped in the distance as the sun's light grew pale in twilight.

Oh'Raum let Haseth roam the small island in search of her dinner and stomped down the knee-high grass into a makeshift mat. In the middle he set a forearm-sized bundle of kindling from the pack on Haseth's rump and removed one of his firelighters from his own pack. Rowan'Gaff had seen Oh'Raum's magic fire before, but it amazed him each time the old wizard produced flame from nothing.

Oh'Raum removed a small stone from his pack and saw Rowan'Gaff intently watching him. A smile crossed his face. "Would you like to light tonight's fire, my boy?"

Rowan'Gaff shook his head and shrank back from the old man. "I... I don't know the magic."

"Knowledge is the magic, Rowan'Gaff." He held the fire lighter out to the boy. "Take this end and strike the white tip across the face of the stone. It will ignite like a torch. Don't be alarmed."

Rowan'Gaff inched closer to the kindling bundle and took the small, white-tipped stick and stone from the wizard. He held the flat rock in his left hand and, as shown, slid the tip of the firelighter across it. The end burst into flame illuminating their small island and Rowan's amazed expression.

"Now place it under the kindling before it goes out," instructed Oh'Raum.

Rowan'Gaff slid the small torch beneath the bound kindling and watched as the dry sticks caught. "How does it work?" Rowan'Gaff slowly asked, still amazed that he had just created fire. He looked up at the old man's face, now flickering in the firelight. "Do I now have magic?"

Oh'Raum stifled a chuckle. "What you have is the beginning and understanding of alchemy and chemistry."

Rowan'Gaff mouthed the strange word. "What is chemistry?"

"It is a natural understanding of how things in our world react to each other. The elements of water, fire, earth, and air work together in ways only a few of us understand. Within each, there is knowledge yet undiscovered. This is the magic of which you speak." He pulled another fire lighter from his pack and held it in front of the boy. He pointed to the white-tipped end of the small torch. "This is part of that knowledge that I have, and you do not."

"What is it?"

"Mostly ground up fish bones."

Rowan'Gaff laughed. "Can I learn this knowledge?"

Oh'Raum considered the boy sitting across the fire. Finally, he smiled and said, "I believe you could, but your destiny lies on a different path." His eyes flashed to Ealhswith, Rowan's sword.

Without thought, Rowan's hand rested against the sword's cold pummel. He also believed his destiny lay on a different path than wizardry. *If I did know this magic, I would be an even more invincible hero.*

Oh'Raum pulled their cooking crocks from Haseth's pack and set them next to the small fire. He half-filled each with water and a generous handful of wild rice grains he had collected from the banks of Lake Fal'Run. Although an experienced traveler, nostalgic thoughts turned his mind to that far-off lake and his small cottage nestled in the foothills of The Great Hooks. He smiled, closed his eyes, and sent positive thoughts to his young ward, Preslovard, who watched over their cottage.

Rowan'Gaff watched in silence, lost in his own thoughts about the great hero he was destined to become.

Rach'Ella Wash

The following day, the weather turned dark as did both their moods. The grove of Emerald Green conifers lingered in Rowan's mind as a far-off memory. The outskirts of the marsh gave way to a stinky, wet bog extending into an opaque wall of gray gloom. Their night on the mound provided little rest for either of them, with the endless trill of countless toads and the descending blanket of fog.

Following a cold breakfast of leftover reed grain, they packed Haseth, who waded cannon deep in muck, swishing her tail at biting flies also looking for their morning meal.

With no clear path to follow, the pair made their way westerly by bounding from one mushy island to another. With their fill of hinny, the bog-biters turned their attention to Oh'Raum and Rowan'Gaff, pestering them throughout the day with puffy, itchy bumps.

"Are we going the right way?" Rowan'Gaff called forward.

"Ahead of us lies the sea," Oh'Raum huffed. "We have no choice but to find it." He slipped on a smooth stone and bumped Haseth who trudged alongside her master. The old hinny had already stopped him from toppling into the water several times. A splash behind them and a curse from the boy meant Rowan'Gaff fared worse over the slimy ground.

"I hate bogs!" Rowan'Gaff shouted.

"Ha! I'm sure they regard us with equal disgust. I much prefer a cool stream and mountain foothills. What say you, young man?"

Rowan'Gaff slapped a gnat from his forearm. "I don't care. Anything but this hellish place."

"Oh, come now. Indulge your fantasy," Oh'Raum said hoping to take the boy's mind off their current plight.

Rowan'Gaff thought while sloshing through the murky water. "I did enjoy D'Grath."

"Ah, the city. What about it struck your fancy?"

"The people, the merchants in particular. I also like the guards and the security of the walls."

Oh'Raum laughed. "D'Grath is only a small trading outpost. Wait until your eyes take in the splendor of a truly great city like Holm'Stad. Even the harbor town of Dur'Loth will set your mind afire with possibilities."

"I made several trading rides to Son'Us from our Longshore homestead," Rowan'Gaff said trying to match Oh'Raum's storytelling but dropping his exuberance at the name of his former home. "It was nothing like D'Grath and you say there are cities more grand?" Rowan'Gaff pulled a boot from the mud with a thick slurping sound. "I will see them all, someday."

"Perhaps you will, young man. You mention Longshore. I travelled there but only once in my youth. Good people of the southwest."

"If you say so. I only knew the stingy traders in Son'Us and my father."

Oh'Raum allowed the comment to hang in the air a moment. "Tell me again about your mother?" He stopped atop a mushy mound of ankle-high grass and turned to face his young companion.

Rowan'Gaff pulled himself from the water and leaned against Haseth's flank. He took in several heavy breaths, his head low. "As I said, I never knew her. Everything I know of her came from my father. He kept much from me; I suspect." Rowan'Gaff looked down and kicked the ground. "All I was good for was labor."

"Why say you this?"

"I felt like not much more than a pack mule for him."

"Did he not feed you, cloth you, and shelter you?"

"Aye," Rowan'Gaff quietly responded.

"Is that not more than he did for his mule?"

Rowan'Gaff shook his head and gave a pitiful laugh.

"Tell us, Master Rowan'Gaff, the stories of your magnificent mother as told by your callous father who, after all, did not clothe his mule." Oh'Raum said, smiling.

Rowan'Gaff laughed at the wizard's joke and watched him wade into the dark water close to Haseth. "My father did tell me she was beautiful, but she was his wife, and what husband would call their wife a hag?" He said and took up their pace.

"Truer words," Oh'Raum agreed.

"I like to think she really was beautiful. I think she had my hair color or close to it."

"You're a fair enough lad, so let's both think of her as a rare beauty."

Rowan'Gaff smiled. "I don't know what she saw in my father."

"Perhaps he acquired his indifference to you as a result of her absence?"

Rowan'Gaff thought about it. "Perhaps. And perhaps he was always a son of a..."

"And what of her lineage?"

"He did tell me that she descended from greatness."

"Greatness, you say?" Oh'Raum chided. "And what would that make you?" He paused to allow Rowan'Gaff to finish the sentence.

"Destined to be a great hero," he answered without skipping a beat.

Oh'Raum laughed.

"And what of your mother, great old wizard?" Rowan'Gaff asked, mocking the old man with his own sense of humor. "Tell us a story of your homeland and spin us a great yarn."

Oh'Raum abruptly stopped laughing. He looked skyward before saying, "Alas, my story pales in comparison to yours, young master. I have no previous life, but the meager existence you see before you."

"But surely, somewhere is your homeland," Rowan'Gaff pressed.

"The wild is my home and has been now for many decades. Any life I lived before is and has been meaningless to me."

Rowan'Gaff pondered the old man's evasion. "Someday, you will tell me of your own childhood."

Oh'Raum smiled. "Perhaps it will be as you say, my young friend, but today is not that day."

Rowan'Gaff put his tongue between his lips and blew out a rattle. "Then tell me the story of where you learned your mystic ways."

Oh'Raum let out a breath, "Oh, what a tale that is, young man."

Rowan'Gaff smiled.

"I was the apprentice of the great Master Hamön Iandīthas. Have you heard of him?"

Rowan'Gaff shook his head. "Never."

"Hamön loved the wild places of this world and traveled fields yet unseen by other folk. It was whispered in the towns he could talk to trees."

"Could he?"

Oh'Raum laughed. "If true, he never passed that knowledge to me. He knew more than most men had forgotten and he gave me a great gift."

"Magic?" Rowan'Gaff mused.

"Nothing so trivial, my young hero. He gave me knowledge and a love for learning. That is where true power exists."

"So, you were apprenticed when you were a boy?"

"I requested it."

"Then you left your home like I did."

"I was older than you when I made my choice and was certainly not following a dream to find and old man on the other side of the world."

Rowan'Gaff chuckled. "I guess not."

"Since I was a boy, I've been drawn to nature and I didn't fit in with my surroundings. My parents were overly protective, and I was always escaping the eyes of my watchers to run through the forests. I can't count the number of times I was recaptured lounging near some babbling brook or merely walking the deer trails in a yet unnamed wood."

"What did your parents do?"

"They allowed my folly as long as I kept up my studies and duties. I wager they thought I would grow out of such nonsense, but the opposite happened. I grew to loathe the city and longed for a time when I could make my own decision about my future. That's when I met Hamön."

"You lived in the city?"

"Yes, and I couldn't wait to leave it."

"If I lived in a city, I would never want to leave. Travel, yes, but I've had my fill of open country."

"So, you say. Each man must choose his own path. Mine lay on a much different track than that chosen for me by my father. When I left my home with Hamön, my parents understood why. My return visits were pleasant enough but grew more and more infrequent. Then my parents crossed the river."

"Have you not since returned to your homeland?"

"Aye. I'm always welcome in that part of the country but have only travelled there a handful of times since they set sail for the afterlife. I spent many years with Master Hamön in his cottage, which is now my cottage." Oh'Raum laughed. "Someday, it will be Preslovard's cottage and his responsibility to pass along my ancient knowledge."

Rowan'Gaff imagined such an existence, living among the forests in a small hut doing nothing all day but learning. The thought did not appeal to him.

"Master Hamön taught me the sciences and how natural things interact."

"What do you mean?"

Oh'Raum looked around the marsh. "Tell me, how do you make mud?"

"Earth and water," Rowan'Gaff answered.

"And fire?

Rowan'Gaff thought for a moment then laughed. "Wood and more fire, or at least your magical fire."

"Ah, but have you ever seen fire come from the sky?"

"I have seen the skies flash with *leiptr* that once caused a fire near our farm," Rowan'Gaff said, remembering how his father cursed the gods and the many buckets of water they hauled to extinguish the blaze.

"And yet, I create the same fire with knowledge of what the people of the black land called, *al-kīmiya*ʾ."

People of the black land, Rowan'Gaff thought. The name felt far away and mysterious.

"Can you also create flashes in the sky?" Rowan'Gaff asked.

Oh'Raum smiled. "Not yet."

They marched in silence for the majority of the remaining afternoon as Rowan'Gaff pondered the powers of this old man and dreamed of the possibilities for himself. He envisioned faraway lands, the adventures he could have venturing there, and enemies he would defeat along the way.

Late in the day, the wetlands gave way to rolling grasslands and firmer ground. The sounds of the coast slowly rolled toward them with each step and sea birds, hunting fish in the shallows, filled the sky.

"Finally," Rowan'Gaff said. "I thought that bog would never end."

"I told you the sea lay head of us."

"Two days in the marsh is enough for the rest of my life," Rowan'Gaff admitted. He made a sound of disgust. "Where can we make camp and dry these britches?"

Oh'Raum surveyed the beach while examining his map. He put a hand to his beard and shrugged. "Right here is as good a spot as any." He tapped the spot on the map indicated in his visions and glanced several times out to sea. *Now what?* he thought and tried to recall scenes from his dreams.

Rowan'Gaff released the strings holding his pack and lowered it to the beach. Pebbles crunched under its weight — pebbles from his nightmares. His pulse quickened and he turned to Oh'Raum expecting him to be standing at the water's edge rocking softly back and forth. Instead, the old wizard leaned against Haseth, scrutinizing his map on her rump.

"What's the name of this place again?" Rowan'Gaff asked, his voice cracking.

"Rach'Ella Wash," Oh'Raum answered. The words rolled from his lips as though exquisitely familiar. He looked out to sea trying to fit frames from his dreams into the real world or vice versa. To his right, the beach trailed away to the northwest and the ground rose to the Or'Nath Hills, small coastal mountains which marked the entry to Helsem Fjord and the deep-water harbors of Holm'Stad.

To his left, the pebbly beach stayed southerly leading to Skorpo Fjord and its sheer cliff overlooks. Beyond the cliffs lay one of King Tyurn's western garrisons and southerly still, the port city of Dur'Loth Harbor.

"Rach'Ella Wash," Rowan'Gaff repeated. "I would have called it Barren Beach or The Deserted Coast." He kicked at the pebbles trying to hide the fear of his nightmare. "So, what do we do now?"

"We make camp," Oh'Raum said.

ଔ   ୫

Rowan'Gaff roused from his blankets, awakened by the lapping of water and the mumbling of an old man. He raised himself to an elbow and looked for Oh'Raum. "Master Oh'Raum?" He called into the fog. In the distance he heard the wizard muttering. He stood, shocked by the cold, wet gravel beneath his feet. A breeze blew from side to side, enough to ripple his undershirt as he gingerly walked toward Oh'Raum. The wind brought with it vapors from the previous day's bog crossing.

Rowan'Gaff continued, crunching stones beneath his bare feet. A dark figure appeared from the haze and Rowan's anxiety diminished. Oh'Raum's long gray hair waved in the breeze and the bottoms of his long cloak scrubbed the beach rocks.

"Master Oh'Raum?" Rowan'Gaff asked.

The old wizard rocked forward and back as though pressing his forehead against a yet unseen obstacle. Above the tide, Rowan'Gaff heard the old man whispering, *"Orbeth Alum. Mur Toolik Sah'yassa, Alum Et. Dur'dortha Lo Aro'um Nen'malli Fer'eth."*

Rowan'Gaff reached for the old man's shoulder.

A gust of wind swirled the fog around Rowan'Gaff, and the sound of the shoreline vanished. "No!" his dream-self cried.

An unseen power pushed Rowan'Gaff from the beach to the

halls of a crowded war tent. Torches burned among the rows of tent poles and towering men lined the aisle he moved along. The men shouted at him; snarled at him; cursed him and spat on him.

He knelt on the worn, grass floor before the glowing visage of the hero.

"Please," Rowan'Gaff begged. "I am your kinsman!" He looked up into the glowing face of Cap'Tian.

Beside Cap'Tian, stood Oh'Raum pleading for the boy's life. "Enough blood has been shed today," the old man cried.

"You are no kinsman of mine," the hero shouted, raised his lance and, plunged it deep into the boy's chest.

"Gods!" Rowan'Gaff yelled and kicked his blankets free. His breathing raced and his clammy skin ran wet with sweat. Across the fire, Oh'Raum puffed on his long pipe intently watching him. "What?" Rowan'Gaff huffed.

The magician took a deep pull from his pipe, let out a long smoke stream, and said nothing.

"Why are you looking at me like that?" Rowan'Gaff pressed.

In a low voice, Oh'Raum calmly said, "Do you think us equals?"

Rowan'Gaff sat up on his blankets. The sound of Oh'Raum's voice crashed into the boy's ears with unusual force. "No, sir," he timidly answered.

"Then do not ask me why I do a thing, or do not do a thing. I do what I please and I look at what I please and if I find meaning in what I look at, then better off am I."

Rowan'Gaff sat quietly.

"And what I see before me is a puzzle. You, young man, torn from your home by a vision to find me, while I, torn from my home by a similar vision to come here. And here we are." He pulled on his pipe stem — cheeks filling with aromatic smoke. "You stir in the night from dark dreams, while I stir tonight by visions I do not fully understand. What haunts your dreams? The truth now! Let's have it."

Rowan'Gaff stood and walked a few steps from the fire. "I dream of Cap'Tian, the great hero of legend."

"Aye, as do I. And dark armies?"

"Not exactly, sir. No."

"What then? The truth!"

"I left my home to find you, this is true, but my dreams are darker still. I wore their armor."

"The black army?"

Rowan'Gaff nodded. "And was pushed forward through their ranks. They split before me and I found myself among the vanguard."

Oh'Raum puffed his pipe while his mind put together pieces from his own dreams.

"Before me stood Cap'Tian."

"The glowing hero," Oh'Raum whispered.

"And..." Rowan'Gaff put a hand to his chest.

"And what? All of it now."

"He kills me."

Oh'Raum stared into the fire. "Dark indeed." He drew from his pipe. "But you sound as though you speak of things that have happened. These are yet the visions you see today behind your eyelids?"

"No, sir."

"Then tell on."

"After you found me in the wood, my visions changed. I no longer wore the dark armor."

"Good tidings, then. Continue."

"My visions now begin here on this beach. You're muttering in an unknown tongue and I believe you hold something in your arms."

Oh'Raum looked up at him, his face dancing in firelight shadows.

"Then I'm pulled from the beach, away from you."

"Pulled?"

Rowan'Gaff looked at his feet. "Drawn away. Pushed. I arrive in a great tent with grass underfoot. The hero is there; and you; and a great company of men."

"Similar visions have been my dreams."

"What does it all mean?"

"What of the child can you tell me?"

"Child? I have dreamt of no child."

"I see." Oh'Raum gazed into the fire again. "Tomorrow is a special day, as *Sköll* will catch his quarry. Have you seen it in your dreams?"

Rowan'Gaff knew the story from his Father and shook his head. "I have not dreamed of the wolves."

Oh'Raum nodded. "I know not what happens from here, young man, but we have played our parts thus far. It appears we have only glimpses of the future." He looked deeply into Rowan's eyes. "Never think your destiny is written, young man. Every decision you make matters." Oh'Raum briefly thought back on this own life's decisions that brought him to this point.

Rowan'Gaff returned to his blankets and sat opposite the fire. "I don't want to die."

Oh'Raum laughed. "We all die. 'Tis the nature of men to die; our final act in this world."

"I want to be a great hero, like Cap'Tian."

"Then be that hero, Rowan'Gaff Vodr," Oh'Raum dryly said. "Be the hero of legend."

Rowan'Gaff smiled. *Could it be that easy?* He laid down, pulled his blanket to his chest, and stared into the thickening gray clouds. "Is it really that easy?" He asked.

"Perhaps we shall see on the 'morrow," Oh'Raum answered and drew again from his pipe.

Sleeper

The Baby in the Boat

A soft rain fell throughout the night. Oh'Raum waited for a sleep which did not come. He stared into the night's sky anticipating what might greet them when the moon set.

When the first rays of morning dawned, a heavy fog followed the rain which came from the north. Oh'Raum stretched his old bones and walked to the shore to empty his full bladder. Waves gently caressed the shoreline while he added his water to the vast Sea of Res'Teran, obscured this morning by rolling fog. Oh'Raum looked into the gloom. *Iver'Cross lay off the coast at over forty leagues,* he thought. He smiled. *I wonder if Hed'Ra still runs the inn.*

"Master Oh'Raum?" A tired Rowan'Gaff called from their campsite.

"I am here, young man."

"Is this it?"

"Is this what?" Oh'Raum asked while walking back to the fire.

"Am I dreaming?"

"I don't think so."

Rowan'Gaff sat up and wrapped his blanket around his shoulders. "It's cold."

"And damp. It rained most of the night."

"I wish we were back at Olva's in a soft bed."

"Many a day's ferry-pulling would you have before you if that were our future."

"I'd pull that silly ferry myself if it meant a soft bed."

Oh'Raum laughed, easing their plight. More rain fell.

"Fetch as much driftwood as you can, and we'll stoke this stubborn fire to life. A hot breakfast will do much to lift our spirits."

Rowan'Gaff stood, stretched, and trudged toward the beach carrying his soaking blanket with him.

Oh'Raum watched the boy. Visions of his own recollections solidified in his mind: the hero, the black army, the prisoner, the dark coffin, and the high walls of Holm'Stad. He poked the fire while thoughts, dreams, intuition, and feelings crashed within him. These dreams had a story to tell and although they both played their parts, their true future remained obscured to him.

Rowan'Gaff emerged from the breaking fog and plopped himself and a small bundle of driftwood next to the fire pit. "What's on the menu?"

Oh'Raum fed the thinnest stick to the fire and fanned it with the corner of this cloak. "I thought a bit of pork and a boiled potato would heat us well this morning." He looked into the sky. "I believe this gloom is breaking, that should also do well to warm us, my young friend."

Rowan'Gaff smiled. He needed his spirits lifted, considering his anxiety. Every pebble on this strange beach brought thoughts of his impending death at the hands of the glowing Cap'Tian. "I'm glad the fog is leaving us. I feel as though I haven't seen the sun in weeks."

Oh'Raum nodded. "Traveling the world can prove difficult at times." He filled one of the cooking crocks with water and plunked in two small potatoes. In the other crock he sliced several blade-widths from the slab of salted pork they acquired in D'Grath. Rowan'Gaff longingly eyed the meat.

Despite the slow, steady rain their fire embers boiled the potatoes and soon the sweet smell of sizzling bacon surrounded the fire. After their warming breakfast, Oh'Raum held his palms to the Eastern horizon, stacking his fingers until he reached the sun. "We have several hours before mid-day."

Rowan'Gaff returned from the shore with their cleaned cooking crocks. "Is mid-day when the sky goes dark?"

Oh'Raum turned and faced him. "Aye."

Rowan'Gaff set the cooking crocks near their fire-ring and squinted at the sun. "I've never seen the sun go dark. I've heard the story of *Sköll,* but I never thought I would see the wolf eat."

"You won't," Oh'Raum said.

Rowan'Gaff faced him. "But the story says…"

"The stories are just stories," Oh'Raum said, cutting him off. "*Máni* moves in front of *Sól* and blocks her light."

Rowan'Gaff looked back into the sky. "I don't see the moon."

Oh'Raum smiled. "You won't."

"This is the knowledge you spoke of?" Rowan'Gaff whispered.

"A fraction."

Rowan'Gaff turned, sat by the fire, and rubbed his eyes. "I wish I had such knowledge."

Oh'Raum closed his eyes and chanted.

> The sun turned south,
> The moon did shine;
> Her right hand held
> The horse of heaven.
>
> The sun knew not
> Her proper sphere;

The stars knew not
Their proper place;
The moon knew not
Her proper power.

The sun turns pale;
The spacious earth
The sea engulfs;
From heaven fall
The lucid stars:
At the end of time,
The vapors rage,
And playful flames
Involve the skies.

Rowan'Gaff sat and listened to the singing old mystic. In some far-off place in his memory, he heard the voice of a woman singing — *his mother?* His anxiety grew like a garden weed and he felt as though he would burst. Oh'Raum sang on about the end of days while Rowan'Gaff floated though his own mind. He saw himself stumbling through the fog toward the old magician then felt himself pulled from the beach to kneel before the great hero, Cap'Tian, his kinsman. His pulse quickened and the air on the beach stifled him. He grew hot and clinched his fists.

When Oh'Raum finished his chant, Rowan'Gaff burst to his feet and stormed away from the fire, clutching his chest where the lance pierced him.

"Are you well?"

"I..." Rowan'Gaff managed but did not turn back.

"While you wander, find us a juicy rabbit or a fat fish for supper, ay?" the wizard called.

Rowan'Gaff ignored the request, lost in the scenes of his

death flowing through his mind. *What am I to do to escape this fate?* he thought. The brisk walk along the crashing waves calmed his mind and soothed his anxious thoughts. "A dream is just a dream," Oh'Raum had said. *Stories are just stories.* "Never think your future is written." *Is this day the end of my story?*

He stopped at a rock outcropping around a small bend in the coastline and found a relatively comfortable seat among the jagged boulders. Crabs skittered among shallow tide-pools searching for a morsel of flotsam. "What say you, crabs? Is it better to be a crab or a man with a dark destiny?"

The crabs did not answer. The clicking of their legs on the rocks and the rhythmic rush of the waves provided a brief relief for Rowan'Gaff. His thoughts turned away from the dark army and the glowing hero. Why he thought about Oh'Raum's apprentice, Preslovard, he knew not. The face of the boy he had only known for a day entered his mind. Preslovard stood in front of Oh'Raum's cottage holding a thick book.

"Hail, Preslovard," Rowan'Gaff called.

Preslovard smiled and extended the book.

Rowan'Gaff took the heavy book and looked at it. Carved into the brown leather, four parallel scratches embossed its cover. Like straight fishhooks, the four lines turned sharply at the top end and curled into a round shape at the other. At the mid-point of each, short, tangent etchings in a four, three, three, six configurations made the sign of the *Svefnthorn,* the Sleep Thorn rune.

Rowan'Gaff looked into Preslovard's smiling face and wavered a step backward, shaking his head.

"No time for..." he managed before the book slipped from his hands and both Preslovard and the cottage fell away into darkness.

CR　　　　　SO

Oh'Raum watched Rowan'Gaff stalk away from the fire. *Was my singing that bad?* he mused. "While you wander, find us a juicy rabbit or a fat fish for supper, ay? A rabbit would do well to fill my belly tonight, for sure," he said under his breath. He took a deep breath and listened to the sound of the waves. The air blew in cool from the sea and gulls chirped in the distance.

He, too, felt the weight of this journey. Their dreams were but fragments in time; sometimes illuminating, sometimes dark and disturbing. Again, he closed his eyes and breathed in a cleansing, salty breath to dispel the dark visions.

With each breath, his thoughts turned away from the dark army and the glowing hero. Another image faded into perception — his cottage in the meadow. The sight of Preslovard emerging from the cottage warmed the old mystic's heart. His young apprentice carried one of his many volumes passed to him from his master, Hamön.

"Preslovard, my boy. Have you been well?" Oh'Raum asked and approached his ward.

Preslovard smiled and extended the thick book to his master.

Oh'Raum looked down to see which tome the young boy presented him. In wide, black, strokes on the rich leather-bound book sat the *Valknut,* three interlocking triangles. Oh'Raum did not take the book from the boy but took a step backward. "Why give you this knot for those fallen in battle?"

Preslovard pulled the book away from his master, turned, and wordlessly re-entered their lodge.

Oh'Raum opened his eyes on the beach to rapidly dwindling light. *Preslovard,* he thought and put his face in his hands.

The sounds of sea birds had vanished, and another sound rose from the sea behind him. The gentle creak of wood and the soft thump of water against a hull.

Oh'Raum stood. High in the sky, *Máni*, the daughter light, began her crossing of *Sól*, her mother. *So, it begins*, Oh'Raum thought and turned toward the sea. As if pushed by an unseen hand, a small boat approached the shore. Her charred mast held the remnants of a burned square sail. Round battle-shields lined the vessel along its stem-posts, their vibrant colors scorched by fire.

Oh'Raum knew the ship from his dreams. He willed his feet to carry him to the shoreline, fighting through the fear in his stomach.

The boat's keel ran aground the pebbly beach, which parted as though to embrace it. Water lapped its strakes and gently swayed its unmanned steer-board from side to side.

Oh'Raum reached out a shaking hand to steady himself on the bow stempost. Two bodies, one male and one female, lay on the keelson charred and black, but clearly not fully immolated.

Seeing the half-burned bodies in the growing darkness, Oh'Raum looked away. "Oh, my dears, your journey is not yet complete," he whispered. "I know not why our paths have crossed, nor at this time, but rest peaceably as I will speed you to eternity as best I can."

He stepped into the water and pulled the small boat further onto the shore then returned to his small cooking fire, now the only point of light in the darkness. He pulled a thick arm of driftwood from the fire and, using it as a torch, returned to the boat.

"May the seas carry you to the afterlife," he said and tossed the torch on deck. The branch thudded on the planks followed closely by an unfamiliar sound. Within the boat itself, came a muffled cry. Oh'Raum, wedged his shoulder into the boat's bow, dug his feet into the pebbled beach, and pushed the barge back to sea. A faint cry reached his ears.

Visions overtook his mind. He had seen this very boat before in his dreams; when he had looked up as arrows blotted out the sky. The cry again — an almost imperceptible sound. *I know this place. Preslovard? The knot for those fallen.*

Oh'Raum rounded the bow, to the lower side of the boat, and put both hands on its gunwale. "Forgive me," he said and hauled himself over the burned side rail.

He threw the torch to shore and moved to the prow of the small craft. Soft cries floated between the planks. He knelt and felt around the damp deck. His finger slipped into a knotted plank which moved freely at his probing. He removed the board and smiled at the treasure that lay within.

Wrapped in a pristine white cloth lay a sobbing baby. "Well, hello little one." Stitched into the blanket's corner, the unmistakable swirling script of the Kingdom of Draer told Oh'Raum all he needed to know. The wizard's breath hitched. He sat on the port gunwale and looked back to the lifeless bodies at the center of ship. "My Lord and Lady Draer," he whispered. His head sunk to his chest. The old wizard sobbed. Mournful tears welled in his eyes then cascaded across the lines in Oh'Raum's face. In his arms, the baby squirmed, coughed, and pitifully cried again. "There, there, young princess. I surely will send your parents across the river, for they are more dear to me than you know." His voice cracked. "As are you, sweet lass."

Oh'Raum dismounted the boat with the baby in one arm, splashing in the water. He fetched another burning stick from the fire and returned to the boat, setting it afire.

"I loved you in this life as a brother and a king, Tyurn. May you and your fair queen find eternity and rest." The white sheet in his arm twitched. "And I will watch over your daughter, My

King."

Oh'Raum re-kindled the funeral barge and pushed the small craft back to sea. He watched the deck planks and gunwales ignite while he stood on the beach rocking the baby in his arms.

He cradled the child and in a soft voice, sang it to sleep. *"Or'beth alum. Mur too'lik sah'yassa, alma et. Dur'dortha lo aro'um nen'malli fer'eth.* Oh, sweet child, there is no need to cry. For as long as the stars shine, I will watch over you."

Overhead, the sun gradually reappeared in the heavens. Behind Oh'Raum, Rowan'Gaff Vodr slowly drew *Ealhswith* from her scabbard.

Sleeper

I

The Road to Dur'Loth

Rowan'Gaff awoke to a hazy twilight. *Have I slept all day?* he wondered. The vision of Preslovard and the *Svefnthorn,* known in some tongues as the Sleep Thorn, flashed through his mind. He looked around at the growing darkness and pushed himself from his rocky chair. After a good stretch, he followed the shore north to their meager campsite, now just a faint orange speck in the distance.

Each of Rowan's labored steps crunched pebbles underfoot as he made his way in the darkness. Fear and anxiety permeated his being when vague images from his nightmares slowly emerged from the fog.

"Master Oh'Raum?" he quietly asked.

Fire grew close to the shoreline and licked along the edges of a dark boat gradually bobbing away from the old wizard. Rowan'Gaff cautiously advanced, his hand on Ealhswith's hilt. The world moved slowly for the young farm boy from Longshore. The song of the sea gulls vanished and the dancing flames from their fire appeared to freeze into the air. At any moment, Rowan'Gaff expected to be ripped from the beach by destiny and forced to kneel before his executioner.

"Master Oh'Raum?" His voice sounded weak and pitiful to his own ears — not a whisper but a hoarse whimper.

Oh'Raum stood at the shoreline, swaying to and fro,

whispering in an unfamiliar tongue.

Rowan'Gaff drew Ealhswith, not sure of what protection his stubby short-sword would provide against Cap'Tian, the glowing hero.

The growing light glinted from the edge of his shaking blade when Rowan'Gaff extended the blade in front of him. *Steady*, he said to himself.

Oh'Raum turned to see the terrified face of his young companion. In his arms, a squirming white cloth cooed.

"What is that?" Rowan'Gaff yelled.

"Calm yourself, young sir. It is just a babe."

Rowan'Gaff looked around, anticipating the beach to vanish around him.

"I see that both our visions have come to pass, but not as we were shown," Oh'Raum calmly said.

Rowan'Gaff lowered his sword, his hand tremors slowing. "I don't want to die," he whispered.

"I don't think that is your fate today." Oh'Raum offered him a smile and walked past him to the fire ring.

Rowan'Gaff watched the burning funeral barge bob in the waves before turning to eye the baby in the old wizard's arms. He sheathed Ealhswith and calmed his breathing. "It was on the boat?"

"*She*," Oh'Raum sternly announced, "was on the boat." His mood grew somber. "With her parents."

Rowan'Gaff sat next to the mystic. "So, she was meant to journey with them across the river?"

Oh'Raum nodded. "It appears such."

"Who would do this to a baby?"

They sat in silence for several minutes watching the baby gnaw at her fingers.

"I think she's hungry," Rowan'Gaff said.

Oh'Raum mentally inventoried their provisions. "We have

nothing for her but water from our skins."

Rowan'Gaff wrinkled his nose. "Phew, she also needs a good cleaning. She smells like Haseth after fording the bog."

Oh'Raum scowled, "Aye, we do need to dry her swaddling clothes and we didn't bring provisions for a yearling."

"What are we going to do?"

Oh'Raum thought about the eleven-day journey back to his cottage. "Come, hold her."

Rowan'Gaff took the baby who whimpered at the change of position. The mystic unrolled the map in his lap and found their location on the coast, Rach'Ella Wash.

"Following the coastline does us no good," Oh'Raum said and slid his finger over the map.

Rowan'Gaff gently bounced his legs and scanned the lines where the old magician slid his finger.

"I think we need to make for Bal'Wern Keep. There will be maids there to care for the little one," Oh'Raum continued.

"But that's days away."

The old man considered their rations. "I can reduce a potato and we have our skins. If we make the Northern Road, we may chance upon a family with a young one."

"Hear that? Potatoes and water for the next few days, kid," Rowan'Gaff said, still rocking the baby in his lap.

"Do you have a better plan, young master?"

"Why not make for the king's garrison at Dilli'Gaf?" He placed his finger in a clump of low hills just south of the Thune river.

Oh'Raum shook his head and his voice grew low. "I doubt the king's men will be in a mood to help us."

Rowan'Gaff looked at him.

"No, we make for Bal'Wern Keep with all haste." Oh'Raum took the baby from her human cradle and the pair packed their blankets and cooking utensils.

"Do you mean for us to brave the bog again?" Rowan'Gaff asked, slung his pack over his shoulder, and took Haseth's lead.

"Nay. I think we head north toward Or'Nath at least half a day. We camp for the night then make easterly until we find the road. If my thoughts are true, we will find no shortage of travelers marching south."

Rowan'Gaff nodded as though the names meant something to him.

Oh'Raum donned his pack and wrapped the baby in his sleeping blanket. He tied the blanket ends around his back to support the infant at his chest. "Ready?" he asked.

"Do you think we'll have new dreams tonight?"

Oh'Raum shook his head. "No, my young friend, I believe our days of prophetic visions may be over."

Rowan'Gaff smiled and turned Haseth's left side to the sea. He took a few steps before stopping and turning back to the old mystic. He nodded to the bundle at Oh'Raum's chest. "And then there were three."

"And then there were three," Oh'Raum repeated.

Rowan'Gaff turned and clicked his tongue at the hinny who dutifully picked up the pace.

Before leaving the rocky beach for a small stand of sand pine, Rowan'Gaff called over his shoulder, "What are you going to name her?"

"What?"

"We can't just call her the baby."

Oh'Raum's thoughts turned to the baby's parents, crossing the river and passing into eternity on their final voyage. *What would you have named your daughter, my Queen?* The dead did not answer. "We will call her, Ra'Chel."

"What does it mean?" Rowan'Gaff asked.

"She came to us at Rach'Ella Wash," Oh'Raum said.

"Welcome to the adventure, Ra'Chel."

Welcome to the adventure, indeed, Oh'Raum thought and smiled.

CR   SO

The company made good time leaving the thickets along the western coast. They soon found clear walking through the wide-bodied oaks of the north and upon re-examination of his map, Oh'Raum decided to set a north-easterly course overland. They finally made camp at dusk under the branches of an ancient tree.

Ra'Chel squirmed in Oh'Raum's blanket and fussed at her empty belly while her soiled cloth dried on a stone near the fire. Haseth tamped and sniffed the oak's thick moss.

Rowan'Gaff hugged the massive trunk and marveled at its girth. "It would take ten grown man to wrap this tree."

"Twelve," Oh'Raum said. "I've seen trees that dwarf this young thing."

Rowan'Gaff laughed.

In his lap, Oh'Raum mashed a previously boiled potato. "It's coming, little one," he cooed at the baby.

"Do you think she'll eat it?" Rowan'Gaff asked and sat next to him.

"I doubt she'll take the skins, but the mash should sustain her until we can find her some proper mother's milk."

Rowan'Gaff looked up at the old man. "Have you tended a baby before?"

Oh'Raum shook his head. "Never, but I know enough to keep her alive until we find someone who has."

Rowan's face grew serious. "I hope so."

Haseth stamped again.

"What is it, old girl?" Oh'Raum asked. He nodded to Rowan. "Tend to her, if you would. She may have one too many biters her tail can't manage."

Rowan'Gaff stood, walk to the hinny, and put a hand on her neck. He rounded her, keeping his hand on her back and spoke to her in soft tones. "What is it, old battle ax?"

Oh'Raum frowned at him.

Rowan'Gaff chuckled and continued his interrogation, "Have you had enough of the old man? What's that? Untie your lead and let you roam among these oaks?" Rowan'Gaff looked at Oh'Raum for his response.

Oh'Raum laughed, lay Ra'Chel on his knees, and unwrapped the loose blanket from her face.

"Hello, sweet one." The baby fussed and looked into his unfamiliar eyes. "Hungry?"

He dabbed a blot of potato on his finger and smeared it on her lips. Wanting to suckle, Ra'Chel pursed her lips several times and kicked her legs when no nipple followed the finger.

"Too many miles on these haunches, old girl?" Rowan'Gaff asked the hinny.

"Oh, there, little one. This is all we have," Oh'Raum sang and smudged more mashed potato on the girl's lips, this time making sure some of it went in her mouth.

Tiny fists pumped and the girl's cry grew.

"Or maybe, this northern grass tastes like bog reed," Rowan'Gaff asked, continuing his show of soothing the animal. He knelt beside her, tore a handful of green moss from the oak's trunk, and held it in front of Haseth's mouth. She sniffed it several times, blowing warm air on his hand. After reaching for it with her lips, Rowan'Gaff let her take it in and went to the ground for more. "Too old to reach the ground, eh?"

The hinny restlessly stomped her feet.

"Master Oh'Raum?"

Oh'Raum turned to his young companion who knelt under Haseth, inspecting her belly. "What is it?"

"She's leaking."

"What?"

Rowan'Gaff moved farther under the animal. "I think she's waxing up."

"That's impossible, she's a hinny and she's older than I am."

Rowan'Gaff reached under and ran his hand along Haseth's teats. She staggered away from his attention.

"Come, watch the baby," Oh'Raum directed. He took Haseth's lead, knelt, rubbed his hand along her stomach, and smelled it. "Oh, my sweet old friend," he said and gently pat her neck. "Pass me your crock."

Rowan'Gaff passed the stone bowl to the old man who hunkered under Haseth and spoke to her as he gently milked. "Was it the baby's crying, old girl? Oh yes, it was, wasn't it?"

Haseth stood motionless allowing Oh'Raum to kneed her. "You're as full of surprises as you are milk, sweet one," he whispered. When finished, he scratched the animal's neck again and poured what remained of his waterskin into Rowan's. In his own, he careful poured the precious jenny milk. "Here, let me take her."

Rowan'Gaff passed the crying Ra'Chel to the old man who poked the waterskin with the tip of his knife and dribbled a few drops onto the girl's lips. Instinctively, the babe pulled the corner of the skin to her lips and the milk into her mouth.

"There you go, little one," Oh'Raum said.

Rowan'Gaff silently watched the girl drain the skin.

Oh'Raum looked at Haseth who had calmed following her milking. "Thank you, girl."

Rowan'Gaff spread his sleeping blanket next to the fire and propped on an elbow. "What are we going to do with her in Bal'Wern?"

"Lord Bohn has many maids in his court. I will ask him to look after the child."

"Will he?"

"For me, he might, but I fear the news from Holm'Stad. I believe the city has fallen."

"But what of our dreams of Cap'Tian?" Rowan'Gaff asked.

"I know not. If speed is on our side, we will reach the road tomorrow after mid-day. If my fears are not misplaced, we will have all the dreadful news we can bear."

Ra'Chel finished the jenny milk and burped, which brought a laugh from Rowan. "Good one."

Oh'Raum smiled, hoisted the girl to his shoulder and lightly patted her back.

Rowan'Gaff rolled to his back and sighed heavily. "Master Oh'Raum?"

"Yes, master Rowan'Gaff," Oh'Raum said, sensing a change in the boy's mood and returning the formality of his greeting.

"Now that the time has passed, I need to tell you the rest of my visions."

Oh'Raum's mind brought forward scenes from his own dreams but said nothing — allowing his young companion to speak.

"I told you I was swept off the beach and into the war tent of Cap'Tian."

"Aye, you did and that he kills you."

Rowan'Gaff drew in a deep breath. "There's more." He put his hands under his head. "You were there, and — and you try in vain to stop him."

"In vain, say you? It is never vain to try and save a life."

"What I mean is that he finishes his work."

"Did your dream come to be this day?" Oh'Raum asked.

"No, sir."

"And were the events this day precisely what you saw in your dreams? Mine were not."

"No sir."

"Then why do you dwell on this now?"

"After the killing blow, you held me, and I apologized to you. For what, I know not."

"Is there something you feel you need to apologize for?"

"No, sir. I just thought you should know the rest of my dream."

"I think you can forget such dark things, Rowan. The day is ended, and we are both on new journeys. If we dream tonight, I pray we dream of oceans and of sweet mountain flowers next to a softly babbling brook."

"Perhaps — anything but the bloody beach and rowdy tent is more than welcome."

"Good night, young man."

"Good night, Master. Good night, Ra'Chel," Rowan'Gaff said and rolled to his side.

"And now, little miss, you and I need some rest." Oh'Raum spread his blanket out, curled the baby against his chest, and pulled his pack under his head.

The night passed thankfully quiet with no visions of the future or impaling nightmares between the two. Following another gentle milking and feeding, they set their course east toward the crossing of the Northern Road and Hill Creek.

"How long will it take to get to Bal'Wern Keep?" Rowan'Gaff asked just after lunch.

"We should be in the court of Lord Bohn four days hence, if the road is kind to our travels."

Late in the evening, the pair reached Hill Creek, south of the crossing with the Northern Road.

"We should camp here tonight," Oh'Raum said. "Roads are useful things, but not places for overnighting."

Rowan'Gaff tied Haseth near a stand of spruce and without prodding set to work finding firewood.

Oh'Raum smiled and lay Ra'Chel in a mossy crag to

unburden Haseth for the night. After ringing several stones, he brought out his last kindling bundle and a firelighter from his pack, and quickly stoked a small cooking fire.

Rowan'Gaff returned with a heavy armload of sticks and stacked it near the stone ring. "There's plenty more should we need it."

"Very well. Fill your skin from the creek and I'll set to dinner."

Now familiar with their routine, Rowan'Gaff had already untied his water skin and drained it before heading to the small stream.

Oh'Raum turned to Haseth. "Have you milk for the little one, old girl?"

The hinny's underside dripped slowly and Oh'Raum took full advantage. He filled his water skin with milk, pinching closed the punctured corner. "Well done, girl," he said and pinched off the final drops of jenny milk.

"I think she deserves a washing tonight," Oh'Raum said to Rowan'Gaff when he returned from the creek.

Rowan'Gaff nodded and pulled several tufted limbs from the nearby spruce grove. He folded them together and spoke quietly to Haseth while pouring cool water over her back. "There you go, old girl. Does that feel good?"

Haseth, swished her tail at the droplets running down her sides.

"Oh, you like the water, eh?" Rowan'Gaff used the spruce sprigs to rub down the hinny's short hair.

Oh'Raum smiled at the liking the boy took to Haseth. "Be sure to get her stomach nice and cool. Right now, it is keeping this little one alive," Oh'Raum said and ran the milk skin over Ra'Chel's soft lips.

Distant shouting startled them. Rowan'Gaff looked at Oh'Raum. "Should I go see what it is?" Rowan'Gaff asked.

Oh'Raum shook his head. "Finish your work and keep a wary ear."

Moving slowly, to limit his own noisemaking, Rowan'Gaff poured water over Haseth and slid the makeshift brush over her back, listening intently to the growing clamor.

"There appears to be a tussle near the road," Oh'Raum said and lifted the baby to his shoulder after finishing her dinner. "We will remain here until morning."

"But we need a wet-nurse for Ra'Chel, don't we?"

"Aye, but the fray on the air is not our concern. Getting to Bal'Wern is."

The shouting faded in the distance followed by a restless night of noises from the road. The only member of their trio to sleep was the baby, who nestled in Oh'Raum's chest barely moved throughout the night.

"Master Oh'Raum?" Rowan'Gaff whispered from across their embers.

"Yes?"

"Is it uncommon for the road to be travelled thus at nightfall?"

"Yes, it is. Rest, we have a long day on the march tomorrow."

Rowan'Gaff rolled to his side. "I don't want to be on the road."

"Neither do I, lad. But it is the fastest route to Bal'Wern Keep."

The road did not turn out to be the fastest route the following morning. After a hasty breakfast, the trio crept through the trees to the Hill Creek crossing.

To Oh'Raum's surprise, a slow-moving procession of travelers stretched in both directions. He and Rowan'Gaff emerged from the wood-line and joined the throng.

"Excuse me, lady," Oh'Raum politely said to a woman

riding a four-wheeled cart. Long, thin poles stretched out and yoked a shaggy cow clopping along the road. "Where does this throng make haste?"

"Holm'Stad, good sir. Five days, we've been on the road, with nary a respite," the woman said.

"And the tidings from Draer?" Oh'Raum asked and swallowed the knowledge of the Royal Court's demise.

"Dark, my lord. A great horde from the east flowed down the mountainside and sacked our homes. I hear tell that King Tyurn and even Queen Frann, gods bless her, were put to the sword when the city fell."

"What do you know of this horde?" Oh'Raum asked.

"Great black, armor-clad beasts they were," said a man from behind Haseth. "The king sent out his host to meet them on the fields of Fire Worm Road, but it was for not."

"The great city of Holm'Stad fell in a single night," the woman whispered.

"A single night?" Oh'Raum repeated.

"Do you hear of any wet-nurses on the road," Rowan'Gaff asked.

"Yes, or any cow's milk for purchase. We have a little one in our company," Oh'Raum added.

"Ephi here barely gives enough milk for me, let alone a babe. I have seen others along the road, but none being milked."

"A laden caravan, looking to barter cheese, passed my camp early this morning. I would look for them a few miles ahead," the man said and pointed along the Southern route.

"Thanks to both of you," Oh'Raum said and tugged Haseth's lead, prodding her along at a faster pace.

"You mean to catch the caravan?" Rowan'Gaff asked.

"That and make for Bal'Wern with all haste. A conquering horde will not linger in Holm'Stad long and these good people have been on the march for five days."

Rowan'Gaff understood their dilemma and wordlessly picked up his own pace.

The large rumbling caravan came into view just after midday on the southern bank of the River Thune. Along the road, Oh'Raum continued gathering bits of news from Draer refugees.

According to the reports, an immense army had crossed the mountains at Far'Verm Pass and the Draer watch-towers high in the mountains alerted the city of the advancing multitude. King Tyurn mobilized his army, whose vanguard intercepted the host on the plains of Fire Worm Road. The Draer knights slowed the throng, which appeared to have no end.

"When night fell, the torches stretched high into the pass, bringing with it the songs of legend," one traveler said and recited a stanza known throughout the Western Kingdom.

Cold and black brisk East winds blew,
Through Far'Verm Pass to Western lands,
To walls of Draer dark shadows drew,
Delivered into evil's hands.

Draer King's army gave valiant defense,
Against the shadow's growing might,
As dusk Sun's light made red intense,
Draer King lay martyred that very night.

Rowan's arm hair stood on end when the man's solemn voice rang out above the shuffling of feet. Several people near him sobbed and picked up the tune, singing in their own low voices.

Unmatched they marched with force of arms,

> Southward evil's dark armies spread,
> Cross rivers and forests and trampled farms,
> With misery, hopelessness, death, and dread.

"Isn't the next part where Cap'Tian arrives?" Rowan'Gaff asked.

Oh'Raum nodded. "It is, but I don't think the rest of the song comes true this day."

Rowan'Gaff looked at his feet.

"Come, the caravan is within our grasp."

The caravan, a large wagon laden with goods, traded with Oh'Raum for a flagon of cow's milk, two pennies of ground rice and information on the invading army.

"One penny weighed it with two pennies counted," the shopkeeper said and held out his hand. Oh'Raum passed several coins to the man and leaned in close at the shopkeeper's bidding. "'Tis the Eastern Horde which routed our good king, my lord. For an age, the mad King Ver'Sin Caropa heard the stories of his forebears and wanted to reclaim said glory for himself."

Oh'Raum nodded, remembering the histories taught him by Master Hamön.

"He knew the songs as well as you, my lord. And he meant to have the fertile Western lands for himself." The shopkeeper chuckled. "Have you been to the lands East?"

"Aye, I know what lies over the Hooks," Oh'Raum answered.

Rowan'Gaff packed the purchased goods away in the bags on Haseth's back and listened intently to the dark news.

"Then you know in recent ages their water runs ruddy and their fields are soured. They mine out the hills like moles and barely a tree stands there still. Gods help us, should they come *víking* south. I think they mean to conquer and never return to those cursed lands east."

Oh'Raum nodded. "I don't think King Ver'Sin would send such force if he meant not to keep the lands won with blood. No doubt his horde is already moving south. Where make you?"

"I planned for D'Grath. From there, I know not."

"Your wagon is much for the ferry to handle."

Rowan'Gaff laughed behind Oh'Raum.

"Your counsel is well taken, friend. I bid you good and safe travel. Where make you and your young ones?"

Rowan'Gaff scowled. "I'm thirteen."

"We make for Bal'Wern and the halls of Lord Bohn."

"You have not heard then. Lord Bohn has barred his gates and evicted all but his garrison. News through the column is that he makes to fortify against the coming enemy."

"Folly," Oh'Raum shouted and slammed his fist on the caravan's counter. "What can Bal'Wern do that Holm'Stad could not in a single day?"

The shopkeeper shook his head and made a sign of friendship with his hand. Oh'Raum accepted it and the two wished each other pleasant and safe journeys before Oh'Raum and Rowan'Gaff continued their march south.

"Madness," Oh'Raum whispered.

"Lord Bohn is making a tactical error?" Rowan'Gaff asked.

"He is doing what he feels is right, but it will be for naught when the armies of Ver'Sin reach his gates. His king is martyred and the towers of Holm'Stad are now the stronghold of the invading king."

"Should he counterattack or strike an accord with this invader?"

"If news we have heard bears true, I don't think Lord Bohn or any of Draer's governors will have any other course but an accord with the new ruler."

"And what does this mean for us? What of Ra'Chel?"

Oh'Raum rested a hand on her head, buried in his chest. "We'll take the Harbor Trail to Dur'Loth. I have acquaintances there who may apprentice her."

"Why can't you?" Rowan'Gaff asked. "Your cottage is hard enough to find. I doubt this black army will ever enter your meadow."

"I am not for rearing a yearling, Rowan. She needs the attention and nurture of a woman's tender touch. There is no wet-nurse in my meadow and the girl can't survive on jenny milk forever. Haseth has been a miracle, yes, but I'm sure her suckling time is nearing an end."

Rowan'Gaff put a hand on Haseth's rump. "What is it like — Dur'Loth?"

"It is safe, my young friend. And that is what she needs right now."

Two days march took the trio past the path to Dilli'Gaf Garrison, a Draer stronghold. Dire news reached them of black raiders from the sea who made landfall in Skorpo Fjord and took control of the garrison. Fleeing Draer fighters joined the refugee column south which swelled to fill the road by the time Oh'Raum, Rowan'Gaff, and Ra'Chel reached Harbor Trail.

"We'll be in Dur'Loth in two days," Oh'Raum said when he and Rowan'Gaff left the main refugee train.

Two days of fast march later they entered the coastal city at just passed mid-day. The Dur'Loth town militia, a group of retired sailors and hobbled farmers, met them at the town's edge.

"Many travelers on the road these days, sir," an old man said when they approached.

"Have you room for these good people of Draer?" Oh'Raum asked.

"Many ships are at anchor and have opened their bunks for a time. The inns are full, but with fair barter and coin, there is always room." He scrubbed at his wiry beard. "Ill tidings from our Northern friends."

Oh'Raum nodded. "I suspect the invaders will come this way in the coming days, either by land or by sea."

"By sea? I've not heard the brigands coming by sea."

"They have longboats beached in Helsem Fjord and have already landed north of Dilli'Gaf."

"Slow going for novice waterman, they stay to the safety of the coast, do they?"

Oh'Raum nodded. "I doubt many from the east can sail more than a river skiff."

"You have acquaintance in town?"

"Aye. I am known to many here and seek Mistress Brune at The Westerly."

The old man nodded and examined Oh'Raum's wrapped blanket, hinny, and young companion. He looked at Rowan'Gaff's sword. "We could use a stout sword in these times, young master."

Rowan'Gaff rested a hand on *Ealhswith*.

"My young friend does fancy himself a hero and he is kinsman of Cap'Tian," Oh'Raum announced.

Rowan'Gaff looked at Oh'Raum in surprise.

"Is this true, lad?"

Rowan'Gaff nodded.

"He is also trained in novice soldiering. With a keen-eyed instructor, my young friend might make a fine beadle."

"Well, pass on then, my friends. We would be honored to have you, young master. See the parish commissioner when your friend has concluded his business at the inn."

Rowan'Gaff smiled and followed Oh'Raum into Dur'Loth Harbor.

They made their way along the narrow streets to the town wharf, hitched Haseth beside several frail donkeys, and entered a two-story longhouse. A carved sign of a blowing gale and square-sailed longboat hung from twisted, wrought-iron bars nailed above the door. Inside the crowded inn, haggard men huddled horns of frothy ale and smoked thin pipes. They shouted above the din just to be heard across roughhewn tables. An old brown-haired woman and a teenage girl rushed between tables, slopping down plates of cheese and vegetables while clearing what horns and mugs they could carry.

"May we share the end of your table, friend?" Oh'Raum asked a group of fisherman.

The leader nodded. "Service is a bit slow 'round here, mate, but you and your young friend are welcome enough to rest your bones."

"Thank you. We're on the road for many a day."

"Fleeing the ravagers?" another man at the table asked.

"Not as such, but we've marched with a column from the north, fleeing all the same."

The company nodded. "We're most the crew of the Wallef. No refugeeing for us, ay mates?"

The men pounded their mugs and sloshed back a hearty gulp.

"And what of you, young sir. You look a stout one," a red-haired crewman asked Rowan.

He looked at Oh'Raum and puffed out his chest. "I am Rowan'Gaff, wielder of *Ealhswith,* and protector of Ra'Chel of the sea."

Oh'Raum turned a smiled at the boy and his magnificent title.

"Well, Rowan'Gaff the mighty, fancy you a mug from one of these wenches?"

"Oh'Raum Yulr," a woman yelled.

The cacophony in the inn subsided and Oh'Raum turned to see Fi Brune gliding around tables in his direction. She freed

146

her arms of plates and mugs before embracing Oh'Raum in a long hug. "My love, you've returned to me," she said.

"Hello, Fi."

"I have missed you." She kissed his cheeks and sidled next to him forcing an arm around her shoulders.

"Mistress Brune, allow me to introduce Rowan'Gaff Vodr and the stalwart crew of the Wallef, of which we have just made good acquaintance."

Fi looked at Rowan'Gaff then beamed at Ra'Chel who squirmed from the noise and smoke in the air. "And who is this young one?" She bent to caress the girls soft cheeks.

"Ah, yes — this is why we're here, Fi. I—"

"Don't tell me this is your daughter from some hag mistress?"

Oh'Raum smiled, "Of course not! You see—"

"Well then, isn't she adorable. Lil'Ith, come look at the baby," Fi called to her teenage barmaid. The girl, unloaded mugs from her arms near a washing station and swept through the inn with practiced ease.

"Oh, isn't she a looker?" the girl said.

"Could we get another round, my lady?" the red-haired deckhand asked.

"In a minute, love," Fi answered. She turned to Oh'Raum. "Have you come to take me away to that hidden cottage of yours?"

Rowan'Gaff laughed.

"Fi, I need you to apprentice this child."

"I have Lil'Ith. She carries her weight well for not yet of marrying age. This yearling needs a wet-nurse."

"I need her safely looked after and I can think of nowhere else for her. I beg you. Apprentice this young one and I will forever be in your debt."

Fi straightened and looked up into Oh'Raum's eyes. "For

you, my love, I will do anything."

"Bless you, Fi."

"But there is a cost," Fi quickly added.

"Of course," Oh'Raum replied and eyed Rowan.

"I will raise her as if she were our true daughter."

"I could ask for nothing—"

"For a husband's true kiss," Fi continued, cutting him off.

"Oy, mate. She's got your scent," one of the sailors joked.

Calls from around the inn heckled Oh'Raum.

"Give her one for me!"

"Lay one on her, my lord!"

"Has he ever kissed a girl?" one patron asked to the laughter of the room.

Oh'Raum glared at the inquisitor. "If this be your price, my lady, I will gladly pay it," he announced to the mob.

Fi stepped chest to chest with him and they embraced. Oh'Raum looked deep into her melting eyes. "You will raise her as our daughter."

"Aye. I will, my love."

"You are one of the most enjoyable reasons I come to this forsaken town," Oh'Raum said and smiled.

"I know," Fi whispered and closed her eyes.

Oh'Raum scanned the room, making eye contact with the assembled, silent crowd and leaned in taking her lips. Hoots and shouts erupted from the inn, louder than the previous clamor. Fi wrapped her arms around his chest and pulled him to her bringing forth more cheers and whistles.

Oh'Raum did not disappoint. When finally they broke their embrace, Fi leaned into his ear and announced, "You can take more than a kiss, my lord. We can make as if tonight is our wedding night, if it please you."

Oh'Raum pulled back and stared into her eyes. "I may yet indulge your fancy, my dear. For tonight, I need to wash the road from my feet and sleep in a bed."

"As you wish," Fi said, smiled, and turned back to the baby. "What is this sweet one's name?"

"Ra'Chel," Rowan'Gaff said.

Lil'Ith returned with freshened mugs and a plate of meat and cheese. Fi unwrapped Ra'Chel from Oh'Raum's blanket and hoisted the girl to her shoulder. "There she is. My sweet, Ra'Chel." She pat the baby's back and danced her around the inn. The men moved aside as Fi twirled by singing, "This is Ra'Chel, my daughter. Lil'Ith, you have a wee sister. Shyla, come see my daughter," Fi called. An aproned woman appeared and cooed over the baby while the inn returned to its former raucous noise level.

Oh'Raum sat to the cheers and hails from the Wallef's crew. Rowan'Gaff watched the inn's mistress dance away with the baby, a concerned look on his face. "So that's it?" he asked.

Oh'Raum drank from a foaming mug. "She'll be safe and in good hands here. If I know Fi, she'll want for nothing. The inn makes her a tidy coin and she is only a fortnight's easy journey from my cottage."

"A fortnight? That's an eternity."

Oh'Raum regarded his young companion. "You could stay and watch over her. I doubt you long for the quiet of my meadow as I do."

"Me? I don't—"

"You long for city life. Well, here you are. You want use of your sword. They need young men in the town militia. You don't believe Fi will mother Ra'Chel well. This is your chance to watch over her."

"Where will I stay? How will I earn coin? I have no acquaintance here," Rowan'Gaff protested.

One of the Wallef crew laughed. "I was but a shoulder taller than you when I signed aboard. What say you, Steersman?"

The red-haired fellow eyed Rowan'Gaff and nodded. "We plan to be at harbor for a goodly time. I could use another strong *holumenn* what with those on the march and their possessions."

Rowan'Gaff looked from the Steersman to Oh'Raum who raised an eyebrow. "Your future is yours to choose, young master," he whispered.

Rowan'Gaff took up his mug and gulped the sweet honey-mead. "To the Wallef," he shouted and smiled a frothy grin.

"The Wallef," the crew shouted and raised their own mugs.

Oh'Raum nodded at the young man and raised his mug in salute. "To the Wallef, indeed."

Part II:
A Desperate Plan

Sleeper

Dreams of Older Men

Freya Danely skipped among the wildflowers in pre-dawn sunlight singing a made-up song. An early riser, Freya often picked flowers to adorn the breakfast table for her master and her brother.

> Flower friends, flower friends,
> come grace our breakfast table,
> Grace us with your sweetness and ...

The thin, eight-year-old stopped at the sloping bank of their babbling creek. She rolled her blue eyes and looked into the sky, searching for the right words. Finally, she smiled and continued her song.

> ... and love us if you're able.

She skipped and hummed the rest of her silly tune all the way back to their cottage, nestled in the foothills of snow-capped mountains. A gentle breeze wafted her blonde curls while the sun's light wrapped around the peaks, inching its way along the ground. The light bathed the colorful flowers and the freckled young girl in a new day's warmth.

Freya stopped at the cottage door, turned back to the ocean of color spread across their meadow, took a deep breath, and crept through the door.

Her brother, Preslovard, slept along a side wall next to the hearth. When she came to Master Oh'Raum's cottage, three years ago, Pres, voluntarily gave up his room which originally housed boxes of foodstuffs and hanging dried meats. He moved his bunk to the corner of the common room and together, they built her a low bed of oak limbs and sweet pine boughs.

Not one for the mornings, Preslovard rolled toward the cottage's wall when Freya quietly closed the door behind her. She walked to the water barrel and filled a mug before arranging the morning's flowers neatly on their small table. She sweetly whispered to the flowers, thanking them for the fresh smells and lovely colors, knowing they would brighten her master's morning.

A thump from Oh'Raum's chamber startled her. The old man moaned softly. Freya inched her way to his door and leaned against it with one ear. There were many rules to learn when first apprenticed by Master Oh'Raum Yulr. One she broke regularly was never to enter his chambers when the common room door stood latched.

Has he fallen? Freya silently questioned and reached for the latch. "Master Oh'Raum," she called, barely above a whisper. She opened the door and slipped inside.

Master Oh'Raum lay on his bunk with beads of sweat running on his forehead. He lurched from side to side a though being prodded by a hot poker and mumbled something Freya did not understand.

"Master?" She tried again.

"My King," Oh'Raum muttered. "My King, I failed you."

Freya inched closer wanting to wake him but thought better of it.

"I know this place," Oh'Raum said amid another sharp jerk to his side.

"Freya," a voice called behind her. She jumped and turned to see Preslovard's scowling face. "Out of here, this instant," he demanded.

The young girl turned and snuck from Oh'Raum's room leaving him to his nightmare.

"You've been told not to go in there. Why can't you follow instructions?"

"I heard a noise and thought the worst."

Pres yawned and watched his father writhe on the bunk before shutting the door. "I have seen this before. Before you came to apprentice, Father had many visions."

Freya plopped into her chair and sulked at her brother's scolding.

"It has been an age since I've seen him thus, and I have no doubt he will tell us about it in his time. For now, we must allow him the dreams. Do you understand?"

Freya nodded. "I just..."

Preslovard sat across from her and reached for her hand. "I care for him too, dear sister," he softly said. The sounds from Oh'Raum's room quieted and Pres smiled at the young girl. "Fetch father his tea while I stoke the fire for breakfast. How feel you about a johnnycake?"

Freya smiled. "With blackberry jam?"

"As you wish, my lady," Preslovard said and looked to his father's chamber door. *Please, not again,* he thought.

Freya hopped from the chair; Master Oh'Raum's night tremors soon forgotten.

Preslovard stood and stretched his six-foot frame. He walked to the wash basin, rinsed his face, and with a thin leather thong tied his black curls into a shoulder-length pony tail. He splashed his face again before setting about the morning's chores.

Oh'Raum sat on the edge of his bunk panting. He looked at the sheaf of paper on his table and frowned. For eighteen years he searched the possible meanings in his previous visions and thus far found no answer — until this morning.

Calmed, Oh'Raum stepped to his chair and rifled through

the parchments searching for his first dream-sketch. He found it on a bottom shelf bundled with various scrolls he referenced during his research.

Faded ink lines slashed across the page dotted with runes and symbols. At the center of the scroll, his quill tore through the paper leaving a sharp gash. His eyes went to the coast, to a small inlet leading to a wide marshland. "Rach'Ella Wash," he whispered, and remorse welled in him. *Eighteen years,* he thought and sighed.

A soft tap on the door roused him from regret. "Master, I have your tea."

Oh'Raum turned. "Come in, little one."

"I crushed a dried tulip petal in it this morning. I hope you like it," Freya said and set the steaming cup on the corner of his table.

Oh'Raum smiled. "You always please me, dear. I have no doubt this will be a most delicious blend."

Freya smiled and hopped on his bed. She swung her legs and looked around his chambers. Oh'Raum took up the cup and blew on the hot liquid. He sniffed it while Freya intently watched his reaction.

"Pres is making johnnycakes. He says I can put jam on mine."

Oh'Raum took a sip and smiled at the refreshing, warm elixir.

"How is it?"

"Lovely," Oh'Raum said and took another sip.

Freya's smile did not last. She looked at her slippers.

"Are you well this morning, dear?"

"I... I heard you when I returned from gathering flowers, and I..."

Oh'Raum faced her but said nothing.

"I crept into your chambers when I heard you talking. I'm sorry," she burst, "I know I'm not supposed to, but I was afraid you'd fallen and..."

The old mystic held up a hand. "Fret not, little one. In my dreaming, I knew you were here with me. It was that which woke me."

"I'm sorry, master."

"I have not had visions as this for many a year — long before you came to apprentice. And long have I searched for their meaning."

"What did you dream?"

"It is not for young ears, my dear. Come," Oh'Raum stood and stretched, "let's find your brother."

Freya bounded from the bunk, took his hand, and walked to the common room. Preslovard turned and smiled at his master. "Good morning, Father."

"Freya mentioned johnnycakes and jam."

"Yeah," the girl squealed and leapt to her seat at the table.

Preslovard produced a stone platter piled with three large, brown pancakes. He set the plate in the middle of the table, refreshed his tea, poured a juice for Freya, and took his place.

Freya scooped a large helping of blackberry jam onto her johnnycake and waited for the others to settle behind their plates before digging in. Throughout the meal, Preslovard watched his master, remembering long ago the first night the dreams assailed him. When their eyes met, Pres offered him a thin smile but did not inquire about the night's new visions.

"Freya, help your brother with the washing then tend the animals. I need to speak to Preslovard alone, dear," Oh'Raum said near the end of their breakfast.

"As you wish, master," the girl answered, not yet familiar enough to call him father.

"The visions again?" Preslovard asked.

"It has been an age, but I again see pieces to the puzzle in my dreams."

Freya drained her mug of sweet juice and she and Preslovard washed the morning's dishes. She dried her hands, kissed Oh'Raum, and left to attend to the animals as instructed.

Preslovard sat across from Oh'Raum, resting his hands on the table.

Oh'Raum cleared his throat. "Eighteen years hence I left you for a quest of which I have never spoken. You know that Rowan'Gaff stayed in Dur'Loth, but that is the extent of your knowledge."

Preslovard smiled. "I know of your work since, Father. I know of your long hours of study into the meanings of these dreams."

Oh'Raum nodded. "Aye. I have spent these dreamless years searching for meaning and keeping the fruits of that quest hidden from the world."

"Have you now new understanding?"

Oh'Raum sipped his tea. "Not fully. The new visions remind me of the past and yet, I feel them leading us toward an unclear future."

"Us," Preslovard quietly repeated.

"When I tell you of the night's dreams, you're place becomes more clear, my son."

Preslovard remained silent.

"In my dream, I emerged in a dark place, black as the day *Sköll* finally devours the sun. Behind me, I felt cold stone as if I stood in the corner of a large room, possibly a hewn cavern. My fingers dived into chips and pot-marks among the smooth stone telling me the age of the strange place.

"I inched away from the corner with outstretched hands. Why I left the safety of the corner, I know not, but I moved toward the middle of the cavern as though drawn to it." Oh'Raum lifted a shaking hand toward Preslovard and closed his eyes.

"In the middle of the room, I found an immense stone box and set on each corner stood horrifying, horned creatures, the likes of which I have never dreamed. I know not how I made out their features, but in my mind I see their ghastly faces watching me still." He sipped at his cup.

"They crouched at the corners of the stone coffin, their muscled arms and taloned hands between their knees as though ready to spring from their perch and attack. Curved stone wings stretched high above them and their studded tail lay wrapped at their clawed feet."

"Goodness," Preslovard said at the image.

"I felt their eyes upon me," Oh'Raum continued, "and when I reached for the sarcophagus, they attacked." The old wizard opened his eyes and offered his apprentice a thin smile. "Years ago, I had a similar vision. The hideous creatures attacked and drove me from the cavern. I now know that my vision was of a tomb. Possibly the tomb of the hero, Cap'Tian. I also know today that it was not I they drove from the tomb," his voice hitched, "but you."

"Me?" Preslovard stood and paced the small room.

"I have shielded you as best I could from my visions and the possible destiny, they have set for me. After last night, I can no longer deny that you, my son, have a role to play."

Preslovard rolled the implications around in his mind, finally taking a deep breath and turning to his mentor. "I will do what I must, Father."

Oh'Raum's pride welled. "Who else could ask for a better apprentice. Now, there is much we need to discuss before we know your true path. A plan we must have. Fetch paper and your quill. I will recount the past as there should be no more secrets."

Preslovard brought his parchments and inkwell to the table and took his seat.

"The boy we found in the woods, Rowan'Gaff Vodr, remained in Dur'Loth with Bodvar Her'On, Steersman of the Wallef. I know not of his current situation. He and I ventured to Rach'Ella Wash on the Northern coast. There, as shown in my visions, floated the funeral barge of King Tyurn and Queen Frann of Draer."

Preslovard looked up from his scribing.

"They were dear to me, Pres. As close to me as you and Freya." Oh'Raum spoke slowly, his emotions surfacing. "In a hidden bow compartment, I found a swaddling babe — the good king and queen's daughter." Memories of the baby cascaded through his mind. "We named her Ra'Chel and took her to be apprenticed by Fi Brune, mistress of The Westerly."

"Why did you not bring her here? Never have we seen the King's Guard this far East. I doubt Ver'Sinian knows of our meadow, his father certainly did not."

"The babe needed a woman's touch, Pres. It was the right choice not to bring her to the cottage."

Preslovard, rarely one to disagree with his master, furrowed his brow, "Do you know where the Draer Princess is today?"

"I do not. And I think it best her true lineage remains in our confidence."

"What of Rowan'Gaff? What does he know of her?"

"He remained in Dur'Loth to watch over her but knew not of her parents." Oh'Raum huffed. "I know not how long he fulfilled his charge."

"So, her secret is ours alone, then." Preslovard said.

Oh'Raum nodded.

"Have you other visions?"

"Many," Oh'Raum answered. "I foresaw the invasion from the East. I believe it the long-forgotten past and our current future mixed as though in a cooking crock. I saw a vast blackness spread from the North before I knew of Ver'Sin's sacking of Holm'Stad and his march south. I witnessed Cap'Tian and his host win back our lands with blood and King Ver'Sinian's forebears driven back over the eastern ranges."

Oh'Raum sipped his tepid tea. "I witnessed his great host rise against the black horde. I stood in his war tent and beheld his deeds. I saw the betrayal of the hero."

"As in the song of legend."

"Just so," Oh'Raum said and nodded.

"And you saw me in a sunless dark place with four hideous demons."

Oh'Raum chuckled. "I saw through you when in the dark place, to be precise. And they weren't more than lifeless gargoyles, to be sure."

Preslovard smiled. "If destiny has her say, I shall be the fool to find out."

"When first I had the visions, I felt drawn to the coast where I set the Draer barge on its path to eternity. When Rowan'Gaff left his Longshore home, a force drew him to our wood, Pres. Today, I feel swept away to a dark future and feel I am pulling you along with me."

"When first you had the visions, you left in haste. Does the same feeling fill you now?"

Oh'Raum nodded. "It does."

"If I am to be pulled with you, father, I embrace it. I shall make ready my traveling pack at once."

"Your eagerness may be misplaced. A last dark vision I must give you to record. When in the tent of Cap'Tian, I besieged him for the life of a prisoner. He refused my counsel and took this man's life. I know not the condemned's identity, but as I held the dying man," Oh'Raum cleared his throat before slowly whispering, "I felt I held you in my arms."

Preslovard nodded. "And yet make out my face you did not?"

"It could yet be a man unknown to us, but nay, I did not make out a face. I had only a glimpsed feeling of you, my son."

Preslovard scribbled the final detail and capped his inkwell. He set the quill beside the parchment and dried the wet ink with several breaths. Neither of them spoke until Freya bounded through the door smelling of muck and humming a tune.

"Animals tended master." She slid into the empty chair and propped on her elbows between them. She rolled her eyes from Preslovard to Oh'Raum and back again. They each gave her a silly side glance which made her smile. Finally, she fidgeted and asked, "So are you going to tell me the big secret, or not?"

Preslovard laughed. "Not I," he said and made a rune sign with his fingers.

Oh'Raum ruffled his beard. "You're brother has spoken his intentions and made the rune of trust, little one. I dare not go against it."

Freya huffed and sat back in her chair. "So be it. Keep your secrets."

Preslovard conspiratorially leaned in and crooked a finger at the girl. She smiled and sidled next to him. He looked up at Oh'Raum while whispering, "We have a great task before us today, little sister."

"What great task?" She whispered in return.

"We must make ready our packs for journeying."

Freya's eyes grew wide. "We're going on a trip?"

"Aye. A quest that must remain our secret," Preslovard said.

Oh'Raum held back his emotions watching his wards. Pride for the man Preslovard had become and uncertainty of his protection for his youngest apprentice. *Am I on the right path,* he silently questioned.

"Now run and gather your boots and such. I feel we must leave sooner than expected," Preslovard said and looked at his master who brushed at his eyes to hide prideful tears.

Preslovard's Quest

Preslovard stood outside the door to the cottage, repeating lines from The Balled of Cap'Tian. He heard Oh'Raum helping Freya pack her last few belongings and give her simple instructions.

"Watch out for your brother. He will rely on your good counsel, young one."

"Yes, Master," Freya replied.

"But also do what he says."

"Yes, sir."

Preslovard sang to himself and aimlessly gazed to the Eastern mountains.

> Foretold the hero of this song bides,
> Until Draer maiden softly weeps,
> When returning horde of evil rides,
> Deep in El'Thune Cap'Tian sleeps.

"Stay off the roads where you can," Oh'Raum instructed and put a soft hand on Preslovard's shoulder, bringing him out of his trance. "We know not the forces arranged against us."

Deep in El'Thune Cap'Tian sleeps, Preslovard thought.

"Protect your sister," Oh'Raum whispered.

"I will, Father."

"Master?" Freya asked in her high, sweet tone.

Oh'Raum knelt. "Yes, dear one?"

"Who will look after you while we're gone?"

Oh'Raum smiled and kissed her forehead. "Don't fret about that, little one. I have business in Dur'Loth and will reunite with you soon after." He looked up at Preslovard but continued speaking to Freya. "At the bridge over the River Thune, two fortnights hence."

"So long?" Freya asked.

"The turning of the leaves will be your sign for when we will be reunited."

"It will pass in no time, little sister," Preslovard added and straightened his shoulders.

"Until then, my dears," Oh'Raum said in a reassuring tone.

Preslovard took a last breath of meadow air and followed the path away from their cottage, Freya a step behind him. Oh'Raum remained at the door, watching them.

Freya gently caressed each flower she passed, like a bumble bee alighting from petal to petal. At the edge of the clearing, Pres and Freya turned and waved a final time to their master. Oh'Raum returned their gesture knowing they stood far enough away to not see the tears coursing through the lines of his weathered face. Eighteen years ago, the scene played in reverse, where Preslovard stood with flowing tears at the cottage door when Oh'Raum waved from the forest's edge.

"Come sister," Preslovard said and took her small hand, "we have a day's walk to the edge of the lake."

"Is he going to be alright without us?"

Pres did not immediately answer. "He has his own path to follow. We shall share tales of our travels in a month's time."

Freya sniffled, turned, and walked out of the meadow with her brother.

Their first day of travel saw them to the edge of Lake Fal'Run, a trip they both knew well. They crossed the creek that fed the lake with mountain runoff before making camp. Freya helped by bringing small twigs and kindling to the fire pit.

Preslovard unrolled their sleeping blankets and built a sufficient fire.

"My legs hurt," Freya said and plopped onto her blanket.

"Wait until morning," Preslovard replied and smiled.

"And we have to do this every day?"

"Every day."

"For how long?"

"It's best not to think about it," Pres answered.

Freya poked a stick into the fire and watched the end ignite. "Are we on our quest, brother?"

"Aye, we are."

She looked up at him. "What is our quest?"

Preslovard sat on his own blanket across the fire. "Do you know the Ballad of Cap'Tian, the song of legend?"

Freya rolled her eyes around her head. "Something about a princess, right?"

"There is a princess, yes. It is about a dark army invading the land and a hero rising from the people to drive away evil."

The girl's eyes grew wide.

"The song says the great hero fell victim to a sinister plot by the retreating enemy king. A foul potion forced the hero into a sleeping death and somewhere, deep in the mountains to the North, he sleeps still."

Freya sat spellbound.

"Our quest is to find where he sleeps."

"Was that Master Oh'Raum's sleeping vision?"

Pres nodded. "One of many." He stoked the small fire and added a larger log. "Long before you came to apprentice with us, he ventured north — called by the visions."

"Do you have them?" Freya asked.

"I do not." He crooked an eyebrow. "Do you?"

The girl giggled. "No."

"Father wants us to remain in open country as best we can. It will make our going slower, but the less we see of Ver'Sinian's troops, the better."

"How far do we have to go?"

Preslovard unrolled his map and Freya shuffled around to look at it. "We're here," he said and pointed to the Northern tip of Lake Fal'Run where two lines stretched into the mountains indicating the feeder creek.

"That's our house."

"It is," Preslovard said and smiled. "We're going here." His finger slid north to a jagged clump of harshly drawn mountains.

"El'Thune Hills," Freya slowly read by tilting her head.

"Deep in El'Thune, Cap'Tian sleeps."

She looked up at him then back to the map, tracing her slim finger along the roads between the mountains and the lake.

"We're going to walk north and tomorrow; we should camp near Middle Marsh. I hope to make the D'Grath Ferry by the night of our third day."

"Are we going to see Mistress Olva?"

"I'm sure she'll have plenty of sweets for you."

Freya clapped her hands. "I hope she has tart biscuits, too."

"I have yet to travel north from D'Grath, so I know not what lies there for us. According to Father, the countryside is grassy plains and low hills. We should make good time."

Freya bent over the map and sounded out the names of the places they were likely to pass. "Where are we meeting Master Oh'Raum?"

Preslovard tapped the map.

"And he is going by way of," she slid her finger to the western coast, "Dur'Loth Harbor."

"Should he leave tomorrow, he will get there about the same time we reach the hills."

"Then he is coming this way and will meet us here." She popped her finger off the parchment.

Preslovard's voice grew firm. "Freya, we are going into unknown country. Neither of us has travelled to this part of the world. We must also remember our charge from Master Oh'Raum to avoid the King's Guard where possible. If you and

I are separated," he paused, "you must find your way home."

"By myself?"

Preslovard nodded. "Many dangers are in the world, especially with Ver'Sinian's soldiers on the road."

"I—I'll do my best."

He smiled. "To that end, it's time you had your own map. You packed your quill, yes?"

She nodded and rummaged through her pack producing her writing utensils and a rolled scroll.

"Tomorrow when we make camp, you can start drawing your own." He rolled his map and tapped it against his palm.

Freya smiled. "Show me again where we'll be tomorrow?"

Preslovard stuffed the map into his pack and turned to cooking their dinner. "If the weather is kind, and your little legs can keep up, we should make just east of the marsh."

"'Tis you that will struggle keeping up with me, big brother," Freya said and stuck out her tongue.

Her prediction did not hold. Having made the journey to D'Grath many times, Preslovard's anxiety grew regarding the thirty miles yet to cover. Freya did her best to keep his pace but required far more rest stops then he normally needed. This put the pair off the pace for reaching Preslovard's intended camping spot by late afternoon.

"How far have we gone today?" Freya asked through heavy breaths.

"Not far enough." He felt bad directing his frustration toward his sister. His true concern, this vague and impromptu quest, ate at him and his commitment to Oh'Raum. He did not want to let his father down but knew finding the legendary resting place set him on a path to failure.

"I didn't know it would be this hard." Freya's voice sounded distant.

Preslovard's mind worked over the problem and explored apologies when he reunited with his father. *I did my best, father, but ... if I had more time, perhaps I could better explore the … it's just a legend after all … I'm sorry I let you down.*

The third day of their trek passed more quickly, and the pair made good time. Freya's aching legs bothered her less when she stretched from her blankets. They talked little as they walked, preferring to let their minds wander. Freya picked flowers and talked to them softly along the trail while Preslovard mentally inventoried their supplies and ran the Ballad of Cap'Tian over and over in his mind, eager to glean new meaning from its singing.

The pair made up the previous days lost ground, reaching the southern bank of the River Mor'Ah late evening on the third day. The twinkling fires of D'Grath glimmered off the slow-moving water, inviting travelers to the shops and inns within the walled outpost. After setting camp, Freya played along the water's edge, happy to see other children splashing among the tall grasses. Preslovard watched her — keeping his promise to protect his sister.

"Sweet girl," a woman softly said and approached his campsite.

Preslovard smiled. "Aye. Which one is yours?"

The woman pointed to a mop-headed boy ankle deep in the muddy water. He and Freya showed each other rocks they picked up with their toes before hurling them into deeper water and giggling. "Rodmar."

"A fine-looking lad."

"It's good to see the children may yet play in these times. Are you traveling north?"

Preslovard nodded. "And you?"

"South to First Town. We have family there."

"The way south is clear to Fal'Run. Where come you?" Preslovard asked.

"Or'Nath. My husband worked the mines," she softly answered. "The king's man conscripted him a fortnight hence."

Preslovard remained silent.

"I know not where he is now. My sister works in a bakery in

First Town so there may be work for me there also."

"Preslovard."

The woman smiled. "Asny."

"A pleasure to meet you."

Asny politely nodded.

Rodmar grappled with an especially large stone, barely heaving it a few feet. The resulting splash doused them both and brought gales of sweet, childhood laughter.

Asny too laughed at their antics. "Where make you?"

Preslovard hesitated. "We are meeting our father in the hills West of The El'Thune."

Asny nodded. "So, she's your sister?"

"Yes. We are both apprenticed."

"I see. Your father is a good man to take you both in."

"That he is," Preslovard agreed.

They watched the children play, now soaked to the shoulders.

"Have you news?" Asny asked.

Preslovard shook his head. "You?"

"The King's Guard patrol the road. Once we reached the Plains, we didn't see many travelers until D'Grath. We have no coin for the inn, so we paid to cross."

"Freya and I need to provision tomorrow in town. Is the market open?"

"A few stalls remain open," Asny answered and looked up and down the bank. "Not too far from shore, you two."

"We should dry them off. Have you supped? You and Rodmar are welcome to join us."

"Thank you, Master Preslovard. That would be nice."

They coaxed the children from the water and hung their sopping clothes on a line to dry by the fire. Preslovard prepared a broth from their store of vegetables and Asny added a half loaf of bread. The children huddled in their blankets, sipping from wooden bowls while the adults ate from the crocks.

"Thank you sharing a meal with us," Asny said when the

washing finished.

"'Twas our pleasure."

The following morning, Freya waved to her new friend as the ferry pulled away from the bank. "He was nice," she said. "Can we visit him again?"

"Perhaps," Preslovard said and turned toward D'Grath. "We have much work to do today. We only have a day here before we head north into unknown country." Knowing they followed in Oh'Raum's footsteps eighteen years hence did not ease his restlessness. *Tomorrow we leave familiar ground.*

"I hope Mistress Olva has fresh tarts."

"We'll know soon enough, little sister."

Mistress Olva did not have tarts. Preslovard and Freya entered D'Grath following several questions by the King's Guard who manned the city gates. Lord-Governor Erovad's men slinked at the side of the armored, pike-wielding guards. When the interrogation ended, the pair walked to Olva's. Refuse littered the D'Grath streets and the smell of human waste replaced the sweet smell of roasted chicken and freshly baked bread.

"What happened here?" Preslovard asked Olva when they arrived at her establishment.

"It is the way of things, young man. A new king sits in Holm'Stad and the country rots."

Freya slumped in a chair, overwhelmed by the state of the once thriving trading town.

"We have coin for a room and provisions."

"A room, I have. Provisions are scarce. You may trade at the market, but I doubt you'll find everything you seek."

Olva's prediction rang true that afternoon when Preslovard ventured through the once great D'Grath Market. Freya remained with Olva to help in her kitchens. Most of the stalls remained shuddered and the shops that did open offered a paltry array of scrawny ground pheasants, virtually meatless fish, and dirt-covered, dehydrated vegetables.

"Did you get what we needed, brother?" Freya asked when Preslovard returned to the inn.

He offered her a thin smile. "We'll need to do some foraging, but I think we'll make do."

"Not what you expected, eh, young man?" Olva asked and stirred a pot of stew.

"No."

"The land suffers under this invader-king." She laughed and coughed at the same time. "Almost twenty years on and still invaders I calls his like."

"Does the rest of the country suffer thus?" Preslovard asked.

"Aye, I should think. The King's Guard care nothing for the people, only taxes and levies. Countless travelers tell of undue harassment and crass treatment by these dark invaders."

"We aim to avoid them."

"And good council this," she said. "But tell me, what news of Oh'Raum. Is he well?"

"He is."

Olva smiled. "Good news is welcome. We are both closer to crossing the river, so hearing of your master's good health is welcome indeed."

"Mistress Olva?" Freya asked.

"Yes, my dear."

"May we make a tart?"

The old woman made a show of puckering her toothless lips. "A tart say you? Well, let me see." She left her steaming pot and rummaged through various boxes and cupboards. "No fruit have I, but if you were to happen upon a sweet potato, we may have what we need, young mistress."

Freya hopped from her stool. "I have a sweet potato, fresh from our garden."

Olva clapped. "Ha! I thought you might."

The next morning, they shared breakfast with Mistress Olva, donned their newly laden packs, and set off north along

The Plains Road. Once out of eyesight of D'Grath, Preslovard turned their course northeast into the wilderness, following Oh'Raum's direction to avoid the roads.

Sloping plains stretched to the foothills to their right. Sparse groves of trees dotted the countryside and made for a pleasant campsite. Each night they stopped; Freya lay next to the small fire copying Preslovard's map. He watched her trace the mountains and roads, adding her own titles and comments. Beside her boxy rendition of D'Grath she scrawled the word *tart* in her wobbling script.

Two days after leaving the city and shortly after a restless night, Freya hit her limit. "Pres," she called from a considerable distance behind him. "I can't take another step."

"Stopping is not an option. We must continue this pace."

"The hills," she panted, "I can't do the hills as you do. Up and down, up and down."

"My goal is to make Tau'Wa Creek tonight and we just broke camp. We've a full day in front of us, sister."

Freya plopped to the ground. "I just can't."

Preslovard knelt next to her. "We'll take more rest breaks, but we can't give up. Would father give up on us?"

"That's not fair," she said.

"Fair or not, it's the truth."

Freya looked down. "No. Father would never give up on us."

"That's right. I'll slow down and we'll stop more. How does that sound?"

"Do your legs not hurt?"

He nodded. "They do."

She pulled her waterskin from her pack and took a long drink. "More stops?

He nodded again.

"And slower. I can barely keep up your pace."

"I promise."

"I don't like questing," she said and stood. "I'd rather be home."

"As would I," he agreed. He looked to the south and thoughts of Oh'Raum flooded him. *I wish you were here, Father,* he thought.

"I wish Master Oh'Raum were here," Freya said.

Startled by her voicing of his thoughts, Preslovard looked over his shoulder and smiled.

"He would walk at my pace," Freya continued.

He took her hand, and they resumed their march north.

"Of that I have no doubt, little sister. Of that I have no doubt."

Sleeper

Ra'Chel the Barmaid

Crisp, morning air chilled Oh'Raum who shivered under his worn traveling cloak. As was his tradition before setting off journeying, Oh'Raum stopped at the edge of the meadow, turned, and looked back at his cottage – empty.

A day had passed since Preslovard and Freya set upon their own trek to the northern El'Thune Hills. Regret and misgivings of sending his wards into the unknown filled the old mystic. He had extinguished the cooking fire, overfilled the animal food troughs, and packed his satchel for a journey of several weeks. Other than the odd trip to D'Grath to trade provision for the winters and receive updated news of King Ver'Sinian's latest atrocity, Oh'Raum and his wards rarely left the seclusion and safety of their meadow.

Ver'Sinian, the youngest of Ver'Sin The Conqueror's sons, assumed the throne four years after his father's invasion of the Western Kingdoms. Ver'Sinian's two older brothers, Ver'Sin II and Ver'Sauren, met suspicious and gruesome ends leading to their younger, more ambitious brother's coronation. Rumors abounded in smoke-filled taverns of the boy-king's hand in the mysterious death of his father, as the consumption of ale exceeded the fear of the king's vast spy network.

Ver'Sin The Conqueror proved a ruthless occupier, sending his black-clad troops south following the fall of Draer and the execution of King Tyurn and Queen Frann. Ver'Sinian continued his father's firm hold of the land and its people for the four years since his coronation.

Oh'Raum sighed, turned, and disappeared into the thick wood line. He followed the trail from his meadow to the northwestern banks of Lake Fal'Run. Where he would normally turn north to D'Grath, the old magician stopped and looked across the river that fed the lake. Two days march ahead of him, Preslovard and Freya walked toward an uncertain future — as uncertain as what he might find in Dur'Loth. Oh'Raum followed the lake south for a day to the small fishing village of Fal'Run.

"Oy'Vid, you old bear," he announced as the door to The Red Rudder, Oy'Vid Ol'Vir's small lakeside tavern closed behind him.

"Oh'Raum, my old friend," the barkeep answered. "Haven't seen you venture along the south shore in quite a while."

The friends embraced and Oy'Vid led Oh'Raum to a recently cleared table. "Sit, my friend." He motioned to a young man for drink and a plate of dried meats before sitting across from Oh'Raum. Oy'Vid's large frame consumed the chair. His dark beard stretched almost as wide as his smile at seeing the famed wizard.

"The lines in our foreheads have grown long, old friend," Oh'Raum said and grasped Oy'Vid's hand. Oy'Vid smiled and shook his friend's hand in return. "I'm glad to know you're still here." Oh'Raum looked around the inn and leaned forward. "What news have you?"

Oy'Vid furrowed his brow and hunched his shoulders forward. "Few spies 'round these parts, Oh'Raum. Can't say the same for the blasted King's Guard. Word is our king is not sleeping well and struck with paranoia. Doubled patrols on the roads, he has."

Oh'Raum nodded.

"Speak plainly, friend. What spurs you from your cottage?" Oy'Vid asked.

Oh'Raum smiled at his friend's perception. "I make for Dur'Loth but need one of your boys to watch over my meadow."

"What of Preslovard?"

"I have sent him into the mountains to follow another path."

Oy'Vid nodded. "Well," the tavern owner said and placed his palms on the table, "I'll send Einar to your cottage at once. He is responsible enough to tend your animals until your return."

"Einar?"

Oy'Vid laughed. "My second youngest. Not yet born since your last pass through this part of the country."

Oh'Raum smiled. "You have yet had more sons?"

"Aye," Oy'Vid said and raised a fisted hand. "Don't let my age fool you. I'm as potent an ox as I ever was."

"I don't doubt it," Oh'Raum said and laughed.

"This is Hott, my youngest," Oy'Vid announced when the plate of meats and two foaming mugs approached their table. Oh'Raum nodded to the boy who returned a large, toothy smile. "His mother never knew what hit her." The boy rolled his eyes before returning to the kitchen.

"A fine lad, to be sure," Oh'Raum said and picked through the meats, eventually choosing a dried lump of spiced fish.

Oy'Vid took a long draught from his mug and wiped a well-used sleeve across his face. "Now, tell me what in Dur'Loth forces you to leave your home."

"I'm looking for someone. I saw her last in Dur'Loth," Oh'Raum slowly said. "I feel led to reconnect with her."

"Please tell me you've finally come 'round to Fi's prodding. She's been a fine catch for most of her life and I know how you continue to spurn her advances."

"Not my dearest Fi," Oh'Raum laughed. "Although I can't rule out a night in her bed before the fates have us cross the river."

"Ah, another lass has your eye then?"

177

"A much younger lass — and no, whatever lustful thoughts are in your deranged mind, my friend, banish them at once. I must find her for other, more pressing matters."

"Well, you're travel should be carefree along the lake trail. The King's Guard watch over Long Bridge and if you mean to avoid them, you'd be hard pressed to cross anywhere for a hundred miles in either direction."

Oh'Raum nodded. "I have no fear of the king's men, although I know it best to avoid them when possible."

"Hott," Oy'Vid shouted, "run to the mill and fetch Einar. I have need of him."

"Yes, father," the boy answered before bounding through the door.

"Don't fret about your cottage, I will make sure it is well tended."

"Thank you, my friend. I have coin for provisions, maintenance and…"

Oy'Vid held up a hand cutting him off. "Don't speak of such things now, Oh'Raum. If settlement is required, we will speak of it after your safe return."

"Thank you, my friend. I do need a full pack for the journey and I'm happy to pay for a room with your softest bed."

"And you shall have it."

A peaceful night's sleep and a day's walk from Fal'Run, Oh'Raum made camp at the intersection of Lake Trail and the Southern Road. Low, rolling hills stretched on either side of the road dotted with other travelers' cooking fires.

Oh'Raum walked a distance off the road and set up his meager lean-to under the branches of an old-growth oak. Normally, the old mystic would simply wrap himself in traveling blankets next to a goodly fire, but as his years proceeded, he found the radiating warmth of a fabric lean-to more to his muscles liking.

After a hearty vegetable soup, provided on the compliments of The Red Rudder, Oh'Raum stretched beneath his shelter and quickly fell asleep to the songs of resident night-birds high in the trees. His pre-sleep thoughts of Preslovard and Freya gave way to images of war tents and victorious soldiers.

"My lord, I beseech you," his dream-self cried to the glowing hero before being wrenched from the immense tent to a dark cavern. Creatures scurried in the shadows, circling him as he crept in the darkness.

"I am Oh'Raum Yulr, he who knows the ancient ways," Oh'Raum's ghost cried into the black cavern. *"Onar'ee dor'sayfum, ed ignatium!"* He yelled and struck a fire-starter against the rough, stone floor. Yellow light erupted in his hand and illuminated the vile creatures lingering in the darkness. Black-skinned dogs, slick with oozing, fleshy oil slinked away from the fire and more red eyes glinted in the shadows. Yips and growls echoed through the chamber followed by the clacking of hungry teeth.

Oh'Raum felt the presence of others with him in the cavern, relieved to not face the inevitable calamity alone. He scanned the room for his companions but saw only the beaming red eyes of several *tu'hünl'volf* and their oily, squirming skin at the edges of his light.

"Now what?" a voice asked beside him.

Oh'Raum wheeled toward the voice. No one stood next to him.

"Do we open it?" another voiced asked. Again, the magician swung the torch toward the question — nothing.

An immense stone box appeared in front of him. Fierce gargoyle faces stared down at him from each corner of the tomb.

"I think we should open it"

"Preslovard? Is that you," Oh'Raum called. "Where are you?"

A jarring scrape filled the room, drowning out the gnashing of teeth in the gloom. The thick stone lid slid to one side. Brilliant light burst from the coffin filling the room with luminosity. Oh'Raum's dream-self squinted against it and the oily, black dogs yelped and ran from its radiance. Blinded, Oh'Raum fell to the floor and shook. He woke in his lean-to — the first rays of morning dancing across his face.

At the southern tower of Long Bridge Crossing, an armored-clad guard shouted at Oh'Raum. "Oy, old man. What's your business on the road?"

Normally, Oh'Raum would not stand for such blatant disrespect and respond with a crushing line of indignation. Knowing the importance of his current mission, he replied in a soft, sincere voice. "Just an old traveler making for the coast, sir."

"Where come you?"

"Two days hence from Fal'Run on the southern shore of the same-named lake." Oh'Raum hung his head and slumped his shoulders to hide his true height and the fire in his eyes. The hood of his cloak lay down his back exposing his long, thin hair.

"No weapons bear you?"

"Oh, no sir. Have no need of weapons do I," Oh'Raum said, betraying no sign that *Óvinr* lay cleverly concealed within his cloak.

The guard looked to his companion opposite the roadway. "What say you?"

"I say, I've been standing here for too long."

The original guard laughed and waved the dirty old man through. Longbridge spanned the Great River Mor'Ah, cutting the country into distinct northern and southern regions. Like a giant snake, it's waters meandering from the Great Hooks, east of D'Grath, to the sea. Its mouth bisected Longshore's southwest Peninsula, fanning into the ocean at a wide river basin. Over a mile at its widest, only four crossings spanned the Great River: the ferry at D'Grath; Narrow Bridge, which lead to the Longshore Garrison outpost; the bridge leading to Son'Us, the kingdom's southern-most city; and Longbridge Crossing.

On the northern bank of Mo'Rah, the road split northwest

to Dur'Loth and north to Bal'Wern Keep.

A week after leaving his meadow, an exhausted and dirty man opened the door of The Westerly. Most of the tables sat open and Oh'Raum noted the mood of the place. *Not the rowdy inn I remember last.*

He sat near the wall and hoisted his pack to the bench beside him. A barmaid approached, greeting him with a gloomy smile. "What can I get you, sir. We're out of most meats," she said and looked over her shoulder at the black-clad men feasting on two huge trays of salt-pork, fish, and chicken. "Our ale is well-aged and..."

Oh'Raum dropped his hood.

"Master Oh'Raum?" the girl asked, unaware at her volume.

Oh'Raum smiled. "I'll have an ale, my dear." He slid a shiny coin across the table. "And you may quietly tell Mistress Brune that I am here."

The girl's lips fell to a frown and tears welled in her eyes. "My lord, my mistress—" she choked on the rest of the sad news.

Oh'Raum reached for her hand. "I see, my dear. Just the ale then," he softly said before the waitress shuffled to the kitchen. Oh'Raum took a deep breath and longed to hear Fi's voice echo through her tavern. "I missed my chance with you, my love," Oh'Raum whispered, and thought, *I should have told you the truth.*

The woman returned with a mug and small plate of cut fruit. Oh'Raum invited her to sit. "Lil'Ith, correct?"

"Yes, milord."

"You don't need to call me that."

"But my mistress told me you..."

"Regardless," Oh'Raum said interrupting her. "I don't require it. Master Oh'Raum, or Oh'Raum, or sir, is sufficient."

Lil'Ith smiled.

"Lil'Ith, you remember my last visit, yes?"

She nodded.

"And the baby girl, your mistress apprenticed."

"Aye, Ra'Chel. She's in the kitchens. Do you wish I fetch her?"

Oh'Raum's breathing hitched and his pulse quickened. "In due time. First, I want to know the happenings here in Dur'Loth. It has been many years."

Lil'Ith lowered her voice. "Dark times, sir. First, the King's Guard came by the road then by the harbor. They conscripted most of the men and pressed many of the ships into service. We have an entire garrison here because of the harbor, but few travelers or merchants come here now."

"And news of the Wallef?"

"One of the first ships conscripted into the King's Navy."

"There was a boy. He travelled with me." Oh'Raum's voice cracked with emotion.

Lil'Ith rolled her eyes. "Rowan'Gaff Grimsson. He's a Nightwatchman."

"Grimsson? When I knew him, he went by Vodr."

"Was he a little *cumberworld* then, too?"

"My dear. Such language," Oh'Raum said. "But you said he's an officer of the law."

"He comes in here night after night droning on about a great warrior and how he is going to do this and that."

"I see."

"I didn't mean to gossip, Master, but he barely covers his tab and can't keep his hands off the maids."

"So, he's a blowhard and a drunkard?"

"He holds his drink just fine, sir."

"And the King's Guard? They do nothing?"

"The less they have to do, the better."

Oh'Raum nodded. "I shall wait for my previous friend, my dear. I look forward to talking with him about his behavior."

Lil'Ith smiled. "Thank you, sir. Would you like to see Ra'Chel now?"

Oh'Raum returned her smile. "If you please."

The girl that exited the kitchen swung between the tables reminding Oh'Raum of how Fi Brune swept through the room.

"You asked to see me, sir?"

Lil'Ith stepped up behind her. "Sister, this is Master Oh'Raum Yulr."

Oh'Raum smiled.

"You're too old for me, if you're looking for a wife," Ra'Chel said, spun on her heels, and returned to the kitchen.

Lil'Ith's face reddened. "Oh my." She panted several times. "I'm so sorry."

Two boys at the end of the dock throwing rocks at the skittering crabs heard Oh'Raum's booming laughter explode from The Westerly. One of the armored guards rose and approached his table. Lil'Ith inched toward the kitchen. "Everything alright here?"

"Quite so. Quite so." Oh'Raum said, still laughing.

"Then let's keep it down over here," the guard said and rested a hand on the hilt of his sword.

Oh'Raum noticed the hand, put both his own on the table, and smiled up at the officer. "There will be no further outbursts, good sir."

The guard looked at Lil'Ith then back to Oh'Raum. "See that there aren't."

The Westerly's door swung open and several men entered, clubs slung on their sides. They clapped each other's shoulders and took up tables near the King's Guard, jostling each other with friendly jibes. The guard near Oh'Raum smiled and returned to his comrades.

Lil'Ith bowed. "I'll fetch Ra'Chel again and—"

"I think it best if I go to her, my dear," Oh'Raum said, stood, and walked to the kitchen.

Inside, Ra'Chel leaned elbow-deep into a foaming sink scrubbing plates and mugs. She turned when the door closed behind her. "Well, you're a persistent, old cuss, aren't you," she said.

Oh'Raum's eyebrows narrowed and a stern expression crossed his face. "That's no way for a princess to talk. Mistress Brune should have taught you better manners."

Ra'Chel laughed and returned to the dishes.

Oh'Raum spoke in a low, menacing voice. "Look at me when I speak to you, barmaid. You have no idea to whom you address."

Intrigued and somewhat embarrassed, Ra'Chel straightened and dried her hands — her face betrayed her indignation. For a moment, they stared each other down. Neither flinched. "Well, whom do I address?" she finally asked.

Oh'Raum took a deep breath and rolled his shoulders to their full breadth. He appeared to grow several inches taller. The room engulfed her. The candle flames danced and flickered as a brisk wind attacked their light. Ra'Chel stepped away from this apparition, bumped the wash basin, and looked for an escape route like a helpless, trapped animal.

"I am Oh'Raum Yulr, master of the elements and wielder of sacred knowledge. It was I who was summoned to the coast by visions of your coming. It was I who pulled you from your parents funeral barge before they crossed the river to eternity. It is I who brought you to this place and set you into apprenticeship with the mistress of this inn." His voice grew calm and gentle. "It was I who fed you, shielded you from the elements, and cleaned your swaddling linens."

He grew quiet and the stifling kitchen released its grip on her.

"And it is I who will see you sit on your father's throne in Draer."

Ra'Chel stood wide-eyed, her chest heaving. "My mother spoke of you often. She loved many men, but only one was she in love with. Only one had her heart."

"In my own way, I loved her as well. Had our lives turned out differently, I would have tried to be a good husband to her." Oh'Raum looked to the ground, ashamed.

Ra'Chel watched the old man, looking for signs of deception or malice. "Why now do you come and tell me these things?" She waved her hands around the kitchen. "I am no princess. Why disrupt my life, such as it is?"

Oh'Raum took a half-step forward. "The visions have returned, my dear. There are great things—"

"I know nothing of your visions. Please, sir, I have dishes to wash." She turned and plunged her hands into the soapy water. Her shoulders slumped and she cried.

Oh'Raum spoke in a whisper. "It is not my intent to hurt you, Ra'Chel. Please let me explain."

She shook her head, drenched her sponge, and jabbed it into a mug.

Oh'Raum backed out of the kitchen. "I understand." Before leaving, he turned. "Did your mother tell you where your name came from?"

She did not turn, only shook her head.

"I named you," he whispered and shut the door behind him.

Oh'Raum returned to his table to find a fresh pint next to the plate of fruit. One of the club-wielding men eyed him from their table, working up the courage to approach. Oh'Raum recognized him and waved him over.

"Master Oh'Raum."

"Rowan'Gaff Vodr," Oh'Raum replied.

Rowan frowned. "I haven't used my father's name in many years. It's Grimsson now. Captain Bodvar gave it to me."

Oh'Raum nibbled an apple slice. "I see. And where is the good Steersman these days?"

Rowan'Gaff sat and reached for a bit of apple without asking. Oh'Raum looked up at him. Expressionless, Rowan pulled the fruit to his lips and crunched through it. "I don't know. I heard the king released the Wallef from service, but they don't stay long in port these days. Nobody does."

"And when you're service onboard concluded, you stayed in Dur'Loth."

185

Rowan'Gaff nodded. "I thought many times of coming to find you."

"To what end?"

Rowan rubbed his face. "I never told her. I had plenty of opportunity, you know."

"I'm sure."

"But I kept your secret."

"What secret?"

Rowan sat forward. "How we found her and brought her here." He looked around the mostly empty tavern. "The dreams and such."

Oh'Raum sat back. "I just told her in the kitchen."

"You did?" Rowan asked and looked to the kitchen. He waved at Lil'Ith to bring another tankard. "What did she say?"

"Nothing."

The door to the kitchen opened and Ra'Chel emerged — her face grim. She walked to where they sat.

"Good day, Ra'Chel," Rowan said. "You're looking as lovely as ever."

Her fabricated smile spoke volumes to Oh'Raum about their tenuous relationship. "Rowan'Gaff, please give us a moment. I believe we have much to discuss."

Reluctantly, Rowan returned to his table without joining their frivolity. Instead, he leered at Oh'Raum and Ra'Chel.

"What about my name?" she asked in a forceful tone.

Oh'Raum smiled at her unwavering demeanor. "Mistress Brune raised you well. I was right to bring you to her."

Ra'Chel remained quiet.

"Eighteen years ago, I experienced dark visions which included many sites I have spent these years examining for deeper meaning. From where these dreams came, I know not. They drew me to the northwest coast where at the exact moment of an eclipse, a scorched funeral barge slid to shore. It happened almost precisely as I foresaw. Onboard were the King and Queen, of the now conquered kingdom of Draer. Also

186

aboard the barge, I found a baby girl, less than a year old."

Tears welled in Ra'Chel's eyes, but she managed to hold back the entirety of her emotions.

"The dreams beckoned me to a pebbly shore called, Rach'Ella Wash. It is there I found you. The young man I traveled with asked what we should call you. I chose to name you Ra'Chel."

Ra'Chel looked up. "Young man?"

Oh'Raum thinned his lips. "You know him as Rowan'Gaff Grimsson."

Ra'Chel whirled in her seat and stared at Rowan who quickly shied away from her gaze. She turned back to Oh'Raum. "That pig?" Her raised voice attracted the glares of the armor-clad King's Guard.

"That pig, was a confused young man with aspirations of greatness. His story is yet to be written."

Ra'Chel's face flushed. "Why are you here? Why are you telling me these things?"

"I loved your father more than even his subjects."

Ra'Chel shook her head.

"I felt compelled to follow as instructed by the dreams," Oh'Raum looked around the tavern, "and here we are."

"I've had no visions. My life is my life," she huffed. "What do you want from me?"

"I can't say. I assure you; I would not do this for just anyone. But I would for the king's daughter."

She again shook her head and quietly asked. "Stop it. Please." Instead of anger, Oh'Raum felt helplessness in her request. Ra'Chel spoke with her head down just above a whisper. "Thank you telling me about my name." She paused. "And for saving my life."

Oh'Raum remained silent.

She looked up at him. "Now what?"

"Now, my dear, we make a plan."

Sleeper

What Preslovard Found

Preslovard jerked awake. "Who's there?" he yelled into the night. Distant, leg-rubbing crickets and a high-pitched yelp from Freya answered him.

"In heaven's name?" she said and shook off a shiver.

"I'm sorry," Preslovard apologized and reclined back to his makeshift pillow — a worn cloth pack. He stared into the sky's oily blackness and remembered his master's commission.

"Find the deep place where the hero sleeps," Oh'Raum had said.

Looking back through his memory, the request from his father now sounded fleeting, almost pleading, like the cries of a desperate man with too much knowledge about things he wished he could forget. Preslovard closed his eyes, soothed his breathing, and focused his thoughts away from the feeling of being watched.

I will not fear, he repeated to himself several times in rhythm to his breathing. *Fear is temporary. It flees from me, as darkness flees candlelight. I am the light that dispels the darkness of fear.*

Successfully calmed, he rolled to his side and watched the embers of their small fire dwindle to blackness as the first blue haze of dawn crept across the sky.

Freya yawned and said in a groggy voice, "It's too early for night terrors, big brother," before rolling to her side and pulling the blanket over her head.

Preslovard stretched under his blanket, sat up, and pulled his half-empty waterskin to his lips. He planned to refill it from the River Thune, which they would reach before midday. He slipped a previous meal's boiled potato from his food pouch and nibbled on it for breakfast.

"If we get an early start today, we can make an early camp."

Freya rolled to her back and huffed under her blanket. "I'm tired of walking."

"So am I, little sister, but father is counting on us."

The girl flipped the blanket off her face and rolled to her side. "I've watched you pour over your maps at night. You don't know where this place is we're supposed to find."

Preslovard knelt and blew onto the remaining embers. "No one does. Father gave me all the information he could. Come on, get up. We have a river to cross today."

"Fine," Freya droned and rolled free from of her blankets.

After watering a nearby privet, Pres secured his bed roll to his pack, helped Freya don her pack, oriented himself with his map, and continued their march north for the El'Thune Hills. After rounding the seaward slope of an unnamed hilltop, the previous day, the ground slowly descended. Looking from an outcrop of rock, the River Thune stretched out before them. Navigating through rough country made the going slow, but refreshing for the young man, even with his younger sister in tow. Freya, for her part, only complained when he forced her out of bed, especially on cooler than normal mornings.

Preslovard appreciated the company, despite the coaxing. He followed his master's commands to the letter and stayed off the roads, which would have significantly shortened their journey.

"We know not what forces are arranged against us," Oh'Raum had said. "Protect your sister."

The weight of these words now sat heavy on Preslovard's shoulders and he pondered their dire meaning until the sounds of rushing water filled the air. The sound escalated with each step and the prospect of fording the River Thune presented a challenge they would be forced to overcome.

After foraging a patch of *Karljohan*, which Freya stumbled into, the pair emerged from a Spruce grove running the length of the river. Pres sat on a large rock and removed his map. He triangulated their approximate position from two visible mountain tops and a bend in the river to his right. According to his map, the Thune ran westerly for half a league before making a sharp bend to the south. To his east, past another slow meander, a narrow spot provided a potential crossing point.

Preslovard replaced his map and clapped Freya, who played in the water, on the back. The two paralleled the river to the northeast and followed the windings until they reached the narrow spot. To their good fortune, a knotted rope spanned the river between two thick-trunked oaks.

"I'll go first," Preslovard said. "Give me your pack."

He removed his breeches and shoes and placed them in his pack. He placed both packs atop his head and forded the waist-high water — one hand on the slick rope.

"It doesn't look deep," Freya called over the rushing water.

"There are a few loose rocks, and the current isn't severe. Keep both hands on the rope and your footing sure and you'll be fine." He dropped both packs a few feet from the water's edge and turned to help Freya.

"Oh, the water's cold."

"Both hands on the rope, Freya."

The girl inched her way farther from the southern shore, taking the fording slowly as Pres had instructed.

"Good girl, you're doing fine."

"I can feel the loose rocks."

"Feel with your foot for a good solid spot before—Freya!" Preslovard screamed.

Freya slipped on a slick river rock and plunged under the moving water. Preslovard stomped from the shore, slipping on loose stones, almost falling into the water himself.

Freya's grip on the rope never wavered and a moment later she pulled herself from the water and wrapped both arms around the rope.

"Are you alright?" Preslovard frantically asked continuing his plunge into the river to reach her.

Freya coughed and hugged the rope tighter while brushing her blonde hair away from her face. "I'm fine," she said though heavy breaths. "You weren't kidding about the rocks."

Pres reached her splashing wildly and drew her to him, looping his arm around her and the rope. "Are you okay?"

She smiled up at him and started giggling. "You look like a drowned rat."

Her contagious humor swept over him and he hugged her tighter, laughing along with her through his own deep breaths.

They made their way slowly to the river's northern shore, dried as best they could, and took a moment to compose themselves. "I don't know that we'll tell Father about this part of our journey," Preslovard said while filling their waterskins. "What say you?"

Freya turned to see the smile on his face. "Only if you promise me, we're taking the road home."

"Count on it."

On the north bank of the Thune, the ground sloped sharply upward toward the high peaks of the twin mountain range. Two snow-covered pinnacles towered over the landscape with several smaller shards of rock jutting into the sky, encircling the El'Thune Hills.

"Why are they called hills?" Freya asked surveying the imposing, craggy heights.

"No one knows. According to legend, somewhere up there a hero sleeps."

"How are we going to find it?"

Preslovard did not answer. Instead, he hiked his pack high on his shoulders and continued climbing away from the river.

They took a break in a clearing midway up the slop. Preslovard turned to Freya. "I think we need to talk about our plan."

"We have a plan?"

Pres laughed. "If we work our way across the southern side of the mountain, we can canvas a good portion of the ground. If we find nothing, we head north, then traverse the slopes westerly."

Freya looked up at the hillside sloping up and away from her. "We zig-zag."

"Right."

"Do we even know which side we should zig-zag on?"

Preslovard turned to the map on his right thigh and shrugged a moment later. "Father didn't know which face of the mountain held the chamber we're looking for." He watched Freya skipping along a bed of blue cornflowers. He hummed softly to himself, running the lines of the old song through his mind.

When from the heart of the Western lands,
Like a brilliant star that comes to Earth,
A shining hero stalwart stands,
Raises sword and shows his worth.

He stood, paced, and sung aloud.

"Cap'Tian, pure of heart and mind of stone,
With sword and shield and spear-tipped lance,
The hero stands — one man alone,
Drives back the horde's conquering advance.

Back to the East flees evil's retreat,
With one final card yet to play,
A feast and trap did lay in defeat,
For Cap'Tian's fate ends would betray."

"What are you singing," Freya asked.

"The Ballad of Cap'Tian."

Freya skipped to where he paced and listened, her head cocked.

Preslovard stopped pacing and methodically spoke the final verses

> "By victory drink was Cap'Tian betrayed,
> To sleep but not to die or rise,
> On windward slopes the evil stayed,
> To perhaps return and claim their prize.
>
> Foretold the hero of this song bides,
> Until Draer maiden softly weeps,
> When returning horde of evil rides,
> Deep in El'Thune Cap'Tian sleeps."

His breathing quickened as his mind ran through the lines again. "East," he said and paused, quickly running through the verses. "West. South." He turned to his little sister. "No north."

Freya watched Preslovard resume his pacing in front of their packs.

"No mention of the north in the song. What if this is by design?"

Freya's huffed. "Then we're on the wrong side of the mountain?"

Preslovard snatched up his map and spun in a half circle to orient himself. "If we trek to the east, we can reach the northern slopes through this gap here." He pointed to a small hilltop on the extreme eastern side of the two main peaks. "We might make that cut by tomorrow night."

Freya made a show of caring about his finger on the map. She much preferred to resume her carefree skipping along the rows of blue, puffy flowers.

When the sun dipped toward the low hills to the west, the

two decided to make camp. They unfurled their bed rolls near soft patches of heather and Preslovard built their cooking fire for the crocks.

"How about we broth those mushrooms you found today?"

Freya smiled and pulled the four *Karljohan* mushrooms from her pack, washed them from her waterskin, and walked them to her brother. Preslovard, took out his dagger and snipped the root ends from the stubby, brown mushrooms.

Freya watched him skillfully work. Plants fascinated him and his love for things that grow evidenced itself in how he handled and prepared their dinner. Not long after, they sipped a mild, nutty broth from their cooking crocks.

"We'll be on the other side tomorrow?" Freya asked and blew steam from the lip of her crock.

"If we get an early start tomorrow morning, we should easily make the other side of the pass."

Freya screwed her face in to pinch. "Always with the early starts. Why is there no sleeping in on chilly mornings on this journey?"

Preslovard sipped his mug. "It took us almost a fortnight to get this far, dear Sister, and we have still longer on our quest before Father is to meet us at the bridge."

"How far until the bridge?"

"We'll spend the next several days searching for where the hero sleeps. If we don't find it in time, we make for the bridge."

She pointed aimlessly into the forest. He smiled and pointed in the opposite direction. "Straight that way, we'll hit a road. Since we're on the northern side of the mountains, we turn left to meet Father."

Freya looked into the dwindling light in the direction he pointed and sipped her crock. "I thought I would like questing more."

Pres nodded. He, too, longed for their cottage nestled into the foothills of the Great Hooks, his studies, and his garden. "We'll both be home sooner than you think."

"By the road, right?"

He laughed, "Yes. By the perfectly smooth, quick-marching road."

After washing their crocks and slipping into their blankets, they both sat quietly listening to the sounds of night creatures emerge from their dens. Freya broke their silence with a long sigh. "The first thing I'm going to do when we get home is go for a long swim in the lake. What are you going to do?"

Preslovard thought for a moment. "Never leave again."

ᚱ   ᛋ

Nine days passed in similar fashion. The pair walked on an east to west path until they crested the foothills for a southerly turn. They would make camp, eat a meager dinner, and get what sleep they could in this unfamiliar country. Freya would complain about another day of trudging on the slanted ground, but once on their way, she stayed with Preslovard step for step.

On the morning of the tenth day, the duo traversed a tree-covered slope high in the El'Thune foothills.

"How high up to you think this place—" she tripped and fell to the hard ground.

Preslovard turned. "Are you okay?"

"I tripped on a stone."

Pres walked to where she sat rubbing her knee and offered her his hand. Something about the shape of the stone caught his eye. "You tripped on this?" he asked and knelt.

"Yes, I—"

"Help me," Preslovard said and scraped away dirt from around the oddly shaped stone. A chipped triangular tip protruded from the loamy ground. Preslovard cleared away fallen leaves and twigs as Freya joined him in freeing the small pyramid.

It turned out not to be a small pyramid but a broken piece of a much larger, flat stone. The shard perched skyward only barely revealing its battered point.

"It's smooth," Freya said.

Preslovard scanned the area around the stone, stood, and shuffled more debris away from where Freya had tripped. Under several inches of vegetation more flat stones emerged. "They're paving stones. Freya, I think we found a road."

"Actually," she paused, "I found a road."

Freya stood and stepped away from where she fell. Cracked gray stones grew around Preslovard as he kicked away the twigs, dead leaves, and undergrowth.

"I think I found the edge. Clear away that side."

Freya kicked and scraped at the debris hiding the stones. Preslovard joined her and together they cleared an area wide enough for Oh'Raum's cottage and just as long. "It's massive," Preslovard slowly said, gawking at what they had uncovered. "It must stretch for miles north into the valley. Perhaps even all the way to Draer."

"How did we not see this before?" Freya asked.

"You didn't fall. We must have passed over it each time we traversed the slope." He walked to the middle of the road and pulled his map from his breeches. "It runs almost due north, south and climbs into the mountain." He looked up the slope. The rows of flat stones vanished beneath the undergrowth several yards from where they stood. Above that, nothing stood out as made by human hands.

Preslovard rolled and stowed the map before turning to Freya. "Come on," he excitedly said and dashed up the ascending slope.

Trees had grown up through the middle of the road, twisting and tossing stones aside like a child's blocks. Lumpy mounds were not mounds at all, but strewn paving stones, weathered by a millennia's erosion — covered by leaves, blown dirt, and decaying branches. Despite this, Preslovard quickly identified the road's course.

Higher and higher the road drew them. After hours of

climbing the ground suddenly leveled. On either side of the road the land dropped away down steep, tree-lined slopes. Above the trees, a sheer cliff loomed over them.

"I think we're on a bridge," Preslovard said.

Freya stepped to the middle.

"No, Frey. Stay to the side with me."

The young girl heard the urgency in his voice and slowly stepped back toward her brother.

"It is going to be strongest here," he said and pointed down the causeway's side. The ruins of a Gabon wall gave way to a chiseled guard rail running both sides of the bridge.

"The trees won't grow without earth beneath them. Stay close to them, as they appear sturdy and long-lived."

Cautiously they walked from tree to tree, carefully looking for any sign that the structure could not bear their combined weight. At the far end of the bridge, they emerged into a small clearing that ran to the base of the enormous cliff.

"I never," Freya gasped. "Pres, we found it."

Cut into the crumbling side of the cliff stood an immense doorway. Countless ages of thaws had cracked the opening's casings almost beyond recognition. The entrance resembled an open, hungry maw with jagged, granite teeth. The remains of the smooth-chiseled casing stones lay in a rubble heap at the base of the colossal cavity.

Freya's voice hitched. "Are — are we going in there?"

Preslovard looked down at her and saw the fear growing on her face at the darkness that loomed before them. "Be brave, little sister. Remember, you are the candlelight that drives away the darkness."

She knew the mantra, as taught to her by Oh'Raum, but peering into the darkness and unknown of that gray cavern felt like icicles dripping down her spine. She looked up at Preslovard. "Can I be the candlelight that you return to from your exploration?"

He smiled. "Let's make camp there," he reassuringly said

and pointed to a flat, tufted clearing to the side of the cave's mouth. "You can wait for me there. I promise I won't venture in far."

"Thank you."

The pair made camp in an ancient meeting place just beyond the imposing gates of the once great Kingdom of Unda'Vager. Preslovard built a small fire for Freya to tend while he explored the cave.

"I'll be right back," he said and wrapped bark around the end of a stick before stuffing it with dried grass, moss, and leaves. From his pack he removed a small pouch of fat he used as seasoning and lathered the end of the torch.

Freya gave him a thin, less than reassuring smile. Preslovard jabbed the torch into the fire, scrambled over the pile of fallen boulders, and disappeared into the darkness.

The road's flagstones continued into the mountain until they slowly gave way to hewn rock. The tunnel widened slightly just inside the cave's mouth and continued until the sunlight from the opening no longer illuminated the dusty floor.

Preslovard held his torch high above him and ran his fingers along the smooth cave walls. They felt cold and slick with moisture the farther he ventured from the bright opening behind him. He inched deeper into the blackness, stopping every few steps to turn and gauge his distance from the opening.

The tunnel into the mountain continued farther than he anticipated, and he felt a tug in his chest to return to Freya and their small encampment, just outside the diminishing point of light behind him.

Smaller side tunnels branched off the main passage into dark recesses and plunged into unknown depths. Preslovard continued inching into the cave, hoping the light of his torch would land on the resting place of the legendary hero with each successive step. He again turned toward the pinpoint of light which represented his only escape from this dark tomb and thoughts of turning back assailed him.

Deep in El'Thune Cap'Tian sleeps, he said to himself and took another step forward.

His footfall missed where he expected the road surface to be and he slipped from the top step of a wide, descended stair. Momentum carried him forward, sending him end over end into the darkness, crashing between the hard walls like a log in a flume. Down he rolled until coming to a thudding stop at the base of the thankfully short staircase.

Preslovard sprawled on the cold, stone floor, his torch weakly flickering behind him on the bottom step. Pain in his ankle sprang to life when he righted himself to take stock of his condition.

A quiet shuffling emanated from the darkness. The tiny sound startled him. "Who's there?" he shouted, his words echoing throughout the tunnels until his own voice meekly answered him moments later.

Preslovard stood and winced from the sharp pain in his foot, leaned against the wall of the cavern, and shifted his weight to his uninjured leg. He limped along the wall toward the stairs and clutched the torch. He swung it in front of him like a sword in hopes the fire might scare off whatever effortlessly moved in the shadows. Slowly he inched toward the sound and fixed his eyes on the circle of torchlight, scanning for anything at the edge of its illumination. Instinctively, Preslovard drew his sword. The sound reverberated from the walls, amplified by the enclosed space.

I am the light that drives away the darkness. The thought wavered through his consciousness.

A small pair of gray feet appeared just outside the circle of light. Preslovard froze. Silently the feet slinked away from the faint light as though harmful to be illuminated by it.

"Hello?" Preslovard called, a quiver in his voice. Despite his growing fear, he inched closer.

Again, the light revealed the tiny feet. The blade of

torchlight rose up two thin, gray legs until it reached the torn hem of brown cloth.

"I'm not going to hurt you," Preslovard softly said and lowered his sword.

Just outside the cone of light, Preslovard recognized the outline of a young girl. She looked younger than Freya and much thinner in build. She wore a tattered, leathery, one-piece smock. The skin of her arms looked gray and mottled. Clutched to her chest she held a small, stringy doll which heaved with her panting and swayed with her forward and back.

"Are you down here alone, little one?" Preslovard asked and moved a step closer. He raised his torch above his head to illuminate a wider circle and called out in horror at the girl's wretched face. "Oh, Gods!"

Her heavy breathing came from an open mouth of sharp fang-like teeth. Drool slipped from the corners of her maw as her wide-set eyes narrowed on him. Dirty, matted hair fell to the sides of her revolting face, clumped in place with knots of muck which swayed in rhythm to her breathing.

Her gaunt face was not that of a lost, trapped little girl but a starving, wild animal driven by a single deadly intent — to feed.

Sleeper

Underground Escape

Freya poked a stick at the fire, sending sparks lofting into the night's sky. The growing darkness filled her with fear for her brother, yet to emerge from the cave, but also apprehension of what night animals lurked about the countryside.

I will not fear, she thought.

The sky to the north flashed, breaking her concentration, followed by distant rumbling above the treetops.

"It's going to be a wet night for Preslovard when he scurries from that cave, Petunia," she said as though a friend sat with her around the fire. Pretending not to be alone always made her feel better at home, but in this strange place with the firelight dancing on the cliff behind her, it did not help as much as she hoped.

"Perhaps, I'll make up a song," she said aloud to the fire.

Freya hummed a melody to herself adding words she thought rhymed and sounded fun.

Buttercups, buttercups growing in a row,
Along comes a gardener, ready to sow.

A smile crossed her face, and she jabbed the fire again.

Preslovard, Oh Preslovard picking edible root,

Her thoughts unexpectedly turned dark as did her made-up song.

Along comes a robber, eyeing his loot.

A cool breeze swept through the clearing. Dancing flames swirled and flickered in the mountain wind. Freya shivered. Large rain drops fell around her hitting the fire's logs sending sizzling plumes into the air.

"Rain, rain, go away, come again another—"

The sky above her sparked with a crackling bolt of light, followed instantly by the crash of thunder. A torrent of rain cascaded from the heavens.

Freya let out a scream and scrambled to gather up their belongings before dashing for the dry shelter of the Unda'Vager gate. Her short arms could not hold everything. After a second trip, she sat just inside the widened part of the doorway soaked from head to foot. Preslovard's traveling supplies lay strewn on the rocky floor, partially drenched. The cooking fire spat and hissed puffs of steam, but soon fell quiet, extinguished by the downpour.

Now in the darkness of the cave, Freya pulled her knees to her chest and wrapped the driest of their two blankets over herself. Behind her lightning flashed, dancing off the interior of the tunnel before her. Thunder echoed through the passage bouncing back to her, reverberating off the craggy walls.

"Rain, rain," she sang more to drown out the rumbling storm behind her than to wish the storm away. From within the black passage an echoed voice sang back, "Rain, rain."

Another flare of lighting slashed through the cavern and Freya thought she saw something glint in that instant of light — two red eyes.

"Come again another day," she croaked, barely able to get the words out.

Again, the eerie echo returned to her, "Come again another

day." This time the echoed voice carried another sound, the low growling of an unseen beast.

ଉ   ଊ

Preslovard stared into the blackness — into the blood-red glint of dozens of advancing creatures. What sounded like a ravenous pack of dogs followed at their heels. The snarling swarm of *tu'hünl'volf* lunged past their masters, snapping their powerful jaws in anticipation of sinking their dripping white fangs into his juicy flesh. In his faint, dancing torchlight, their handlers looked just as fierce. Greedy, hungry mouths huffed strings of white drool at the edges. Large, black eyes, bulged at the thought of their next succulent meal.

Preslovard held his torch and sword in front of him, defensively holding his attackers at bay. The horde descended on him, scratching and biting. Preslovard stabbed and slashed at the greasy animals. He parried several spear thrusts from the creatures behind the dogs, quickly realizing he stood outmatched. The unleashed *tu'hünl'volf* ripped and tore his clothing, snarling alongside their monster masters.

Despite his efforts, bite after bite tore into him and pain erupted throughout his body. His shrieks echoed in the tunnel. Pres swung his torch like a club, bashing into anything it connected with. His sword blade glinted in the torchlight as it worked its deadly business.

Several animals lunged for his throat to find instead, the flesh of his defensive forearm and either a fiery club or the deathblow of his sword.

"*Et Tuwet!*" One of the handlers yelled. On command, several of the *tu'hünl'volf* broke off their attack and ran past him in search of other unfortunate explorers that ventured into their domain.

A sharp pain in his right hand ripped the sword from his grip and it clattered to the floor. Preslovard swung his torch stabbing embers into two dogs on his left. He punched and kicked his attackers, both creature and *tu'hünl'volf*. A biting pain in his right calf dropped him to the hard floor. He rolled from side to side and fought to his knees, elbowing anything within reach. He scampered away, swinging wildly in the darkness. His torch all but extinguished from the fierce melee.

Behind the creatures, a faint light emanated farther down the tunnel, just enough to give them direction toward their prey.

Preslovard darted into a side opening, right of the stairs, feeling with his hands as he went. Behind him, the animals nipped at his fleshy calves. He turned, kicked, and crazily swung his bloody fists while scampering along the side tunnel. The corridor opened into a larger room where the crushing *tu'hünl'volf* dragged Preslovard to the floor.

Preslovard lay on his back fighting off the dog's bounding attacks. He shuffled away from the flashing teeth and felt himself slip backward, like falling from stool. Rushing wind whipped past his ears and the growling disappeared in the distance, far above.

Preslovard curled into a bloody ball, not knowing what horrible death lay at the bottom of this new nightmare. His left side scraped past a stone outcropping. The rock tore into his hip and arm. He tucked his head and yelled into his chest, sucked in a deep breath, and tightened all his muscles in anticipation of a crushing landing to shortly follow.

Preslovard hit what, at first, felt like stone. The stone opened beneath him — swallowing him. His ears bore the brunt from the wall of water collapsing over top of him. It bit his wounds and he convulsed at the stinging erupting throughout his body. In complete darkness, Preslovard floated. The pressure in his ears paled in comparison to his desire to breath. He kicked his legs and swam toward the decreasing pressure in his ears, breaking the surface after several painful strokes.

He faintly heard, high above him, thundering shouts and

the echoes of growling dogs. Preslovard took in several deep breaths and slowly swam forward. He rolled to his side and forced his body to make slow, even stokes. With each reach of his lead hand, he wished to make contact with a solid object.

A brilliant dot appeared in the distance, casting faint light over the water and illuminating a series of black bumps rising above the glittering reflections. Preslovard angled for one of the bumps. His hand reached out, mid-stroke, and grazed the cold stone of a stalagmite. He gripped the cone of rock, a tiny island in the black sea, and pulled himself from the frigid water.

The distant torch swept the water from side to side. Beneath the torch's light, Preslovard made out the thin shape of a man and a knee-high dog. Each sniffed the air, walked from side to side, and looked out over the water — hunting.

Tiny ripples peeled away from Preslovard with every chest heave. *Calm yourself. You're alive,* he thought. *Oh gods, Freya.*

The point of light above the scrawny figure bobbed out of sight, plunging Preslovard once again into darkness. He slid from the stalagmite, cringing against the cold water, and cautiously swam to where the light vanished.

After hitting two more rocks jutting from the water's surface, Preslovard crawled from the icy lake to a small, rocky beach. Faint, torchlight glowed down a narrow tunnel set into the wall. He brought his knees to his chest to both wring water from his clothes and conserve what little body heat remained. Droplets splashed the underground lake and resounded through the chamber. He shivered in almost complete blackness while dark thoughts and misgivings rippled through his mind like the distant echoes. *Freya. Father. I failed you both.*

Something skittered in the shadows, slinking among the rock flakes. Preslovard jerked, sat up, and groped for a defensive weapon — a hand-sized shard. Motionless, he listened and squinted in the faint tunnel-light.

To his left, a hairy leg appeared from behind a rock. Slowly, another reached out, feeling along the rock-strewn beach. Pres stood and backed away when an enormous spider emerged from behind the rock. It moved deliberately, gently searching out its path. Easily larger than his hand, the spider groped along in the darkness to the water's edge.

Preslovard's body ached from oozing bites, bleeding scrapes, and the tenseness of battle. Though hobbling, he kept his footing and crept deeper into the mountain. Scraping echoed from side passages forcing him to crouch or press himself against the tunnel wall.

The end of the main passage opened into an enormous cavern. Torch-lined walls disappeared toward a high ceiling with immense pillars supporting the space. More torches surrounded each pillar illuminating a throng of gray-skinned creatures. They crawled over each other in a huddled orgy of arms and legs.

Circling the vast chamber, torches bobbed above scrawny frames with oily, black bogs at their heels. Howling voices and running feet approached from the chasm's opposite end. Torches flooded the opposite wall, spreading out through the cavern with searching orange light.

Preslovard slid from the passage and crept along the wall. In front of him, a giant boulder blocked his path — a fallen piece of ceiling. He found an open cleft and pressed himself between the wall and the huge rock. He crouched in the shadow and held his breath.

Glistening, black *tu'hünl'volf* dashed past him into the corridor leading to the subterranean lake, followed by running, ghastly figures. One of the hideous men stopped at the tunnel entrance.

"*Dri'ang ner'd lo kru'nem,*" he hissed. Bulging eyes peered into the hallway from a gaunt, skeletal face.

"*Ma'nim,*" a voice shouted back.

Torches swung around the area, searching for signs of the intruder.

Preslovard tucked his head to his knees and sank deeper into his hiding place, a slender crack in the wall behind the boulder.

From the middle of the cave, the horde wailed. Echoing shrieks erupted throughout the grotto and torches flashed around the room. Oil-slick dogs dashed from place to place, yipping and nipping each other as the mania grew.

Preslovard inched into the crack, expecting discovery at any moment.

"Met'met en pre'ang," one of the torch-wielders shouted and approached the fallen boulder.

A high-pitched child's scream pierced the black halls, reverberated, and cascaded through the underground city.

"Ah'oo! Ah'oo!" The creatures screamed and scurried for side tunnels.

Freya?

The torchlight around Preslovard faded, leaving only a sliver of light in his hiding place. Running and scraping echoed through the expansive cavern. He relaxed and slid deeper still into his narrow, protective fissure. His eyes fluttered either from exhaustion, blood loss, or both. Preslovard's forehead rested against the stone fissure and he unwillingly lost consciousness.

A swollen bladder forced him awake. During his rest, his body relaxed and wedged even farther in the narrow crack. Preslovard groped in the dark for a handhold but found only cold, smooth stone. His stomach ached for release. He wriggled side to side and managed to straighten himself, relieving the pressure on his knees.

With each tiny movement, Preslovard inched deeper into the cleft. He reached with his right hand to place his palm against the rock wall for leverage. In the almost complete darkness, his hand wrapped around the corner of another crack. He exhaled and pulled on the corner, slipping from the fissure and falling to the floor. A faint ribbon of torchlight cut through the crevice like a sunbeam.

Preslovard stood and felt the slit in the wall. It ran from floor to ceiling just wide enough for him to slide back in. He looked around this new room, squinting in the available, dim light. Stones, covered in a generous dust layer, littered the smooth floor. The sleek walls showed their own age marks.

Pres slid along the wall allowing his eyes to adjust in the dull light. A few steps along the wall he came to a sharp, chiseled corner and pressed his back into it. From the corner, he stretched his arms out and stepped toward the middle of the room. Something appeared in his vision — a dark box. The muted light shaft ended at its base and Preslovard fixed his vision there. He made out etched runes and the figures of men and horses as though they marched around the base of the platform.

He followed the figures to one corner and looked up. Preslovard fell away from the hideous face above him. A massive, winged creature bore down on him. With aching legs, he pushed away from the monster and it vanished in the darkness. Pres stopped, his heart pounding and his bladder screaming

A voice deep in his memory sprang forth — his father. *'Twas not I who they drove from the tomb, but you.*

Preslovard stood and marched to the fierce gargoyle. He put his nose an inch away from the monster's snarling face, untied his britches, and relieved himself on the gargoyles corner pedestal. His water washed away the dust below the gargoyles clawed feet, exposing more engraved runes. Three interlocking triangles etched in the stone box — a *Valknut.*

"The knot of those fallen in battle," Preslovard whispered.

He moved to his left, the box's long side, leaned across its broad top and felt for more runes.

Can it be?

Preslovard turned and followed the faint ray of light to the opening in the wall. Before squeezing into the narrow cleft, he turned back toward the sarcophagus, invisible in the blackness then inched from the tomb toward the Unda'Vager city common. Behind the boulder, Preslovard watched the creatures skulking in faint torchlight. Along the right wall, the light faded to almost utter darkness and potentially a possible escape route.

Preslovard inched along the wall, feeling his way in the dim light. He passed the tunnel to the lake and reached the cavern's dark corner. He crouched in the corner expecting to hear a whooping alarm. *Ah'oo! Ah'oo!*

His eyes adjusted to the light and he watched the creatures' movements. Thin legs supported boney frames, spindly arms, and large heads with taught, ashy-gray skin wrapped like leather over gaunt bodies. Many of the creatures slept in churning mounds on the stone floor. One monster wriggled deeper in the pile while another squirted out, like a litter of puppies squirming for their mother's warmth.

The ambulatory beasts walked with slow gates supported by thick pikes. They slumped forward, sliding their feet on the floor as they went.

Preslovard stood and mimicked their hunched back and labored walk. Ahead of him, a blocking stone barrier butted against the cavern wall. Above it, a thick, white netting extended, from the top of the lower rock fence, toward the distant ceiling like a trellis. Hanging from it, bulbous, dark sacks spread across the netting. Pres moved closer. One of the sacks moved and the trellis rippled.

Preslovard froze and remembered the huge spider near the lake. The dark sacks came into focus with another step. The heavy netting — layers of spider's web — stretched high on the cavern's wall. It ran the length of the waist-high stone fence enclosing an immense cage.

Preslovard followed the low wall, careful to not skip loose rocks and mindful of every noise. Clicking and skittering within the web-pen masked his movement and the groaning of sleeping creatures echoed from the walls.

The web-netting turned a corner and led to a roughly hewn double gate system. Preslovard peered through an opening in the gate's slats. Inside, hundreds of yellow-striped spiders inched across the floor. Huge, puffy birthing sacks clung to the web strands strung from one side of the enclosure to the other. Like enormous crabs scampering among tide pools in search of food, the huge, rabbit-sized spiders moved along the webs from sacks of stored food.

"Ah,oo! Ah,oo!" a voice screamed behind Preslovard. He whirled to see a scrawny creature running toward him in the darkness. The warning echoed in the cavern and replies returned from around the city common. Pres backed-peddled and fell against the gate. The ghastly creature rushed him, snarling.

With his teeth bared, the monster slammed into Preslovard and clawed at his face and neck. Pres wildly swung his fists, deflecting the frenzied attack. Pain erupted from his shoulder and warm blood gushed from a deep bite.

Pres punched the side of the beast's head and slammed it against the stone floor. Thick, hollow thuds echoed around the room, followed by a high-pitched crack.

"Ah,oo! Ah,oo!" Hundreds of shouting horrors descended on him.

The damaged gate burst open and a surge of huge spiders erupted from the holding pen. They spilled over his legs and the injured freak like water breaching a levy. Preslovard pushed away from the imposing wave of critters. The floor of spiders moved with remarkable speed, not creeping cautiously in the dark, but running on the points of thick, hairy legs.

A crush of underground creatures flooded toward the panic and screamed at the sight of the spider stampede. Oil-slick, black *tu'hünl'volf* tore into the freed spiders in a growling feeding frenzy, only to receive harsh punishment from their master's pike.

Preslovard loped along the outer wall among human bones and discarded animal carcasses. On the cavern's opposite side, he turned up the, main passage and moved quickly along the tunnel wall. Behind him, shuffling and scurrying creatures hurried to round up the remnants of their spider herd — the cacophony dying to a distant rumble.

At each junction, Preslovard stopped and listened, hoping for a telltale sound to direct him to the exit. The biting, subterranean air warmed with each cross passage and soft gusts guided him to freedom from the hellish Unda'Vager tunnels. The corridor ascended its way through the mountain, ending in a double staircase and a distant point of brilliance.

Outside, sunlight softly bathed the tunnel and Preslovard squinted against it the closer he inched toward freedom.

Just inside the Unda'Vager Gate, he found the remains of their belongings. "Freya," he tried to cry, only managing a pitiful dry squeak. "Freya?" Their packs and blankets lay strewn about the opening, torn and slashed. Dark splotches of dried blood streaked the ground. He looked into the gate's open maw and pushed away dark thoughts of his sister's fate. *Oh, Freya.*

Preslovard rummaged through the debris and found a few drops remaining in his torn waterskin. He tested the fire's heat and found none. He searched the area for tracks leading away from the gate, hoping to find a trail of small footsteps running for safety.

Again, he peered into the cave. Part of him wanted to return to that hellish nightmare for his sister's sake, but another part hoped her death was quick and painless. His rage flared.

"Freya!" This time his voice did not fail him. His call resounded through the halls like a fierce death cry. A sickly echo cried back moments later. *Freya.*

Red eyes flashed deep in the cave accompanied by growls.

Preslovard backpedaled to the safety of sunlight, still holding the torn waterskin. He hurled it into the cave and howled in agony, a sound the *tu'hünl'volf* and their *Vernönae* masters well understood.

Pres turned and limped across the causeway working his way down the mountain. He followed the mountainside until he found, Hill Creek, a trickling stream of snowcap runoff. The water tasted cool and refreshing. It quenched his parched lips and soothed his dry throat. Pres removed his tattered shirt, rinsed it, and tore bandage strips from it. He drenched them in clean water, scraped away as much scab and cave muck as he could, and wrapped them around the numerous bites on his legs and arms. The longest strip he saved for the grievous wound on his shoulder. A breeze swept passed, cooling his wet bandages and relieving some of his throbbing pain.

Keep going, Pres, he told himself. He pushed to his feet and lumbered through the forest. In his mind, Oh'Raum waited for him at the River Thune Bridge. He projected a mental map of his journey focusing on his impending rendezvous in between bouts of grief and remorse over his lost sister. Preslovard stumbled west until the sun sank behind the mountains. With no more energy, he passed out in a grove of tall spruce.

The following morning, Preslovard woke cold and stiff. His stomach growled and his improperly mended wounds ached and throbbed. According to his internal map, half a day's walk and he should reach his father. He crossed Hill Creek knowing it intersected the North Road and attempted to stay well off the road for fear of the King's Guard.

After mid-day, Preslovard reached the River Thune and followed it southwest to the bridge — the northern most point of King's Road. He drank his fill of cool water and collapsed in the bridge's shadow, expecting to see his father's pleasant face.

Instead, salty tears for his little sister cut clean lines down his cheeks.

Oh'Raum's Plan

Crackling firelight danced throughout the small room as Oh'Raum, Rowan'Gaff, and Ra'Chel huddled over the old mystic's worn map.

"If there were any other way, we'd take it," Oh'Raum said and looked at Ra'Chel. "The three of us traveling together is out of the question."

"I don't trust him," Ra'Chel said and leaned away from Rowan.

"I've shown you nothing but kindness," Rowan objected, trying to look as wounded as possible.

"Kindness, Rowan? Perhaps to me, but to no one else. You can't keep your hands to yourself and you are mean to the people."

"Master Oh'Raum, I swear..."

"Enough. You two need to square and soon. Rowan, this is your chance to prove your worth. Ra'Chel, he must accompany us. Why, I do not yet know, but I'm certain of it."

"Like the visions. I'm destined to come with you."

Oh'Raum nodded and turned a menacing stare at Rowan. "I need to know where your loyalties lie, Rowan'Gaff."

"With you," he quickly said.

Ra'Chel laughed under her breath.

"Then I will travel by road," Oh'Raum continued and pointed to the map. "You will go by sea to Skorpo Fjord and follow the river to the bridge. It is my hope Preslovard will be there with fair news of his findings."

"The Wallef entered port last night and is moored at the bay's far end," Rowan said.

"Good. Send word to Steersman Bodvar with my compliments. Invite him to meet with me."

Rowan nodded.

"I still don't understand why I can't come with you along the road," Ra'Chel asked.

"I overheard the King's Guard in The Westerly at mid-day meal. Word has spread of an old man and young woman traveling together. I can only assume a well-positioned spy in Fal'Run heard me talking to an old friend."

"The king's spies are known to me," Rowan said.

Ra'Chel eyed him.

"I'm not one," he blurted.

"We'll know soon enough," she sneered.

Oh'Raum tapped the map. "Your journey will take two days. From there, it is two days overland to the Bridge at the River Thune. I will leave several days before you. This will allow my old legs a generous lead and dissuade any suspicion of my going. Also, if Preslovard and Freya trek south, I will meet them."

"What will we do when we get to the bridge?" Ra'Chel asked.

Oh'Raum smiled. "We'll discuss that when appropriate."

"My rounds begin shortly," Rowan said. "I'll send word to Bodvar to meet you at The Westerly."

"Good."

"When?"

"As soon as he is able. Time is not our ally."

Rowan nodded and turned to Ra'Chel. "Good night."

She did not return his goodbye.

"Master Oh'Raum, why do you put such trust in him?" Ra'Chel asked when only the two of them remained.

"Why do you hold him in such contempt?"

"Since my coming of age, he has courted me. None of the townsfolk like or respect him. He holds himself in such high esteem, it's nauseating. He—"

Oh'Raum held up a hand. "I can't attest for any redeeming qualities, but he must journey with us."

"I don't trust him."

"If we are arrested before morning, your fears will be warranted. Remember, he still does not know you're heritage, nor does he know of my ultimate goal."

She shook her head. "I still don't believe it all myself." She laughed. "Me, a princess?"

"This is why Preslovard's success is so important to our cause."

"And what success is that?"

Oh'Raum did not respond but allowed a thin smile to betray his deep anxiety. "We must follow the path put before us."

Ra'Chel stood, unwrinkled her smock, and huffed. "My path leads to the kitchens. I'm sure Lil'Ith is furious with me by now."

Oh'Raum stood and moved to the door. "I'm sorry I took you away from your work."

"Oh no. It's not every day you learn you're royalty."

"Indeed," he said and bowed. "Until tomorrow, Your Grace."

Ra'Chel giggled and returned an exaggerated curtsy. "Milord."

"Oh, Master Oh'Raum will suffice."

"As you wish, Master Oh'Raum." She laughed again and they exited into the night.

The following morning, Oh'Raum sat in The Westerly enjoying a hot bowl of raisin oatmeal when Bodvar Her'On entered.

The burly Steersman sat across from the old mystic. "Your beard has a bit more gray than I remember, old man."

"And your belt struggles to hold your girth more than I remember, Steersman."

The two stared at each other before Bodvar laughed heartily and slapped the table with both hands. "A truer word was never spoken!" He twirled a finger at Lil'Ith to bring him his own bowl. "Grimsson sent word of a meeting last night. Fortunate for you we are at port — the waters south team with *Zander*. If not for my men nearly mutinying for time with their women, we would yet be at sea."

"Fortunate indeed," Oh'Raum said after Lil'Ith sat Bodvar's bowl of oatmeal on the table and returned to the kitchens.

"What can I do for you, Oh'Raum? More runts you wish me to apprentice?"

Oh'Raum laughed. "Rowan tells me your ship was conscripted."

Bodvar nodded. "Aye. We ferried the king's troops along the coast." He looked around the inn and leaned forward. "Old bastard barely paid us enough to eat. Piss on him and his usurper heir, I say," he whispered and sat back in his chair. "Once freed from that mess, we returned to fishing The Res'Teran, and much happier a lad sailed on the old Wallef — let me tell you."

"To be sure," Oh'Raum agreed. "And what of Rowan? Was he a good mate?"

"He's a better watchman than a deckhand, if that's what you're asking." He spoke through a spoonful of oatmeal. "He pulled his weight, I guess, but nary a day passed without him grumbling. I see why you wanted to offload him."

Oh'Raum shook his head. "The choice was his." He laughed, "And yours."

"True — true," Bodvar agreed.

"Is that why he goes now by Grimsson?"

Bodvar laughed and slid his empty bowl aside. "The men called him that for his poor attitude. When I began using it, the boy took it as his last name, like a badge of honor. He yet calls himself that?"

"He does," Oh'Raum said.

Bodvar shook his head. "A strange one he is."

Oh'Raum nodded.

The Westerly's door opened, and Rowan entered. He waved at the pair and approached.

"Someone's ears are aflame," Oh'Raum said and shifted his eyes over Bodvar's shoulder.

Rowan sat. "Captain," he said and nodded to Bodvar.

"Well, Master Grimsson," the Steersman bellowed. "Been reminiscing about your youth with our old friend here."

"I merely asked about your adventures on the Wallef," Oh'Raum corrected.

Rowan whistled at Lil'Ith for his own breakfast. "I see."

Bodvar spread his hands, "Now that we're all here, Oh'Raum..."

"I have need of your ship."

Bodvar nodded. "Where do you sail?"

"Not I. Two other passengers; to Skorpo."

"Easy enough," Bodvar said. "Any cargo?"

"None. Just passengers and their belongings."

Lil'Ith delivered Rowan's breakfast, collected the finished bowls and scowled at Oh'Raum.

Bodvar rubbed his face and elbowed Rowan'Gaff. "What say you, Grimsson? You up for a sail on the old Wallef?"

"He is one of your passengers," Oh'Raum said.

The Captain nodded with interest. "And the other?"

"The barmaid," Rowan said.

Bodvar looked to The Westerly's kitchen, frowned, and turned to Oh'Raum, puzzled. "What game is afoot, wizard?"

"A most serious one; and one that is in need of discreet passage to Skorpo Fjord."

"I see. I see. Then discreet passage they shall have."

Oh'Raum set a fat leather purse on the table. Rowan'Gaff stopped mid-bite at the sight of the bulging moneybag. "I have coin for both your service and your silence," Oh'Raum said.

Bodvar eyed the purse and instinctively licked his lips. "A fair offer indeed," he said and reached for the bag.

Oh'Raum's speed of hand stunned both his companions. In a flash, the purse vanished, and the old mystic munched on a slice of green apple. "Half when they set sail and half when we meet again in the north."

Bodvar looked at Rowan. "Such a bargain, he sets before me, eh?"

"A fairer offer you won't get from the bastards in black," Rowan said.

"'Tis true, my young friend. Half when we set for the sea and half," he paused, "where in the north?"

"River Thune Bridge," Oh'Raum answered.

Bodvar nodded. "Two days from landfall in Skorpo to the bridge and the same back. How much in is that purse?"

"Enough to buy another ship."

"Then you have an arrangement. When do you sail?" Bodvar asked Rowan'Gaff.

"Four days hence," Oh'Raum said. "I will settle with the inn and make for the road tomorrow. If the road is favorable, we should meet at the bridge in five days."

"That will give me time to settle the men and make ready the ship," Bodvar said.

"Rowan will have your coin. I put these young people in your charge, Steersman. Treat them as you would me."

Bodvar nodded, stood, and extended his hand Oh'Raum shook to affirm their agreement. "Four days then." He slapped Rowan on the shoulder and left The Westerly.

Lil'Ith approached. "Who is paying for that scoundrel's oatmeal then?"

Oh'Raum smiled. "Allow me."

"You may want to add a decent gratuity for the extra work I did last night while you and Ra'Chel schemed all night."

"Such language — schemed, she says," Oh'Raum said to

Rowan, who laughed. The old wizard handed her a shiny gold coin. "And please keep the balance as recompense for yester-night's offense."

Lil'Ith's eyes grew wide at the sight of the greater coin. "Milord, please forgive—"

Oh'Raum held up a hand, stopping her disrespectful onslaught. "No, lady, it is I who should apologize. I took your sister away from her duties and I must do it again four days hence."

Lil'Ith smiled. "Ra'Chel told me."

Oh'Raum scowled.

"Oh, she didn't betray details, just that she was traveling, and I would need to cover until her return." She flattened her smock and looked at the floor. In a timid voice she asked, "Would you know when that would be, Master?"

Oh'Raum shook his head. "I know not, sweet lady, But I will endeavor to have her home safe and sound when our business is complete. You have my word."

Lil'Ith smiled. "Then that shall suffice."

Rowan burped and handed her his empty bowl.

She frowned, took the bowl and shuffled to the kitchen.

"So, you trust Steersman Bodvar?" Rowan'Gaff asked.

Oh'Raum's eyes burned into him. "Did nobody teach you manners or the least bit of courtesy?"

Rowan remained silent.

Oh'Raum leaned forward. "From this moment forward you will treat the people that prepare your food with the respect they are due. They are not your servants."

"Master—"

Oh'Raum ignored his plea. "You will do well to not arouse my ire again, sir. Do I make myself clear?"

Rowan felt small and looked at the table. "Yes."

"Excuse me?"

Rowan looked at him. "Yes, Master Oh'Raum."

"I may have done you a disservice leaving you here in the

care of Master Her'On. The reports of your behavior are unacceptable and if I were not following the path of greater force, you would not be on the Wallef when she sails."

Rowan's face went slack.

"But you are a part of our band, Master Grimsson, and this may yet be your chance to prove a hero lives within you. I charge you to change your ways from this moment forward."

"Yes, Master."

"Then let us not speak of this again. You have four days to make ready. Off with you."

Rowan'Gaff stood and slinked from the inn, punching the doorpost on his exit.

Oh'Raum shook his head. He finished his plate of apples, visited Dur'Loth's many shops through the afternoon, and inventoried his traveling provisions by candlelight after nightfall.

The following morning, he, Rowan'Gaff, and Ra'Chel coordinated their plan before setting out upon Harbor Trail for King's Road. Slowed by numerous inspections and checkpoints by black-clad soldiers, his first day's travel fell short of his ambition.

Oh'Raum reached King's Road following two full days on the march. Ver'Sinian's Guard patrolled in tight formation and scrutinized the old traveler at every opportunity.

"Traveling alone, old man?"

"Aye."

"And where are you off to this day?"

Oh'Raum smiled and leaned on his staff. His answer changed with each interrogation. "Holm'Stad, sir. My grand-daughter serves our king, and it has been an age since we last united." Oh'Raum coughed and shuffled his feet. He hunched over his walking stick and exaggerated his hand-shaking when the solders inspected his small pack.

"Have you seen any other old men traveling with a young woman?"

Oh'Raum shook his head. "No, sir. Not many travelers on the road these days. I did pass a woman selling almost turned turnips yesterday. Rank they were. Do you like turnips? They tend to give me gas, especially—"

"Alright, on your way!"

Oh'Raum struggled to don his pack and muddled on his way, silently laughing.

Sleeper

Ra'Chel's Road

The days following Oh'Raum's departure passed slowly for Ra'Chel. She unpacked and repacked her knapsack half a dozen times, adding this bottle or removing that trinket.

"I've never left Dur'Loth," she said to her sister, "I have no idea what I need for a journey of unknown days."

Lil'Ith sat cross-legged on her bunk and watched Ra'Chel fret over each item. "I wish I was going with you."

Ra'Chel turned to her older sister. True, aching concern pulled her brow low and taught. "Oh, sweet sister, I wish you were coming, too. What a comfort it would be." She crossed the room, sat beside Lil'Ith, and faced her. "What would mother say right now?"

Lil'Ith laughed. "Those tankards don't wash themselves, girls."

Ra'Chel nodded and joined her laughter. She furrowed her brow, scowled, and lowered her mocking voice. "You two are slower than snails through syrup."

Lil'Ith grabbed her sides and rocked back on the bunk with gales of laughter.

Ra'Chel fell beside her and stared at the ceiling. "She would also say that we are all we have."

Lil'Ith smiled and snuggled beside her baby-sister. "No matter what happens in the world, girls, you will always be sisters. No man has the power to break that bond."

"I don't intend to be gone long."

"I know, but it won't be the same without you here," Lil'Ith said. "I asked Anora Kard'Tor to help at the inn. Her family welcomed the extra coin. We may keep her on when you return."

Ra'Chel rolled forward and returned to her bunk. She dumped out the pack and scrutinized each item before replacing it.

"You sail tomorrow?"

Ra'Chel nodded. "We leave harbor at first light." She stuffed a rolled parchment bundle into the sack and faced Lil'Ith, her face wet.

"Oh, my dear," Lil'Ith said and embraced her. "Trust Master Oh'Raum. Mother loved him."

Ra'Chel dried her tears. "I know. I still can't believe the things he says, but in here," she tapped her chest, "they feel right."

"Then trust those feelings, Sister."

Lil'Ith released her. Ra'Chel turned back to her half-loaded backpack and upended it. Lil'Ith placed a soft hand on her arm. "I think you've packed it enough."

Ra'Chel flopped on the bunk's edge and huffed.

"Go to bed, you have an early day tomorrow," Lil'Ith said and refilled the pack.

Ra'Chel looked up at her, desperately longing to tell her sister the truth — to divulge her secret. *Master Oh'Raum claimed me a Princess!* she screamed in her mind. Oh'Raum's warning also echoed in her memory. "Tell no one. Ver'Sinian won't hesitate to finish what his father began when he martyred your parents." Ra'Chel resigned to keep her secret. "I'm going to miss you," she whispered.

Lil'Ith set the backpack on the floor and sat next to her. "We're going to get through this."

Ra'Chel faked a smile, hugged her sister, and walked to her bunk.

Lil'Ith blew out the bedside candle and pulled her covers to her chin. "Ra'Chel," she whispered in the dark.

"Yes?"

"I love you."

"I love you, too."

Ra'Chel stared at the ceiling in complete darkness. Her mind clouded with jumbled thoughts of recent events. Four days ago, her most pressing concern was making sure the opened mead casks had not turned. Then the old wizard arrived with wild claims of her heritage; utter lunacy to be sure. In another life, she would see the humor in it and be off about her business, but in this life, her heart ached at the truth of it.

Images of Fi Brune danced through her memory like the mistress herself danced between The Westerly's tables. "We all have our happy-ever-after's, sweet Ra'Chel," her mother would sing. "Yours being closer than most, my little princess."

Did she know? Ra'Chel questioned. She allowed the happy memories to drift through her and slowly fell asleep.

Like her mind, a heavy fog rolled in during the night and blanketed Dur'Loth Harbor. The following morning, she stood at the south end of the port awaiting her tender to the Wallef.

Rowan'Gaff emerged from the fog. "A gloomy morning for sailing," he said.

"No more obscure than this foolish quest."

Rowan laughed. "This is my second foolish quest, lady."

Ra'Chel detected a subtle change in his normally superior demeanor. "Why did you never tell me?"

"I felt bound by Master Oh'Raum."

"He ordered you not to tell me?"

"No. He charged me to watch over you." He looked at his dirty boots. "In that I failed him and you, I guess."

Contrition? Genuine remorse?

A slim skiff approached the dock and heeled alongside an attached wooden ladder. "It may be as Master Oh'Raum said, your chance for Rowan'Gaff Grimsson to prove his worth." She mustered a fake smile, descended the ladder, and sat in the rickety boat. Rowan followed and took up the port oar.

The Wallef, a wide-bottomed *knörr,* held a dozen men and smelled of fish. Her captain, Steersman Bodvar Her'On, stood tall at the stern of the single-masted ship, shouting orders when the skiff pulled alongside. "Stow that bundle, Gudrod! You move like you're green, man," he shouted. "What took you so long, Thorvald?"

The skiff's starboard oarsman made a rude sound. "This murk, captain. 'Twas lucky I—"

"Get our passengers aboard and secure that skiff, you worthless cuss," Bodvar yelled.

Rowan'Gaff took Ra'Chel's traveling sack and hefted it over the gunwale. He smiled and offered his hand to help her climb aboard the merchant ship. Ra'Chel warily eyed him. With one hand on the gunwale and the other on Rowan's shoulder, she hopped aboard.

"A woman?" one of the crew yelled.

"She is my personal guest, Hroar. You will treat her with respect."

Several of the men grumbled but returned to their duties.

"Skiff secure," Thorvald announced.

"Bergvid, pull the stone," Bodvar ordered. "Run out the oars to bay's end. Grimsson, to the bow with you."

"Aye, Captain," Rowan'Gaff answered and shuffled along the side of the ship. At the bow, he hung on a mast line and scanned the fog ahead.

"Alright lads, heave to."

In unison, the Wallef's crew leaned into their oars and rocked back, seated on planks spanning the deck. Ra'Chel felt the ship move under her.

"Clear ahead," Rowan shouted.

Again, the crew pulled against their oars. The ship creaked around them and cut a clean line forward.

"Sloop to port quarter, Captain. A dozen *faðmr* at most,"

Rowan yelled.

Bodvar leaned the tiller left and the bow of the ship swung to the right. Ra'Chel stood at the port gunwale and watched a larger ship glide passed, hidden mostly in fog. She inhaled deeply. Her lungs filled with damp air and her mind with adventurous thoughts.

A day's sail north from Dur'Loth the fog broke and clear evening skies emerged overhead. Rowan'Gaff took to the rocking boat with practiced ease while Ra'Chel struggled to maintain her footing. She felt queasy from the moment she stepped into the skiff, intensifying when the Wallef left Dur'Loth Harbor's calmer waters.

The Wallef's square sail flopped in the dull, inconsistent wind, slowing their passage. The crew stoked a small cooking fire and dragged grungy nets aboard teaming with colorful fish.

Ra'Chel marveled at the abundance and variety. "I've never seen such a thing," she said.

Rowan'Gaff smiled. "The small ones get tossed back. The larger ones we'll be eating shortly."

"Right from the sea?" The thought of food wrenched her troubled stomach.

He nodded. "I didn't know how much I missed this, until we boarded this morning."

She looked at him. "Why did you leave?"

He rested a hand on his sword. "This was not my destiny."

"I hope you're hungry," Hroar said and pushed past them carrying a red-bellied Arctic Char longer than his arm. The fish whipped its tail against his hold. The *holumenn* swung the fish high above his head and crashed its skull against the ship's gunwale.

"Oh my," Ra'Chel exclaimed.

"You may not want to watch this next part," Rowan said.

"I've seen the fish unloaded at port, but I had no idea it was such gruesome work."

Rowan laughed. "That's not the gruesome part."

Hroar hung the fish over the gunwale, inserted a slender blade in its belly and slit it from tale to chin.

Ra'Chel recoiled. A thick slosh of innards rolled from the fish and slid over the ship's side.

Rowan'Gaff steadied her. "Don't worry, it will taste delicious."

Her stomach-ache receded when the sweet smell of grilled fish wafted around the ship. Bodvar enthusiastically ordered the ship's stores opened and a potato per man cooked for evening meal. The crew cheered the order and soon wooden plates passed between them, piled with blackened meat and a steaming potato. They opened a cask of ale and sat with their backs against the ship's hull enjoying the hot meal.

The men washed the plates in salt water and hung them in nets to dry. They cleaned the deck, stowed bundles, and worked while humming various shanties. The melodies leapt from man to man like fire through underbrush. Ra'Chel listened, trying to distinguish the songs.

"Captain, Bodvar. What do the men sing?"

"Oh, well, any number of unsavory tune to pass the time. Mostly each man sings his favorite."

"I see."

"Lads, let's have a song for the lady," Bodvar yelled.

"Oh, no. You don't have to—"

One of the crew at the bow shouted, "I don't know any song fit for a lady's ears, Captain." The crew laughed.

"Nor did I expect such an imp as you to answer otherwise, Sigvat. Mind your nets."

"What about *To Holm'Stad and Beyond?*" shouted one mate.

"No, no," Bodvar said.

"*A Rose for Epona?*" yelled another.

"A song of war? What's wrong with you, Hermund?"

One of the mates stood and belted an off-key tune. His mates joined in on the opening note:

He sees himself as the savior of the world,
His will is strong and he's feeling good.
I've known him since the first taste of beer,
I will meet him many times in a year.

Happy little, happy little, happy little boozer
Happy little, happy little, happy little boozer
Happy little, happy little, happy little boozer
Happy little, happy little, happy little boozer

"No, no!" Bodvar yelled. "Come on lads, have we not one
song we can serenade to this woman?"
Rowan'Gaff stood and cleared his throat.

Fly, gallop my *hepos*,
Fly, gallop the frost brush,
Swing across the fabric countries,
New countries and new places.

What is this when traveling?
What's up here,
Everything I can do is travel 'on the shaft',
Everything I need.

Much seen in the world,
Lots more to see
Many countries for me to go,

Hear those stories.
I sing, dance, play, I play,
I tear the joy out of these roads,
Of these, of you, of life

Here at the North Star.
This is my home,

> This is the end point of the trip,
> Heposeni's stable place,
> The birthplace of the cloth brush
>
> Keep on galloping
> My black horse
> Carrying me
> To unknown Shores
>
> Keep on galloping
> My black horse
> Carrying me
> back home.

He held the last note and cheers rang from the crew.

"Well done, Lad," Bodvar roared.

Ra'Chel clapped when the final note faded. "Wonderful," she said.

Bodvar stepped beside her. "Come now, lady. Grace us with song."

She blushed. "Oh, I don't—"

"Aye!" the men shouted and clapped.

Ra'Chel looked to Rowan'Gaff and his broad smile. "You run a tavern, you know at least one song, I'd wager."

"None fit for this occasion," she said.

"Then sing us a new song," Bodvar urged.

"I guess I could." She stepped away from the gunwale and took deep breath.

The crew fell silent when she closed her eyes and softly sang:

> I dreamed a dream last night
> of silk and fair furs,
> of a pillow so deep and soft,
> a peace with no disturbance.

And in the dream, I saw
as though through a dirty window
the whole ill-fated human race,
a different fear upon each face.

The number of their worries grow
and with them the number of their solutions —
but the answer is often a heavier burden,
even when the question hurts to bear.

As I was able to sleep just as well,
I thought that would be best —
to rest myself here on fine fur,
and forget everyone else.

Peace, if it is to be found, is where
one is furthest from the human noise —
and walling oneself around, can have a dream
of silk and fine furs.

Ra'Chel opened her eyes to the Wallef's crew stunned faces.

"Never has such a sweet sound been heard on this ship, lady," Bodvar whispered.

Rowan added, "And I doubt ever will again."

Ra'Chel returned to the side of the ship, blushing.

The youngest mate, Thorvald, stood, rubbed his hands down the front of his shirt and bowed to Ra'Chel. "Thank you, my lady."

The rest of the crew nodded and muttered their own appreciation.

Ra'Chel, still blushing, returned their bow.

Thorvald walked to the base of the ship's mast and stoked the fire. Orange light danced among the crews' faces while he took up his own song.

When Rowan'Gaff heard the lyrics, he stood and reverently listened to Thorvald's sweet voice.

> Cold and black brisk east winds blew,
> Through Far'Verm Pass to Western lands,
> To walls of Draer dark shadows drew,
> Delivered into evil's hands.

Rowan and many aboard the Wallef stood and joined Thorvald.

> Draer King's army gave valiant defense,
> Against the shadow's growing might,
> As dusk sun's light made red intense,
> Draer King lay martyred that very night.

Ra'Chel listened to the men slowly sing. The words flowed into her and welled deep-rooted, unfamiliar emotions. *They sing of my parents.* Tears flowed on her face.

> Unmatched they marched with force of arms,
> Southward evil's dark armies spread,
> Cross rivers and forests and trampled farms,
> With misery, hopelessness, death and dread.

One by one, each crew member stood and joined the song until the sea filled with sounds of their combined voices.

> When from the heart of the western lands,
> Like a brilliant star that comes to Earth,
> A shining hero stalwart stands,
> Raises sword and shows his worth.

Finally, Bodvar's baritone joined the men's chorus. Their voices rose to a crescendo at the mention of the legendary, shining hero. Emotion spread among them like smoke and many fought to maintain their composure.

Cap'Tian, pure of heart and mind of stone,
With sword and shield and spear-tipped lance,
The hero stands — one man alone,
Drives back the horde's conquering advance.

Back to the east flees evil's retreat,
With one final card yet to play,
A feast and trap did lay in defeat,
For Cap'Tian's fate ends would betray.

Ra'Chel watched in awe. The crew draped steadying arms over each other and sang with passion and reverence.

By victory drink was Cap'Tian betrayed,
To sleep but not to die or rise,
On windward slopes the evil stayed,
To perhaps return and claim their prize.

Foretold the hero of this song bides,
Until Draer princess softly weeps,
When returning horde of evil rides,
Deep in El'Thune Cap'Tian sleeps.

Until Draer princess softly weeps, deep in El'Thune Cap'Tian sleeps, Ra'Chel repeated in her mind. Memories of Oh'Raum flooded her and understanding exploded her thoughts. *This was his plan all along.* She turned to Rowan'Gaff and caught him wiping his own tears.

"I guess that's enough for tonight," Bodvar muttered. He nodded to his men. "Man your bunks, you lot. Thorvald, sling two hammocks for our guests."

The men rearranged the *Wallef's* deck to reconfigure her for sleeping. They hung hammocks between the gunwales and spread blankets beneath for the lower ranking crew.

"We'll be at the bow tonight," Rowan'Gaff said and pointed to several ropes slung across the ship's prow. The crew hung thick blankets over the ropes and folded them to form two secure sleeping sacks.

The cooking fire died to embers and countless stars appeared overhead. Ra'Chel's hammock swung to the boat's rocking rhythm.

"What do you know of this quest?" she quietly asked Rowan'Gaff.

"Only what you know."

"Then tell me of your previous journey with Master Oh'Raum."

After a moment, Rowan said with a low voice, "Perhaps tomorrow."

The bustle on board slowed as each man found his birth until only the ocean's gentle rocking remained.

Are you seeing the same lights, Oh'Raum, Ra'Chel thought and fell asleep.

Early the next morning, Ra'Chel slipped from her rocking hammock. She steadied herself on the starboard gunwale and crept to the ship's stern. The crew snored and rolled with each pitch.

"Good morning, lady," Bodvar whispered. He swayed side to side against the tiller when the Wallef crested then dipped into another swell. "The Res'Teran is up a bit this morning."

"Forgive me, Steersman Bodvar, where can I, uh," she paused and looked over the ship's side.

He watched her dance, stifled a laugh, and looked round the ship. "I guess you could hang over the side from the tiller here. You can wrap in a blanket for a bit of privacy as well."

Ra'Chel stepped behind him and worked out the maneuver in her mind. "You'll come back for me if I fall in, right?"

"I don't get my coin if I don't," he said and laughed. "But I like you well enough to come 'round otherwise."

"Thank you," she said when done relieving herself. She stepped beside him, wind whipping her hair. "Will we make land today?"

He nodded. "We should."

The Wallef's bow slid into Skorpo Fjord's sandy shore just after mid-day. Rowan'Gaff vaulted the gunwale and, with the help of several crew, tugged the ship to higher ground. He turned and helped Ra'Chel disembark the ship. At first, firm ground felt strange under foot and she found herself awkwardly swaying with each step.

"It takes a bit to get used to," Rowan said.

"You heard me," Bodvar said behind them. "You will make camp here until I return."

Hroar shrugged. "As you wish, Captain."

A commotion in the forest — raised voices and an approaching cohort startled the ship's company. The men of the Wallef armed themselves against the advancing, unknown foe. Ra'Chel stepped behind Bodvar and eyed Rowan'Gaff.

The bushes parted and a stream of black-armored guards burst forth like a swarm of huge ants.

"Drop your weapons in the name of King Ver'Sinian," they shouted.

"Stand down, men," Bodvar yelled.

One of the soldiers approached and removed his helmet. "Who is your commander?"

"I am Bodvar Her'On, Steersman of the Wallef." Bodvar made a show of bowing.

"What business have you here?"

"We came ashore to provision the creek's fresh waters. And ..."

The officer saw Ra'Chel and stepped past Bodvar. "Who is this woman?"

Rowan'Gaff, clutched the handle of his sword and stepped forward to meet the soldier. "My wife."

The soldier momentarily considered them, turned, and returned to the wood line. "Take them into custody."

Rowan'Gaff drew his sword.

Bodvar yelled, "On what charge?"

"We have orders to detain any young women traveling with an old man. She is a young woman and you," he looked at Bodvar, "are an old man."

"These passengers are under my protection!"

"You're welcome to come with them. Once we verify, she is not who we are looking for, you'll be free to continue your voyage."

The Wallef's crew grumbled and readied for Bodvar's order to attack. He turned and nodded to Rowan to sheath his sword. "You have your orders, Hroar."

"Aye," the mate responded.

"Leave all weapons," the officer said. "You won't need them."

Bodvar, Rowan'Gaff, and Ra'Chel stowed their packs abroad the ship. The steersman turned back to the officer, unceremoniously bowed, and said in a mocking tone, "At your convenience."

Preslovard's Prison

Preslovard's eyes flickered and the fog in his mind slowly cleared. He stretched and rolled to his side. A chain near his feet rattled and tugged at his ankle. He tried to sit up.

"I wouldn't do that just yet, lad," a man said. "We was taking wagers on whether you'd make the night."

Preslovard rolled to face the voice.

"Cost me a lesser coin, you did."

Pres opened his eyes and squinted in to a dark, leathery face.

"There he is," the man said. "Oy, pass that ladle this way boys. Need to take water, this one does."

Preslovard felt tepid water run across his lips and stuck a bulging tongue from his mouth like a snake tasting the air.

"Easy, lad," the voice said.

"Where am I?" Preslovard croaked.

"In his grace's finest accommodations," another voice called, accompanied by the jangle of heavy-sounding chains.

"Dilli'Gaf," the first voice answered.

Preslovard took a longer drink.

"Save some for the rest of us, will ya?" Pres did not recognize the voice's accent.

"How did I get here?"

"The column's dog team found you at the Thune. The commander thought you dead." The man laughed. "Might've been better off had you been. They loaded you in the cart and on the column marched."

"My father? I—"

"Forget him, I says. Your old life is gone, lad."

Preslovard struggled. The man helped him sit against a cold, stone wall. In front of him, a screen of dark, gray bars faced a wooden shelf on which the men sat, aligned like bread loves in a bakery. Several men on either side of him filled the bunk. Above his head, another rack ran the cell's length. A thick chain stretched the ledge's length attached at one end to a huge, metal ring imbedded in the wall. The chain wound through the men's anklets and clanged when any one of them moved.

"I must get back—" Pres tried.

Laughter broke out among the men. Calls of "I must get back," and "Me too," echoed throughout the cell.

An armored guard approached and slammed a thick club against the bars. "Silence, you dogs!"

Preslovard's entire body ached. His smaller wounds itched and the gash on his shoulder throbbed. A dirty, thick bandage rubbed his neck. He tried to lift it and peak underneath.

"Cleaned it as best they could. It was that or leave you for dead," the man said.

"Thank you."

"Weren't I," he said and laughed. "Were those bastards in black and they weren't doing you no favors."

Pres took another sip of water. "Is there any food?"

"I'd imagine you're hungry enough to eat through these chains."

"You haven't earned food," the man to his left said.

The chain slid through their anklets, its end whipping. One by one the men slid to the end of the bunk and hopped to the dirt floor.

"Get moving," the guard yelled and bashed his club against the bars.

Preslovard inched forward and took his place in the line of

prisoners. His stomach growled and his legs barely held his weight. The line of men shuffled through the bars and into a wide central courtyard where two parallel lines of sticks lay on the ground, stretching the yard's length.

"Put this on," another guard said and tossed a grimy, undershirt at Preslovard's feet.

The prisoners formed two lines, each behind a stick, facing a wooden platform on which stood a huge man adorned in shiny black armor. When the line of men finished moving and the square grew quiet, the commander spoke in a bland, uncaring voice.

"Congratulations. You wretched bastards are getting a second chance at life through honorable service to his Grace, Ver'Sinian the First."

Guards patrolled the gathering with stern faces, inspecting the rabble for signs of disagreement.

"Look around you. Many of these King's Guards were conscripted as you have been. Through loyal service to the crown, they have regained their honor, as you will. Those of you that excel will be rewarded. Those that don't, will die before you become a larger problem. Your training begins now."

An imposing man marched in front of the gathering, slapping his club in one gloved palm. "I am Tola Serendian and I am your lead instructor. You will address me and all your instructors as, Sir. Welcome to your new life. Reach down and pick up your weapon." The conscripts followed his instructions. "Front row, turn around."

A frail man turned and faced Preslovard, his expression a frightening, gray death-mask.

Doors near their cell opened and several men exited carrying trays heaped with food. Delicious smells of boiled eggs, charred bacon, and baked bread wafted through the assembly area.

Preslovard's opponent licked his chapped lips and gripped his stick in anticipation of the instructor's next command. His own stomach growled, and he eyed the mounds of food — as did Preslovard.

"The victorious eat," Tola yelled. "On my command," he said and raised an arm.

A shrill broke out at the far end of the prisoners. One trainee lunged at his adversary wildly swinging his weapon like a berserker. The two clashed and quickly fell to the ground grappling. They punched, kicked, and clawed one another until several guards clubbed them apart.

"Disobey a command and you will starve," Tola shouted. He raised his arm again, "On my command." He paused waiting to see if any of the other new arrivals attacked. Satisfied, he yelled, "Fight!"

Preslovard stepped back with his right leg and raised his stick seconds before his challenger charged him screaming. Despite his weakened condition, muscle memory moved him deftly away from the frenzied attack. He stepped around his challenger and swatted him high on his back.

The man staggered forward before whirling back toward Preslovard. His face looked more like a deranged animal than a human. Images of hideous cave monsters flashed through Preslovard's memory and he readied himself for a second, vicious attack.

Guards formed around the pair and jeered.

"Come on you," one yelled.

"You gonna let him do that?" another shouted.

Veins on the man's neck pulsed with anger and his chest pounded as though his heart might burst forth like cannon fire.

"Only one of you will eat," a guard taunted.

"I'm going to kill you," the man roared and circled.

Preslovard remained calm and shifted his feet as Oh'Raum taught him.

The attack came as a charging, overhead swing Preslovard easily parried. Instead of another strike across the back, Pres closed the distance and unleashed a volley of successive strikes to the man's right shoulder, left abdomen, and sword hand. He fell to the ground under the onslaught, dropping his stick, and curling into a ball at Preslovard's feet. He cried and begged for mercy.

The guards erupted with laughter and kicked dust on the wailing man before moving toward the food table.

Preslovard dropped his stick to follow.

"Where did you learn the sword?" Tola asked. He held his club out like a barricade.

"My father."

"I see," Tola growled and stepped inches from Preslovard. "I'll be watching you, bridge boy."

Preslovard turned for the food line, stopping after a few steps. "It is permissible to give him half my ration?"

Tola laughed and shook his head. "You're one of those, eh? We need soldiers, not monks. He may eat at mid-day, if his skills improve."

Preslovard took his place at the end of the serving line where a boiled egg, single strip of pork, and fist-sized loaf were dropped on his plate. The victorious prisoners sat against a wall and gobbled their breakfast while the losers went to work cleaning the cells, his morning challenger among them. The man rubbed his throbbing knuckles.

"It doesn't take long to make enemies here."

Preslovard turned to the man who spoke to him in the cell. "I have no enemies here."

"You will, lad."

"My name is Preslovard."

"Ka'Dal," the man replied.

Preslovard scanned the fortification; four high towers connected by a stone wall. A single gate flanked by guards — the only entry and exit point. More guards patrolled the stone wall and the square towers.

"Forget it, boy," Ka'Dal said.

Preslovard looked at him.

"You're in no condition to make a decent escape. You'd be nothing more than sport for the tower archers."

Right of the gate, thatched huts ran the wall's length at ground level. Hammers clanged from a forge and sparks flew from grinding wheels within the armory. Larger rooms, built along the back wall, served as guard barracks, kitchens, and cells for conscripts and prisoners. Left of the gate, a covered stable housed numerous horses and left of that, a makeshift pen held the garrison's livestock.

"On your feet," the guard yelled and clapped his club against the wall. He split the conscripts into three groups. The first group practiced thrusts on straw-stuffed sacks with their practice swords. The second group learned to move as a unit and follow barked orders from their leaders, who did not hesitate to meet out harsh discipline for the slightest mistake. The third group, among whom Pres stood, learned pike techniques with long poles. Four rows of conscripts faced four dangling canvas sacks.

"Thrust!"

"Ha!" The front line of trainees shouted and bashed the ends of their poles in the targets.

"Hold!" Tola said. "*Lepo!*"

The first line relaxed and stepped aside.

"Thrust! Hold!" He paused. "*Lepo!*"

Preslovard, watched the guards patrol the stone wall. He counted their steps and calculated distances between the towers and the thickness of the rampart.

"Thrust!"

Preslovard stepped forward and slammed his pole into the target. "Ha!" He yelled in unison with the three men beside him.

"Hold! *Lepo!*"

Pres relaxed and stepped to the back of his line. The practice continued several more rounds until the guard yelled for the three groups to rotate. Between each grueling training session, the conscripts gulped water and found what cool shade they could.

Following a complete circuit of training, the exhausted trainees repeated their earlier formation, each standing behind a stick on the ground. The guards made a show of shuffling the conscripts around, jeering and taking bets on entertaining matchups.

"Before we see who eats, I want you to see what happens to those who think escape is possible. He pointed his club to the pike training area where round after round of men smashed and thrust the canvas targets. Two guards released the hanging sacks. The bags hit the ground, spilling bound and bloodied men. Like a nightmarish birth, they squirmed from their canvas prisons — some alive, some not.

"They dreamed of returning to their miserable lives. Now they are nothing more than targets for better men." He paused to let the horrific sight burn into their collective memories. Finally, he turned. "Make ready."

The conscripts retrieved their weapons and faced off. A tanned, muscled man turned and nodded slightly to Preslovard who returned the acknowledgement. Pres watched his opponent set his feet and position himself in the southern fighting style. He smiled and remembered his master's voice. *The men of the wastes dance with curved blades and talk a lot.*

"Fight," their instructor commanded.

Preslovard's challenger slid to his left, scraping the balls of his feet on the sunbaked dirt. Pres countered, probing the distance with his sword at blocking height.

The dark-skinned man's eyes widened in recognition. He smiled. "Although you are schooled in our ways of fighting, I will be eating today, my friend."

"That is yet to be—"

The attack came at mid-sentence with a speed that caught Preslovard off guard — an upward stroke from Preslovard's weak side, while moving his back leg. He bent away from the slash, dropped the tip of his stick and clipped the incoming strike just enough to deflect it. He stumbled forward, spun, and reset his feet while his opponent formulated his next attack.

Preslovard shook his head and stepped forward.

The man smiled. "Drop your sword. I eat. I am better than you."

"But I'm hungrier," Preslovard said and launched into a series of blinding strikes.

The guards cheered when Pres scored several hits, driving his rival staggering backward. He hit the wall of armor-clad soldiers who pushed him back into the melee.

Preslovard pushed his advantage by closing the distance swinging his stick as Oh'Raum taught him. *The sword is a tool, you are the weapon, my boy.* His anger bubbled to the surface and instead of a fellow conscript, Preslovard saw a vicious subterranean monster. He slashed at the creature, releasing his rage for what they did to his sister as well as his own failure to protect her.

The beast fell.

"Enough!" Tola shouted and struck the stick from Preslovard's shaking hand.

Pres stood over the crumpled heap beneath him, panting. Not a beast any longer, but a man not dissimilar to himself; captured, tortured, and beaten.

The guards erupted in cheers for Preslovard. "He's a man for our cohort, if there ever was one," one yelled. "Well done," another said. "Aye, did you see the rage?"

Preslovard fell to his knees in front of his bloodied victim. Shame engulfed him and he bent his face to the dust.

"Get up, monk," Tola said. "You've earned food."

"Give it to him," Preslovard whispered.

"That's not how things work around here. Now get up."

Oh'Raum's voice slashed through his mind. *The turning of the leaves will be your sign for when we will be reunited.*

Preslovard ate his mid-day meal in contemplative,

scheming solitude. Ka'Dal approached.

"Your remorse will end your life, young man."

"I'm not a soldier."

"You have the skills to be."

"You mock me?"

"No. You are the perfect conscript for these bastards to mold."

"I have already been molded," Preslovard said.

"By your father, no doubt."

Pres nodded.

"You saw the men in the canvas today. They were molded, too."

Preslovard looked at him.

Ka'Dal stood. "If the guards think you have a friend, they will make you fight him."

"Do I have a friend?"

"Only until I get hungry," Ka'Dal said and smiled.

Following the mid-day meal, the brutal training continued long into the afternoon. The guards pushed the conscripts to the edge of exhaustion and, with the ends of their clubs, beyond.

When the sun dipped below the western wall's rim, the guards called the men together.

"Line up, you lot. You know the drill by now."

Each man found a spot behind a grounded stick, stood at attention, and sized up their opponents.

"Front row, turn around," Tola ordered.

Several man bent to retrieve their practice weapons, receiving instead sharp rebukes from the guards.

"Follow instructions, you! I gave no order to pick up your weapons." Tola strolled between the rows of conscripts tapping his club against his thigh. "Hand to hand — make ready!"

Preslovard squared off against a tall, thin man with slumped shoulders. Each raised their dirty fists, awaiting the trainers next order.

"Fight!"

His opponent quickly closed the distance, forcing Preslovard's retreat. He struck a pack of taunting guards who jostled him back to the fight. Punches pummeled him until he fell to the ground and curled into a ball.

"Oh, come on now, charity-case," Tola chided, "you can do better than that."

The tall, thin man backed away and looked at the head guard while several prisoners lined up for evening meal. He licked his lips.

Preslovard stood.

"Now then. Let's try that again. Fight!"

Again, the tall fighter marched forward. Preslovard poorly avoided several jabs and body blows. A sharp hook to the chin sent him back to the dusty ground, dazed. His opponent stepped away.

The guards shouted their indignation. "Oh, come on! — That's pathetic!" — He won't last long."

"Right, get in line," Tola commanded. He walked to Preslovard's side and knelt. "That was disappointing. Your fighting skills better improve. Now off to the cell with you."

Preslovard stumbled to the cell and flopped on the sleeping ledge. He spat a mouthful of blood, tore a piece from his trouser legs, soaked it from the water bucket, and lightly dabbed it to his bleeding lip. He rolled against the bars and blankly stared into the next empty cell. In his mind, Preslovard pondered his options for escape, calculating odds and probabilities. Flashes of bloody men rolling from target sacks assaulted him. He drove away the gruesome images and focused on the wall's height, the number of guards on the rampart, and how to create a distraction to facilitate his plan. *I'm coming, father.*

Days passed in similar fashion and thoughts of escape slipped further from his mind. Doubt, failure, and fear replaced his observations, calculations, and optimism. At morning meal, the trainees fought with wooden swords; at mid-day the guards provided a variety of weapons, and each evening they faced off with only their fists.

As expected, Preslovard stood victorious each morning where none met his sword skill. He proved capable with a staff and club for their mid-day sparring sessions but fell short each evening. Day after day, the nightly beatings progressed and took their toll on his failing body and his weakening mind.

"Still dreaming of escape?"

Preslovard silenced his sobbing and rolled away from the bars to face Ka'Dal with one open eye. His left, blackened and swollen, remained closed. "Always," he whispered.

"Perhaps, you should turn your talents to fighting."

Preslovard shook his head.

"The sooner you face it, the better off you'll be. This is your life now," Ka'Dal said.

Pres did not answer. Instead, he slowly rolled to face the bars, pulled his knees to his chest, and returned to scheming.

The horses, he thought. *They are the key.*

Sleeper

Betrayal at The Beach

Ra'Chel, Bodvar, and Rowan'Gaff silently walked through the forest following their captors.

"Captain, may I ask where you're taking us?" Bodvar asked.

"You may not."

"I can assure you; we are not your quarry. I only met this woman last week."

Ra'Chel scowled at Rowan'Gaff.

"What?" he asked.

"I knew you would betray us," she growled.

Rowan protested. "I haven't done anything."

She shook her head. "How else would they know where to find us, you creep?"

"I don't know."

Bodvar turned around. "I suggest you two keep quiet. The less you say, the better."

"But she thinks—" Rowan'Gaff tried.

Bodvar's expression stopped Rowan in mid-sentence.

After half a day's march, the company emerged from the forest into a broad valley. A road from their left led to a massive stone garrison at the valley's far side. A rider exited the garrison to meet them.

"Send word to Commander Nerayo. I have a young woman and an old man in custody as instructed."

The rider wheeled his horse and galloped to the garrison.

The company stopped at the closed front gate, where the officer turned to Bodvar. "We wait here."

The rubble-strewn area around the garrison smelled and forced several in the group; to cover their faces. A black and red stream of filth ran from a metal grate to the right of the gate.

"Captain, my ship served the king honorably and…"

The soldier stopped him with a raised gauntlet. "Then you understand following orders. Not another word from you until my Commander allows it."

The gate swung open and the company entered the fortified garrison's central courtyard. To their right, a shabby fence held half a dozen pigs and several chickens. Horses in tight stalls champed beside them and the stench from outside the wall doubled.

Groups of armored guards shouted orders at scrawny trainees, occasionally delivering a club to the backside when they did not move with alacrity. The men fought, hand to hand, in the yard.

The gate closed behind them. The Captain removed his helmet when Commander Nerayo approached. "Sir, as ordered I have found a young woman traveling with an older man."

The commander stepped around the captain to inspect Ra'Chel and Bodvar. "And the other?"

"He claims to be the woman's husband, sir."

"I see," Nerayo said. "How fortunate for her."

Ra'Chel stepped behind Bodvar who spoke quickly.

"Sir, a pleasure to make your acquaintance, this young couple travels from Dur'Loth aboard my ship, the Wallef. Perhaps you've heard of her. We ferried the king's troops during our honorable service to…"

Commander Nerayo turned to the captain. "Take them to a holding cell."

"Sir, please," Bodvar protested.

The commander continued, "And dispatch a rider to Dur'Loth."

Pike carrying guards surrounded the trio.

"You will be our guests until word comes from Dur'Loth. Enjoy your stay," Nerayo said, turned, and made a show of inspecting the trainees.

"This way," ordered the Captain.

A wide sleeping bench ran the length of the cell's back wall. Ra'Chel kicked the dirt floor, scattering dust and rocks into a toilet bucket set in one corner.

Trainees shouted in the courtyard and the ever-present clanging of practice weapons echoed from the cell's walls.

"What are we going to do?" Rowan asked Bodvar.

The Steersman sat on the bench and shook his head. "It's going to take days to get a report from Dur'Loth," he whispered.

Rowan stepped toward him. "And what is that report going to say?"

Bodvar frowned. "Keep your voice down. We have no idea what the report will be."

Ra'Chel wheeled on Rowan'Gaff. "How long will you keep this up?"

Bodvar looked at her.

"Did you sell out Master Oh'Raum as well, blackguard?"

Rowan'Gaff retreated from her when she advanced.

"Ra'Chel, I swear to you, I am no spy."

"Stop it, Rowan! Call the guards to release you. You've done your job well, toad."

Bodvar took her by the shoulders, sat her on the bench, and turned to Rowan'Gaff.

"I'm no spy, Captain," he pleaded.

"If you are, I'll let your blood flow myself, boy."

"What do I have to do to prove it to you?"

Ra'Chel looked up. "Break us out of here."

"Aye," Bodvar agreed, "wouldn't that be a thing."

A guard approached. "You there," he said to Bodvar. "Commander wants to see you."

Ra'Chel stood. "Captain?"

"It will be alright, my dear."

She glared at Rowan and slumped on the cot.

"Fight!" a guard shouted.

The trainees charged at each other in a storm of flailing fists.

"My god," Rowan said.

Ra'Chel covered her ears to the fighter's screams and animalistic growls.

A guard approached their cell carrying two wooden platters piled with steaming food. "Your companion sups with the commander."

Rowan took the food. "Thank you." He handed a platter to Ra'Chel who shook her head. Dirty, battered, men shuffled into the cell opposite them, eyed their food, and flopped on the long sleeping shelf. Many tended bloody wounds with swatches of torn cloth. The prisoner closest to the bars stared past them through a single glazed eye.

An hour later, Bodvar approached led by a guard. Ra'Chel and Rowan'Gaff met him at the cell door.

"Are you okay?" Ra'Chel asked?

"I'm fine dear." Bodvar smiled and clapped Rowan on the shoulder.

"What did they want?" the boy asked.

"Information." Bodvar sat on the bunk. The cell door clanged shut causing a shudder to ripple through the prisoners in the opposite cell. He beckoned them close and whispered. "They are indeed looking for our friend and his companion. The commander doesn't believe we are their quarry but must make sure before he releases us."

"Will he release us when word comes from Dur'Loth?" Rowan asked.

"I don't think so," Bodvar said and looked at Ra'Chel. "But I do know Grimsson did not betray us."

She looked at Rowan. "Then how did they know where to find us?"

"They have a contingent stationed on Skorpo Overlook. The moment we entered the fjord, they alerted the garrison of our landing."

Rowan paced the small cell. "We need to get out of here. We must make the bridge by three days hence."

"The commander called me his guest. We are free to leave the cell, but he thinks it best if we remain here." He looked at Ra'Chel.

"You mean, it's safer if I remain here."

He nodded. "The conscripts are unpredictable, and many haven't eaten in days."

"If I attack a guard, you two can leg it," Rowan'Gaff said under his breath.

Bodvar laughed.

"What happens to you?" Ra'Chel asked.

"That's not important."

"Okay, just stop, Grimsson. You are not attacking a guard."

"You have a better plan?"

"Not at the moment. We have several days before word arrives from Dur'Loth. This is not the time for rash action."

Ra'Chel joined Bodvar on the bench.

He smiled at her. "I've been in tough spots before. Tonight, we sleep. Tomorrow, we start looking for a way out of here."

None of them slept. Bodvar rolled every few minutes on the uncomfortable sleeping ledge. Rowan'Gaff's mind meandered through possibilities for escape. Moreover, he pondered ways of earning Ra'Chel's respect — possibly her love.

Ra'Chel rolled to her side and found Rowan'Gaff staring at the ceiling.

"I'm sorry, Rowan," Rachel quietly said.

"For what?"

"For accusing you of treachery."

He laughed. "I haven't done anything in my life to make you think otherwise."

She smiled. "Still. It was unfair of me."

"Apology accepted. Speak no more of it." He rolled to face her. "I'm more concerned about getting out of here."

"Bodvar is a man of honor."

Rowan'Gaff nodded. "He will do everything he can to see us safely to the bridge."

"I fear for Oh'Raum."

"That old wizard can take care of himself."

"And his apprentice?"

"I only met him briefly the one time. Oh'Raum's visions took us to the coast not long after."

"What was that like?" Ra'Chel asked.

"The journey with Oh'Raum?"

"Having prophetic dreams."

"My visions weren't prophetic. They were a jumble of images — nightmares really. I was but fourteen when they first came."

"You dreamed of me, like Master Oh'Raum?"

"No, I had no visions of you. I dreamed of the hero, Cap'Tian. He is my ancestor."

Ra'Chel remained silent.

"I felt led to leave my home and travel the length of the country. I almost died from the journey. Master Oh'Raum found me and took me to his cottage. He too had visions, but although similar, his were," he paused, "more pleasant than my own."

"Do you yet remember them?" Ra'Chel asked.

He nodded. "They are seared in my memory."

"Tell me one."

He took a deep breath. "I was but fourteen when I first saw the black army in my dreams. I could barely lift a sword and," he laughed, "remember dragging it behind me. I marched with an army, wearing armor for a grown man. I did my best to blunder along in the heavy boots. At times it felt like the armor would crush me."

"That's terrible," Ra'Chel said.

"It was that first dream that drove me to leave my home in search of the old man."

"What do you mean?"

"I remember waking from that dream with an itch in my chest." Instinctively, a hand moved to his heart. "A longing to leave that very moment, everything else be damned."

"And that's how you found Master Oh'Raum?"

"Something like that."

She stared at him, waiting for the rest of the story.

"I was a young fool. My father left for the markets of Son'Us and without packing properly, I started walking. I'm surprised I made it at all."

"Was it not the adventure you imagined?"

Rowan'Gaff searched his thoughts. "I don't remember much of the journey itself. I walked where I was told. Each night I had another vision. When hungry, I ate and when I came across water, I drank."

"Sounds like something protected you."

"Master Oh'Raum and his apprentice found me in the forest, near death."

"Oh my," Ra'Chel said.

"After a day of nursing me to health, we left his cottage and walked for days to the Great River." He laughed.

"What?"

"The ferryman tried to cheat me a day's wages because I didn't know my numbers then. Oh'Raum intervened and we all got full shares. That was in D'Grath."

"That is in the far East of the country?"

"Aye. A small trading outpost. Oh'Raum walked with this old she-mule." He looked past her. "What was her name?"

Ra'Chel remained silent.

"When we found you, she gave milk to feed you." He shook his head again, trying to jar the memory free from its hiding place. "I bought my first sword in D'Grath." He smirked. "Nothing more than a large dagger, but it fit me well. Master

Oh'Raum taught me to fight with it." He smiled. "I brought it on this journey."

"You have it still?"

"She is on the Wallef. I named her *Ealhswith* — Strength, in some lost tongue."

Bodvar yawned. "And quite the swashbuckler you were, Grimsson, always waving the thing around the deck."

Ra'Chel laughed.

Rowan'Gaff rolled his eyes. "We walked for almost a fortnight before we got to the beach. That's where we found you. As I was drawn to find Master Oh'Raum, he was drawn to find you."

"And you took me to Mistress Brune."

"Yeah, that was Oh'Raum's idea."

"She was a wonderful mother," Ra'Chel said.

"She hated me."

"Most people in Dur'Loth did."

Rowan'Gaff rolled to his back and crossed his arms.

"I'm sorry."

"No, you're right." He laughed. "Master Oh'Raum gave me every chance to change, but I never did."

"He wasn't the only one," Bodvar said.

Both men chuckled at the jab.

"Bodvar," Ra'Chel said.

Rowan'Gaff raised a hand. "No, he's right. I was a little scoundrel."

He rolled to face her again. "Oh'Raum was also right. He charged me to change, to prove my lineage, and show what hero lives within me."

"Rowan, it is that kind of talk that kept you from making friends in Dur'Loth."

"This is my chance, Ra'Chel. I will get you out of here."

"Have you a plan?"

He shook his head. "Each sunrise brings us closer to discovery on horseback from Dur'Loth."

"I'm afraid we will never make our rendezvous with Oh'Raum and Preslovard." Tears welled in her eyes. "All is lost."

"Hey," a scratchy voice called behind her.

Ra'Chel rose to her elbows and, in the dim light, made out the gruesome face of a battered conscript. He waved her closer.

"Ra'Chel, no," Rowan'Gaff said.

Again, the man beckoned.

Ra'Chel walked to the bars and knelt out of arm's reach.

"Your friend called you Ra'Chel?"

She nodded.

"And you seek Master Oh'Raum?"

"Yes."

Emotion flooded the prisoner. He closed his puffy eyes and his body shuddered. "The hinny's name was Haseth," he said through flowing tears. Angry determination ripped across his face. "I am Preslovard, and I have the plan you seek."

Sleeper

Escape from Dilli'Gaf

Ra'Chel turned to Rowan'Gaff. "Haseth. The name..."

Rowan'Gaff slid next to her. "Preslovard? What? How did you get here?"

They grasped hands between the bars.

"I was conscripted at the River Thune crossing — six, maybe eight days go."

"My god," Ra'Chel said. "Does Oh'Raum know you're here?"

Pres shook his head. "I swooned beneath the bridge and woke here, near death." He kicked his leg causing the chain to ripple down the line of prisoners.

"Bodvar," Ra'Chel quietly called.

The Steersman rose to his elbows. "What?" he managed. At first, he thought the prisoner had ahold of Ra'Chel through the bars. He leapt to his feet ready to attack.

"It's Preslovard," Ra'Chel said.

"Oh'Raum's ward?"

She nodded as hot tears cut tracks on her cheeks.

Rowan shook his head. "Bodvar, we can't wait."

Bodvar put a hand on his shoulder and nodded. "In good time, my boy."

Preslovard look at Bodvar.

"This is the Steersman of our ship," Ra'Chel said.

"Oh'Raum charged me with delivering them to the bridge."

Pres nodded. "How did they capture you?"

"Skorpo lookouts. They knew right where we would make land."

"And my master?"

"He took the road north several days before we left by ship. He feared missing you at the bridge."

"I agree with Rowan'Gaff. We can't wait."

"You have a plan then?" Rowan asked.

"Each morning the victors are served fresh bread. I know not when it is baked, and I have seen no laden wagons. I also count twelve stabled horses." He looked past them for the guards.

"The sacks of flour are our diversion."

Rowan'Gaff looked at Ra'Chel and back to Preslovard, a confused look on his face.

"First we must gain access to the stables, specifically the horses' bits and reigns."

"You mean to ride out the gate and billow the flour behind us?"

"No, I mean to blow up the kitchens."

Bodvar laughed. "With flour and strips of leather?"

"Each horse reign is taller than a man, yes?" Preslovard asked.

They nodded.

"We must braid them, as a mother braids her daughter's hair. Three together should form a leather thong thick as my thumb."

"And by tying them together," Rowan'Gaff interrupted, "we can make it safely over the wall."

Preslovard smiled. "We need the guards focused on the havoc in the kitchens so as to make our escape. We assault the northern rampart near the tower. How far do you make the wood line?" He looked at Bodvar.

Ra'Chel answered. "That was the closest, yes."

"We may have the tower guard to contend with."

"I can handle that," Rowan'Gaff said and puffed his chest.

"Best leave that to me, Grimsson," Bodvar said. "I wager, Master Preslovard has you in mind for kitchen detail."

"Rowan, you need to find the flour sacks, and—"

"I know my way around a kitchen. It should be me," Ra'Chel said.

"I think it best if you're in charge of the ropes. The work at the kitchens will be dangerous," Preslovard said.

"The rider from Dur'Loth won't be here for several days," Bodvar said.

"You three have work tomorrow."

Ra'Chel took Preslovard's hand again. "Can you last several more days?"

"I never cared for hand to hand." He smiled. "I fair well with sword against this lot and hold my own at mid-day. I'll be fine."

The following morning, after the conscripts filed from their cell, Bodvar, Rowan'Gaff, and Ra'Chel set about their tasks. Rowan, with the subtleness of a novice pickpocket perched beside the kitchen door and made idle conversation with anyone who entered. "So, the men get bread each morning?" and, "Looks like you need a hand with that tray. Here, allow me." The guards shook their heads and gathered for the morning's entertainment.

Ra'Chel, accompanied by a guard, asked about the horses, feigning care. "How often are these poor animals bathed?"

"We take them to the river once a week," a scrawny man said.

"And their tac? Is it properly maintained?"

He pointed to rows of bridles hanging from nails and nodded. "It's all-in working order."

Ra'Chel surreptitiously counted the long, leather straps. Her guard-escort leaned against a stable post, bored with the interrogation and wishing he could get a better view of the morning's swordplay.

In the yard, two rows of dirty, bruised conscripts readied

for their morning ritual. Bodvar stood next to Tola and shot a wry smile to Preslovard who squared off this morning against a short, fat man with a puffy, closed left eye.

"Make ready," the instructor shouted.

The men bent and retrieved their training weapons.

"Fight!"

Each line of fighters crashed into the other in fierce melee. Bodvar watched Preslovard parry and dodge his attacker's crude swings. The young man's wounded eye slowed his movements, but he proved no match for the shorter conscript.

"The monk has an easy one this morning," Tola said. "You there," he called at a black-skinned man who stood over a bloody, defeated foe, "that one." Tola pointed at Preslovard. The dark-skinned man bowed and marched toward his new opponent. Without warning he surged past Preslovard's fat opponent, joining in a two-on-one sword fight.

"Now we see if he eats this morning," Tola said, smiling.

Bodvar watched the men fight. Preslovard took several blows before recovering and sliding away from this new, faster attacker on his weakened side. Pres disarmed the short man, sending him to the ground with a sharp whack to the back of the head. The move cost him a hard hit on his left side.

The assembled guards reacted with hisses and exclamations. "That one hurt, eh lad?" One shouted.

"There we go," Tola said and pumped a gloved fist.

"You mean to break these men?" Bodvar asked.

"Only the breakable ones. The rest receive the honor of becoming King's Guard."

Preslovard skipped away from numerous thrusts and arcing swings. He rolled to his left and rose holding the fat man's practice sword in his left hand. His dark-skinned opponent backed away from Preslovard's spinning wooden swords and quickly lay in a bloody puddle at his feet.

The guards erupted in cheers at the carnage. Had the swords been steel, Preslovard might have cut his way through the entire garrison to freedom. Instead, he faced Bodvar and Tola, spat, dropped the practice swords, and walked triumphantly to the food table.

The instructor made a noise under his breath.

Bodvar turned toward him. "What?"

"Did you see the look on his face?"

"He looked determined, proud."

"He looked defiant. I've seen it before. He's a scheme about him."

Bodvar watched Preslovard take his plate and sit with the other victors.

"Do they fight like that every morning?" Ra'Chel asked the stable master.

He nodded with a painful expression.

"Did you once fight like that?"

"Aye. I was rubbish at arms and nearly starved when I was first conscripted. My horse knowledge saved my life."

"How long have you been here?"

"Dunno," he replied.

The garrison's exterior wall, supported the stable's broad sloping roof. A wide, central path allowed access to the numerous stalls, most occupied with horses. At the path's end hung each horse's tack.

"What can I do to help?" Ra'Chel asked.

"If you'll fill the feed bags, I'll fill the water trough."

"Gladly."

Rowan'Gaff watched her across the garrison's training yard. He stood beside the kitchen door working to gain access to the ovens.

"Do you need help cleaning that, sir?" Rowan asked a man carrying an empty tray.

The skinny man muttered something before entering the kitchen.

"I can help prepare lunch," Rowan tried again when a guard walked up carrying a bulging potato sack.

"Move."

Rowan talked himself into the kitchens by offering to mop the floors between meals. The kitchen-hand stood watching in the corner, happy to oversee the young man perform his duties. "Get the mop good and wet, then sop it back up."

The outer kitchen, just inside the door from the courtyard, contained a preparation area. Long wood-hewn tables ran its length where servants retrieved laden trays. A small fire burned inside a brick hearth at one end of the room and an archway led to the main cooking area.

Through the archway, Rowan'Gaff found an immense, open-face brick oven. Dangling chains held blackened, metal pots and a huge caldron sat bubbling among the flames. Dirty, sweating men worked at a fever-pitch skinning, chopping, and preparing meats and vegetables for the next meal.

"I got me a mopper, lads," the kitchen-hand roared over the clamor. Rowan grumbled and scanned the sweltering room. A smaller doorway led from this roiling room to a storage area and a dry cellar.

"In here, just push everything to the refuse port," his handler said and pointed to a hole in the back wall.

Rowan'Gaff slopped more mop-water, creating tiny rivers of debris flowing for the hole. The kitchen workers moved from their stations only long enough to allow him to slop his mop by and move on. In the dark storage area, he found the reason for his labor. Massive flour sacks lined an entire wall, piled waist-high.

When he finished the mopping, Rowan slopped up the dirty water and followed the kitchen-hand back to the courtyard.

"You dump it in the horse trough."

Rowan'Gaff nodded. "Say, friend. Would it be possible for me to help tomorrow morning as well? I hate sitting in the cell just waiting."

"I don't see why not. I'll need to ask, Virin, but it shouldn't be a problem."

Rowan smiled, lifted the dirty water, and walked past Bodvar on his way to the horse trough.

Bodvar nodded and ascended the creaky steps to the Northern Rampart. At the top, he looked out over the treetops and scanned the ground for obstacles between the wall and wood line. The guard, manning the tower, warily eyed him.

Bodvar put on a fake smile. "Anything interesting happening up here today?"

The guard flatly responded, "Nothing interesting happens up here."

"Heck of a view," Bodvar tried.

"Same as yesterday — same as tomorrow."

I'm going to have to kill this one, Bodvar thought. He smiled. "Have a good night then."

"Uh, huh." The guard watched him descend the steps to the courtyard, between the stables and the animal pen. At the bottom of the steps, he found Ra'Chel at the end of the stables. The two exchanged a surreptitious glance and went about their business.

Preslovard fought well at mid-day, earning what he hoped was his final meal in this hell. His opponent proved no match for his pike fighting ability. As usual, a group of guards jeered the combatants, disappointed by the brief display Preslovard afforded them.

Rowan'Gaff worked the serving line behind a heaping tray of boiled white potatoes. "Well done," he whispered when Preslovard moved past his station.

"No talking, you," a guard yelled.

Preslovard smiled, accepted a potato, and silently moved down the line.

Before the evening meal, following an intense day of sparring, Preslovard faced off against the black-skinned man; the second opponent he bested before morning meal. The fury in the man's eyes burned through Preslovard who stood against him with only fists.

"This looks like retribution," Bodvar said, standing next to Tola.

The instructor answered with a chuckle.

"Bad blood between these men will hinder—"

Tola wheeled on Bodvar and cut him off in a growling tone. "You train your men your way. Allow me to train mine, my way. Fight!" He shouted without looking away from Bodvar.

Preslovard raised his hands and squared his feet.

The dark man moved closer, his own weapons at the ready. "You owe me a meal," he said.

"Then beat me and get on with your feast," Preslovard said.

The dark man feigned left and swung a crushing blow down with his right hand. Preslovard ducked his head, raised his left arm and deflected most of the impact to the side of his head. A hail of strikes quickly followed the initial volley. Pres managed to escape most of his opponents punches, save for a few that landed hard to his ribs and head. The fight provided minimal sport for the men watching but allowed Tola to make his point when Preslovard lay in a bleeding heap under his victorious opponent.

"And he learned what?" Bodvar asked.

"That no matter what he thinks, he isn't in charge here."

"If that was to be his lesson, I guess it was effective."

"It always is," Tola said and walked to Preslovard. "You going to live, charity-case?"

"That is yet to be seen," Pres quietly answered.

"I don't suppose there remains anymore defiance under that blood, eh?"

Preslovard shook his head.

"I thought not. Off to the cells with you," Tola said and kicked his rump.

Pres rolled to his knees, stood on wobbly legs, and shuffled for his place on the sleeping bench.

"I brought cheese," Rowan'Gaff whispered when he entered the cell.

Ra'Chel and Bodvar knelt near the bars, Ra'Chel holding Preslovard's battered hand.

"Oh good." Ra'Chel took the small block, broke off a piece, and passed it through the bars.

"How is he tonight?" Rowan asked.

"I'll live," Preslovard quietly replied between bites. He held up the morsel. "Thank you."

Rowan'Gaff sat beside Ra'Chel. Deep inside, a spark of jealousy ignited at the sight of her holding Preslovard's bloody hand. "I found the storeroom. They have an entire wall of flour sacks."

Pres nodded.

"And I know right where to find the bridles. It won't take me anytime to braid them."

"Well done," Preslovard said.

"I will most likely have to incapacitate the tower guard, but that shouldn't be a problem," Bodvar added.

"And I will be earning my morning meal." Pres tried to laugh but winced in pain instead.

"So, we go tomorrow morning, then?" Rowan asked.

Pres nodded and looked into his eyes. "Your task is most dangerous, Rowan. When the cooking fire is at its highest, you must unleash the flour into the air, spreading as much of it as you can in the room."

Rowan'Gaff nodded. "I will make a cloud so thick; they'll think a fog has rolled in."

"Be warned. When the flour ignites, it will do so most violently."

"I will stand near the door and make my escape."

"Will he have time to make it to the rampart," Bodvar asked.

"We will see that he does."

Rowan'Gaff put up a courageous front. "Regardless, you three must make your escape."

Ra'Chel offered him a thin smile and set a gentle hand on

his arm. "We shall all make our escape."

Rowan looked at her hand. It felt as heavy as the Wallef's stone anchor on his arm and its heat penetrated deep into his heart. Rowan'Gaff hoped his smile said more than his agreement. He hoped it hid his true fear.

"I thought about spreading oil along the wall to spread the kitchen fire," Bodvar said. He turned to Rowan. "What does the kitchen do with its greases?"

"I can spread it along the walls to the stables," Ra'Chel said.

"You will need to wait until the food is served," Rowan'Gaff added. "I think I can gather the morning's greases for you."

"Then that is our signal. When the food comes from the kitchen, Grimsson will hand Ra'Chel the oils. She will spread it to the stables. I'll be watching you fight, Pres. When the fire starts, I'll make my way to the rampart and handle the guard if needs be."

"I'll be at the stables braiding like a crazy woman," Ra'Chel said.

"Don't be in there when the fire reaches it," Preslovard warned. "I'll head for the rampart."

Rowan'Gaff moved to the bunk and put his face in his hands. Ra'Chel turned to him. "You okay?"

Again, he lied, "Yeah. Just getting myself ready. Never escaped a garrison before." Outwardly, he presented an air of fearlessness. Inside, his tumultuous spirit whirled like a hurricane, reminding him of his time aboard the Wallef. Each battle brought his deep-rooted fear closer to the surface, which forced him to smother it in false bravado. He would swing *Ealhswith* wildly and make grand claims about the battles he would eventually win and the foes he would vanquish.

As a Dur'Loth watchman, his brash nature alone quelled most of the disturbances and the few times requiring him to display what little swordsmanship he did possess, his opponents were often too drunk to stand, let alone fight. This escape presented Rowan'Gaff his first real moment of courage and he doubted he could follow through on his promises. One thought permeated his growing fear. *For Ra'Chel. I'll finally be the hero she needs me to be.*

Bodvar sat next to him. "I know that look, Grimsson."

Rowan smiled. "I'll do my duty, Captain."

"As will we all, son."

Rowan'Gaff smiled, enjoying the word. He looked at Bodvar and felt true kinship with the Steersman. *As will we all — father,* Rowan wanted to reply, but held back.

Before sunrise, Rowan'Gaff left for the kitchens as arranged by Virin, the kitchen boss. Not long after, Ra'Chel requested to again work the stables and as Bodvar had become a familiar sight at Tola's side for the morning fights, the guards allowed them free.

The conscripts' chains were removed, and they moved to the training yard in a shuffling line of battered, beaten, and hopeless men. Each lined up behind a training sword, scrambling for position to find a weaker opponent.

The kitchen doors swung open and Rowan'Gaff appeared, carrying a large tray laden with slices of cooked ham. He set the tray on the feeding table and tucked a brown waterskin against the table's leg.

Bodvar watched Rowan's jerky movements and eye flicks.

Rowan'Gaff took a deep breath and returned to the kitchens, passing several other servants carrying their own trays. Bodvar looked back to the waterskin — gone.

"Make ready," Tola yelled.

Preslovard raised his sword. Behind the crowd of guards, Ra'Chel moved along the courtyard wall, the waterskin at her side.

"Fight!"

The first line of conscripts crashed into the second, wooden swords clattering. Preslovard easily spun away from the initial attack and countered with a riposte to his left.

A commotion near the kitchen doors distracted Tola and

several other guards from the melee.

"No!" someone in the niche yelled.

The kitchen door blew from its hinges. A massive orange fireball burst into the courtyard. Two guards, stationed near the kitchen, fell to the ground unconscious. A third victim flew with the door.

The conscripts turned to the explosion and guards rushed the area. Prisoners dashed for the food tables, grabbed what they could, and shoved it down their gobs before the guards' clubs found their backs.

Bodvar ran for the stables. Preslovard ran for the kitchen looking for Rowan'Gaff.

"Fetch water! Hurry!" Tola commanded.

The kitchen inferno blazed through small windows. Inside, people screamed. Preslovard pushed his way through the guards who paid him no mind. He tried to enter the kitchen when a hand grabbed his shoulder.

"They're done for," Tola said.

"We have to try," Preslovard shouted, shook free of Tola's grip, and slammed into the flames.

Bodvar reached the stables where Ra'Chel sat braiding long strips of leather. "Almost there," she said when he passed on his way to the rampart. "Where is the fire?"

Bodvar stopped midway to the rampart. "Damn! It remains inside the kitchens. I'll go…"

Preslovard emerged from the kitchen carrying a badly burned servant and the fire itself.

"Well done, monk!" Tola bellowed.

Press, dropped the servant and fell on the spot where Ra'Chel spilled the oil. Flames licked his legs, forcing him to roll and extinguish them.

Bodvar snapped his fingers and smiled. *You sly devil.* He turned and ran up the stairs.

Tola barked orders. The fire spread, outpacing the guards who fought to put it out. It followed the dribbled oil past the animal pen, ingesting the hay within the horse stables.

"Get those horses out of there! Open the gates!"

Bodvar mounted the rampart to find the tower guard gawking at the frenzy below.

Preslovard stood and limped along the fire's path. Half way to the animal pen he found Rowan'Gaff lying face up, unconscious.

"Rowan! Get up!"

Rowan'Gaff remained motionless. Pres knelt beside him and hoisted Rowan to his shoulder. Barely able to stand, Press lurched toward the stables.

Ra'Chel emerged with a coil of thick leather and bolted for the stairs. Atop the rampart she found an unconscious guard and Bodvar holding a hefty brick. He tilted his head and gave her a thin smile. They tied the leather rope around a crenelation and tossed it over the edge.

Preslovard reached the rampart and collapsed. Rowan'Gaff tumbled to the floor beams. "Get her over the edge," Pres said.

"But," Ra'Chel tried.

Bodvar took her. "No, miss. You need to go now." He helped her through the crenelation and over the wall's edge. "As soon as you're down, make for the wood line. If we aren't right behind you, make for the Wallef as fast as you can."

"Please be right—" she started and slipped over the edge.

Bodvar turned, grabbed Rowan'Gaff's arms, and pulled him to the edge. Preslovard stood and met him. Together they tied the end of the leather rope around Rowan, lifted his legs over the edge and lowered him to the ground.

"You next," Bodvar ordered.

Preslovard pulled himself over the wall and shimmied the rope landing on Rowan'Gaff. There he untied the rope and dragged him a few steps from the garrison's outer wall.

Flames licked the rampart below Bodvar sending ash over the wall. An orange hue cascaded above Preslovard. Horses burst from the open gates, followed by running guards and escaping conscripts.

Bodvar slid to the ground and hoisted Rowan'Gaff to his shoulders, sending Preslovard ahead to Ra'Chel in the wood line.

"Is he alive?" Ra'Chel asked.

Panting, Preslovard answered. "I believe so."

Bodvar joined them and knelt. "We can't linger."

"Is he alive?" Ra'Chel asked again.

Bodvar turned Rowan'Gaff's face to her. "He is!"

"I've got him," Bodvar said.

"We must make the river by nightfall," Preslovard said and gasped for air.

"We must make the Wallef by nightfall," Bodvar argued.

They set off at a slow march, the pace set by Bodvar carrying Rowan. Preslovard offered to carry him and each time Bodvar refused.

"He's the closest thing I've got to a son."

Pres nodded and continued their march north to the River Thune. At mid-day they reached the river. Bodvar sat Rowan'Gaff against a tree while Ra'Chel brought cool water in the cup of her hands.

Preslovard walked downstream and waded into the rejuvenating water — bubbling ecstasy escaping him once fully submerged. Bodvar dunked his head and drank his fill.

"He's coming round, Bodvar," Ra'Chel called. She rubbed water across his forehead.

Preslovard pulled himself to the bank, reveling in the soothing water.

Rowan'Gaff's eyes rolled around in his head before finding their focus. He blinked several times, recognizing Ra'Chel's face first.

In a groggy voice, he said, "I guess we made it."

"We did!"

Bodvar sat next to him. "You blew yourself up and Preslovard set himself on fire to make our escape."

Rowan looked at Pres.

"He carried you to the rampart," Ra'Chel added.

"Where are we?"

"The Thune," Bodvar said. "We'll be back abroad the Wallef shortly."

"No," Rowan'Gaff tried. "We have to reach the..."

"We have no provisions, Rowan," Ra'Chel said. "The closest safety is the ship. They have food and medicine."

Rowan nodded.

"Can you walk, Grimsson?" Bodvar asked. "I'm a bit tired of carrying you, son."

"You carried—"

"You're not as light as you used to be." Bodvar took Rowan's hand and hoisted him to weak legs.

"I could use more water."

"Of course," Ra'Chel said and returned with another handful.

"Thank you," Rowan said before her fingers touched his lips.

They moved quicker along the river bank, stopping to listen for signs of pursuit and giving Rowan'Gaff brief respites. Preslovard's urgency to reach the bridge grew with each step in the wrong direction. *We're going the wrong way,* he thought, but forced himself to keep walking as fresh provisions and armaments were promised by Bodvar as soon as they reached his ship.

Hroar saw them first. "Oy!" he shouted when Ra'Chel emerged from the trees, followed by Bodvar supporting Rowan'Gaff, then Preslovard.

"Make ready the boat," Bodvar commanded.

"Make ready the boat, you lot," Hroar repeated. He helped Ra'Chel and Rowan'Gaff over the gunwale. "Course, captain?"

"Dur'Loth with all haste."

"No!" Preslovard shouted.

Hroar eyed the stranger.

Bodvar turned to Pres and placed a hand on his shoulder. "The ship departs for Dur'Loth. *We* make for the bridge following the northern bank."

"Sir?" Hroar asked.

"Bring our belongings and find this man a pack and provisions. We haven't much time."

"And a sword," Preslovard coldly said.

Bodvar smiled. "And a sword."

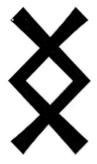

Alone at The Crossing

Brilliant sparks floated from his fire when Oh'Raum prodded it back to life. He hated waiting. After arriving at dusk, two days hence, Oh'Raum expected to see Freya galloping toward him each time he looked into the forest, followed by a smiling Preslovard. She would recount their adventure together between gales of sweet laughter before getting down to serious business about what they discovered.

Each glance to the wood line brought the old mystic closer to despair. The nightly dreams did not help calm his apprehension at this entire business. Why had he set the princess on a different course than his own? Did he truly trust her companions?

Oh'Raum watched his coals glisten with each gentle breeze. *Where are you, my son?* he pondered.

"Ho there, friend," an accented voice called.

Oh'Raum turned and peered into the darkness.

"May we share your fire?"

"You may." Oh'Raum placed a hand on his sword until the smiling, tanned face of a tall man and a woman's shrouded form appeared from the shadows.

The man raised empty hands and helped the woman sit. "Thank you," he said. "I am Oubin. This is my wife, Ashanti."

"Oh'Raum." He placed his right hand over his chest and bowed slightly.

Oubin repeated the gesture and smiled. "You honor us."

"I know your people's ways."

The travelers warmed their hands against the fire before Ashanti removed a small bundle from Oubin's pack and prepared their evening meal.

"Have you eaten?" Oubin asked.

"I have," Oh'Raum answered, "but please."

Oubin smiled again and nodded at Ashanti. "You travel south on King's Road as well?"

Oh'Raum hesitated. "What news from the north have you?"

"We left Holm'Stad, three days hence. My wife's sister married a north-man, and we are blessed by the creator to have the means to visit."

Oh'Raum nodded, knowing the beliefs of the southern desert dwellers.

"A contingent of men left before us, did you see them?"

"Aye, they passed me on the road, many a day hence," Oh'Raum answered.

"Ah," Oubin said and awkwardly paused. "And what news do you share?"

Oh'Raum returned a thin smile. "Many inspections await you on the road south."

"I see."

"The questions are about an old man traveling with a young woman." Ashanti's eyes flicked to Oh'Raum. "Are there King's Guard on the north road?"

Oubin shook his head. "None that we encountered."

"You will encounter them south. I was stopped and questioned even though I travel alone. I imagine they will take special interest in you two."

Ashanti looked at Oubin, exchanging silent words. Without removing her face covering, Ashanti said. "We heard rumors."

"Rumors, you say?"

Oubin side-glanced his wife. "It is better not to speak of such things."

"I have heard no rumors."

"It is said the king has nightmares," Ashanti said.

"Ashanti, alsamt. La tatahadath 'akthar min hadha," Oubin scolded before smiling at Oh'Raum.

"We all have nightmares, lady," Oh'Raum said. He turned to Oubin. "Allow us to speak truth without fear, sir. The king has nightmares of his downfall?"

"So the rumors say."

Oh'Raum nodded and poked the fire again. "Your holy book says those who acquire power with violence will lose it with the same."

"Tabarak alkhaliq," Ashanti whispered.

"Indeed." Oh'Raum paused. "Our king has done much violence to gain his power."

Oubin looked into the shadows. "We should not speak of these things."

"Perhaps not," Oh'Raum said and offered Oubin a reassuring smile.

After finishing their dinner, Oh'Raum wished them a pleasant night and the pair moved a short distance from Oh'Raum to unroll their sleeping blankets.

When sleep finally took him; Oh'Raum stood on a rocky shoreline among a great throng. To his left and right, mourners stretched into the hazy distance. Out to sea, a faintly recognizable boat drifted on a glassy, smooth surface.

Like orange lightning bolts, flaming arrows erupted overhead and rained down on the boat. In their orange glow, Oh'Raum made out the ship — the Wallef. Fear overtook him along with a deep desire to know who drifted on the funeral barge.

"Hello?" His mind called to the person next to him. "I say, who crosses the river this day?"

Before anyone answered, Oh'Raum felt his spirit ripped backward through the crowd. The shoreline vanished from view. Backward he flew, through a massive gate and along narrow streets. He spun around corners, zipped past dark shops, crashed through doorways and corridors until coming to rest in a dark, echoing tunnel.

Torches lined the roughly hewn walls, illuminating the dirty floor and jagged, low ceiling. Shapeless black figures rushed past him, like strong wind gusts, pressing him to the cold walls. *Running men?* In his mind, the question escaped him accompanied with a blast of steam. He shivered.

Oh'Raum awoke to a biting, cold dawn. Hoping to see Preslovard and Freya, the old magician rolled to his side and stretched under his blankets. He slowly sat up and wrapped his blankets around him.

Do I wait another day? He shivered. *Do I venture to the hills?*

Oh'Raum turned to where Oubin and Ashanti made camp and saw no trace of them. He stood, walked to nearby tree, relieved himself, and stoked a few remaining coals for a hot oatmeal morning meal.

The food warmed him and gave him more time to think about a course of action. "I know where Ra'Chel should be, and Preslovard should be here," he said and scraped the last morsels of oatmeal from his crock. "The known is the river, eh?"

As though receiving an answer from the forest, Oh'Raum looked south and smiled. "Right, the river it is then." He washed his utensils, packed his bedding, and set about marking sign for Preslovard should he emerge from the forest the moment Oh'Raum broke camp.

Oh'Raum allowed himself one final, desperate look northeast. With a sigh, he turned and set off along the bank in search of Ra'Chel and Rowan'Gaff.

A steady rain fell, slowing Oh'Raum's progress along the bank. A hard mountain snow in the El'Thune Hills swelled the river, making it almost impossible to ford. Twice, he avoided travelers on the southern bank looking for a place to cross.

Under a cloudy mid-day sun, Oh'Raum stopped for a break and a bit of food. He perused his map and gauged his progress. Instinctively, his eyes fell on the spot, just to the north, where he first met Ra'Chel and his mind pulled the memories forward; the eclipse, the funeral barge, and the baby hidden in the boat. The gloomy weather reflected his mood.

Often, he wondered how the baby came to be in the secret bow compartment. *Did a wet-nurse steal her away in the midst of battle and imagine her safe on the boat? Did the invaders spare her the sword only to burn or drown her away to the afterlife?*

Oh'Raum crumpled the map and stuffed it in his pack. Thoughts of the departed Draer King and Queen bubbled rage within him — energy he would use to quicken his pace.

The rain gave way to a soggy, red-sky evening when Oh'Raum made camp. He passed no sign of Ra'Chel or Rowan'Gaff. *Could they have ventured on the opposite bank?* His dark uncertainty kept pace with the setting sun and drove any evening-meal appetite from his thoughts.

Oh'Raum silently sat against a thick tree, draped his blankets over his legs and shoulders, and stewed in his burning doubts — his only heat. Oh'Raum's eyes fell closed and he calmed his breathing to oblige the day's engulfing exhaustion.

"We'll make camp shortly," a hushed man's voice said from the darkness.

Oh'Raum roused from sleep but remained motionless.

"We should've hours ago," said another quiet, disembodied male voice.

"How can you see anything?" a soft woman's voice asked.

"There's yet a sliver of moonlight," the first voice answered.

Best to let these strangers pass among the dark trees, Oh'Raum thought.

"Bodvar, I can't take another step," the woman called.

Oh'Raum sat up.

"Did you hear that?" the man asked.

"Bodvar Her'On?" Oh'Raum whispered.

"Who's there?"

"A friend," Oh'Raum said and unfurled his blankets.

"Oh'Raum?"

"Oh'Raum?" Ra'Chel called.

"What?" the other male voice asked.

"Rowan?" Oh'Raum answered.

"Father?"

"Preslovard?" Oh'Raum called, emotion filling his voice. He removed a fire-lighter from his pack and struck it. Orange light filled the forest, dancing in and out of shadows.

"Father," Preslovard said again, emotion hidden in his plea.

"Master Oh'Raum," Ra'Chel cried before tears flowed down her face.

Bodvar shook the old man's hand. "You're a fair sight."

Confused, Oh'Raum asked, "What's happened? How come you this way?"

They cobbled together a meager campfire around the fire-lighter and Bodvar went for wood.

"We were captured as soon as we made landfall," Rowan'Gaff said.

Oh'Raum's eyes danced from face to face. Finally, he asked, "Where is Freya?"

A thick silence descended on the company, so heavy even the wind held its breath, awaiting an answer.

Preslovard allowed his buried emotions to claw their way out of him. He put his face in his hands and wept. "I failed to protect her," he managed through his tears.

Ra'Chel cried with him and comforted him.

"Please, no," Pres said and pulled away from her. "Do not lighten this burden from me. I deserve not your forgiveness."

"And yet," Oh'Raum said in a solemn tone, "you shall have it." He allowed a moment of crackling fire to reinforce his fortitude. "Look at me, son."

Preslovard did as instructed and swiped at the tears on his

bruised face.

"You have never failed me, Preslovard."

Bodvar returned with an armload of wood, set it next to the fire, and quietly sat next to Rowan'Gaff.

"I left her alone, Father."

Oh'Raum nodded. "Many stories we will hear around this fire. That is but one, my son. Save it for the appropriate time." He turned to Bodvar. "Captured?"

The Steersman nodded. "The Garrison had lookouts on Skorpo Overlook. I assume they signaled the garrison when we entered the fjord."

"It was awful, Master Oh'Raum," Ra'Chel said. "Preslovard was forced to fight to stay alive."

"The guards took us into custody because," Bodvar mimicked the officer, "She's a young woman and you're an old man."

Oh'Raum nodded.

"I was conscripted not a day after reaching the Bridge," Preslovard said.

"Conscripted?"

Pres nodded. "For three days I lay unaware while those bastards stole me away to Dilli'Gaf."

"If not for Preslovard, we would yet be there," Ra'Chel said.

"We all had a part in our escape," Rowan'Gaff blurted.

Oh'Raum faced him. "And what part did you play, hero?"

"He blew himself up," Bodvar said.

"I was the diversion, thank you."

"And an effective one, I have no doubt," Oh'Raum said and look to Bodvar. "And no guards followed you?"

"We made for the ship, sent her to sea, and fast-marched the northern bank. We had no idea you'd be heading south."

Oh'Raum took up his pack. "I have medicine, should you need it — and food."

Rowan'Gaff fed the fire a few sticks and brought out his dinner pouch.

Oh'Raum turned back to Preslovard. "Now, my son, you have much a tale to tell."

Preslovard drew from his waterskin and focused on the growing flames. "We found it."

The words hung in the air until the fire's heat lofted them skyward.

Preslovard looked at Oh'Raum. "Freya found it," he whispered and took a deep breath. "She tripped on an upturned paver. That lead us up the mountain where the road became a bridge leading to a great opening in the mountain's side."

"Unda'Vager," Oh'Raum whispered.

"We made camp just outside the entrance and I went in to explore the tunnel." He shivered. "There are people — creatures in the cave."

Oh'Raum shook his head. "I am so sorry, my son. The failure was mine as I should never have sent you to such a place."

Preslovard scanned the fire-lit faces. "The monsters have mottled gray skin, command packs of ravenous dogs, and cultivate great nests of enormous cave spiders."

"My god," Ra'Chel muttered.

Rowan'Gaff snickered at the terrifying description. Inside, his hidden fear churned.

"Inside the entrance tunnel, I found a set of worn stairs. It was at the bottom of those stairs I was first attacked. Sentries patrol the tunnels with their slimy, hairless beasts at the heel. During the melee, I fell through a shaft and eventually splashed into a freezing, subterranean lake."

"The entire horde searched for me with faint torches and their ever-barking dogs. Somehow, I swam to shore and found my way into a large, obscured crack in the wall, except it wasn't a crack. I kept wedging my way deeper into it, until I fell through into a larger room. It is there, I found Cap'Tian."

Rowan'Gaff, disinterested with Preslovard's obviously made-up nonsense, looked up at his legendary ancestor's name.

"Tell me what you found, son," Oh'Raum pressed, already knowing what Preslovard would say from his own dark dreams.

"Four large gargoyle's guarded the tomb, one on each corner."

Oh'Raum nodded.

"And chiseled runes encircled the sarcophagus."

"Precisely as I've seen it." He looked at Ra'Chel. "When returning horde of evil rides, yet deep in El'Thune Cap'Tian sleeps."

"You don't mean to go back to this place he talks about?" Bodvar asked. "Hairless, slimy dogs? Gray-skinned spider herders? Our bargain was to safely deliver these two to the bridge, not venture into the underworld with them."

"And no one has asked you to do anything less," Oh'Raum said. "You will receive payment when at the bridge, as promised."

"I'm not afraid," Rowan'Gaff announced. "It can't be as bad as he says."

Preslovard stood and grabbed Rowan's shirt. "They killed my sister and may yet gnaw on her bones, *skreyja bacraut*!"

Rowan'Gaff stood at the insult and drew *Ealhswith*. "How dare—"

"Rowan!" Oh'Raum shouted, his voice echoing among the trees.

"Did you hear what he called me?"

"Put it away, Grimsson," Bodvar said.

Oh'Raum turned to his apprentice. "Nothing you do here tonight honors your sister."

Preslovard released Rowan's tunic and faced his father. "They bested me once, father. It will not happen again. That cave will run knee-deep with their wretched blood." He spat into the fire and stormed into the shadows.

"Preslovard," Ra'Chel called.

"Ra'Chel," Oh'Raum said, "let the man be with his

thoughts."

"Aye." Bodvar said and placed a hand on her arm. "Best he finds his own way to heal from this."

Rowan'Gaff sheathed *Ealhswith* and sat. "Scared of the dark, he is."

Bodvar sat next to him. "You'd think twice pulling a blade on him, Grimsson. He's twice the swordsman you are and the reason you're sitting here tonight."

"Will he be alright, Master Oh'Raum?" Ra'Chel asked.

"He's a stout heart, dear. For now, his mind is filled with vengeance, but in time he'll find himself again."

"The king's men will soon cover the countryside like fleas on a dog," Bodvar said.

Oh'Raum nodded. "Tomorrow, we head north along Hill Creek. The black knights will most likely stay along the Thune and avoid the marshes."

"Marshes?" Rowan asked. "Why always marshes with you?"

"They will search where it is easiest. We will go where it is hardest," Oh'Raum said. "When we reach the Hill Creek crossing, your charge will be complete, Master Steersman."

Bodvar nodded.

"We will continue to Unda'Vager, find the tomb and," he looked at Ra'Chel, "see if a prophesy awaits us."

The following morning, they ate a hasty breakfast, rolled their blankets, and headed north along the River Thune. Not long after sunrise, a small tributary marked the junction of the Thune and Hill Creek — a trickling marsh runoff.

"Fill you skins from the river," Oh'Raum said. "You don't want to drink this water until we're past the bog."

At mid-day the air filled with the stench of decaying plants and swarms of biting insects crowded the air around them. Birdsong gave way to croaking frogs and splashing lizards.

"Is this the same swamp we walked through eighteen years ago?" Rowan'Gaff asked.

"Indeed," Oh'Raum answered.

"I hate it just as much today as I did then." He slapped a biting insect on his exposed neck.

"And it hates you," Bodvar said and slapped his shoulder.

"These damned bugs don't."

"You must have sweet blood," Ra'Chel said. "But as long as they have you to eat, they aren't bothering me."

"And I've too much salt in my veins for the little blood-suckers," Bodvar added.

Rowan, swiped at another sting. "And let me guess. You've cast some spell, so they leave you alone."

"Garlic and onions," Oh'Raum said.

"What?"

"I eat lots of garlic and onions. I grow them in my garden."

"That's dumb," Rowan said and crushed an attacker against his arm, leaving a thin streak of blood.

"And that, my young friend, it why I'm a wizard and you are food for insects."

Bodvar laughed. "Aye, he's got you there Grimsson."

Preslovard remained silent, setting the pace at the front of the troop. Each step closer to Unda'Vager felt like a spike driven into his memory. He replayed the fight at the bottom of that first staircase. A thrust here — a parry there. His torch cut slashes of light across his dark thoughts and his ears remembered the snarling *tu'hünl'volf*.

"How much longer must we endure this place?" Rowan'Gaff asked.

"At least another day," Oh'Raum said. "We should reach the Hill Creek crossing by this time tomorrow."

Rowan made no attempt to hide his disgust.

That night they made camp at the northern edge of the marsh on a patch of dry ground just large enough for the five of them. Ra'Chel set to frying a sack of golden chanterelle they picked at dusk and a bit of salted pork Oh'Raum won in a trade with a fellow traveler.

"Not bad for a thong of leather," Oh'Raum said when the

sweet bacon smell wafted passed him.

"A good trade indeed," Bodvar agreed.

Preslovard nibbled at his portion and skipped the nightly talk around their small fire. His mind filled with echoes of dripping water and the warning cries of gray-skinned sentries. *Ah'oo! Ah'oo!*

He closed his eyes against the memories agonizingly cascading through his mind. He opened them and they flicked from face to face around the fire. Finally, they landed on his father, who locked eyes with him. For a split second, Preslovard wondered if his master could read his thoughts. *What does he think of me now?*

Oh'Raum watched his ward and knew painful memories assaulted him. The jovial, flower-loving Preslovard he knew sat across the fire smothered in guilt — his face a mask of revenge and shame.

Just after mid-day the company approached the Hill Creek crossing. They mustered in a small grove of birch and scanned the area for signs of the King's Guard.

"I'll go ahead and scout the crossing," Oh'Raum said and pushed past Preslovard.

"So, you're leaving then?" Rowan'Gaff quietly asked Bodvar.

"The Wallef needs her Steersman."

Ra'Chel let out a whimper.

Bodvar turned to her. "I was asked to bring you this far, my dear. I have done my duty." He paused. "Barely."

"I'm sorry to see you off," Rowan said.

"I'll miss your sword," Preslovard coldly added.

Oh'Raum approached. "The road is clear." He reached into his cloak, retrieved a bulging purse, and handed it to Bodvar. "Thank you, my friend. I release you from a job well done."

Bodvar accepted the money pouch and looked in the old man's eyes. The weight of the coin in his hand felt unbearably heavy and an unfamiliar feeling welled within him — guilt. He scanned the faces of his companions, stopping on Ra'Chel's sullen face. *Why am I feeling this way?* he silently questioned. In a cracking voice he asked, "Oh'Raum, may I speak to you?"

Oh'Raum extended a hand and the pair crossed a clearing to a nearby tree. "What is it, my friend?"

"I need to know," Bodvar said, stuttering to complete his demand. "I need to know who she is. Why you're doing this? Why is the king seeking you both? Something in me begs to know."

Oh'Raum put a steading hand on his shoulder, thought for a moment, and nodded. "You've earned that right." He cleared his throat. "She is the daughter of King Tyurn."

Bodvar's heart pounded in his chest. He turned and looked at Ra'Chel across the small clearing.

Oh'Raum continued, "She is the heir to the throne of Draer, and for my part, I intend to see the usurper vanquished and that girl enthroned."

"My god," Bodvar whispered.

"You must keep these tidings behind your lips, old friend. Ver'Sinian knows of us and yet seeks our deaths. How he has come by this information, I know not."

"He has spies everywhere and—"

"And until we are either victorious or defeated, we must protect her with our lives. You've played your part. Now return to your ship and speak of this never again."

Oh'Raum traversed the clearing and made ready to continue their journey. Bodvar stepped beside him and hiked his pack on his shoulders. "So, we're off then?" he said.

"You're staying with us?" Ra'Chel asked.

Bodvar turned and faced her. "Aye, lady. I am."

"The road we travel is a treacherous one, Steersman," Oh'Raum said.

Bodvar cleared his throat and smiled at Rowan'Gaff. "And we will travel it together," he paused, "to either victory or defeat."

"As it should be," Rowan'Gaff added.

"We should reach the cave by nightfall tomorrow," Preslovard said. He turned and faced them. "Unless there is more to say here."

"Lead on," Oh'Raum said and smiled at his apprentice.

Preslovard led them across Hill Creek and onto the slopes of The El'Thune Hills. He retraced his steps from a month earlier, climbing higher into the mountains and churning inside for the fight to come.

The following evening, under an orange sky, they crossed the ancient road leading up the mountain.

"This is where Freya found the road," Preslovard coldly said. He rested his foot on the skewed paving stone and pointed up the slope. "The city entrance is there."

"Lead on," Oh'Raum said, watching emotions cascade through his apprentice.

Preslovard turned and followed his previous steps up the mountain. Bodvar tugged on Oh'Raum's arm to slow him to the back of the pack.

"Is he up for this?" Bodvar whispered.

Oh'Raum stroked his beard. "I know of nothing else that may satisfy his taste for revenge."

The Steersman nodded. "Be wary. I've seen men avenge loved ones in battle at the cost of their own life. This need not be a funeral march for your apprentice."

"With all that I am, it will not be so."

Pres led them through the moss-covered stone debris to where the slope suddenly leveled. The sun's orange light shined high on the mountain above them.

"What is this?" Ra'Chel asked panting.

"A causeway to the entrance," Preslovard answered.

"Looks like just more road to me," Rowan'Gaff said and continued walking.

"I'd watch my step," Pres said. He turned to Ra'Chel. "Stay close to the trees. The ground is safest there."

"Where you go, I follow," she said and blushed as soon as the words left her lips.

Preslovard's heart momentarily softened and for the first time in a month, he smiled. An instant spark returned to his eyes, quickly extinguished by his impending vengeance.

They traversed the causeway with Preslovard continuously warning Rowan'Gaff about loose stones and cracked beams. Pres led them to a grove of trees growing through the road surface from a tall support pillar below the bridge. Opposite the stand, the entrance to Unda'Vager opened before them like a gaping wound on some immense monster. Long, black cracks slashed the rocks above the cave, fallen stones littered the causeway, and rivulets of water dripped from what looked like jagged stone teeth.

Preslovard drew his sword.

"We're not going in now?" Rowan'Gaff asked. "It's almost nightfall."

Preslovard walked to the remains of Freya's meager encampment and wheeled to face his companions. Oh'Raum barely recognized the fierce, revenge-filled face of his apprentice.

"Be it night out here, or night in there, this battle we fight in the dark," Preslovard said, turned, and vanished into the darkness.

Sleeper

Part III:
Army of Legend

Sleeper

Nightmares of Kings

King Ver'Sinian Caropa writhed as though rolling on burning coals. The sweat-covered boy tugged the thick blankets of his massive bed and shouted at enemies in his mind.

In his nightmare, the boy-king marched among his army wearing heavy, oversized, black armor instead of his glistening, feather-light plate mail. Normally the king sat between his generals far from the battle, maneuvering the legions of worthless men to either their deaths or his victory. In this nightmare, Ver'Sinian marched forward with the dregs in slow, cadenced steps. With each footfall, steam billowed in thick clouds from face slits in their black helmets. His own lungs burned, and he grunted with each lumbering lurch forward.

Just a dream, just a dream, he yelled in his mind.

A distant voice roared a command and the legion abruptly halted. In front of him, brilliant light flooded through cracks in the wall of black armor like crepuscular rays of sunlight through menacing clouds. His army undulated within its ranks as though collectively panting from their march. One moment Ver'Sinian felt their crushing closeness and the next he felt naked and exposed.

Whispers floated through the throng: "Cap'Tian," and "*Uykucu.*"

Ver'Sinian's skin crawled at the name of his country's most hated enemy. *Uykucu,* The Sleeper, defeated the boy-king's ancestor, Se'Vin The Great, when he ruled these lands. Hisses followed the whispers and several among the army spat to remove the vile taste of his name from their lips.

Although only seventeen, Ver'Sinian's schooling included many lessons on *Uykucu* and how, in defeat, his ancestor tricked the fool into drinking poison. Se'Vin's potion masters assured the king of the enemy's horrific death, no doubt with the proper amount of pain and agony to usher him to the afterlife. When word arrived, the poison had not killed the enemy, but merely put him to sleep, Se'Vin promptly executed his potion masters for their failure. That is what kings did. Now, in the boy-king's mind, he stood as one of his foot soldiers trying to get a glimpse of the dreaded enemy.

Another roaring command engulfed the company and without hesitation, they flew forward — a great mass of men, armor clanging, chests heaving, and throats raw with guttural shouts. Like a leaf on a river, Ver'Sinian flowed along with them, as if his feet no longer touched the ground. A shout churned within him, bubbled to the back of his throat, and burst forth like a geyser spewing boiling water from an unknown roiling depth. No ardent battle cry escaped his lips, but a terrifying, fearful shriek.

The army in front of him split open and flowed around an intense bright light. At the center of the light, Ver'Sinian made out the shape of a man — *Uykucu*, The Sleeper, Cap'Tian. The blinding orange and yellow light burned Ver'Sinian with its radiance and he squinted away from it.

Ver'Sinian continued forward long after his army abandoned him to the left and right. He feared he might fly into the shining orb and be lost in it, unable to find his way back to the real world — the living world.

Just a dream, he shouted again in his mind.

A glistening shield slammed against his left side and sent him thundering to the dirt. His black armor rattled around him and his helmet rung like a mission bell calling congregants to worship. He threw the helmet to the ground before tight fists closed around his arms, righting him before the immense, glowing form. Sā'Ben and Ver'Sen, his brothers, held him forward.

"Brothers, please," he pleaded.

His oldest brother, Ver'Sin, put a hand on the back of his head, leaned close and whispered in his ear. "This is the throne you've won, little brother."

The glowing hero raised his lance and thrust it into the boy-king's chest while his ghostly brothers continued rushing him forward. The lance passed through his black armor as though nothing more than cheap linen. Ribs shattered under its weight, making way for the sharp point to first compress then bifurcate his frozen heart.

In his twisted nightmare, Ver'Sinian experienced the horror as both the executed and witness — his consciousness continuously jumping perspectives.

The lance pushed through his chest, bursting from his back in a shower of blood, meat, and bones. The spear's long wooden shaft slid through the hole while Ver'Sinian moved past the glowing hero, propelled by the echoing words of his brothers. "... the throne you've won, little brother."

The dream-world around him grew dark and another presence entered his vision. An old man approached and knelt on a grassy meadow. Slumped in his arms, the body of a young man lay like a worn blanket. Ver'Sinian felt the intense grief emanating from the old man. Ver'Sinian's dreamworld spun and now he lay on the floor in the old man's arms. He looked into the tear-filled eyes, searching for recognition.

"Father?" Ver'Sinian asked in another man's weak voice. The boy-king looked down at himself. Blood dried on his hands and a gaping chest wound oozed thick, red foam.

The grieving apparition lay him gently on the grass and floated away. The floor beneath him rippled and roiled. It opened, like a great mouth, and swallowed the boy-king into darkness. Before covering his eyes, the face of a beautiful woman hovered over him. Devoid of expression, the girl queerly examined him, tilting her heard from side to side to look deep into his eyes — through them. She opened her mouth and Ver'Sinian thought she might kiss him. Instead, a scream exploded from her lips. The ground around him shook as it swallowed him whole like a snake eating a mouse.

Ver'Sinian shrieked.

"My King?" a voice inquired. Ver'Sinian shot from his blankets and scratched at his heaving chest.

"Arbas?"

"It is I, My King. The guards called me."

Ver'Sinian's breathing calmed and he looked around his bed chambers. He moved to a small table and poured a mug of water.

"Is it the same dream, My King?"

"Have we found the old man or the girl?"

"No, Sire."

"Assemble the advisors."

"My King, it's the middle of the—"

Ver'Sinian hurled the mug against the hard-stone wall and whirled on his aid. "Assemble my advisors, now! And summon a chambermaid to clean that up." He pointed to a cluttered desk opposite his four-poster bed. Ancient books, scrolls, and scribbled writings covered the desk's surface. "I have gleaned nothing from this nonsense."

Arbas bowed low and scurried for the door.

An hour later, Ver'Sinian, flanked by his personal guard, marched into his war room. Behind him, Arbas, *Vücut Yardimi* to his highness, and the chambermaid carried the remains of Ver'Sinian's desk.

In the gathering room, a group of aging, bearded men sat at a long table awaiting the unpredictable boy-king. They moved to stand when he entered, but Ver'Sinian dismissed them with a gloved hand. "Keep your seats," he said and motioned to

Arbas and the chambermaid before continuing. "You, gentleman, are the most enlightened men in my kingdom and among the most renowned mystics in the land."

The gathered smiled and nodded to each other at the collective compliment. The king's personal aid and chambermaid deposited the bulging bundle of papers and books on the table.

"This mess is the accumulated histories and legends surrounding *Uykucu*. Each of you has instructed me to read this material to gain insight into finding and possibly destroying this mythic *canavar*."

The men regarded the papers with reverence, having scoured the ancient writings countless times themselves.

Ver'Sinian moved to a nearby tapestry flanked by small, mounted torches. "I have spent the last month reading this tripe and can any of you tell me what knowledge I've gained?"

The advisors mumbled, none wanting to speak first or risk becoming the target of the king's rage.

Ver'Sinian removed one of the torches from its mount and turned back to the gathering.

"Nothing!" he yelled and tossed the torch on the table.

The spreading flames eagerly licked the dry parchment and covered the meeting table in a fine, fiery orange and yellow tablecloth.

"My king!" one of the mystics shouted.

"These scrolls are priceless," another yelled and feebly pulled documents from the table to extinguish the charred paper.

One of the advisors made for the door.

"Leave and be cut down!" Ver'Sinian shouted. His guards slung their pikes forward, blocking the escape. The king calmly walked to the head of the table. "You will have me fight a myth, a legend? You know of my visions and have me scouring the country for those within them. I doubled guard patrols and our garrisons are at capacity. I have prisons overflowing with old men and yet my visions continue." He looked around the smoldering table. "So, tell me, what is next? Shall I start executing everyone younger than Arbas?" He pointed to his aid.

"My King?" A cloaked mystic at the far end of the table raised a shaking hand. "The song speaks of *Uykucu* yet sleeping in El'Thune Hills. Perhaps we dispatch scouts to the mountains to search for him?" he said as more of a question than a suggestion.

"Arbas," the king said.

The king's aid stepped forward. "Yes, My King."

"Send a garrison to El'Thune. I want this myth found and killed."

"A garrison, Sire? We have but reserves in the city as it is."

Ver'Sinian turned on him. "I don't care if you conscript every man and boy in this city." He turned to his gathered advisors. "Start with this lot. I want a garrison in El'Thune immediately."

"Yes, My King," Arbas said.

Descent into Darkness

Oh'Raum stepped forward and rapped the foot of his staff on the causeway flagstones. An echo shot around the canyon and reverberated deep in the mountain's root.

"Preslovard Parn," Oh'Raum said in a low, rumbling voice that almost shook the bridge apart.

His companions felt the change and backed away a step. To Bodvar, Oh'Raum appeared to grow taller. His call, like a cannon shot, flew into the cave mouth, bouncing from its walls, and struck Preslovard in the back.

"You have forgotten your place," Oh'Raum continued.

Preslovard emerged from the void with his head hung low.

"You are not some mindless berserker."

Preslovard walked to Oh'Raum, whose voice softened, and he appeared to return to his normal size.

"You are the heir to ancient knowledge. You are my apprentice," Oh'Raum paused, "and my son."

Preslovard sheathed his sword.

"We do not fight after a full day's march when our enemy is fresh, and we are not. The hole in this mountain will be there after a hot meal and a night's rest."

"Yes, Father."

Ra'Chel watched Preslovard's face. He looked at his feet, ashamed of his rash action and his forgetfulness of his father's teachings. Her own emotions churned alongside Preslovard and her breath hitched when the thought of them together struck her mind.

"So now what?" Rowan'Gaff asked.

"We make camp in the stand, eat our fill, and sleep before moonrise," Oh'Raum answered.

"I'll take first watch," Bodvar said when the company reached a stable camping site within the grove.

They unrolled their blankets and brought out their dinner supplies. Bodvar and Preslovard scoured the causeway and stand of trees for fire-twigs while Ra'Chel and Rowan set to preparing dinner.

Full darkness descended on them and the temperature, high in the mountains, quickly dropped. Ra'Chel wrapped herself in her blanket and sat close to their small fire.

Oh'Raum tugged on his pipe while staring at the dancing flames. He broke the silence so abruptly, even Bodvar jumped. "Tell me again of your fight in the cave, son."

Preslovard, who also watched the ballet of fire, took a deep breath. "I left Freya at our camp, just outside the cave's mouth. The first tunnel stretches a good way into the mountain with numerous side rooms and passageways. Where they lead, I know not." He looked around the fire to see who was watching him or merely listening. Ra'Chel watched him. "The far end of the tunnel leads to a short stairway, just taller than a man. It was there that I was attacked."

Oh'Raum, who never took his eyes off the fire, nodded.

Pres continued, "I injured as many as I could, but every thrust of my sword was met with several bites from the dogs."

"*Tu'hünl'volf,*" Oh'Raum whispered.

"I had both torch and sword, but there were too many. I fell and crawled backward into one of the small side chambers. Instead of my back against a wall, I fell into a hole," he paused, "or off a cliff."

"Or down a well," Oh'Raum softly echoed.

"Eventually I crashed into the underground lake, made my

way to the edge, and found the tomb by sheer luck."

Oh'Raum laughed, "Luck, say you?" He shook his head. "Another word, I believe, is more appropriate. But tell the rest of your story."

"A rock outcrop at the lake's edge leads to another wide passage. I followed this to a great room filled with the vile creatures."

"And where within does the tomb lie?"

"Behind a fallen boulder along the wall. I hid behind the boulder as they searched for me. It is there, I found the entrance crack."

"Can we all fit through this crack?"

Preslovard scanned his companions before nodding. "I believe so, father."

"Very good," Oh'Raum said and smiled at his ward.

"You have a plan then?" Bodvar asked.

"Not as yet."

"Must we all go into this place?" Rowan'Gaff asked and looked around the fire. "Surely, some of us can wait out here."

Oh'Raum pulled on his beard and let out a breath. "Ra'Chel and I must do this, the rest of you..."

"I won't let either of you go in alone," Preslovard blurted.

Ra'Chel smiled.

"I've come this far," Bodvar added.

Rowan'Gaff glanced around the fire, puffed his chest and announced, "If Ra'Chel must go in, then I go as well."

Ra'Chel laughed, "With so many protectors, what am I to do?"

"Finish your dinner and sleep warm in your blankets," Oh'Raum answered.

Each did as he recommended. In time, the entire company fell asleep in the grove, save for Bodvar who kept the watch and Preslovard who slept on his side and also eyed the gaping cavern. Sleep finally found him under a clear, star-filled sky.

The following morning, Preslovard roused to Bodvar

sleeping against a nearby tree. "Did you keep the watch all night?"

Bodvar shook his head. "Oh'Raum relieved me at high moon."

Pres shivered under his blanket, rolled to his knees, and scanned the stand for his master. "Where is he?"

Bodvar wordlessly lifted his chin in the cave's direction.

Preslovard stood, his blankets draped around him like a cape. "He went in?"

"Not an hour ago."

"Why did you not wake me?" Preslovard demanded. He dropped his blanket, drew his sword, and stormed toward the cave mouth, stopping where their mound of dirt met the planked causeway. A sudden, terrifying thought struck him. He turned and searched their campsite. "Where is Ra'Chel?"

"I'm here," she called back.

A breath escaped Preslovard and he sheathed his sword. "You didn't go with him?"

"Go where?"

"Into the cave?"

"Master Oh'Raum went in without me?"

"What?" Rowan'Gaff asked and wiped sleep from his eyes.

"Oh'Raum went into the cave without any of us," Bodvar said.

Preslovard turned on him. "How could you let him go by himself?"

Bodvar laughed and looked at him. "If you think I am such a man to stop, Oh'Raum Yulr, from anything, you think too highly of me, young man."

"Stop me from what?" The clear, low voice came from behind Preslovard and stirred the entire company.

Preslovard whirled. "Father, I..."

Oh'Raum wiped blood from *Óvinr* and slid the gleaming sword neatly into her sheath.

"I didn't know you were going in this morning. I would have

304

gone with you," Preslovard said.

"Of course, you didn't know. That was by design, my son. I needed more information and any of you accompanying me would have been a distraction."

Bodvar nodded to the blood on his rag. "Did your quarry provide the information you sought?"

Oh'Raum tossed the soiled rag near his pack. "I'm afraid I don't speak their tongue, but I found out what I needed."

Ra'Chel stepped beside Preslovard, too close for Rowan'Gaff's liking. "What did you need to know?"

"How to get safely and quietly to the tomb."

"And how are we going to do that?" Rowan asked, his question laced with sarcasm.

Oh'Raum smiled. "By making rope, young man."

ᘓ   ᘔ

Oh'Raum stood at the cave mouth amidst the debris of Freya's camp. Not much remained. In his mind, he saw her wrapped in her blankets, huddled against the cold mountain wind, taking what heat she could from the fire, and waiting for Preslovard to emerge from his reconnoiter.

Unda'Vager's entrance passage stretched deep into the mountain, a foreboding reminder to those seeking entrance of the kingdom's greatness and power. Oh'Raum stepped passed the threshold and the remnants of a massive portcullis, flanked by small guardhouses hewn from the rock. The side chambers, some cut deep into the mountain at varying intervals, served as administrative offices, shops, counting houses, farriers, granaries, wheelwrights, and passages to other parts of the city.

Wide enough for two carts to pass, the tunnel closed in and the morning's light quickly faded behind him. Shallow wheel ruts scarred the corridor's floor, an archeological reminder of the commerce that once flowed through this long dead stronghold.

The passage gradually narrowed, and the air cooled. Oh'Raum drew his sword and sniffed the air at each side opening. He moved silently, with slow, deliberate steps which drew him deeper into the mountain's darkness. His senses reached into the darkness, smelling for mordent odors, and listening for abnormal echoes. Behind him, the opening to the surface world now looked like a distant, nighttime star.

He paused at the precipice of a short staircase — his muscles coiled and the grip on his staff tightened.

The attack will come at the bottom, he thought, *just as it had for Preslovard.*

According to Preslovard, the bottom step opened to a larger room, bordered by openings.

One will be descending stairs, one will be where he fell, and one will be where the sentry waits.

During Preslovard's descriptions of his previous encounter, Oh'Raum constructed a rudimentary map of this room, a wide landing with two staircases and two side chambers. Oh'Raum assumed the descending stairs would be directly across the steps leading to the entrance. Preslovard said the attack came from his right side and he had backpedaled to the other opening where he fell away from his attackers.

Oh'Raum pressed his right shoulder to the wall and descended the stairs. He paused at the bottom step and listened for signs of the sentry's impending attack.

The beasts are well trained, Oh'Raum thought before spinning the corner and stepping into the sentry's alcove.

The *tu'hünl'volf* sat at its handler's feet, patiently waiting for slack in its lead, a silent order to attack. The sentry stood, hidden in a deep alcove where even the faintest light dared not go.

Oh'Raum advanced with silent, practiced speed. He lunged right, and a moment after the sentry released his hound, a blinding upward swing sent the animal's head bouncing to the back of the alcove. With his sword now over his left shoulder,

Oh'Raum brought it across the sentry's neck. The blade's tip bounced against the alcove's wall sending a ringing echo through the cavern.

Oh'Raum turned and sank into the alcove, listening for raised alarms deeper with the mountain. When assured his presence remained undetected, he emerged from the guard's post and pulled a small, corked bottle from within his cloak. Inside the grimy glass, pale green light emanated from several small mushrooms growing within the bottle. He inspected the descending stairs, directly across the exit stairs, as he suspected.

In the room where Preslovard fell, Oh'Raum found the remnants of a stone ring and a wide hole in the floor. Above the ringed hole, at head level, a large timber stretched the length of the room. Wedged from wall to wall, rope grooves confirmed what Oh'Raum suspected. He moved back to the alcove, collected the *tu'hünl'volf 's* head, and dropped it into the hole. Several seconds later a distant splash echoed from the depths.

Oh'Raum smiled.

ભ   ଛ

"Rope?"

"You mean to climb down to the lake?" Preslovard asked.

Oh'Raum nodded. "From there we can swim to the tunnel you followed to the city's heart."

Pres nodded.

"How much rope do we need?" Bodvar asked.

"A decent length. The vines along the causeway should give us a good start."

Ra'Chel looked around the bridge. "We passed a thick patch of nettles we could use as binder strands. I'll go harvest those."

Oh'Raum nodded. "We can set up a rope run between these trees," he said and pointed to the two most distant trees of the grove.

Bodvar looked at Rowan'Gaff and smiled. "Ready to get to work, Grimsson?"

"Someone needs to protect..." he paused and abruptly changed his stance, "assist Ra'Chel." Ra'Chel looked eagerly at Preslovard who moved to the causeway's rim and pulled on a large clump of hanging vines.

"Right, we each have our duties then," Oh'Raum announced.

Mid-day's light filled the canyon when they pulled the thirteenth length of thick rope from the rope run. Bodvar turned the coiled fibers over in his hands, inspecting it for potential flaws. "I've made a fair share of twist in my day Oh'Raum, and I'd be damned to see a finer length of vine-wound strand in any costal harbor from here to Sal'Sund."

Oh'Raum smiled. "You'd be surprised what skills quiet cottage life demands."

They both laughed.

"We're going to need several stalwart branches to span the opening," Oh'Raum said.

"Here, father," Preslovard announced.

They wound the final length of rope, hoisted the logs on their shoulders, and moved to the cave mouth.

"Our movements will be slow and our breaths like a quiet wind," Oh'Raum said. "This is an exercise in patience and deliberate action."

Preslovard smiled at his father. He turned to the company. "He means to move slowly and quietly until it's time to run for our lives."

Ra'Chel let out a soft laugh.

"Thank you, my son. That is precisely what I said, though a bit more eloquently. From this moment until we reach the hero's tomb, we try not to speak. We communicate by touch and hand signal where there is light."

They nodded, released their final apprehensive breaths, and walked slowly into the mountain.

When the light dwindled, Oh'Raum withdrew his mushroom bottle and looped its string around the shaft of his staff. A smile crossed his lips at the astonished looks on his companions' faces.

"*Mycena chlorophos*," he whispered.

The group entered the well room where Preslovard stretched the logs over the opening, wedging the logs between the damaged rock walls. He lashed the three logs together in a pyramid shape with nettle-twine creating a strong beam which spanned the hole. Bodvar stepped forward with the rope and looped a seafarer's knot around the logs, leaving enough length to tie off to the large support beam running the room's length.

Preslovard sheathed his sword, sat at the well's edge and used the logs to lower himself down the rope. Once Preslovard reached the water, he swished the rope, signaling the next climber. Oh'Raum nodded for Ra'Chel to follow Pres.

Ra'Chel's heart thumped in her chest. The light from Oh'Raum's bottle vanished above her. She felt the closeness of the walls, like being entombed alive. Ra'Chel gripped the rope with all her strength and wrapped both legs around the bumpy rope. Slowly, she descended through the blackness. Several slips down the rope, Ra'Chel felt the walls fall away and an impression of open air filled her mind. Down she slid, waiting for the first splash of icy water to grab at her foot.

Below her, Preslovard held the wet rope steady without adding his own weight.

Ra'Chel's foot slipped into the lake, sending a chill up her spine. Preslovard had recounted the cold water, but this felt like icy knives sliding up her legs. She held her breath to keep from calling out in the darkness. Then Preslovard pulled her close and even in the frigid water, she felt his warmth.

One by one they slipped into the well and shimmied down the rope. Finally, a faint green light swayed and spun in the air above them. It slowly descended and joined them in the water, the green mushrooms bobbing in the safety of their enclosed bottle.

Oh'Raum indicated for them to clump together. "All but Pres, close your eyes," he whispered. He instructed Pres to turn where he thought the opening might be. Oh'Raum held both hands above his head and clapped two small stones together. A spark of white light erupted over the lake and instantly burned a faint image into Preslovard's vision. Pres slowly swam for the small, rocky beach. Oh'Raum tapped each person to follow his ward and soon they pulled themselves from the icy water.

Shivering and dripping, they moved to the tunnel where Preslovard pointed in the mushroom's dull, green light. Oh'Raum returned his *Mycena chlorophos* bottle in his cloak, crept forward, and inspected the tunnel, ready for an attack — his acute senses attuned to the shuffling and grunts at the far end of the passage. The company followed a short distance behind.

Oh'Raum slid along the left side of the corridor to Unda'Vager's vast city center. He looked back and silently called for Preslovard to assume the lead when rounding the corner. Pres took a deep breath and crept around the corner, taking up a familiar position behind the large fallen boulder. He felt for the slim crack that led to the tomb.

One by one, they moved from Oh'Raum to Preslovard, who directed them into the crack. First, Rowan'Gaff, then Ra'Chel, followed by Bodvar, the fattest of the group. Pres pushed him deep into the crack against Bodvar's huffing protestations. Oh'Raum moved to the crack and shimmed his tall, lean frame inside.

Preslovard inched his way through the crack and reentered the hero's tomb.

Oh'Raum gathered them together, removed the green bottle and smiled at each one of them. "Well done," he whispered. "I didn't think we'd make it this far."

"What—?"" Rowan'Gaff said.

Preslovard stifled a laughed.

Bodvar smiled and shook his head.

Ra'Chel looked around the room under the faint green light. "Now what?"

A lump grew in Oh'Raum's throat and his mouth suddenly went dry. His faint memory and this terrifying reality crashed together in the sweet innocence of her question. *Now what, indeed?*

Rowan'Gaff walked to the center of the room and put a hand on the gargoyle-defended stone box. He turned, "Do we open it?"

Oh'Raum put out a hand and tried to speak, but nothing came from his mouth. He walked to the sarcophagus to stop Rowan'Gaff.

"I think we should open it," Rowan reiterated.

"Wait," Preslovard whispered, watching his master's movements.

Oh'Raum rested a hand on the coffin's lid and let out a ragged breath.

Bodvar stepped forward. "I think Oh'Raum needs to make that decision, lad."

"I want to read the runes," Oh'Raum finally said.

Rowan'Gaff stepped away from the stone box and snarled at one of the gargoyles. "Read on, sir," he mocked.

Oh'Raum moved the dangling green bottle close to the carved runes and whispered, *"Valknut."* He slid around the tomb's base, examined the chiseled letters, and rubbed away debris. He rounded each corner below the gargoyle's clawed feet, mumbling. He straightened and rubbed the coffin's wide top. The old mystic drew in a deep breath and blew dust from obfuscated letters scratched at the center of the stone. Oh'Raum leaned the glowing green bottle over the lid and said aloud, "Until Draer Princess softly weeps."

His eyes sank and a mournful expression crossed his face. He looked at Ra'Chel. They all looked at Ra'Chel.

"What?" Rowan'Gaff asked, breaking the silence in the

tomb. He looked from Ra'Chel, to Oh'Raum, and back to Ra'Chel.

Her pulse quickened and her face flushed. Her lips curled and she suddenly felt very exposed.

"She's the—?" Rowan'Gaff started to say, shushed by Bodvar's hand on his shoulder.

Oh'Raum walked to her and lifted her sunken chin. Tears welled in her eyes. "Up until this moment, a sliver of me wished you were just an old crazy man."

He smiled.

"But," she continued through a fit of sniffles, "now I know it's all real, isn't it?"

He nodded and gave her a thin smile. "For this moment, you were born, your highness," he said in a low voice.

Slowly, Preslovard knelt beside the tomb.

"No, please," Ra'Chel tried.

Bodvar, lowered to a knee as well. Rowan'Gaff stood frozen, his mouth agape until Bodvar tugged him to the ground.

Ra'Chel's emotions burst forth like an erupting volcano. The truth of her existence, the secret of her ancestry, the prophecy in front of her, and the sacrifices of these men flooded through her like a torrent. Oh'Raum caught her by the shoulders, turned her to the stone coffin like a weapon, and commanded his kneeling companions, "Open it!"

The Battle of Unda'Vager

The fools, Marden thought from his vantage point. *What are they doing among the stinging nettles?* The spy watched the pair. They trudged among the stinging plants, lopping them at the root. The boy lopped and the girl added the useless plants to their growing bundle.

Marden watched in silence.

"Scout the area," Captain Caton had commanded before the scout left the garrison's camp two days ago and today looked like another boring day skulking among the bushes. Then he had happened upon the nettle-pickers.

While the garrison's main body enjoyed dry tents, hot food, and blankets on soft hay, he scoured the hillsides foraging berries and mushrooms, drinking earthy-tasting creek water, and struggling to make his meager supplies last.

Could they make tea from the leaves? Marden wondered. *I guess I should follow them.*

Marden expected the nettle-farmers, he like that moniker best, to lead him to a ramshackle homestead hidden on the forested mountainside. To his surprise, the nettlers, that sounded like a good name too, led him higher into the mountains and through an almost invisible cut in the hillside.

The scout followed, before hunkering behind a fallen boulder to watch the two. They joined three men who pulled and stripped lengths of twisted vine between two trees in a small grove growing on the causeway. Opposite the stand of trees, the bridge led to a massive cave opening, cut directly into the sheer mountain's face.

Marden smiled. *An old man and a girl.*

Back among the garrison, Marden immediately reported to Captain Caton.

"Rope, you say?" Captain Caton asked. He looked around the tent at his lieutenants. "It's the best lead we've had since entering these foothills. And you definitely saw an old man and a girl?"

Marden nodded. "Aye, four men in total."

Caton looked to the man on his right. "What say you, Keene?"

The assembled leaders looked at Caton's second in command, who shrugged. "Maybe there's something valuable in the cave."

The gathering laughed and several nodded.

Caton stood. "We're not here to mine." He sternly scanned the room before a wide smile crossed his face. "But treasure hunting is better than boredom." Smiles returned to his commanders. "Break camp," he ordered. "Marden, will lead us to this cave."

Marden raised one side of this mouth in contempt. He had not thought of treasure.

✢   ✣

Rowan'Gaff, Preslovard, and Bodvar rose and put their shoulders into the sarcophagus' stone top. Harsh scraping echoed around the chamber. The men grunted at its weight, adding to the noise bouncing around the cavern. Slowly, the top of the stone box slid to the side. It teetered before toppling to the floor with a deafening crash. The company sank away from the box and the thundering sound.

"*Ah,oo! Ah,oo!*" echoed throughout the cavernous city.

Oh'Raum shot Bodvar an alarmed look. The Steersman drew his sword and rushed to guard the crack, their only escape route. Rowan'Gaff and Preslovard stepped behind Oh'Raum, who prodded Ra'Chel forward. She expected to see a revolting, decayed corpse, wrapped in moldy cloth strips, under a covering of thick, brown dust.

Rather than an ashen-faced cadaver, inside the stone coffin lay a pristinely preserved man — a sleeping soldier. His armor reflected tiny glints of faint mushroom light and his weapons looked newly forged. No debris littered the inside with him and not even a sheet covered his head. Neck-length blonde hair cropped his brow and draped his chiseled face. A broad shield on his chest lead to leather britches, greaves, and thick hide boots. To his righthand, a long, spear-tipped staff stretched the length of the coffin.

Ra'Chel nearly shouted when his chest heaved in a deep breath. Oh'Raum pulled her away moments before the man sat up sending his shield clattering to the foot of the stone box.

His hands reached for the side of the box and he pulled in another deep breath. He whipped his head toward Oh'Raum and Ra'Chel. Rowan'Gaff drew his sword.

Cap'Tian vaulted from the sarcophagus, grabbed his lance and shield and crouched ready for the fight.

Oh'Raum stepped between the two men, his hands outstretched. "Wait, please."

"Who are you?" Cap'Tian demanded, his voice deep and strong.

"Keep your voice down," Oh'Raum said. "We are not your enemy. Our mutual enemy heard your awakening and searches for us even now."

Cap'Tian lifted his chin to Rowan'Gaff's sword.

"Put that away, boy," Oh'Raum said.

Rowan grudgingly complied.

"Ah,oo! Ah,oo!"

Cap'Tian's posture did not change when Oh'Raum turned

to face him.

"You are Cap'Tian?"

The hero nodded.

"I am Oh'Raum Yulr. The rash young man is Rowan'Gaff. We are here with several others."

"Where is here?" Cap'Tian's question matched Oh'Raum's volume.

"Yes," Oh'Raum gingerly said, "this is a very different place than the one you remember."

"I was toasting my men, now I am here." Cap'Tian kept his spear poised on the lip of his shield ready to kill this stranger with a thrust.

Oh'Raum nodded and licked his lips. "That was a very long time ago. The drink you toasted with was laced with poison."

Cap'Tian tensed.

Warning calls bounced around them, *"Ah,oo! Ah,oo!"* The sound of running feet drifted through the crack.

Oh'Raum quickly continued, "Instead of doing as Se'Vin's potion-masters intended, you fell into a sleep. The magic of this spell is unknown." He looked to Bodvar. "Are they coming?"

Bodvar shook his head. "It sounds as though they scurry about."

"Searching for the source of the sound," Preslovard added.

Cap'Tian's eyes flicked from person to person in the faint light.

"According to the runes on your tomb—"

"Tomb?" Cap'Tian asked, his voice louder.

Oh'Raum stepped aside and lowered his green bottle to the stone, rune-covered box. "The words tell of what happened after you fell to the poison. Your men thought you dead, but those with ancient knowledge found you only asleep. Every attempt to wake you was made, to no account. They decided to rest you in the safest place they knew of at the time, the great storehouse of Unda'Vager."

Cap'Tian looked into the darkness around him. "I know of

Unda'Vager, the mountain city."

Oh'Raum smiled. "It is far from the greatness you remember." Again, Oh'Raum looked to Bodvar for information. Bodvar shook his head.

"Where are my men?" Cap'Tian asked.

"Long dead, I'm afraid. You've been sleeping for over eleven-hundred years."

Cap'Tian looked at the floor. "It is hard to accept your story."

Oh'Raum said nothing.

"It could be that you drugged me and brought me here not a day later."

Oh'Raum nodded. "Yes, I see how that could be equally plausible." He turned and invited Ra'Chel to join them. "This is Ra'Chel Brune. She is the only daughter of King Tyurn and the Lady Frann of Draer, whom both have crossed the river."

"I know not these names," Cap'Tian said.

Oh'Raum nodded. "This is Rowan'Gaff Vodr, your direct descendent on his mother's side."

Cap'Tian eyed Rowan.

"We are here to fulfill, what is to us, an ancient song. The song tells the story of your victory over Se'Vin, the invader, and how his last act before escaping across the mountain was as I described."

Cap'Tian surveyed Ra'Chel. Her smiling face eased his cautiousness.

"The song tells how the tears of a Draer Princess wakes the legendary hero — you."

Cap'Tian laughed. "Again, possibly more deception."

"True, but here we are."

Cap'Tian nodded to Bodvar. "What does he guard against?"

"He guards our only known escape from this place. The city you once knew is home to vile underground people, no longer human and no less vicious than their oily, black dogs."

"I want out of this place," Cap'Tian said and adjusted the

grip on his spear.

"As do we all," Rowan'Gaff agreed.

Bodvar shushed them. "It sounds like fighting."

Ra'Chel, Rowan, and Pres joined Bodvar at the cut and listened to the sounds wafting into the tomb. Oh'Raum invited Cap'Tian to join the group.

"I know that noise," Cap'Tian said.

The unmistakable sounds of battle echoed from the cavernous walls.

"Who are they fighting?" Ra'Chel asked.

Bodvar nodded at her question. "Give me your string."

"What?"

"You hold one end. If I tug on it, follow. If I let it fall, stay put."

Ra'Chel tied one end of the nettle thong around his hand before he shimmied through to the great room. Several tugs on the string followed in quick succession.

"He means for us to follow," she whispered.

Preslovard inched through the gap, followed by Rowan'Gaff and Ra'Chel.

"This is the only way out?" Cap'Tian asked.

Oh'Raum stepped in the cleft. "To my knowledge, yes. Come with us, please." He turned and inched his way through the crack.

In the great room, the battle sounds reached a fever pitch. Mottled, gray creatures, slimy black dogs, and armor-clad soldiers battled. The *tu'hünl'volf* growled from every direction, echoing among clangs of metal and blood-curdling shrieks.

"Unda'Vager is not what I remember it to be," Cap'Tian said from behind Oh'Raum. "It appears part of your story holds true."

"Preslovard, you and Rowan take the vanguard. Cap'Tian, follow with the Lady Ra'Chel. Bodvar and I will be your rear-guard."

"The stairs are closer along this wall," Pres said and set off in the opposite direction from where he encountered the spider farm.

In a single file, each with a hand on the tunic in front of them, they swept along the outer wall, moving as a single, wormlike unit from boulder to enclosure to concealment point. Preslovard stopped at each corridor and quickly peered around its corner for signs of their enemy. The melee consumed the central part of the city with smaller skirmishes within the sprawling corridors.

"We need to make those stairs," Preslovard said and pointed past a group of fighters.

"Then our part of this battle starts there," Bodvar said.

They stood and sprinted for the stairs. Like film on water, the battle lines undulated with one side gaining an advantage only to lose it with an influx of snarling *tu'hünl'volf*.

A group of fighters, alerted by their rapid movements, broke off to block the stairs. Preslovard waded into their lines like a master tactician. He ducked feeble attacks only to deliver devastating thrusts and slashes with deadly precision. Rowan'Gaff entered the melee with the grace and style of a hurled stone. He swung wildly at any opportunistic target, even striking several soldiers on their way to the afterlife, already incapacitated by Preslovard's effortless technique.

Ra'Chel and Cap'Tian advanced though the hole created by Preslovard's opening salvo. Cap'Tian's lance shot from its resting place atop his shield, piercing vulnerable openings between armor plates. Ra'Chel shrank back. Rowan'Gaff's approach of wildly swinging his heavy blade until it made contact with a solid object, hopefully an opponent, slowed their escape.

Oh'Raum and Bodvar guarded the company's rear, each taking an exposed quarter.

Preslovard cut his way to the base of the stairs, turned the corner, and climbed to the first of five landings. Rowan'Gaff followed, continuing to bludgeon foes with each step. The company proceeded upward, fighting at each landing and never turning to look back into the city's dark depths.

Oh'Raum and Bodvar turned to quicken their pace when the rear looked clear. Oh'Raum clutched Cap'Tian's cape and Bodvar secured a hand to Oh'Raum's cloak.

Up they climbed. Preslovard bounding from level to level, following an instinctive map burned into his memory from his first haggard escape from this hell. When the enemy ranks thinned, Rowan lowered his sword, his chest heaving from the exertion, and grasped Preslovard's tunic. He felt Ra'Chel tugged on his own shirt.

Still, they ascended. When creatures blocked their path, Preslovard unleashed his burning vengeance upon them. Snarling and shouting followed them from level to level. The sound right on their heels.

At the second to last landing, Oh'Raum felt Bodvar tug the end of his cloak. Without breaking strike Oh'Raum turned to see Bodvar's hand slip free.

They locked eyes for a split second and Bodvar shook his head. Oh'Raum watched Steersman, Bodvar Her'On, disappear in a cresting wave of blood, teeth and oily, black skin. Oh'Raum understood his friend's final moments. *Do not stop for me,* his eyes said.

Oh'Raum honored Bodvar's sacrifice. He turned and pressed the escaping company forward.

Preslovard crested the final stair to the exit tunnel and the faint point of light at its far end.

"There it is!" Rowan'Gaff shouted amid heavy breaths.

"Keep moving!" Oh'Raum yelled. "Don't stop and don't look back." Behind him the growling *tu'hünl'volf* advanced, pausing momentarily at the shaft of pale light.

The company emerged from Unda'Vager into a clear moonlit night. They raced across the causeway, loping down hillsides and sliding on their backsides down steeper parts. Preslovard guided them east, away from the known roads, stopping only when the land flattened, and the sound of barking dogs died far behind them.

Panting, the company stopped and fell against the thick trees to catch their breath.

"I hope I avenged you, Freya," Preslovard whispered.

"We need to keep moving," Oh'Raum said.

"Where's Bodvar?" Rowan'Gaff asked, his voice alarmed.

Oh'Raum straightened.

"He was with you." Rowan stared at Oh'Raum.

"He slipped from my grasp, young man," Oh'Raum said in a conciliatory tone. "When I turned," his voice hitched, "he was consumed."

Rowan stepped forward. "And you didn't go back from him? You didn't alert us?"

"He waved me on."

"I'm going back." Rowan'Gaff put a hand on his sword and marched up the hill.

"He's gone, Rowan'Gaff. He slowed the beasts for us to escape."

Rowan'Gaff turned, his face red. "You don't know that!" he shouted.

"I do," Oh'Raum softly said.

Ra'Chel cried.

Cap'Tian stepped beside her and looked up the hill at Rowan'Gaff. "Your friend is a hero."

Rowan stomped down the hill, "He wasn't my friend!" He stared into Cap'Tian's unwavering eyes as tears rose in his own. "He was—"

"The only father you ever truly knew," Oh'Raum finished for him and placed a soft hand on his shoulder.

Rowan tore away from his touch. "Why didn't you go back?"

"It would've cost us more than your father and my daughter."

Preslovard stepped closer. "We avenged Bodvar as well this night."

Rowan glared at him.

"It is a sacrifice we won't soon forget," Ra'Chel said. "We all owe our lives to him."

"Aye," Cap'Tian agreed.

"We can mourn him when we are assured of safety," Oh'Raum said. "Know this, Rowan'Gaff, had it been within my power to save him, I would have."

"Then tonight of all night's, your power failed us," Rowan muttered.

"Perhaps," Oh'Raum quietly agreed.

"Where do we march, Father?" Preslovard asked.

"Make for our meadow by way of D'Grath."

"We might make the easterly river by mid-moon," Pres said and trudged into the woods, continuing downslope.

Ra'Chel, Cap'Tian, and Oh'Raum fell silently into step behind him. Rowan'Gaff followed many steps behind. Inside, he seethed with a bubbling caldron of loss, anger, and denial. He stared at the back of Oh'Raum's cloak, carefully picking spots in which to plunge, *Ealhswith*.

They made camp on the northern shore of the River Thune, not far from where Preslovard and Freya crossed weeks earlier. It felt to Preslovard like a lifetime had passed since he and his little sister ventured north in search of the hero's resting place. Now, that hero sat across their small fire from him. Pres silently watched Cap'Tian. *I hope her life was worth yours*, he pondered.

Rowan'Gaff sat away from the fire, brooding.

"I want to go talk to him," Ra'Chel said.

"His loss is fresh, lady. It is best to allow him time."

"I've lost many men in battle, but none like that," Cap'Tian said. "I honor his sacrifice. We should all live lives worthy of the blood he paid."

Rowan'Gaff heard Cap'Tian's pledge. He looked from face to face around the fire and dark thoughts pushed away his grief.

"You showed true courage today, sir," Cap'Tian said and

nodded to Preslovard.

"Yes," Ra'Chel agreed, "leading us from that blackness. Thank you."

Rowan shook his head. *I was right behind him, ungrateful wench.*

"I will miss my friend," Oh'Raum said and watched the flames dance from one charred log to another. "He will be greatly missed among his shipmates."

"I grieve for Bodvar and Freya as well, Father," Preslovard added.

Rowan'Gaff looked at Preslovard's orange, glowing face. *We went in because of you.* His eyes flicked to Oh'Raum. *And he died because of you. You didn't go back for him, you bastard. You didn't even give me a chance to save him.*

"We make for your home?" Cap'Tian asked, looking at Oh'Raum.

Oh'Raum nodded. "It seems like the truest course. I believe there, we can prepare for the next part of this adventure."

"And what part is that?"

"The part where you save us all from our ancient enemy," Rowan announced and joined them around the fire.

Cap'Tian laughed and addressed Rowan. "If your old friend speaks true, my enemies are long dead." He looked at Oh'Raum.

"The invaders from the east have once again taken the land, and—"

"And we just ran for our lives from a den of vipers with you in tow, so you could fight them all for us. Just as you did in the stories of old," Rowan'Gaff spat.

Oh'Raum glared at Rowan for the interruption.

Rowan did not back down. "So, what say you, hero, up for more killing? You fit for waving your sharp stick around a few times and slaying our enemies tomorrow?"

"Rowan'Gaff," Ra'Chel said.

Cap'Tian's face remained stoic. "I know the pain you feel,

young man, so I will forgive your tone."

"You know nothing of my pain, and you can take my tone and—"

"We need," Oh'Raum sharply announced, "to make a plan. We need to spread word of Cap'Tian's return, as the song foretold. From there, I recall no visions."

"You've mentioned this song before. You claim it speaks of me?"

Oh'Raum nodded. "It tells the story of a great hero and is called *The Ballad of Cap'Tian*. Cold and black brisk east winds blew, through Far'Verm Pass to western lands, to walls of Draer dark shadows drew, delivered into evil's hands."

Preslovard took the next two verses, "Draer King's army gave valiant defense, against the shadow's growing might, as dusk sun's light made red intense, Draer King lay martyred that very night. Unmatched they marched with force of arms, southward evil's dark armies spread, cross rivers and forests and trampled farms, with misery, hopelessness, death and dread."

Rowan'Gaff stood and walked away from the fire.

"Where are you going?" Ra'Chel called.

"To relieve myself," Rowan called back. "And be sick," he said under his breath.

"When from the heart of the western lands, like a brilliant star that comes to Earth, A shining hero stalwart stands, raises sword and shows his worth," Oh'Raum rhythmically said. "Cap'Tian, pure of heart and mind of stone, with sword and shield and spear-tipped lance, the hero stands — one man alone, drives back the horde's conquering advance."

Ra'Chel looked at Cap'Tian. He listened like a child hearing about magic for the first time. His pulse quickened and his eyelids blinked.

"Back to the east flees evil's retreat, with one final card yet to play, a feast and trap did lay in defeat, for Cap'Tian's fate ends would betray. By victory drink was Cap'Tian betrayed, to sleep but not to die or rise, on windward slopes the evil stayed, to perhaps return and claim their prize."

Ra'Chel cleared her throat and in barely a whisper finished the song with goosebumps growing on her arm, "Foretold the hero of this song bides, until Draer Princess softly weeps, when returning horde of evil rides, yet deep in El'Thune Cap'Tian sleeps."

Cap'Tian stared into the fire long after the song's words floated into the night. "You think me this hero?"

"Here you sit," Oh'Raum said.

Cap'Tian looked at him. "Are you familiar with black root?"

Oh'Raum smiled. "Oh yes. We call it black radish."

"That's what I farm." Cap'Tian held his hands in front of him, envisioning a mound of radishes. "I've pulled black root from my land the size of your fist. That's what I do. Not this," he said and kicked at his lance.

"You're a tiller?" Ra'Chel asked.

Cap'Tian nodded. "I took up arms to protect my land. I joined a small band of men, harassing small groups of Se'Vin's soldiers. We had a few victories and each time, the men claimed it was because of me. More men heard their stories and next I knew; I was their leader. We marched north as more men joined the fight."

"So, you were a great leader?" Ra'Chel asked.

"No, lady, I was a free man fighting for my home."

Oh'Raum stroked his beard. "And that's what we need again. I think I have a plan."

Rowan'Gaff also had a plan. He stood just outside the firelight and eavesdropped. *So, the great hero is nothing more than a dirt farmer.* Memories of his worthless father pierced his hatred. He pulled *Ealhswith* from her scabbard, rolled up his sleeve and slid her across his forearm. He closed his eyes in ecstasy. Each drop of blood felt like a gush of revenge flowing from him. One drop for the needless death of Bodvar, another for Ra'Chel shunning his affections, a third for the pathetic upstart Preslovard, and a final drop of vengeance for the hero, on who he based his life, being nothing more than a liar. Rowan gritted his teeth. They would see his courage after all.

"You will all be witness to what a true hero looks like," he whispered and drew another red line with *Ealhswith*.

Six Day March

The following morning's crossing of the Thune proceeded without incident and the group set their compass south toward D'Grath. The cold mornings ached Oh'Raum's joints and gave Ra'Chel the chance to prod him about Cap'Tian being much older and complaining much less.

"When my age you reach, Princess, more years lay behind than before," he said after a gale of laughter.

Princess, Rowan'Gaff thought and shook his head.

They walked quietly in a wide valley, which sat between the southernmost El'Thune peak, called the Southern Sister, and the foothills of the Great Hooks farther east. South of Tau'Wa Creek, the land opened into the broad, grassy A'Or Plain that stretched from mountains to sea.

"Cap'Tian, where was your farm?" Ra'Chel asked breaking hours of silence.

"Near Bal'Verin Village."

Ra'Chel looked at Oh'Raum unfamiliar with the settlement's name.

Oh'Raum smiled. "Bal'Wern. Today, it's a major trading post and a vassal of Draer."

Cap'Tian nodded. "I have much to learn about this new world."

"I'm sure there will be plenty of land for you to work when Oh'Raum releases us from this quest," Rowan'Gaff said.

"I hold no one against their will."

"Yet here we are."

"You're free to leave," Preslovard said and turned to face him.

The two men glared at each other.

Rowan'Gaff shook his head. "I know I don't match your sword skill."

"And I can't match your ability to complain."

"The road is long, gentleman. We've no time for juvenile squabbles," Oh'Raum said, attempting to diffuse the tension.

Rowan smiled at Preslovard's jibe. "There will come a time when we finish this," Rowan'Gaff said and puffed his chest.

"At your convenience," Pres fired back, turned, and resumed his place at the head of the column.

To their fortune, sparse snowfall in The Great Hooks slowed the waters of Tau'Wa Creek, making their dusk fording easier than expected. They unfurled their blankets under a clear sky, kindled a generous fire, and ate a small dinner.

"How come you to find me?" Cap'Tian asked between slurps of broth.

Ra'Chel looked at Oh'Raum.

He cleared his throat and smiled at the question. "It started with night visions, many years ago."

Cap'Tian looked around the fire. "You all had these visions?"

A sharp pain rose in Rowan'Gaff's chest like a lance driven through his memory.

"Only Rowan'Gaff and I had such visions," Oh'Raum said and looked at his companions. "Unless they've failed to tell me."

Ra'Chel and Pres both shook their heads. Ra'Chel smiled.

"I suppose I dreamed of you because we're kin," Rowan'Gaff said.

Cap'Tian nodded and took another pull from his soup bowl.

"The visions first led me to Ra'Chel along—"

"Mine brought me to Oh'Raum's cottage," Rowan interrupted. "And together we found Ra'Chel."

Oh'Raum let out a breath. "'Tis how it unfolded indeed."

"Do you know where theses visions emanated?"

Oh'Raum shook his head.

"And you've gleaned meaning from them?"

"Aye. I follow this still, I believe."

Cap'Tian nodded again, his eyes roaming from face to face. "The Mystic, the Princess, the Apprentice, and the," he paused at Rowan'Gaff, "Hero?"

"I have no title among this company," Rowan coldly said.

"Rowan?" Ra'Chel said.

"Oh, no," Oh'Raum said. "I think Hero is appropriate, sir. You showed your worth alongside Preslovard in the depths. You played your part in watching over Ra'Chel."

"You made our escape from the garrison possible," Preslovard added, following his father's lead.

"You never left my side," Ra'Chel said.

Cap'Tian looked at Rowan'Gaff. "Sounds like you've lived up to my name fairly well."

"They boast for my sake. As Master Oh'Raum likes to say, I yet have a part to play."

"And there it is," Oh'Raum said.

"Master?" Cap'Tian asked. "You're a master mystic?"

"Titles aside, studying and unlocking the world's ancient knowledge has indeed been my life's pursuit."

Cap'Tian smiled. "When this is concluded, perhaps you will make an offering for fertility over whatever land I till."

Oh'Raum smiled. "It would be my honor to sow with you."

"I still can't fathom that yesterday I stood among my men and today is a thousand years hence."

"What was it like?" Ra'Chel asked.

"What was what like?"

"Living so long ago."

Cap'Tian set his bowl aside and took a deep breath. "Until

Se'Vin's fire worm attacked the north, we lived very peacefully. I bartered with the people of the village and they dealt fairly with me. Rarely did we come to conflict."

"Sounds nice," Ra'Chel said.

"Sounds like our cottage," Preslovard added, "a simple existence."

"And what of this world? What wonders have transpired while I slept?"

"Your victory secured the peace we've all known," Oh'Raum said. "Until eighteen years ago when Se'Vin's descendant— Ver'Sin—once again invaded the north. It was then my visions began. It was then we found Ra'Chel under a covered sun, and it was then I started to glean meanings from it all."

"That's right," Rowan said. "I almost forgot the convergence."

"What?" Ra'Chel asked.

Oh'Raum turned to her. "On the day you floated ashore, *Sköll* devoured the sun."

"As was the day of our victory," Cap'Tian whispered. "We used the conjunction to hide our movements into the city."

Oh'Raum tugged on his beard, his unconscious gesture when deep in thought. "The world has its own sense of time. I take this as another sign of our path. Where I thought it started with my visions, it now looks to have started long before our age."

"And to me, it is yet another sign that what you speak is true, Master Oh'Raum. What can this farmer do to free our lands once again?"

Oh'Raum smiled. "You, my friend, may have the lightest burden of us all."

Rowan'Gaff's stomach churned. He would play his part of this game until his opportunity came. He looked from face to face and thought about the glorious time when they would all see him as he saw himself — and what sweet revenge it would be. Hidden rage boiled over in his heart and all he wanted to do was release more of his pain to the ground, a drop at a time.

They all looked at Oh'Raum. "When we reach D'Grath, our young friends will surreptitiously spread word of your return and if fate is our ally, rally an army." He looked at Preslovard. "I can't stress the covert nature of your task. The King's Guard are alerted, so much so they somehow followed us to Unda'Vager."

Ra'Chel looked at Rowan'Gaff.

"Cap'Tian and I shall continue to the cottage and await your word."

"Should we split up?" Rowan'Gaff asked.

Oh'Raum shook his head. "Sticking together is best for now." He looked at Ra'Chel. "I charge you with keeping these two off each other. And I expect you both to put her well-being above your own."

"Always, Father," Preslovard said.

"I have done nothing else for eighteen years," Rowan added without looking at her.

"That means, putting aside whatever about the other vexes you," Oh'Raum continued.

"Whatever her fate be, father, I will see it done."

Rowan'Gaff nodded, hiding his dark intentions. "As will I."

"Then start in D'Grath. Spread rumors among the pub-goers and square vendors. Be mindful of the ears that hear your words."

Preslovard nodded.

"Then make for Bal'Wern. Lord Bohn will get wind of your gossip soon enough. It is my hope that word reaches Dur'Loth before you. If so, with all haste, find us at my cottage."

"And if none believe us?" Rowan'Gaff asked.

No one answered.

Finally, Ra'Chel said, "Then I go back to my sister to run The Westerly together. This will all be a memory."

"Then Freya and Bodvar crossed the river for nothing," Preslovard whispered.

331

Ra'Chel put a soft hand on his arm.

"The people will rally," Oh'Raum said. "There is yet more to unfold," he looked at Rowan'Gaff, "and great deeds to be done."

Rowan nodded.

The day's march south across the plains passed quickly under a cool and cloud-filled sky. Preslovard spent much of the day showing Ra'Chel the abundant wildflowers growing in this part of the country. Each step not only brought him closer to home, but closer to her. She enjoyed this side of him.

"This one is especially sweet," he said and directed her to a purple bell-flower.

"Oh my."

"It makes a wonderful Summer tea."

Rowan'Gaff walked behind the pair, decapitating flowers with a long, thin reed he picked up the previous day. He watched them frolic like children among the flowers. With each smile and laugh, his cane lashed another stem, lopping off its top half.

Oh'Raum and Cap'Tian took up the column's rear and talked over his plan.

"With speed, they can reach the harbor and back to the cottage within a fortnight," Oh'Raum said.

"So much has changed since last I saw a map of our land."

"Countries are just lines on paper, my friend."

Cap'Tian chuckled. He looked down at the crushed path they walked, cut by their company ahead. Oh'Raum felt the heaviness of his breath. "I never wanted this," Cap'Tian softly said and shook his head.

"We rarely choose the burdens put on us. All we can do is live with them as they come."

"Ha. Spoken in riddles likes a magician true to his secrets."

Oh'Raum smiled and tipped his hat.

Two days passed in the plains before the D'Grath's central tower crested the horizon. They camped in the open, choosing to avoid the trading outpost for another day.

"Although I'd much prefer a soft bed at Olva's, I think it best that Cap'Tian remain free of its trappings," Oh'Raum announced.

"But isn't he the reason we've done all this?"

"Yes Rowan, the time fast approaches when he will do what must be done. For now, speak only of the returned hero in whispers. His symbol can be a far greater ally at this stage."

Cap'Tian shook his head at the word, hero.

"Tomorrow morning, we will ferry to the southern shore and continue to the cottage. You three spend the day's first half in D'Grath and then march to Bal'Wern with all haste."

Preslovard nodded. "What of those south of the Great river?"

Oh'Raum tugged his beard. "I'm afraid they will need to hear the news from different lips."

"Shouldn't this magical army we raise meet somewhere?" Rowan asked.

"I'm trusting those logistics to Lord Bohn. If I know my old friend, he will rally what men gather along the road."

"You're sure they will come?" Ra'Chel asked

"I believe so, my lady. My vision revealed a great army, just as in Cap'Tian's time." He paused. "I believe men will rally to Cap'Tian's banner once again."

"If they want their freedom, they will. But I can't speak to the men of this age," Cap'Tian added.

"I believe they will," Ra'Chel said.

"As do I."

She smiled at Preslovard's assurance.

"We'll know in a few days," Rowan'Gaff muttered and rolled into his blankets.

Dawn broke over the Great Hooks with a crispness in the air that brought rolling steam clouds into the plain's lowlands.

"I wish I was going home with you," Preslovard admitted. He stoked the early morning coals and rubbed his hands together.

"As do I, son. Your part of this was not what either of us intended."

"If not for your training, I don't know I could have made it this far."

Oh'Raum smiled and placed a hand on Preslovard's arm. The young man looked into his father's eyes. "Above all, son, you are my finest accomplishment in this world."

Preslovard returned his smile.

Rowan'Gaff, lay among his blankets, watched their exchange, and remembered Bodvar's tutelage onboard the Wallef. Had he and the Steersman ever had such a moment? He did not recall. Life on the ship fell into two routines: preparing the ship for departure from port and preparing the ship for arrival in port. Within his heart's dark places, his anger toward Preslovard boiled like black oil for having what he could not.

"Someone mentioned a soft bed last night," Cap'Tian said and stretched. "I know I've been asleep for a while, but I don't remember it being so uncomfortable."

"Two days hence, my friend, you'll enjoy the down of a proper bunk."

Cap'Tian smiled at Oh'Raum. "I look forward to it."

"But don't get too used to my bed," Preslovard said. "I plan on returning to it when this business is done."

"Do all men talk so much in the morning?" Ra'Chel asked from under her blanket.

"Only the good ones," Oh'Raum answered to the laughter of his fellows.

After breakfast they packed and crested the low hill to D'Grath.

"With all haste," Oh'Raum said and looked at Preslovard.

"Yes, Father."

Ra'Chel hugged Oh'Raum and Cap'Tian before heading to the outpost gates with the younger men.

Oh'Raum and Cap'Tian watched them from the hilltop until

they passed the city gates. "If we make good time, we will reach my cottage in two days," Oh'Raum said and hiked his pack.

"Then we shall make good time."

"I don't like leaving them," Ra'Chel said when she looked back from the gate.

"I'd be more worried about our lot," Rowan said. "They trek overland, while every guard in the kingdom looks for you."

She shot him a stern look.

"Highness," he whispered with a touch of distain.

"We have work to do," Preslovard said. "Remember my Father's charge; spread rumors but be mindful of the ears who you whisper to."

Preslovard led them through the narrow D'Grath streets to what served as the outpost's pub.

"I've never been in here," Pres admitted. "We normally stay close to Olva's."

The dark tavern smelled like a musty barn stall mixed with the sweet odor of grilled meats. The only light came from the opened door and a smoldering central fire pit. Shanks of meat hung from the ceiling, slowly spinning on chains.

"Close the bloody door," a hoarse voice called from the back of the joint.

Ra'Chel held her nose while following Preslovard to an open table. "My mother would never allow The Westerly to get to this state," she whispered.

Where she looked out of place, Rowan'Gaff looked right at home. He waved over a short, thin man wearing a stained apron. "I'll have a pint and what do you have to eat?"

The waiter pointed a gnarled thumb at the swinging meat. "One coin for the drink, two more for the meat."

"What if I don't like the meat?"

"An additional coin for complaining," the old man said and held out his hand.

Preslovard and Ra'Chel laughed while Rowan handed over his three lesser coins. The old man looked at them.

"We're fine," Ra'Chel said.

"You're not having anything?" Rowan asked.

Ra'Chel leaned over the table. "Not from here."

Rowan'Gaff shrugged, pulled out *Ealhswith*, walked to the fire, and lopped off what he considered a sufficiently cooked piece of meat.

"You're not really going to eat that?" Ra'Chel asked.

"The last good meal I had was at the garrison," he said. "Besides I paid for it." He took a huge bite and relished the flavor.

"What garrison was that?" a voice whispered from behind Preslovard.

Pres and Ra'Chel turned toward a frail man with a swatch of cloth wrapped over this left eye. "My friend never learned its name," Preslovard said.

The man nodded, pulled from his mug, and leaned closer. "I hear tell of an attack on Dilli'Gaf, on the coast near Skorpo. Nothing left but a stony ruin."

The old waiter set a frothy mug in front of Rowan'Gaff.

Preslovard looked from side to side and whispered. "I heard rumors of Cap'Tian's return."

The old man's good eye widened. "The hero, you say?"

Ra'Chel nodded.

"Now that would be a thing."

The trio spent the morning whispering their rumors at market stalls, smithy anvils, and street corners. At every opportunity, they cut their eyes and spread the seeds of rebellion in D'Grath.

By mid-day they set out for Bal'Wern Keep, a three-day journey. At almost a run, they reached Lord Bohn's former stronghold in just over two days and set right to work, carefully whispering their subversive news.

In Long Bridge Tavern, Preslovard returned to their table with fresh mugs. At the end of their table, a stranger sat talking fervently to Rowan'Gaff and Ra'Chel. The man scanned the room often and spoke to Rowan under his breath. He left when Preslovard sat.

"Mission accomplished," Rowan said and took his mug.

"I know we're to keep covert, but everyone at the bar is talking about Cap'Tian. I think tomorrow we can move on to Dur'Loth, then head for the cottage."

"I look forward to seeing my sister," Ra'Chel said.

"I wonder if the Wallef is at port," Rowan said and drained half his cup. "I need to give them news of Bodvar." The name stuck in his throat.

Pres and Ra'Chel remained quiet. Slowly Preslovard raised his mug. Ra'Chel joined him. Rowan'Gaff looked into their eyes and forced himself to continue his charade. He raised his cup to theirs.

"To Bodvar," Pres said.

"For Bodvar," Ra'Chel quietly repeated.

"Bodvar," Rowan'Gaff whispered.

ↂ   ↂ

The trio made excellent time on Keep Road, from Bal'Wern to Dur'Loth Harbor, despite the constant requests to slow down from Rowan'Gaff.

"I thought you wanted to reach your home?" Preslovard asked.

"I do, but I don't want to be whipped like a worthless mule getting there."

At the intersection of Keep Road and Harbor Trail, a day's walk from Dur'Loth, they encountered people streaming north. Men, dressed in makeshift armor, carried farm tools and women toted bandage bushels.

"Where march you?" Preslovard asked.

"To join Cap'Tian against the usurper pup," one man cheerfully answered.

"What?" Ra'Chel asked.

A plump woman trailing her man answered, "Have you not heard? The hero is returned. He attacked the king's garrison at Dilli'Gaf, not a fortnight hence." She laughed. "Burned it to ruins, he did."

Another man chimed in. "I heard he routed an entire garrison in El'Thune. Word came from Holm'Stad of the poor king's rage, not two days hence."

Several of the column laughed at Ver'Sinian's plight.

"How many men are on the road?" Rowan asked.

"The makings of a cohort, at least," the woman answered before shuffling to catch up to her husband.

"Now what?" Rowan'Gaff asked.

"This can't be from our doing," Ra'Chel said.

Preslovard shook his head. "No," he said and stepped off the road. "I think we need to make for the cottage."

"We're not continuing to Dur'Loth?" Rowan asked, distain in his voice.

Preslovard shook his head. "No."

"I'm pressing on. I'd like to sleep in my own bed."

Ra'Chel looked at Preslovard. "I, too, long for home." She paused and looked at the ramshackle soldiers passing by. "But I fear Cap'Tian's army rallied without him."

"So, you're going with him?" Rowan'Gaff asked.

She looked at Rowan and her expression softened. "I am."

"Right then," Rowan said, turned, and set out for Dur'Loth.

Ra'Chel stepped after him until Preslovard's arm softly caught her. "His path lies upon a different road," Pres said.

Ra'Chel looked deep into his eyes.

"Ours lies together, Princess," he whispered.

Rowan'Gaff fumed. Each step felt like a knife driven into him by their eyes. He knew the fools watched. He forced himself not to look back for fear of looking weak. *Tonight, I will sleep in my own bed*, he thought, *and tomorrow I find the Wallef.*

Cap'Tian's Army

Oh'Raum and Cap'Tian left the thick wood line and entered a wide clearing, backing up to the foothills of The Great Hooks. The secluded cottage sat nestled in the middle of the clearing lined with animal pens and colorful garden rows.

Oh'Raum smiled at the vegetables nearing harvest. "I'll need to pay Oy'Vid a visit with these good crops his sons tended for me."

"A good harvest indeed," Cap'Tian agreed.

A cool mountain breeze ushered them to the cottage where Oh'Raum opened the door and invited Cap'Tian into his home. They set their packs near the central table and Oh'Raum drew them fresh water mugs.

"You have a wonderful, secluded home, Master Oh'Raum."

Oh'Raum returned a wide smile and looked around the common room. "It has served my purposes."

As agreed, Oy'Vid's sons made regular visits to the cottage to look after the animals, tend the garden, and maintain the house. His belongings were right where his long memory expected them, and some items appeared to be freshly cleaned or mended.

Cap'Tian drew long from his mug, the cool, sweet water sapping the heat from the day's march. Neither of them spoke the question burning through them both. *I wonder how our young friends are getting on?* They talked of other things:

history, politics, and how the world had changed since Cap'Tian's victory over Se'Vin.

Word would come when it came and neither an eleven-hundred-year-old farmer, nor a renowned wizard could change that.

That news came six days later when a breathless Preslovard staggered into the cottage and collapsed into a chair. Ra'Chel trailed behind him, equally haggard.

"What has happened?" Oh'Raum asked and handed them both water.

"We nearly ran here from Dur'Loth," Pres said.

"Were you pursued?" Cap'Tian asked.

Ra'Chel shook her head and answered while Preslovard drank deeply. "An army marches north, six days hence."

"What?"

"Your army," Preslovard added.

"Where is Rowan'Gaff?" Oh'Raum asked.

"Remained in Dur'Loth."

"We must leave at once," Cap'Tian said, anger burning his words. "An army marches in my name and here I am sleeping on a soft bed half a country away."

"These two are in no condition for more days on the road."

Preslovard shook his head. "We need to go now."

Ra'Chel nodded. "We'll be fine," she laughed, "as long as Preslovard isn't setting the pace."

Oh'Raum looked at Cap'Tian. "Pack your things. We leave at once."

An hour later, the four left the tranquility of Oh'Raum's cottage for the Lake Fal'Run trail. Instead of heading north, as custom dictated, they headed due west for Long Bridge Crossing.

Cap'Tian pestered Pres and Ra'Chel for information.

"We didn't do much," she confessed. "We followed Master Oh'Raum's instruction and carefully spread rumor of your return."

"By the time we reached Bal'Wern, word spread that you had sacked Dilli'Gaf," Preslovard added.

Ra'Chel laughed.

"But I didn't."

"We know," Ra'Chel said. "We did."

Oh'Raum smiled. "The symbol is often greater than the reality."

"Word came of the king's displeasure of losing an entire garrison in El'Thune Hills. You did that as well."

Cap'Tian shook his head.

Oh'Raum placed a hand on his shoulder. "Let the people have their hero."

"They make me out to be something I'm not. How do I live up to the stories?"

"You don't have to," Ra'Chel said and looked at Oh'Raum.

They walked at a faster than normal pace and reached Long Bridge at dusk on the third day. Men strew the ground and numerous small fires burned along the shoreline. Women tended wounded men while others picked through the debris and the dead.

"We must cross tonight," Oh'Raum said and ushered the company north.

"They skirmished for control of the bridge?" Cap'Tian asked.

"This was not where we crossed," Ra'Chel added.

"Cap'Tian," a weak voice called. "Cap'Tian."

Cap'Tian followed the pleas through the mounds of fallen soldiers to a leather-armored, muck-covered man. Blood stained his tunic, hands, and face.

"Cap'Tian, my commander," the wretch moaned.

"I am here, friend." Cap'Tian knelt beside the man and clasped wrists with him.

"We cleared the bridge of those black armored devils." He coughed several times and spat blood.

"You did well," Cap'Tian said, pausing awkwardly.

"Iro'Far."

"You did well, Iro'Far."

Iro'Far coughed again and smiled at the commendation. "I am not long for the river, commander. Would you help me sit?" He coughed and winced when Cap'Tian lifted him.

Oh'Raum stood behind Cap'Tian. Ra'Chel tore a swatch from her blanket, moistened it, and offered it to Cap'Tian.

Iro'Far looked into Cap'Tian's face and smiled while he wiped the cool rag on the man's forehead. "Have I earned your blessing?"

Ra'Chel's breath hitched. Preslovard drew her close.

Cap'Tian picked up a nearby sword and lay it across the wounded man's chest. Iro'Far clasped it, his knuckles whitening. "Iro'Far, my soldier, my friend, I salute you and lift my mug to you."

Tears rolled from Iro'Far's eyes, cutting clean lines down his dirty cheeks. His eyes fluttered and his grip on the sword faltered. "We gutted the bastar—" Iro'Far's head sank to his chest and he dropped the sword.

Cap'Tian's chest heaved. He gently rested Iro'Far to the ground and remained by his side, his own head lowered. "May your journey across the river be swift," he whispered.

Cap'Tian stood. Fury boiled within him. He turned to Oh'Raum, the setting sun bathing his face in fierce orange light.

Oh'Raum nodded and turned for the bridge. No words needed speaking.

Preslovard and Ra'Chel fell in behind them, still holding each other.

ରୟ   ฅ

The Wallef's single mast bobbed in the morning fog, familiar and recognizable from Dur'Loth's long dock. Rowan'Gaff expected Hroar and the men sleeping one off at The Westerly, but the inn sat virtually deserted.

Rowan'Gaff climbed down the slick ladder to a poorly tied dory bobbing in the water. He boarded the slim rowboat, took up the oars, and slid cleanly away from the dock pillars.

"Ahoy, Wallef," he called when the gunwales appeared in the mist.

"Ahoy," a voice called back.

"It is I, Rowan'Gaff."

"Grimsson?"

"Aye."

"Is Bodvar with you?"

Rowan'Gaff did not answer.

"Oy, mates. Master Rowan brings our steersman."

Groggy voices rose from the decking, some asking questions, others cursing the mist and the hour.

Rowan'Gaff pulled the boat alongside and tied off.

Her'Jolf's sunken face peered over the gunwale and scanned the empty row boat. "Oy, where is Bodvar?"

Rowan climbed aboard the larger ship. "Permission to come aboard?"

"You're already on board. Where is Bodvar?" a stronger voice asked from behind him.

Rowan'Gaff turned. Hroar, Bodvar's First Mate approached. The two shook forearms and Hroar stepped back awaiting an answer.

Rowan looked at the ship's decking and allowed his anger to rise like a rushing torrent. "Oh'Raum Yulr let him die."

"What?" one of the deckhands asked from the ship's bow.

Hroar stepped closer.

"We were..." Rowan paused. "His apprentice led us into a cave." He looked around at the deckhands. More rose from their blankets to hear the story. "We fought our way out. I was in front. Bodvar was near Oh'Raum behind me. I must have killed a hundred creatures."

"Creatures?"

"Oh'Raum never said a word during our escape. Bodvar

was consumed and Oh'Raum kept running. I would've gone back for Bodvar had I known. Oh'Raum let him die."

Hroar turned and walked the length of the ship. Several deckhands whispered farewells to their friend and Steersman. At the bow, Hroar turned and addressed the crew. "Our Steersman has crossed the river. Mourn him in your own way. To many of us, he was more than the captain of this ship, he was our friend," Hroar looked at Rowan'Gaff, "and the closest person we could call father."

Rowan'Gaff nodded. "As a person who called him father and the only person with him at the time, I have a request. I plan to avenge him, but I need your help."

"Name it," Hroar answered.

"I need passage to Helsem."

Hroar silently looked him up and down, considering what could be going through the young man's mind. The Wallef's crew turned to face Hroar, awaiting his decision.

"I hear of an army marching on Holm'Stad," Her'Jolf said to his mates' agreement.

Hroar scanned the crews' faces. "Bodvar left us to honor his word to Oh'Raum Yulr." The deckhands nodded. "He also left for promised coin, and part of that coin belonged us all. If what Grimsson says is true, we all own a part of Bodvar's death."

The deckhands looked at each other.

Hroar continued, "I would repay that by honoring Grimsson's request."

"As would I," Her'Jolf said. Many of the crew agreed. Some muttered but kept their protestations to themselves.

"When do we sail?" Hroar asked Rowan'Gaff.

"At your convenience, Steersman."

Hroar nodded. "Make ready for departure," he shouted.

ॐ   ℘

The Long Bridge battlefield stretched a furlong passed the

bridge's northern shore. Women tended what wounded remained alive and old men carted the dead away on makeshift blanket stretchers.

Cap'Tian walked in silence, his focus on reaching the vanguard of the army fighting in his name. Calls for the hero came from the roadside, and each time he heard his name, Cap'Tian stopped and soothed the wounded and dying. His presence and blessings ushered many across the river.

"How long can he keep this up?" Ra'Chel asked.

"As long as he must," Oh'Raum answered.

They made camp on the eastern slopes of Lash'Rin Bluffs, ate a wordless dinner, and wrapped in their blankets for an early sleep.

Ra'Chel lay on her side looking at Preslovard. He also lay watching her. They stared into each other's eyes which made Ra'Chel giggle every few minutes. Even under the cloud of war and despair from the day's long march, the two lifted each other with nothing more than a smile and a wink.

The next morning, they rose early with the intent of making the fork at Harbor Trail and King's Road. Cap'Tian set the pace, pulling the rest with his will to reach the impending battle.

The road teamed with refugees, wounded, and families returning south. Cap'Tian asked each for news.

"The King's Guard broke and ran at the River Thune."

"Cap'Tian freed the conscripts at Or'Nath."

"What an honor to fight next to Cap'Tian," a man on a rough-hewn crutch said.

The news sped their march and just after sunset they camped outside a field hospital north of the Harbor Trail fork.

Oh'Raum aided in treating the wounded with an abundance of remedies found in his pack while Cap'Tian toured the strewn soldiers. They lay on bloodied blankets, some conscious, some not. Some recognized him. Most did not.

Many called his name. "Cap'Tian, why are you not at the front of the column?"

"I wanted to see that your hard-earned wounds are properly tended."

"Is that Master Oh'Raum, the mystic?"

"Aye," Cap'Tian answered and smiled.

"Brothers, Cap'Tian has a brought a powerful wizard to heal us," one man called.

"Hail, Cap'Tian!" they shouted.

Ra'Chel assisted the nurses while Preslovard worked with Oh'Raum to dispense herbal pain medicaments.

"I don't know what's going to happen when we reach the columns vanguard," Cap'Tian said when they gathered around their nightly fire.

"We're not leaving you."

"I don't think that's what he means, lady," Oh'Raum said.

"For too long, my world has been warfare. Be it before my treacherous sleep or after," Cap'Tian admitted and stared at the flames for answers. "I wish this torment to end," he whispered and looked at Oh'Raum.

Oh'Raum shook his head and searched his memory for an answer. Visions flooded the old mystic: the glowing hero, the dying man, the prisoner.

"What have you seen, wizard?"

"For many years I have searched my dreams for answers and although they follow our course, I'm not able to see them beforehand. Neither do I clearly see the players." He locked eyes with Cap'Tian. "I have not seen you cross the river." He turned to Ra'Chel. "I have also not seen you enthroned."

Preslovard waited for his master's pronouncement on his behalf. When Oh'Raum said nothing, Pres said, "I'm looking forward to the quiet of the meadow."

Oh'Raum smiled. "As am I."

"I heard that many a conscript turned when their cohort engaged our countryman," Preslovard said. "I am glad they are free from that tyranny."

Ra'Chel put a hand on his arm. Oh'Raum smiled at their

growing relationship. "It is fitting for those forced to fight to do so against their tormentors."

Cap'Tian slammed a fist on his thigh. "These invaders have much to answer for."

"Indeed," Oh'Raum agreed.

"My rage will not be content with taking the city." Cap'Tian stared into the fire. "I shall send this boy-king across the river." His impassive tone sent chills through Ra'Chel.

"And his dark host will accompany him," Preslovard added.

Oh'Raum stroked his beard. "Dark thoughts lead to dark deeds, friends. We know not what tomorrow brings. If we must fight, then we fight. I prefer to look forward to the installation of the rightful heir." He smiled at Ra'Chel who flushed.

"That prospect scares me," she admitted.

Oh'Raum laughed. "As it should, dear. It is no small thing to rule."

"I'm afraid I won't do very well."

"First we focus on winning the peace, then we shall worry about keeping it."

"Agreed," Ra'Chel said.

Two days later, they crossed the bridge at the River Thune where Preslovard recounted his exhaustion and eventual conscription.

Encampments grew in number the farther north they trekked. Groups of men huddled around small fires, some tending wounds and others keeping watch.

"We've secured the bridge, commander," one said and saluted when Cap'Tian approached.

Cap'Tian returned his salute and nodded.

"What news do you bring of the battle?" another asked.

Cap'Tian looked at Oh'Raum. "When we reach the city gates, we shall expel the usurper!"

Hails and cheers rippled through the men. They ogled Cap'Tian when he passed. Several asked to join him and return to the front.

Oh'Raum stepped in to placate the requests which eased Cap'Tian's discomfort. "Valiant men are you," he would say. "Rest here knowing the battle goes on."

"Hail, Cap'Tian!"

A similar scene played out at the Hill Creek crossing and the trail to the Or'Nath mines. The road clogged with fighters heading north and wounded heading south. Calls of, "Hail, Cap'Tian," and, "Our commander," grew more frequent when they reached the tail of the main body.

Those who did not recognize Cap'Tian spread stories of his deeds at the front of their column, "He slew five men with one thrust of his lance."

"I stood beside him in battle."

"He rallied us on the northern road before the king's scraps broke and ran for the city?"

Those who did recognize the hero of legend, asked for his blessing and good tidings of the victory to come.

Cap'Tian played his role with each step north and used every word to spur his inner fire. He smiled at stories of his battle prowess and gave praise when asked for it. Leagues further on, he sheltered the wounded and thanked the nurses who tended them.

Oh'Raum and Preslovard, scoured the forests nightly to replenish their medical supplies. Ra'Chel cooked, brought food to the wounded, and kept their encampment fires burning with fuel.

At mid-day on the tenth day after leaving the cottage, cries of, "Hail, Cap'Tian!" broke among the front lines facing Holm'Stad's high walls. The army camped outside arrow shot of the battlements with tents lining the road in neat rows. The rows led to four large, command tents.

"Lord Bohn," Oh'Raum called to his companions and pointed at a banner flapping from one of the larger tents.

Soft, tufted grass led through the tent flap and spread from wall to wall. Oh'Raum stopped just inside the tent's opening at the sudden color change — from soft green in direct sunlight to brighter, bolder green within the tent. A jagged memory shot through the old mystic's mind. *Men die here,* he thought and shuddered.

"Master Oh'Raum!" Lord Keir'Gim Bohn announced when the mystic entered the long tent. Keir'Gim showed a genuine smile and walked forward, his hand outstretched in greeting.

Cap'Tian, Preslovard, and Ra'Chel entered behind Oh'Raum. Lord Bohn turned to his attendants. "Bring food and cold water for these important travelers." He invited them to unburden and rest while his attendants arranged refreshments on the long, central table.

"You know Preslovard, my apprentice," Oh'Raum said, making introductions. Lord Bohn welcomed Pres. "This is Ra'Chel Brune," Oh'Raum hesitated and looked into Ra'Chel's smiling face.

"My favorite traveling companion," Preslovard said.

Oh'Raum spoke slowly, "And this is Cap'Tian Vay'Mar."

"My Lord Cap'Tian." Lord Bohn whispered and knelt.

"Please, friend," Cap'Tian said and lifted Bohn. "We are brothers here."

"A greater compliment I have never received," the master of Bal'Wern Keep said.

Oh'Raum nodded and turned to Keir'Gim. "Rumors we heard on the road."

Lord Bohn joined them at the table and thinned his lips. "Of Cap'Tian, no doubt. The men claimed seeing the hero among them in battle. Others made reference to his great deeds which they claimed to witness. To my shame, I did not discourage such things." He beamed at the legendary hero at his table. "But now here he sits. I still can't really believe..."

"And what of your plans for the city," Oh'Raum asked.

"We prepare for siege. Tell me, friend Cap'Tian, how did you take the city in your day?"

Cap'Tian laughed. "Twas not the city you see beyond that

curtain. My enemy did not also have..." he looked at Oh'Raum.

"Eighteen," Oh'Raum said.

"Eighteen years of control over the land," Cap'Tian concluded.

Bohn nodded.

"Ver'Sinian is a pup," Oh'Raum said. "He knows not the damage a prolonged fight would precipitate. I also suspect he will sacrifice his entire army to cover his own retreat."

"And lest we forget his family's history of treachery?" Preslovard added.

Cap'Tian nodded. "We should anticipate his ultimate cowardice. Have you a map?"

Lord Bohn showed them to his planning table where a large map lay. Small, wood-carved figures stretched like chess pawns, from Hill Creek to the Cher'Ul Hills, north of Holm'Stad.

Cap'Tian tapped Far'Verm Pass. "Have you dispatched scouts to the pass?"

Lord Bohn shook his head.

Cap'Tian looked at Oh'Raum. "Do so."

"If we have the reserves, send a band of men to the northern mines as well," Oh'Raum added. "There is a slippery means of escape there."

"It will be done," Bohn said and smiled at his old friend.

"Do we know of ships moored in Helsem?" Cap'Tian continued.

"My scouts have reported a scant few. No warships."

"I don't see Ver'Sinian going to sea," Oh'Raum added. "His homeland lies East. It is the pass or nothing."

Cap'Tian nodded. "Do we know the king remains in the city?"

"They are hold up like ants in a winter downpour," Lord Bohn answered.

"Then we shall crush them like ants," Cap'Tian said and slammed a fist on the city of Holm'Stad.

The Fall of Ver'Sinian

The Wallef's bow carved a clean line in the mud upon reaching the beach at the apex of Helsem Fjord.

"You have done a great service this day," Rowan'Gaff called to the ship's men.

"In fond memory of Bodvar, Grimsson" Hroar said and clasped wrists with the young man before Rowan vaulted the side to the marshy shore. He pushed the ship from the mud, waved, and followed the path leading to the walled city's western gate. Half a league south, Cap'Tian's army prepared their siege while inside the walls, the remnants of Ver'Sinian's Guard prepared their defense.

Alone, Rowan'Gaff walked to the gate, easily within bowshot from the rampart.

"Look mates, the enemy army approaches," a voice called out from above the gate. Laughter rippled along the wall and men crowded the crenelations to see the fool outside the gate.

"Are you lost, son?" another solder called.

"I seek an audience with the king," Rowan returned.

More jeers and laughter erupted within the walls.

"Move along, boy. This is no place for jesters."

"I will not move on and I will speak to the king before the end of the day, sir."

Mutterings broke out among the solders. "Brave or foolish, this one is," and "Does he wish an arrow now or an arrow later?"

"Call for Jawaad," a man of the watch called.

A moment later, the form of a taller man rose above the wall. "I left my lunch for you, boy. My men tell me you wish to speak to the king."

"Your men speak true," Rowan'Gaff shouted.

"And why would our king parlay with you?"

"I know something he doesn't."

The assembled laughed at this fool's reckless bravado.

Jawaad looked to his men, smiling. "And what would that be?"

"I know where the old man and the girl are."

The battlement fell silent. Rowan'Gaff stood his ground and stared at their commander, awaiting the inevitable question.

"Where?"

"I answer that question to the king alone," Rowan said.

A small door opened in the imposing city gate and the tall, armor-clad man approached. "You play a dangerous game, young man."

Rowan'Gaff smiled. "I play no game."

"After you," Jawaad said and fell in behind Rowan.

Rowan'Gaff stepped through the wicket. Inside the gate, a row of pike-wielding soldiers greeted him.

"You'll leave your weapons here," Jawaad said after joining him.

Rowan'Gaff set his pack on a nearby bench, loosed his baldric, and lay *Ealhswith* atop the equipment. "I expect it all back," he said.

"If the king doesn't like what you have to say, getting your equipment back will be the least of your worries. Follow me."

Rowan'Gaff followed the guard-captain through the city's narrow streets. They approached a heavily guarded central keep and a large pair of wooden gates. A portcullis hung over the entrance like a castle within a castle.

"Wait here," Jawaad commanded and entered the keep.

The guards eyed Rowan'Gaff, not as a threat but a curiosity. "So, what are you then?" one asked.

Rowan did not answer.

"I asked you a question."

Rowan turned to the guard. "Mind your door."

"You hear how he talks to me, Yusri?"

The guard opposite the door looked at Rowan'Gaff. "Perhaps a lesson this one needs."

"I have information vital to the king. Consider that when administering your lesson," Rowan said and stepped closer. "Would be a pity should he not receive what I carry," he whispered.

The guard stood motionless.

Jawaad appeared in the opened doorway. "Come with me," he ordered.

Rowan'Gaff smiled at the gate guard and moved into the inner keep. The change in opulence struck him. Beyond the gatehouse, dirt roads led through narrowly placed houses and shops. Inside, a wide courtyard extended between column-lined walkways. Large paving stones covered the expansive plaza.

The two crossed the yard and entered an ornate door. They followed several twisting corridors before stopping at another guarded double door.

"Should you leave this room, I'll have your things brought to you," Jawaad coldly said before leaving him outside the door.

The outer guards knocked lightly on the door, which opened to reveal two inner guards, who carried long, black pikes and waited to escort him forward.

King Ver'Sinian Caropa sat on a massive throne, raised slightly from the floor on a gleaming white dais. On his right sat an old, bearded man dressed in a fine robe. Behind the king, four guards lined the audience chamber's rear wall. A balcony ran the length of the room on which archers stood at even intervals. A shaft of light penetrated a high window behind the throne casting a long shadow on the marble floor.

Rowan'Gaff approached the king, flanked by the two enormous guards. He felt naked without *Ealhswith* but forced his feet forward on raw vengeance. He stopped where the shadow ended and bowed to the young king.

Ver'Sinian interlaced his fingers and watched Rowan'Gaff. Finally, he asked, "Who are you and how do you know of the old man and the girl?"

"I am Rowan'Gaff Grimsson and I am deep in your enemy's camp, Great King."

Ver'Sinian looked at his advisor.

"Explain," the old man said.

"Many years ago, I had night visions of the old man and fell under his spell. His bastard son and the girl you seek led my father to his death."

"Where are they now?"

"I seek to pour out my vengeance upon them," Rowan'Gaff continued.

"Answer Arbas' question," Ver'Sinian said.

"They are on the road north to join the army at your southern gate. They may yet be plotting their attack on this city." He paused allowing the echo of the room to fade. "They have awakened Cap'Tian."

Several archers gasped at the name.

"My spies have only rumors," Ver'Sinian said.

"Rumors spread by the girl and Oh'Raum's apprentice — but rumors no longer as I have shared many nights in Cap'Tian's counsel."

"Deep in their camp, indeed," Arbas whispered.

"You speak of vengeance. What plan have you?"

"A friend they yet regard me and welcome I am in their tents. I wish a painful end on them for my father's death," Rowan sternly said.

Ver'Sinian turned and whispered with Arbas who looked at Rowan'Gaff several times. Finally, the king straightened.

"What have you to prove your claims?" Arbas asked.

Rowan'Gaff smiled. "I know the truth of what happened in El'Thune." He looked to the king. "A garrison you lost there?"

The king remained still and awaited his evidence.

"Your men found our trail, how I know not. They followed us into the cave where Cap'Tian slept. Hideous creatures live in the depths. Where we crept passed them to the hero's tomb, your men walked into their lair. We opened the tomb and the girl's tears sprang him to life." He shook his head. "I still can't believe it was all real."

"As the song says, majesty," Arbas quietly said.

"And this girl claims to be a princess? She wishes my throne?"

Rowan did not answer. "When we emerged from the tomb, your men were engaged with the cave's inhabitants. We cut our way through the fighting and escaped." Rowan cleared his throat. "Your men apparently, did not."

"Rumors are dangerous things, majesty," Arbas said. He turned to Rowan. "You saw this man rise with your own eyes? You swear it on your father's name?"

Rowan'Gaff stared the old man down. "I did," he paused, "and I do."

Arbas leaned in close and whispered in Ver'Sinian's ear. The king nodded.

"Would you gain access for our men to the enemy's tent?" Arbas asked.

"I will," Rowan said.

"And identify our enemies?"

"I will."

"And kill them yourself to avenge your father?"

Rowan'Gaff hesitated and shifted his eyes from Arbas to the king. "I will."

"It shows great courage to commit such treachery," Ver'Sinian said. "Your ancestors would be proud."

Rowan'Gaff laughed. *If only you knew my ancestor,* he

thought.

"When our spies confirm our enemies are outside the gate, you will leave the city and rejoin your former compatriots."

An attendant showed Rowan'Gaff to a small, but comfortable, room. Servants brought him food and when he left to explore, an escort never stood outside of arm's reach. The king's proxy, Arbas, scrutinized his every move and, no doubt, reported it to the king.

Word arrived that the old man and the girl were among the encamped following two days within the city. In the audience chamber, Rowan received his instructions.

"These three men will accompany you," Arbas said. In front of him stood three men in similar dark clothes. Hoods covered their faces. "They will assist in resolving our mutual problem."

Rowan'Gaff eyed the trio.

"Tonight, you will leave through the western gate. Our scouts report minimal activity along the coast. From there, we are relying on you."

Rowan nodded and a smirk grew at the corner of his mouth.

ෆ ෧

Cap'Tian stepped next to Lord Bohn and Oh'Raum out of bow shot from Holm'Stad's Southern gate.

"Ver'Sinian Caropa!" Cap'Tian yelled. "The free people of the Western Kingdoms demand you hear us."

The assembled army behind him shouted. This brought a similar shout from the king's army lining the city's high walls.

"This is your one and only chance to leave these lands with your life," Cap'Tian shouted.

"Go home, farmer," a soldier on the wall yelled back to the jeers and laughter of his comrades.

"Your men, however, have already sealed their fate," Cap'Tian hurled back.

"No Caropa minion leaves this field alive," Bohn shouted.

Cap'Tian's army roared their agreement behind Lord Bohn's statement.

The army on the wall quieted when a short man appeared over the gate's rampart. His golden and silver armor gleamed in the morning sun.

"I wonder, do rumors bleed?" He did not shout.

"I will find out, My King," one among his company said.

Ver'Sinian smiled and looked from one end of the assembled to the other. "Not much of an army you have. Who tends their crops while they stand before me playing soldier?"

"If the king had ever set foot outside his keep, perhaps he would know," Oh'Raum called forward. "Too busy counting his taxes and plotting his brothers' murders."

Sneers arose among the troops at the jibe.

"And what know you of death, wizard? Bring forth your upstart wench so I may show her my favor."

The king's men hooted and laughed.

"How long does this go on?" Ra'Chel asked Oh'Raum.

"I don't know. I've never sieged a city before," he said and winked at her.

Cap'Tian turned to Lord Bohn. "The princess is right. We take this city."

Lord Bohn nodded and walked the line to Cap'Tian's right.

Preslovard, who stood next to Oh'Raum turned and smiled at Ra'Chel. "I will find you after."

She smiled before he turned and walked the army's front line to Cap'Tian's left.

Cap'Tian raised his lance. Bohn and Preslovard drew their swords to the cheers of the men. The army beat their weapons against wooden shields, driving thundering jolts into the ground and readying themselves for the charge.

"Shields together!" Cap'Tian shouted.

The army's front lines slid together, interlocked their shields into a two-high wall. A third row held their shields above their heads and linked them with the second row at a backward angle. The next several rows of soldiers followed this pattern until the entire cohort inched forward under the shield wall's protection.

"Forward!" Cap'Tian ordered.

Slowly, three groups of raised shields moved forward to the base of Holm'Stad's walls. Archers rained flaming arrows on the interlocked shields. Behind the first wave, archers shot men from the walls behind large, moveable barricades.

Cap'Tian and Oh'Raum, protected within the central shield wall, inched toward Holm'Stad's vulnerable wooden gate. Arrows pummeled the shields and when a lucky shot penetrated the armor, a solder in reserve quickly filled the breach.

Oh'Raum, protected by a second layer of shields within the outer layer, cradled a loaf-sized pouch.

"What is this concoction?" Bohn had asked the night before while Oh'Raum prepared the compound.

"We don't have a word for it," Oh'Raum had replied, smiling. "Needless to say, neither do our enemies."

Oh'Raum had poured several oil drops into a stone mortar and carefully ground its contents.

Preslovard had turned to Bohn. "It smells bad because of the guano."

"As I've never made this before, I'd appreciate some quiet," Oh'Raum had said.

"And if you mix it wrong?" Bohn had asked and took a step away from the mortar.

"We all cross the river."

The shield wall reached the massive wooden gate under a hail of arrows. Boiling water, poured from the ramparts, broke the rear of their formation. The remaining solders quickly recovered only after several of their comrades fell to multiple arrow hits.

Oh'Raum stepped forward, opened the stopper on his pouch and spread a generous bead along the gate's frame. He spread a thick layer around the wicket and plunged the remainder between any exposed beams.

"Right," he called.

"To the rear," Cap'Tian shouted and the remaining shields moved out of bowshot.

Bohn and Preslovard pressed their cohorts to the wall. "Ladder," the Bal'Wern governor called forward.

The shield wall split, bifurcated by a tall ladder. Several men on each leg hoisted the ladder to the rampart and anchored by hanging beneath it from its lowest rungs. The moment the ladder smacked the crenelations, soldiers scampered up it while arrows dropped the stragglers.

Orders flew along the walls to reinforce fighting positions and bring forward poles to topple the ladders. Cap'Tian's archers zeroed in on the ladder summits, aiming for anyone trying to push the ladders over. Soldiers streamed forward and mounted the tall ladders taking the fighting to the rampart.

Cap'Tian leaned close to Oh'Raum. "You sure this is going to work."

"Archer," Oh'Raum called, "loose your arrow."

The archer, tapped his arrowhead against a nearby torch, drew back, aimed, and launched his missile at Holm'Stad's southern gate.

The flaming arrow struck the gate's lower third. Orange flames danced upward while dribbles of flaming oil trickled down the beams.

Cap'Tian gave Oh'Raum a sideways glance.

The gate erupted in brilliant orange fire. The explosive concussion pushed Cap'Tian back a step and threw several soldiers from Holm'Stad's walls. Massive chunks of support beams bounced among the soldiers and splinters flew in all directions, flung from the rampart like shrapnel.

"Lords of the underworld," Cap'Tian said.

Oh'Raum smiled. "Not bad for iron forge scrapings and bat sh—"

A shouting horde of armored knights poured from the gaping hole where the thick, oak gate once stood.

"Forward," Cap'Tian shouted.

The hero's front lines charged forward, crashing into Ver'Sinian's onrushing soldiers in fierce combat. Cap'Tian led the charge with his lance thrusting forward like a snake's tongue tasting the air. Bright blood splattered his shield with each lightning-fast thrust of his spear. Beside him, Oh'Raum moved with the speed of man half his age. He danced around slashing swords and parried pike jabs. His own sword worked among the crushing enemy. Black-armored soldiers fell to his masterful strikes.

Cap'Tian led his forces steadily forward until the rush of Ver'Sinian's men dwindled. "Reserves!" He shouted. His command echoed behind him, rippling through the ranks.

Ra'Chel stood at the rear of the battle, flanked by rows of white tents. Beside her, a dozen of Bohn's hand-picked guards encircled her. "Now!" she screamed.

On both sides of the road, men burst from the tents and ran forward, shouting. Although at a full sprint, they stayed abreast in advancing rows like waves crashing along a bloody shore.

The reserves entered the fray, filling empty positions, scrambling up ladders, and pushing the king's guard from the battlements. Cap'Tian pressed forward with renewed vigor.

The army broke Ver'Sinian's lines and took the bailey just inside the southern gate.

"Left side — secure the gate," Cap'Tian commanded. "Right side — with me." He looked to his right and two dozen men stepped forward awaiting his next order. Cap'Tian smiled and dashed through the streets toward the keep.

Lord Bohn's contingent secured the eastern wall while Preslovard set watches along the western ramparts and held the west gate. Oh'Raum, winded from the battle, remained near the main gate. He looked south, across a sea of slaughter, to the encampment and rose his sword to Ra'Chel.

A cry rolled through the city from east to west. "Huzzah!"

Oh'Raum raised his bloody sword and echoed the triumphant call. "Huzzah!"

The call echoed around Cap'Tian. He led his men through the narrow city streets, bursting into the keep's central courtyard. "Fan out," he ordered. "Bring me the king."

Remnants of the King's Guard put up little defense within the keep. Their lines broke against the rushing, frenzied enemy. Cap'Tian slammed through the throne room doors expecting to be met with a barrage of arrows. Inside, he found an old man sitting to the right of the immense wooden throne.

"Where is he?" Cap'Tian thundered and lowered his lance at the man's chest.

The old man stared defiantly at his attacker. "I am Arbas," he said in a calm voice. "I am his majesty's *Vücut Yardimi.*" He paused. "Aid, in your tongue. I..."

"Where is the boy-king?" Cap'Tian asked again, cutting off the old man's words.

Several fighters joined Cap'Tian in the main audience chamber.

"We did not anticipate the use of magic during your siege," Arbas said.

"Cap'Tian, we've searched the keep. There's no sign..."

Arbas interlaced his fingers and set them in his lap. "So, you're the Sleeper of legend?" Arbas asked.

"Last chance, Aid," Cap'Tian spat. "Where did he go? Answer or meet your fate."

Arbas' expression changed. A shred of doubt slithered across his tanned face like a lizard. "I expected more from you, *Uykucu.*"

Cap'Tian lunged forward in practiced elegance, raking his spear across the brow of his shield. His lightning-fast thrust struck Arbas in the chest, piercing his opulent rope. Blood sprayed the back wall when his lance exploded from the old man's back.

Cap'Tian withdrew his lance and returned to his previous position; lance resting atop the lip of his shield. Gore dripped from his spear and sloshed the marble floor.

Arbas looked down at the gaping hole where his chest had been. His arms drew up and his hands curled into malformed claws before the old man fell to the floor, dead.

Cap'Tian turned to his men. "He was left here to give the rat more time to run."

"Where did he run?" one of the men asked.

Cap'Tian's face grew into a snarl. "He fled east. Come, we must outpace him," he said and shouldered his way through the men.

Cap'Tian ran through the city for the remnants of the main gate. "The welp is not in the keep, Master Oh'Raum," Cap'Tian said between heavy breaths.

"I did not expect him to be."

"The mines?"

Oh'Raum nodded.

"Then our work is not done here," Cap'Tian said and walked through the breached southern gate. He walked to the middle of the battle, raised his lance, and addressed the city walls. "Men of the west, hear me."

A hush passed through the victorious.

"The usurper has escaped our grasp. We cannot let him pass through the mountains."

The men listened and muttered their grumblings.

"We have men on the pass, and I mean to join them. I will not let another Caropa escape these lands."

The murmur grew and shouts of, "We're with you, Cap'Tian," and, "Lead on, Commander," rained down.

Cap'Tian turned and set off for the Eastern mountains at a slow jog. Fighters fell in behind him in orderly rows which filled the width of Fire Worm Road.

Preslovard descended a flight of steps beside the main gate rampart and joined his master. Oh'Raum hugged his son.

"A gruesome affair, father."

"You accorded yourself well. Leading men in battle is no small thing."

Preslovard scanned the dead and wounded outside the gate. "I see now that slaying the cave dwellers was no less gruesome."

"Men must do what they must, son. You saved more lives than you've taken."

"Perhaps."

Oh'Raum watched Cap'Tian's division jog into the distance. "Do you not join the hero for this final battle?"

"No father. I prefer a more enjoyable mission," Preslovard said and waved at Ra'Chel who returned a beaming smile.

"Careful, my son. That is a princess over which you swoon."

Preslovard smiled. "It is not I who swoon, father. Any word of Lord Bohn?"

"None yet. No doubt we will find his lordship lounging in his opulent tent eating roast pheasant."

"I will hold you to that."

Oh'Raum clapped his son's shoulder and they walked through the carnage to rejoin Ra'Chel.

Sleeper

The Last Attack

Sixty-one able-bodied men followed Cap'Tian along Fire Worm Road toward the Great Hooks. Cap'Tian set a moderate pace without any intention of stopping the first night. After the morning's battle for Holm'Stad, men quickly fell off the pace and either made camp beside the road or returned to the city.

On the morning of the second day, Cap'Tian and twenty-three fighters connected with the reserve element previously ordered to patrol the road by Lord Bohn. Together they secured the pass and sent scouts farther east in case they missed the escaping king.

"Take positions at intervals along this stretch," Cap'Tian ordered. "We should know soon if he indeed evaded us."

Concealing themselves in pairs, fighters left the road and waited. The sun danced across the sky, sweeping passed a pleasant mid-day. A chill cascaded down the mountain's slopes, cooling the valley and Far'Verm Pass.

In late afternoon, when the sun scraped the western summits, two black-clad soldiers appeared on the road's northern side. They moved cautiously onto the road, paused to survey the area, and continued steadily east.

Cap'Tian smiled and stepped from his hiding place to block their way. They approached, making no aggressive move. "Hail, travelers," Cap'Tian said. "From the city, are you?"

The soldiers did not answer.

Cap'Tian continued. "I wager you're a dog team for his majesty."

The men looked at each other.

Cap'Tian nodded. "And your boy-king is not far in the woods behind you."

"We wish to pass peacefully, sir," one of the men said.

"Your forces gutted us at Holm'Stad. The king retreats," said the other.

"And you wish to return home to your families?" Cap'Tian asked.

"Aye."

"Your king has led you to ruin. You and your comrades appear honorable men, why do you follow such a tyrant?"

They looked at each other. Finally, one said, "He is our king."

"Does he deserve such an honor?" Cap'Tian let the question linger in the air. "Your contingent has made the road. Perhaps together we should ask them that question."

Behind the pair, a dozen armored men stepped from the northern wood line onto the trail. Cap'Tian and the two soldiers approached, causing the larger group to take up a defensive posture.

"I come to parlay," Cap'Tian said and raised his lance above his head. He scanned the group for Ver'Sinian's customary silver and gold armor. "Your friends have asked to peacefully pass. In return, I have asked a question they have yet to answer."

The soldiers looked at each other. "And what question is that?"

"After the defeat you suffered at Holm'Stad, why do you yet follow such a king?"

"Because he is our king," a voice called from the cohort's rear.

"The same answer as your comrades, here. Does he yet deserve such fealty?"

"Of course, he does!" shouted the voice. "He is our king."

Cap'Tian smiled. "Bring forth the boy-king so he may answer for his crimes and you men will return safely home."

The troop turned and mumbled to each other.

"Kill this man and we can be on our way," the voice called. "How dare you! Don't push me!"

A jostling erupted from the back of the company. The soldiers pushed and prodded one of their men forward. One row passed the soldier forward while he fought against the rush. Cap'Tian's men emerged from the wood line and joined him on the path.

"Unhand me!" the soldier shouted.

The Caropa soldiers forced the man to kneel.

"I'll have your heads for this betrayal," Ver'Sinian yelled. He looked up at Cap'Tian, a barely audible growl growing in his throat.

"Ver'Sinian Caropa — usurper of throne and lands. I am Cap'Tian Vay'Mar—"

"Cap'Tian," and "*Uykucu*," the soldiers whispered.

"He's just a man! Kill him," Ver'Sinian yelled and looked around at his men.

Cap'Tian swung his shield and slammed it into Ver'Sinian's side. The boy flopped to the ground, his black armor clanging. The young king removed his helmet and threw it at Cap'Tian. Two gloved hands grabbed each of his arms and sat him upright.

Ver'Sinian looked up, his vision clouded. Behind his blurry vision he saw his long-dead, brothers' faces. "Sā'Ben?" He whispered. "Ver'Sen?"

Cap'Tian raised his lance, "This is the throne you've won."

"Brothers, please," Ver'Sinian mumbled before the lance pierced his throat.

The downward strike slipped through the king's trachea, behind his sternum, and plunged into his heart. Cap'Tian pulled the spear free, spraying the boy's dark blood across the path. The king's body convulsed several times and his soldiers let him fall forward.

"You men are free to go," Cap'Tian said and rubbed the king's blood from his lance.

Cap'Tian's men gathered around the armored cadaver and awaited his next order. "Remove his armor and gather wood."

"You mean to burn him? I say leave him for the mountain creatures," one of the men called.

Cap'Tian looked at the man. "When your turn comes to cross the river, heed those words, I hope your enemy does not. Now gather wood."

The men did as ordered and built a high bonfire beside the road.

Cap'Tian turned to the remaining King's Guard. "I know not your final rights. Do with him as your people intend."

"Why do you honor their rituals?" one of Cap'Tian's cohort asked.

"Although forsaken by his own men and a tyrant, he is still a man. In this life, it is not us who are the judges. He is to be ferried across the river for a higher judgment."

Ver'Sinian's men removed the king's borrowed armor and dressed his wound as best they could. When dusk fell on Far'Verm Pass, Cap'Tian and his men marched west. Behind them, the last of the Caropa invaders crossed the river atop a blazing pyre. One by one, the men of the east passed Ver'Sinian's charred corpse and continued their course home.

CR   SO

"Master Oh'Raum, I have word from the pass," Lord Bohn said when he entered the tent.

Ra'Chel warmed her hands over the central fire and Preslovard organized a bundle of linen he planned to take to the hospital. Oh'Raum stood and greeted his friend.

"A scout has just returned. Lord Cap'Tian returns this night with tidings of victory."

Oh'Raum nodded.

"So, it is done then," Preslovard whispered.

Ra'Chel said nothing.

Bohn turned to his servants. "Prepare a feast."

"I like feasts," a familiar voice called from behind them.

"Rowan'Gaff!" Ra'Chel called.

"Well, my boy," Oh'Raum said. "I suspected you'd show up here."

Rowan flushed at the announcement but quickly recovered by nodding at Preslovard. Pres returned the gesture.

"Did you make it home?" Ra'Chel asked.

"Slept in my own bed, as I said I would."

"Odd that we did not see you on the road north," Oh'Raum said.

"I came by sea."

"Indeed."

An awkward pause hung in the air.

"You must be Lord Bohn," Rowan'Gaff said and greeted the Bal'Wern noble. "Master Oh'Raum has told me much about you."

"Have I, indeed?"

Lord Bohn looked to Oh'Raum.

"Forgive me. Lord Keir'Gim Bohn, this is Rowan'Gaff," Oh'Raum paused and glanced at Rowan.

"Grimsson."

"He traveled with us in the depths where we woke Cap'Tian," Oh'Raum finished.

"Well," Keir'Gim said and shook the young man's hand. "Any friend of Lord Cap'Tian is welcome here."

"Lord Cap'Tian?" Rowan asked.

"Rowan is his descendant," Preslovard paused, "on his mother's side."

"Even more welcome, young man," Bohn trumpeted.

Rowan'Gaff nodded and tightened his face into a

deceivingly convincing smile.

"Father, I'm off to the hospital."

Oh'Raum nodded.

"Pres," Rowan said, "I'll come with you. There's something I need to take care of. With your leave, my lord," he said and bowed to Lord Bohn.

Oh'Raum and Ra'Chel watched Rowan's unusual behavior in amazement. He appeared polite and genuinely cordial.

Something's amiss, Ra'Chel thought. "Rowan'Gaff, did you see my sister when you were home?"

"No," he said and left the tent behind Preslovard.

"Master Oh'Raum?"

"Yes, dear?"

"Something isn't right with Rowan'Gaff."

Oh'Raum pondered the statement. Finally, he answered. "Has anything ever been right with him?"

Ra'Chel pursed her lips and returned to the fire.

"Some battle, eh?" Rowan asked Pres while they walked through the encampment.

"Of the one battle I've been in, I guess it was typical."

"That bundle for the hospital?"

Preslovard nodded.

"I'll walk with you."

Pres looked at him. "Didn't you have something to do?"

"We can do it after."

Soldiers cooked early evening meals over small fires — vegetables boiled within cooking crocks and strong herbal infusions simmered in kettles. Preslovard and Rowan'Gaff weaved through the tents and groups of huddled men.

For those with less than severe injuries, nurses moved from tent to tent administering ointments and changing soiled bandages. Those gravely wounded found themselves in one of several hospital tents. Healers leaned over unconscious patients, cutting away dead flesh, removing cleaved limbs, and sewing chest and abdomen lacerations. The hospital's stale air smelled like a pigsty mixed with competing herbal fragrances.

Preslovard deposited the linen bundle at the rear of the tent and walked between the rows reassuring those men he fought alongside. Rowan'Gaff stood by the tent-flap and watched him. Images of Bodvar whipped though his mind and fed his raging inferno of hate. The bodies of the wounded looked like the horrific gray creatures, their mouths dripping at the thought of Bodvar's juicy flesh. Like a gray tsunami wave, they engulfed Bodvar, biting him and tearing him to bloody pieces.

"Are you looking for someone?" a woman asked.

The question startled Rowan'Gaff. "No," he whispered.

Preslovard approached. "Ready?"

"I have to stop by a supply tent."

Preslovard held out a hand toward the hospital's exit. Outside the tent, Rowan'Gaff drew in a deep breath.

"You okay?" Preslovard asked.

"Fine," Rowan'Gaff answered and walked away.

The two passed through the encampment, taking a different path back to Lord Bohn's command tent. The sun dipped lower on the horizon and a quiet murmur spread though the men. "Cap'Tian has returned."

"Just here," Rowan said and opened the flap of an outlying supply tent.

Preslovard walked past him. "What do you..." Preslovard started, his words silenced by the sharp pain in his back. He fell to the ground, *Ealhswith* protruding from beside his spine. Preslovard's hand drew to his chest and his right leg kicked uncontrollably several times.

Rowan'Gaff's chest heaved. He wiped his bloody right hand on his tunic and walked a circle around the twitching Preslovard. Three dark-clothed men emerged from behind the high-stacked bushels.

Preslovard reached for the blade jutting from his back, but only managed to feel its pummel. He locked eyes with Rowan'Gaff and snarled, "Of whose business, are you?"

"My own," Rowan'Gaff answered, his face red.

One of the mercenaries drew his sword and one took Rowan'Gaff by the arm. "We have work to do."

Rowan pulled away and knelt in front of Preslovard. "Your death is just the beginning, bastard. The blood of your father and your beloved will avenge my own."

"Get him out of here," one assassin called and pointed with his sword.

"Their deaths will be slower and more agonizing," Rowan crowed before being pushed from the supply tent.

The second man drew his sword and tilted his head to look into Preslovard's face. "I didn't think your friend had it in him. He's the nature of a coward about him."

Preslovard calmed his body. "You know him well." Warm blood flowed down the back of his right leg. He rose to his knees, right leg barely cooperating.

"Don't want to die with your face in the dirt? I don't blame you."

"Your king is dead," Preslovard said and straightened, *Ealhswith's* blade digging deeper into him. He coughed and blood rimmed his lips.

"That sort of thing tends to happen to poor kings," the assassin said and laughed.

"There will be others," his companion added.

Preslovard coughed again and smiled blood-red teeth. "You'll be joining him on the far shore, soon enough."

The assassins looked at each other. "You're the one with the knife sticking out of his back."

Preslovard weakly drew his sword, letting the tip drag the ground in front of him. "Finish this," he taunted.

The sword-wielding assassin stepped behind Preslovard and raised his weapon. Pres watched the assassin's face in front of him. A smile crossed his lips.

Preslovard collapsed. He dropped his chest to his knees, spun around and thrust his sword upward, catching his executioner between his right thigh and crotch. Blood spewed from around *Ealhswith's* hilt, drenching the ground.

The assassin's swing drove him left and he spun down on Preslovard's upward thrust.

Pres pushed with his left leg and drove the sword through his opponent's pelvis, stomach, and left lung. The other assassin, sword at the ready, stepped forward. Pres pulled his blade free, swung it across the advancing assassin's path, and sprayed his face with his companion's gore.

The swing pulled Pres off-balance. He stumbled on his right leg and crashed into a pile of grain satchels.

The second killer wiped his face and lunged in for another attack.

Preslovard, parried the jab, spun, and fell again on his weaker, right side.

The supply tent resembled a battlefield in microcosm. One man lay dead, blood still flowing from between his legs. Blood-splatted, trampled grass and red footprints looked like small bloody lakes cut into the Earth. Preslovard squared off against the Caropa assassin, his own blood oozing down the back of his right leg, filling another tiny lake at his heel. Pres teetered, but did not falter.

The two men stood silent. Preslovard lowered his sword, which grew heavier by the minute. The assassin flicked his sword in the air, readying himself for the final blow. He feigned left then lurched right and swung for Preslovard's neck.

Preslovard raised his sword with lightning speed. He swiped away the high attack, turned, and thrust the tip of his sword into the side of the assassin's neck. He gritted his teeth and slid the blade deeper, slicing through the killer's throat and severing his neck.

Both men fell to the muddy ground, the killer dead — Preslovard from exhaustion and blood-loss. Thoughts of his father and Ra'Chel meandered through his mind before the supply tent fell dark around him.

ॐ   ॐ

"Welcome back, Lord Cap'Tian," Keir'Gim said when Cap'Tian entered the command tent.

"I am no noble, friend," Cap'Tian said and shook wrists with those assembled.

"What of the king?" Oh'Raum asked.

"Joined his kin across the river," Cap'Tian said. "A cohort of his men are yet on their way east."

"A wise move to let them spread the word of this victory," Lord Bohn said.

"Perhaps peace we may finally have," Oh'Raum added.

At the back of the tent, long tables held platters of roasted meats and vegetables. Bread loaves stretched from end to end and against one wall, a stack of barrels.

"A victory feast is prepared," Lord Bohn said.

"A wonderful site, my lord," Cap'Tian replied. "I think it appropriate if this contingent feasts before us."

Cheers from the men erupted.

"As you wish," Lord Bohn said and looked at Oh'Raum.

Oh'Raum smiled.

"Welcome back, kinsman," Rowan'Gaff said. "Congratulations on your great victory."

"Thank you, Rowan'Gaff." They did not shake wrists and Rowan awkwardly kept his right hand within his stained tunic.

"What of an ale for your victory toast?"

Cap'Tian nodded. "Ale all around, Lord Bohn," he crowed and smiled.

The gathered men whooped and cheered.

"This is the victory I was once denied!"

"Huzzah," his men shouted.

Rowan'Gaff moved to the stacked barrels. Another man joined him and together they poured two casks worth of Lord Bohn's finest brew. Mugs passed from hand to hand until everyone in the tent held a full, frothing pint.

Cap'Tian stepped on a bench, raised his mug, and shouted. "Huzz..."

The tent's forward flap ripped open and two men rushed in dragging a limp and bloodied Preslovard. Ra'Chel screamed.

Oh'Raum turned and ran to his son. "Preslovard!"

"Rouse my doctor," Lord Bohn shouted.

Cap'Tian ran forward, joining Oh'Raum.

Rowan'Gaff watched the company converge around Preslovard and stepped away uncertain of his next move. *He is supposed to be dead*, a shrill voice screamed in his mind.

"Where did you find him?"

"On the path, my lord," one of the men said.

"Preslovard," Oh'Raum gently prodded. "Oh, my son."

Tears streamed down Ra'Chel's face.

Preslovard's eyes blinked open. His mouth cracked into a blood-red smile when he locked eyes with Oh'Raum. "Father," he mouthed. "Treachery," Preslovard croaked through blood-cracked lips.

Oh'Raum felt the sword's hilt jutting from Preslovard's back. "Bring linens!" The wizard pulled the blade free and his face pinched with instant, painful recognition.

"Rowan'Gaff," Oh'Raum whispered and tossed the bloody weapon at Cap'Tian's feet.

"You!" Cap'Tian roared and pointed a finger at Rowan'Gaff.

Oh'Raum pressed thick, clean bandages to Preslovard's back, fighting emotion.

Preslovard's eyes rolled to Ra'Chel. "You yet live, my love."

"I do," she managed between sobs. "My hero, you are."

Pres mouthed several unintelligible words, before ending with, "not worthy of a princess."

Ra'Chel leaned over him and whispered, "I am but a barmaid, my love."

Preslovard's head rolled from side to side. "So much more," he managed.

Oh'Raum cradled Preslovard's head in his arms while blood trickled from his back. Their eyes met again and Oh'Raum lost his battle with composure. Before him lay his son, the boy he apprenticed in Bal'Wern so many years ago. The stalwart student, eager to learn the world's mysteries and his vast storehouse of ancient knowledge. His boy, Pres, lover of flowers and all of nature's growing things. The assistant who brought his morning tea and mediated with him long into the night. The adventurer who re-discovered the lost city of Unda'Vager and battled its terrifying subterranean demons. His sweet son, with whom long walks in the forest were the highlight of their day. His progeny that would carry on the teachings of his master and his master's master. Preslovard the brave. Preslovard the wise. Preslovard the innocent.

You are my finest accomplishment in this world, Oh'Raum reminisced.

Preslovard's eyes fell closed and his breathing faltered. In a weak, distant voice he asked, "have I made you proud, Master?"

Oh'Raum looked deep into the young man's eyes. "Oh yes, my boy." Tears flowed like rivers along the lines of his cracked, bearded face. His own voice cracked, sounding unfamiliar and alien. "I am no longer your master."

Preslovard's face momentarily lit with Oh'Raum's blessing. His eyes opened wide as though gazing across a distant shore.

Oh'Raum looked up at Cap'Tian who raised his lance high over his head. He cleared his throat and said. "Hail! Master Preslovard, mystic of legend!"

The tent echoed with the sound of steel ripped from leather scabbards. The assembled joined their leader, "Preslovard!" they thundered.

Oh'Raum looked at Ra'Chel then back to his son. The young man's eyes stared blankly at the heavens. Oh'Raum closed Preslovard's eyes, leaned over him and whispered a blessing of safe travel, in an ancient tongue. "My son, Preslovard, has crossed the river," Oh'Raum whispered.

"Release me!" Rowan'Gaff shouted.

"Take him outside," Cap'Tian ordered.

Four men dragged Rowan'Gaff through the tent's rear flap. They led him beside the small kitchen tent and around the penned livestock.

"Get your hands off me. I demand—"

A gloved hand slammed into the side of his face, cutting off his order. "Speak again and I'll slit your throat," one of the men said and pressed a gleaming blade against his neck.

Cap'Tian, Oh'Raum, Ra'Chel, and Lord Bohn appeared from the back of the command tent. For the first time in his life, Rowan'Gaff read anger in the old mystic's face. In his hand, he carried *Ealhswith*.

The four soldiers holding him forced Rowan to his knees. From behind Cap'Tian two more soldiers approached and dropped the dead assassin in front of him.

"An agent of our enemy you have become, Rowan'Gaff."

"Oh'Raum ... I ... Ra'Chel."

Oh'Raum held *Ealhswith* before him and looked into his eyes. "I remember the boy who bought this. He named it, *Strength*." The wizard shook his head. "I shall have it melted down into a garden implement. It will spend the rest of its days bringing life and beauty to the world."

"A fitting penance for the life it has taken," Cap'Tian whispered.

"No Caropa minion leaves this field alive," Lord Bohn said.

"Kinsman, please," Rowan'Gaff begged.

"You are no kinsman of mine, fiend," Cap'Tian replied in a low tone.

Oh'Raum turned, wrapped an arm around Ra'Chel, and led her back to the tent.

"Master Oh'Raum," Rowan frantically called. "In my dream, you pleaded for my life. Please—"

Oh'Raum turned, sighed, and looked back at the condemned man. "And in my dreams, my son yet lived. Come dear, we must prepare our beloved for his journey to the afterlife."

Sleeper

The Girl in The Woods

Water lapped the sides of the Wallef. She floated west, free of moorings, in Helsem fjord toward the wider and deeper Sea of Res'Teran. Amidship, Preslovard lay wrapped in clean white linen.

Oh'Raum, Ra'Chel, Cap'Tian, and the remaining army lined the rocky shore and watched the ship bob its way through the fjord.

"Archers," Lord Bohn quietly said. A row of archers knocked arrows and plunged their heads into waiting fires. "Draw. Loose." Flaming arrows filled the sky over the fjord and struck the ship's decking and sails.

Ra'Chel fought back tears. Before pushing the funeral barge from the bank, she and Oh'Raum washed Preslovard and carefully wrapped him in the sparkling white sheets. "Do not despair, my lady," Oh'Raum had said. "He will be waiting on the far shore for us both."

Flames licked the Wallef's mast and spread across the stained sale.

Several other boats launched from the fjord, slowly following Preslovard across the river. Down the shore, a woman's voice rang out in somber song.

"You will be free from the bonds that bind you. You are free from the bonds that bound you," Oh'Raum whispered.

Cap'Tian watched the fiery ship sail from the fjord, leading

379

the armada of the dead to the afterlife. *How many times was this meant to be me?* he thought.

Lord Bohn dismissed the archers, though many lingered by the shore wishing their comrades safe journey.

Oh'Raum held Ra'Chel close, more for his own emotions than hers — a fact he would never admit. While he comforted her, she comforted him more. His thoughts turned briefly to Rowan'Gaff and his unceremonious end among Caropa's fallen, buried in a mass grave dug along Fire Worm Road. *He proved his worth after all,* the old mystic thought. A pang of sadness for the boy he once knew overtook him and he leaned on Ra'Chel all the more.

"Come, Master Oh'Raum," she whispered, "a warm fire awaits us. Perhaps we may speak of fond memories."

"Indeed, my dear. Indeed."

Beside Lord Bohn's command tent, Cap'Tian spoke to the men of the Wallef. "You men are free to go. Your part in Grimsson's treachery is paid."

Hroar stepped forward. "Had we known the truth, my lord, we would yet be at harbor in Dur'Loth. May the Wallef's last voyage ferry more than just young Preslovard across the river."

Cap'Tian nodded. "Your Steersman's honor is yet intact."

"Steersman Hroar," Oh'Raum called.

Hroar approached and bowed. "Master Oh'Raum."

"I could not have asked for a more fitting vessel to ferry my son across the river."

Hroar bowed again.

"Your master and I had an arrangement, which I feel is yet unfulfilled."

Hroar held up his hand.

"I insist, sir," Oh'Raum said. Before Hroar could object, the old mystic reached into his cloak and produced a sizable leather purse. "This is what Bodvar earned by bringing the Lady Ra'Chel to me safely. It is right that you and your men should share in his honor."

Hroar looked to the Wallef's crew before taking the money. Oh'Raum leaned in and whispered, "There is enough here to buy a new vessel, should you desire it."

Hroar smiled. "I shall name it, The Her'On, sir."

Oh'Raum smiled and allowed Ra'Chel to lead him through the tent's flaps. Inside, a group of elderly men and women rose when he entered. They beamed at Cap'Tian, who walked beside him.

A robed man stepped in front of the gathering. "The cost of freedom is high," he said, addressing Cap'Tian.

"High indeed," Cap'Tian agreed.

"Hero, I am Bei'Nir Wouters, spokesman for this council."

Ra'Chel and Oh'Raum sat next to the fire.

"We have come to speak to you about lordship over our lands."

Cap'Tian looked at Oh'Raum who remained silent.

"Friends, I appreciate this honor, but my task here is done. We have won the battle, vanquished our enemies, and secured the peace. I have slept for over a thousand years and I am finally free to return to my previous life."

"Forgive me, Lord Cap'Tian, but what life is that? We offer you a kingship."

"I am a farmer, sir."

The ministers muttered to each other; no doubt amused.

Bei'Nir turned to Oh'Raum. "Lord Oh'Raum, you then, must ascend the throne."

"I gave up that life, many years ago, minister," Oh'Raum said.

"But surely, as the late king's brother, the crown falls to you," Bei'Nir pleaded.

"What?" Ra'Chel asked.

Oh'Raum smiled and Cap'Tian turned to the old wizard. "You're—"

"Your uncle, dear," Oh'Raum said and stood. "Honored council-folk, I will not assume that which is not mine to assume. I have lived my life as I wished, among the wild places of this world, and far from courtly matters. My brother, Tyurn, and your beloved Queen ruled this land as I know his daughter will."

Again, the ministers whispered.

Oh'Raum stretched a hand to Ra'Chel. "It is my honor to present you, Princess Ra'Chel, my brother's only daughter, and rightful Queen of Draer."

Bei'Nir looked from Ra'Chel to Oh'Raum then back to Ra'Chel. Oh'Raum nodded. Slowly, those gathered council members bowed low before their Queen. "Your majesty," Bei'Nir said. "We are honored if you would ascend the throne of your mother and father."

Ra'Chel stepped forward, her cheeks flushed. "Please—" she said and asked them to rise. "I," she looked back to Oh'Raum, "accept."

"Wonderful."

"Provisionally," Ra'Chel blurted.

The council remained silent.

Ra'Chel turned and walked to Oh'Raum. "My provision is that you stay with me as advisor, Master Oh'Raum."

"I thought such a request would be made of me, my lady. I humbly accept your provision."

The tent cheered. "Hail, Queen Ra'Chel!"

Oh'Raum beckoned Cap'Tian. The mystic withdrew a wrapped parchment from his cloak and handed it to Cap'Tian.

"What's this?"

"A letter from me for any who come calling. I am leaving care of my cottage to you. It is yours to do with as you please. The cool Spring mornings are especially wonderful medicine for the soul."

Cap'Tian looked at the proclamation. "Master Oh'Raum, I..."

"It is done, sir. Very few know of my meadow. You should be very well insulated from the world. It is time for you to live free from your long burden."

"Thank you," Cap'Tian managed.

Ra'Chel approached. "I don't know what to say, uncle. You knew all along?"

"Aye, your majesty," Oh'Raum answered.

Ra'Chel looked at Cap'Tian who shook his head.

"I abdicated when the calling of ancient knowledge welled within me. I did all I could to distance myself from nobility, not from shame, but from a desire to give myself thoroughly to the mysteries of this world."

Ra'Chel nodded. "Thank you," she whispered.

"It is my honor to serve you, my lady."

"A toast," Lord Bohn announced and lofted a foaming ale mug.

"You changed the casks, eh?" a voice called from the crowd.

"Indeed," Bohn yelled. "My private reserve has never known a finer brew."

"My lady," a woman asked and approached Ra'Chel.

Ra'Chel smiled.

"I am Eléonore Catteau, a member of your council, I'd like to talk to about your coronation."

Oh'Raum smiled. "By your leave, majesty," he said and left the two women to speak.

CR   SO

A fortnight later, Lil'Ith Brune followed her escort, Mag'Nus, through the western gate of Holm'Stad as restoration of the southern gate continued.

Her small pack slung over one shoulder carried her meager traveling possessions as well as a kitchen knife in case the well-dressed messenger or any vagabond tried to take advantage of a woman on the road. *These are dangerous times,* she told herself before setting off north with Mag'Nus.

The official summons arrived eight days hence, delivered

by the handsome, young man in fine attire. "Are you Lil'Ith Brune? Mistress of The Westerly?" He had asked.

Lil'Ith had nodded.

The man smiled and bowed. "Please to meet you. I am Mag'Nus Henderlamb, Lord Bohn's courier," he said and handed her a wrapped bundle.

Inside, Lil'Ith found a carefully folded piece of golden parchment and a small purse, weighted by several coin. Written on the parchment, in the finest script she had ever seen, was written...

To: The Lady, Lil'Ith Brune, Mistress of The Westerly, Dur'Loth Harbor
From: Lord Bohn, Governor of Bal'Wern Keep and the lands South

Dear Lady,
Your presence is hereby requested to be my guest in Holm'Stad at a most important occasion, a fortnight hence. Enclosed you will find sufficient coin to charge a trusted person on the watching over of your establishment. I am honored to make this invitation and look forward to meeting you.

Yours,
Keir'Gim Bohn, Lord of Bal'Wern

Lil'Ith looked questioningly at Mag'Nus.

"Yes madam?"

"Lord Bohn wants to have dinner with me?"

"I am not privy to the contents of my master's correspondence. I am to deliver the bundle, collect you, and return with you to Holm'Stad."

"I can't just up and walk to Holm'Stad," Lil'Ith protested.

Mag'Nus uneasily smiled. "It is imperative we arrive in

time."

"In time for what?"

"Dinner."

A day later, Lil'Ith made her arrangements, packed her small satchel, and headed north with Mag'Nus — after all, *it is not every day one receives an invitation to dine with a noble.* Accustomed to the road, Mag'Nus set a blistering pace, insisting they could either walk faster or farther each day. Lil'Ith did her best to keep the pace which would have them arriving at the realms northernmost city in six days. Along the route, Lil'Ith pestered Mag'Nus with questions. Most he did not answer.

On the afternoon of the sixth day, they entered the walled city, which bustled with activity. Shopkeepers barked at passing customers about gifts for the coronation, couriers bolted through the narrow streets carrying important correspondence, and minstrels played happy music at every street corner. The city looked nothing like she knew in Dur'Loth. Streamers bobbed overhead, strung from balcony to balcony. Revelers danced and sang their way from shop to shop and the entire city felt like she imagined the inside of a bee hive must be like.

Mag'Nus led her through the narrow streets, emerging into a central plaza encircled by high walls. Two guards stood at a heavy door checking credentials and welcomed well-dressed dignitaries in two reception lines. Although not opulently dressed and feeling sheepish, Lil'Ith followed Mag'Nus to the front of the queue to the grumbles of those waiting their turn.

"Everything is in order," the guards said to the man at the line's front. "Welcome to Holm'Stad Keep, Sir Berg'Thor." The guard bowed and stepped aside, allowing the nobleman and his companion through the gate.

Lil'Ith and Mag'Nus stepped forward, dwarfed by the huge guard. Mag'Nus turned and held his hand to Lil'Ith. "I bring a guest of Lord Bohn," he said.

The other guard admitted a finely dressed woman. "Good day, sir," the guard said to a middle-aged man, next in line.

"Good day, I need to see Master Oh'Raum Yul..." the man started.

"Do you have an invitation?"

"Lady?" Mag'Nus asked. "I need your invitation please." Lil'Ith fumbled with her pack listening to the man's plea for entry.

The man shook his head. "No, but this is..."

"I'm sorry, sir. I can't let you in without an invitation," the guard said, interrupting him.

"But..."

"You'll need to step aside, sir."

Lil'Ith handed forward her invitation.

The guard bowed. "Welcome to Holm'Stad Keep, Lady Lil'Ith," he said.

The middle-aged man pressed. "I am a friend of Mast..."

With his pike at chest level, the guard stepped menacingly forward. "No invitation, no entry!"

The guard in front of Lil'Ith stepped aside. "My lady, if you please," he said and gestured for her to pass.

Mag'Nus stepped through the gate, turned, and smiled at Lil'Ith. Outside the man continued to plead with the guard for an audience with Master Oh'Raum.

"If you'll please follow me," Mag'Nus said.

Lil'Ith followed Mag'Nus through a maze of corridors, leading her to an opulent waiting apartment. Inside, a young woman smiled and curtsied when they entered.

"This is Sib'Be. She will attend you," Mag'Nus said, bowed, and left the two women alone.

Lil'Ith stood awkwardly by the door, looking at Sib'Be.

Sib'Be smiled. "Does, my lady, want to bathe before dinner?"

Lil'Ith let out a long breath. "I'm sorry. This has to be a mistake."

"Excuse me, my lady?"

"Please," Lil'Ith said, "I don't know why I'm here. I got this letter from Lord Bohn and I thought I'd be in trouble if I didn't come. Then all the, my lady, stuff, and the escort, and now you're treating me as if I'm special." She sat hard on the bed. "I'm so confused."

Sib'Be smiled again.

"What does Lord Bohn want with me? Is he courting me? Does he think he can—"

"My lady," Sib'Be interrupted, "I have served Lord Bohn for ten years. He has never done what you're suggesting with anyone. He has invited you to dinner. I suggest you enjoy the evening."

Lilith sighed. "It took me eight days to get here. Better be the dinner of my life."

After a gloriously long bath, Lil'Ith sat in front of a large mirror while Sib'Be brushed her hair. The gown they chose highlighted Lil'Ith's thin build and she questioned the decision of wearing someone else's dress to the dinner.

"I still don't know what this dinner is about," Lil'Ith said while Sib'Be worked the straps across her back.

A knock on the door startled them. Sib'Be opened the door and Lord Bohn entered, smiling. "Welcome Lil'Ith."

Lil'Ith awkwardly bowed. "My lord," she said.

Bohn acknowledged her and gestured for his wife to enter the room. "My I present my wife, the Lady Siv Bohn."

Lil'Ith bowed again.

"Oh my, dear," Siv said, "how lovely you are." She smiled at Sib'Be who nodded at the wordless praise.

"I'm so glad you made it in time. Siv and I were delighted at the opportunity to have you as our dinner guest."

Lil'Ith looked up and sighed. "From your note, I thought..."

Siv laughed. "Wasn't that just scandalous? That was my idea."

Lord Bohn straightened. "Are you ready?"

Lil'Ith looked at Sib'Be. "Yes, my lord," she said.

Lord and Lady Bohn escorted Lil'Ith through the keep to a massive reception room. A u-shaped table, lined with elegant settings, circled the room. A tall wooden throne dominated one end of the room and a balcony ringed the entire building.

Lord and Lady Bohn stopped short of the door and waited for the couple in front of them to enter. The guard saw them and smiled. He wrapped his pike against the floor three times and in a booming voice announced, "Lord and Lady Bohn, escorting the Lady Lil'Ith Brune, sister of the Queen."

Keir'Gim and Siv Bohn entered the room which fell silent at the announcement of Lil'Ith's entrance. Everyone turned and smiled at her.

Lil'Ith stood in the doorway unable to move. *Sister of the Queen?* she thought. The attendees stared at her with many wondering why she had not moved.

"Allow me, my lady," a familiar voice said.

Lil'Ith looked up into Oh'Raum's smiling face. He offered her his arm, which she took, and together they slowly walked among the gathered.

"Sister of the Queen?" she asked in a whisper.

"Indeed, lady," Oh'Raum answered.

He escorted her to the head of the table and sat her to the left of the seat reserved for the queen. Once seated, the room regained its previous activity with dignitaries sharing stories and making deals.

"I—"

"This is your sister's coronation dinner," Oh'Raum explained.

"Ra'Chel is—"

"Your sister is my niece and, following dinner, will officially be crowned Queen of Draer." Oh'Raum sat on the opposite side of the queen's chair and drank from a shiny goblet.

"I can't believe this," Lil'Ith said, her face flushed.

"Keeping it a secret was your sister's idea. She thought you would like the surprise."

"I'm going to kill her," Lil'Ith said and laughed.

Oh'Raum joined her in laughter. "I wouldn't say that too loud."

Lil'Ith picked up her own goblet and smelled the sweet wine within it. She took a long drink and looked around the room. Abruptly she asked, "Master Oh'Raum, did your friend find you?"

"I'm sorry?"

"There was a man at the gate when I arrived. He said he was a friend. The guard sent him away. No invitation."

Oh'Raum stroked his beard and shook his head. "I invited no one. Do you recall his name or the look of him?"

Lil'Ith thought for a moment. "Tall; tan; balding; short black beard."

"I know many men of that stature," Oh'Raum said and laughed.

"He had a child with him," Lil'Ith said.

"Indeed? Perhaps I shall look for this man tomorrow."

Lil'Ith took another drink from her goblet which a servant immediately refilled. "Sounded desperate to find you," she said.

Oh'Raum sighed. "A walk to the gate will do me good." He finished his mug, stood, stretched, and walked behind her. "Don't let them eat without me," he whispered.

"I'll do what I can," she said.

"I have every confidence in you," he paused, "my lady."

Oh'Raum notified Lord Bohn of an urgent matter which required attending and left the reception hall. He wound through the keep's passages, arriving at the heavy wooden gate. Two burly guards stood on either side watching the festivities happening on the street.

"Excuse me, gentleman," Oh'Raum asked. "I was told a man came to the gate looking for me."

Minstrels played outside the keep and jugglers flung balls

high in the air. Vendors rolled carts through the crowd barking their sales with sweet-smelling meats swinging on racks.

"Oh, Master Oh'Raum. Yes, sir. There was a man earlier. We had to turn him away, sir."

Oh'Raum nodded. "I understand. Do you know where he went?"

"No, sir," the guard said.

Dancers whooped to the festive music and waved flags.

"Thank you, gentleman," Oh'Raum said, turned, and stopped just inside the door. Something above the raucous merrymakers caught his ear. He turned back and scanned the crowd.

Across the plaza a man frantically waved and shouted. "Oh'Raum!"

Oh'Raum, unable to make out the man's features in the torchlight waved back and gestured for him to come. The man disappeared into the crowd.

As though materializing from a thick fog, Freya emerged from the crowd propelled forward by Oy'Vid Ol'Vir. Oh'Raum's mind stumbled in recognition of his daughter. He had grieved for her, blessed her river crossing, and shed his private tears for her.

"Master," Freya cried and bolted forward.

The sound of her sweet voice shot through Oh'Raum's heart like a lance. The old mystic fell to his knees, his arms wide. His breath hitched and he uncontrollably cried great gasps. "My Freya! Oh, my dear!" He looked up at Oy'Vid, who joined in their tears. "How?"

"My son found her at the cottage," Oy'Vid said. "She's been with me ever since."

Oh'Raum pulled Freya close to him and enveloped her in his robes. He ran a hand through her hair. "I heard—" he started, unable to say the rest.

"When word reached us of your victory, we set right out," Oy'Vid continued.

"What a gift you have brought me," Oh'Raum said through more tears. "Come." He led them passed the guards, through the corridors, and into the reception room. The well-dressed dignitaries watched the frantic wizard set the young girl in his seat and demand food and drink for his roughshod companions.

A loud banging signaled the entrance of another important guest. "Her majesty, Ra'Chel Brune, Queen of Draer."

Seated attendants rose and those engaged in conversation quieted. A flushed-face Ra'Chel entered, wearing a sparkling, dark-purple gown. Lil'Ith barely recognized her sister. A handsome, young soldier stepped forward, bowed low, and extended her his arm. Ra'Chel smiled and accepted the ambitious young man's escort.

He led her to the front of the room, each attendee bowing as she passed. They rounded the corner of the table and Ra'Chel met Lil'Ith's eyes. Tears welled within them and a loving smile grew on her face. The young man released her hand, bowed, and back away allowing the sisters to finally embrace.

Ra'Chel turned to Oh'Raum, his face and eyes red. His hands rested on the shoulders of a young girl. "Master Oh'Raum, are you well?"

"My lady, my daughter—" he managed and pulled Freya close again.

"Freya?" Ra'Chel gasped. She knelt and hugged the girl. "How is this possible?"

"She has been under the care of my friend here," Oh'Raum said.

Lil'Ith looked at the girl, her own emotions surfacing. "Had I known, Master—"

"Oh no, dear. You did your part." Oh'Raum gave her a genuine smile.

"My lady," a servant quietly asked, "would you like us to begin serving?"

"Oh, yes please."

Another staff hitting the floor indicated the start of the formal dinner. "Please find your places. Dinner is served," shouted the herald.

"Make places for our honored guests," Ra'Chel said.

Servants made a place for Oy'Vid while Freya sat on Oh'Raum's knee and picked at the previously brought plate.

"Freya?" Ra'Chel asked, "can you tell us how you came to the cottage? We heard a—" She paused and looked at Oh'Raum.

Freya sipped a water mug and swallowed a mouthful of soft bread. She scanned the room with an expectant expression. "Pres went into the cave and I stayed on the bridge. I bet his story is better than mine."

Servants fanned throughout the room carrying trays of food. Drink fillers moved from goblet to goblet pouring wine and water.

Oh'Raum cleared his throat. "Your brother told us you were gone when he emerged."

"It started raining. Then the monsters came," she said. "I'm sorry for not meeting you. I knew I shouldn't have run and left Pres, but I was so scared, and it was night, and they were growling at me."

"It's okay, love. I'm glad you are safe," Oh'Raum said and looked at Oy'Vid.

"She walked all the way back to the cottage by herself," the innkeeper said.

Conversations around the long table ranged from battle stories to profits made in exotic ports. Music from the coronation street party wafted through the windows adding to the dinner's festive mood.

"I didn't have the rest of my map." Freya shrugged. "I followed it backward."

"So you did," Oh'Raum said. "How did you cross the river? What did you eat?"

"I thought about going back in the morning, but wanted to just get home with you," she said and looked at the old wizard.

He smiled.

"I thought about stopping at Olva's for her treat but was scared to go into the city. So, I pulled myself across the river on the rope. I ate what Pres told me was safe."

"Einar found her hiding in the cottage."

Oh'Raum nodded at his friend. "It's a good thing, too. It could be a while before we return to the meadow."

"Oh?" Oy'Vid asked.

Ra'Chel smiled. "Would you like to live here with us in the castle, dear?"

Freya popped a chunk of roasted chicken into her mouth and nodded. "Do you have a garden?" She asked through her mouthful.

"A glorious garden," Oh'Raum answered.

Freya clapped and swallowed her bite.

When the dinner wound down, the servants prepared the dais for Ra'Chel's coronation ceremony and the attendees turned their chairs to face the enormous carved throne. Beside it lay a glimmering crown on a plush pillow and a thick purple cape lined at the neck with white fur.

Left of the throne, a stand held Cap'Tian's worn armor, his sword, a glimmering silver shield, and his legendary lance. Guards stood on either side of the armor stand.

Oh'Raum cleared his throat, set Freya down, and proceeded to the dais. "Honored guests," he said, quieting the room. Bei'Nir Wouters and Eléonore Catteau rose and joined him beside the throne. "It is my honor to begin the coronation of my lady, Ra'Chel Brune."

Lil'Ith put a soft hand on Ra'Chel's arm. Ra'Chel drew in a deep breath, stood, and stepped to the platform. She faced Oh'Raum, her faced flushed. Oh'Raum gave her a brief smile and turned to Bei'Nir.

Eléonore moved to the side table and lifted the crown.

A horn blast rose from the keep's rampart and the street merrymakers paused in reverence.

"My lady, are you willing to take the Oath?" Bei'Nir asked.

"I am," Ra'Chel said.

Oh'Raum smiled and nodded at the small stool before him. Ra'Chel knelt. "Do you promise and swear to justly govern the people?"

"I so promise."

"Will you, to your power of law, justice, and mercy, execute all your judgements?"

"I will," Ra'Chel answered, her voice solemn and quiet.

Oh'Raum continued. "Will you, to the utmost of your power, maintain the laws of our lands? Will you maintain the rights of our free people? And will you defend the land?"

"All this I promise to do."

Eléonore approached Ra'Chel's right side and passed the crown over Ra'Chel's head to Bei'Nir, who stood on her left. Bei'Nir turned to the assembled and thrust the crown in front of him. Everyone rose.

"As Council spokesman, I hereby complete the Council's will," Bei'Nir announced. He turned, passed the crown over Ra'Chel's head, and handed it to Oh'Raum.

"That which has passed from my brother, shall pass to his daughter." Carefully, Oh'Raum rested the crown on Ra'Chel's head. "Ladies and gentlemen, her majesty, Ra'Chel Brune, Queen of Draer."

Ra'Chel rose and turned to face the bowing crowd. Trumpets again blasted through the windows and a cheer rose throughout Holm'Stad. An accompanying ovation erupted in the reception hall.

"As my first official act," Ra'Chel announced, quieting the applause, "I hereby release Cap'Tian Vay'Mar from his charge as protector of the realm." Ra'Chel stepped in front of the armor stand. "Our hero's armor will remain here, ready for another to come forward from the people when we need a hero." The crowd cheered.

"Lord Bohn," Ra'Chel called. "Please come forth and kneel."

Lord Bohn stepped onto the dais and did as commanded.

"Lord Keir'Gim Bohn, for your leadership in our recent triumph, I hereby elevate you to Protector of The Realm and charge you with command of the army. Rise, sir."

"Hail, Lord Bohn!" shouted the reception hall.

A scribe, near the door, feverishly recorded the events, sending runners to the walls to announce the new queen's actions and proclamations. Cheers of, "Cap'Tian," rose from the masses outside the keep. Among them, a cloaked Cap'Tian, joined in the chanting of his own name.

"Cap'Tian! Cap'Tian," he cheered. He smiled, turned, and disappeared among the revelers.

Shouts of, "Hail, Lord Bohn," drifted over the keep's walls.

Ra'Chel turned to Lil'Ith and gestured for her to join the newly crowned queen. "My sister, Lil'Ith. I invite you to join my court. I further ask that you guide me in the well-being of all women and children within the kingdom."

Lil'Ith's tears signaled her acceptance.

"And finally," Ra'Chel said. "As I have no heir, until such time as I bear a child," she turned to Oh'Raum, "my Uncle's daughter, my cousin, Freya Yulr, shall be heir to my throne."

Ra'Chel waved for Freya to join her. Slowly the girl stepped beside the queen.

"Hail Princess Freya," the room echoed in approval. Oh'Raum beamed.

Freya looked up at Ra'Chel. "I'm a princess?"

Freya's name boomed from the windows accompanied with cheers and resumed music.

Ra'Chel smiled. "Yes, little cousin. You are a princess."

Sleeper

A Time to Cross the River

One hundred archers lined the banks of Helsem Fjord and raised their flaming arrows to the sky. In the distance, a woman's soft voice wafted through the gathered and the funeral barge tipped and bobbed its way from the harbor.

Queen Ra'Chel silently stood on the same spot where, eighteen years earlier, she stood when Preslovard crossed the river. Beside her, Princess Freya fought back tears.

Ra'Chel nodded to her recently installed counsellor, Lord Keir'Gim Bohn. "Loose," the old man ordered.

A flock of arrows burst into the blue sky, arcing toward the small boat.

"Chin up, cousin," Ra'Chel said in her soft, regal tone. "Your father journeys to meet our beloved Preslovard."

Freya straightened, looked to the sky, and closed her eyes. In her mind, her brother stood smiling on the river's far bank awaiting Oh'Raum's arrival.

Behind the stoic pair, a small boy played among the crowd, followed closely by a plump, exhausted woman. "Come young master. We must pay our respects to your kin," the woman whispered and snatched the boy by the arm.

"But, Ayah," the boy whined. He struggled and squirmed in the au pair's arms.

"We send our family to the afterlife, for when our time comes to cross the river, we too want our family sending us off," the Ayah said.

The flaming arrows descended on the wooden ship and the linen wrapped body, quickly engulfing both. Sobs and wails rippled through the crowd lining the rocky shoreline.

When the barge floated from sight, the gathering fell silent. One by one, they left the shoreline for their shops and homes within the walled city. Ra'Chel and Freya lingered, as did Lord Bohn.

Feeling the emotion around him, the young boy wriggled from captivity and tottered toward the Queen and Princess. Along the way he pulled several bright flowers from tufts of long grass.

He slid between the two, smiled up at them, and held up his spontaneous bouquet.

"Well, hello, brave knight," Ra'Chel said and smiled at the flowery gift.

Freya hoisted the boy to her hip and pointed to the flowers. "Do you know what these flowers say?"

The boy considered the question then smiled. "Master Oh'Raum told me. They don't speak because I picked them," the boy whispered.

"That's correct, Preslovard," Ra'Chel said and smiled.

Preslovard returned her smile. Overhead, the moon began its slow passage across the sun's face.

A New Song Sung in Draer

Come gather round the hearth to hear,
The Ballad of Cap'Tian newly told.
A tale of magic, men, and darkest fear,
Of heroes, princesses, and betrayals of old.

Peaceful mystic lived in eastern meadow,
Of great renown and power unknown.
Visions had he of conjunction's shadow,
And by force of arms the invader de-throned.

Upon this course the wizard did scheme,
To search in earnest for hero's lost tomb.
Mighty Preslovard did fulfill the dream,
Leading them deep inside El'Thune's gloom.

For behind the blackness of Unda'Vager's gate,
Live horrors this song dare not say.
For a single noise would seal their fate,
And none would live to see light of day.

A thousand years, the hero slept,
In blackest dungeon and coldest night.
Until Draer princess softly wept,
Awakening him to lead our fight.

Word spread like wildfire,
From field and stream and trading post.
Cap'Tian has risen, with one desire,
To utterly destroy the enemy's host.

From farms and villages and cities wide,
A great army arose from Western Lands.
North, they marched by Cap'Tian's side,

To delivery victory into our hands.

"Oh hero," cried Draer, "become our king,"
"Nay," said Cap'Tian, "I am but a soldier."
"Tis for commoner's courage we need to sing,"
"And Queen have you, of heart much bolder."

Cap'Tian, risen, defeated our foes,
But kingship not sought he in Draer,
Peace and freedom our hero yet sows,
Among good, tilled Earth and clean mountain air.

And so, in peace we may live,
For prophecy unfolded before our eyes.
The ultimate sacrifice so many did give,
When our country calls and need arise.

Map of
The Western
Kingdoms

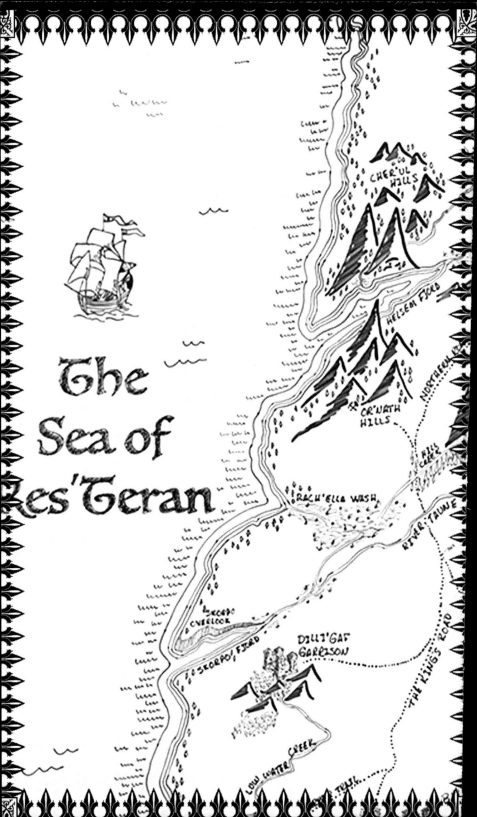

Other Exciting titles from Jumpmaster Press™

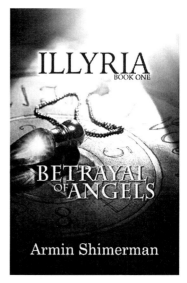

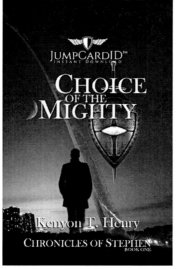

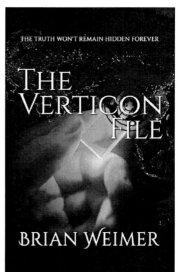